Promises To Keep

Promises To Keep

Anne Griffiths

PIATKUS

This novel is dedicated to the memory of
the British and French resistants who so
courageously risked torture and death
on our behalf

First published in Great Britain in 1997 by
Judy Piatkus (Publishers) Ltd of
5 Windmill Street, London W1

**The moral right of the author
has been asserted**

*A catalogue record for this book is available
from the British Library*

ISBN 0–7499–0378–3

Phototypeset in 11/12 pt Times by Intype London Ltd
Printed and bound in Great Britain by
Mackays of Chatham, Plc, Ltd.

The woods are lovely, dark and deep,
But I have promises to keep,
And miles to go before I sleep
And miles to go before I sleep

Robert Frost

Part One

Chapter 1

Paris, August 1939

'You say I'm to leave Paris?' Misha heard herself stuttering. She'd been day-dreaming over the lunch she didn't want. And her father'd been casually threatening the end of her new and perfect world. 'Why d'you want to send me away from the only place I've ever felt at home?' She'd have liked to leap up and scream but she'd never defied him – she'd never had so much to lose until now. 'I can't,' she said. 'I won't.' She sounded like a child. 'I've got my class to go to and a room I feel is mine at last. I know everyone in the flats, and the shopkeepers, the baker saves me his broken biscuits . . .' Panic was forcing out the silliest statements. She mustn't let him see how much more there was. He was going to laugh of course.

Michael Martin threw back his head with a shout of mockery. 'Well, well,' he said. 'What an achievement! You've developed the same trivial mind as your mother.' He leaned back in the restaurant chair, adjusted his silk cravat and gazed round at the fashionable midday crowd on the terrace of the Brasserie Lipp. 'I tell you this lot'll disappear fast when war's declared. Hitler's planning to send Nazi jackboots stamping along their precious boulevards. They won't like that and nor will you. So yes, you are to leave Paris.'

Misha felt a creeping chill of fear. What if he meant it? Sometimes his plans came to nothing. But Hitler couldn't have anything to do with her. Hitler couldn't mean never

3

watching for Philippe again, never sitting at this very table where she'd once seen him. He'd had the glossy dark-haired woman beside him. She didn't matter today. 'Nobody believes Hitler will get to Paris, surely? The army'll fight off the Nazis and everyone'll stay safely at home. And Paris is our home, isn't it, *Maman*, ever since Dad brought us here from that freezing lodging house in Switzerland? You've made friends, haven't you? We were never anywhere long enough before.' Heels drumming in her hot dusty sandals, Misha willed a silent plea for help across to her mother.

Yvette Martin, pushing bread amongst the chicken bones on her plate, didn't see her daughter's plea. 'We've certainly had a number of temporary homes,' she said. 'Several in London, after your father decided England was the place to be. Then it was a cottage in Ireland, for tax reasons, I believe. My memories are mostly of damp and the bailiffs knocking on the door, certainly not of friends.'

'You've forgotten Spain,' Misha cried. But her father was tapping his knife on the table. They were irritating him. 'You were selling something to the government in Spain, weren't you, Dad? It was nice there, I think. I don't really remember. I just know Paris is where I want to be now. Please, Dad.' A shameful cajoling tone had crept in. Her feet were burning and the chill had lodged somewhere in her chest. She'd seen other girls cajoling fathers. Often at restaurant tables like this one. They were asking for simple things though, more ice cream or money for the cinema.

'. . . and if your father had allowed me to give you a proper French upbringing,' Yvette Martin was saying, 'instead of trailing us around Europe, neither of you would have anything to complain about.'

'You're certainly betraying your upbringing, my dear,' Michael Martin said, through his teeth. 'I've asked you not to wipe up your food like the peasant you are when you're in a restaurant with me.'

Misha watched his pale eyes grow colder as he drew himself up and leaned his elbows on the table. His shadow cut out the sunshine on his wife's hat, a pretty blue pillbox with a blue spotted ribbon. She'd made it herself from sale

4

oddments. All her hats were made from nothing. There was never enough money and she sometimes had to beg for credit from the coalman. Yet Misha knew his own hats came from Savile Row, like the jacket he was wearing. This'd been tailored in the finest tweed, a gingery colour exactly matching his hair and moustache. And only the barber at the Savoy in London was allowed to cut and trim those. She realised she'd never questioned it before. Why should her father also indulge himself with two cars and golf when her mother had to count the sous for their clothing? She didn't know him, she realised. How could she persuade him to change his mind? She must make the subject return to her before they launched into one of their arguments. Forcing a piece of meat into her mouth, she said, 'I can't swallow this. I don't like eating animals. I have told you and you keep deciding to forget. If you think of this stuff as pot-corpse of chicken! Why can't I have a fried egg? I don't actually see why I can't eat as I please . . .' She removed the lump of matter from her mouth and waited for his usual response.

He was ready. 'You know very well the chickens reared to drop eggs from their behind also have their throats cut and are eaten like the rest. And what about your shoes? Some little cow gave up its life in the slaughterhouse for those and they cost God knows how many francs to buy. You two think I'm made of money.'

'But we won't be able to afford the ferry fares, will we?' Misha was flooded with hope. Here was reason enough! He wouldn't want the expense of taking her across the Channel.

He wasn't listening. He was staring at her mother's hat. 'How much did that thing cost me?' he said.

Misha too stared at the hat. The day she'd seen the glossy woman with Philippe, she'd been wearing one very much like it, but black, with a black and white polka-dot ribbon. Ever since, she'd been looking for the ribbon, on every terrace, at every café table, dreading to see it in case Philippe was there too, smiling at the glossy sheen of perfect hair, at the perfect, olive-skinned face. Her mother's hair had a sheen too, red, and she had sculptured bones and eyes like a pretty fox's, whereas she herself had neither. She looked more English, like her father, than French. Her skin was pale, though prone to fierce blushing which left it a patchy pink, and her hair was a nondescript brown. Maybe if she had inherited her mother's looks there would have been more warmth between them. But they'd been all right together, hadn't they? Look up at me, *Maman*, she thought, help me. Remind him how much he says we cost him.

Yvette placed another piece of bread on her plate to show she wasn't listening to her husband's most patient voice, the one he used to emphasise his superiority and her dependence.

'I tell you the girl will be safer with her great-aunt and uncle in England. They're hardly likely to bomb sunny Bournemouth. She can go to school there. She knows nothing, she's as ignorant as you are.'

'School!' Misha shouted. 'But I'm nearly seventeen!' She'd been in enough schools, in enough countries and they'd all had the same blur of strangeness, with children who stared at her because she didn't belong and hadn't lived there all her life as they had. Philippe knew she'd had no education ... Another idea hit her. She dropped her fork; her hand was trembling from a fresh surge of hope. 'I can go to the Sorbonne!' she cried. 'It won't cost you anything, only the books.' And she'd have glorious days catching sight of Philippe, darkly mysterious, dashing about the old stone corridors, gown flying, papers falling ...

'For heaven's sake, keep your voice down and choose a dessert. The man's waiting and you're making me look a fool.'

Misha chose fruit to placate him, because it was the cheapest item on the menu. Her mother chose *caramel au riz* because it was the most expensive, having in it a shocking number of egg yolks and an unknown quantity of cream. She saw her father hesitate between accusing her of wasting a restaurant meal and refusing to pay for the caramel. Instead, he tapped impatient fingers and ordered a sweet dessert wine no one would want. 'A university wouldn't take you. There's a little matter of examinations to pass first.' He leaned back, his face like an overweight schoolboy's. 'The answer's no,' he said, 'and you're being

6

particularly obtuse today. Now listen, I'm not staying the night but will take the Jag down to Lyons where there's some business I have to attend to. This war could well give me the break I deserve. There's always money to be made in a war if you know what's what. I'll be back in a few days and I'll take Michèle to England with me. Your mother, Misha, doesn't wish to go with you so she'll stay here, or if she decides to be sensible, go to her parents in the south where I've told her she'll be safer. Perhaps down there, she can try and be some sort of mother to her son.'

Recklessly throwing aside the idea of the Sorbonne, Misha had another thought: for the first time, she was going to be in control of herself. This was the best day of her life. She'd been threatened with disaster only to be lifted up again by her own cleverness. 'I can't leave the country, Dad,' she said, keeping her voice very calm. 'What if Félix has one of his bad turns? If there's going to be a war, I ought to be with him. And you'll know we're both safe as houses down there in the Languedoc. The Germans won't attack that far south.' Then she thought, wilder than ever, that she'd bring her brother back to Paris, they'd sit out the war together. She'd still have everything that was precious to her, and looking after him would be an occupation, the way it had before he'd been sent away. Her father would never realise, or not until it was too late. He might not come back to Paris for months.

'How d'you know how far the Germans'll go!' he yelled. 'Such foolishness makes me realise I've made the right decision. Your brother of course remains with your grandparents who can look after him properly. You go to Bournemouth and stay with your cousin Janet. It's all decided.'

Misha watched the waiter arranging fruit bowl and cutlery in front of her with hands that bore a tracery of scratch marks. She might ask him if he had a kitten at home and they could have a conversation and that would stop her second or was it her third shout. Until an hour before, her life had been the same, the daily routine, her own little world, and that precious moment every evening when she waited with Frou for Philippe. And she'd learned nothing

7

new about her father since she could remember. He would arrive for brief bickering visits, upset her mother, and be off again in his perpetual flight to something important. 'My cousin Janet?' she said, in a reasonable, mature tone. 'I didn't know there was any family on your side but that old aunt and uncle you said brought you up.' She looked at her mother for confirmation of her own surprise, but she was occupied with a remaining wedge of golden rice. 'Did you know there were cousins, *Maman*?' She had always wanted more family to give her a sense of who she was. With a father so rarely with them, it was difficult to feel quite English yet she didn't have her mother's essential Frenchness.

Her father shifted in his chair and poked a fork into his *tarte aux prunes*. 'They're only distant relations. But your aunt's taken in Janet and her brother for the duration of the war. Their mother's in the services, a colonel or something perfectly ridiculous for a woman to be, so their flat wherever it is has been closed up. You, young lady, are to be taken in as well, whether you like it or not, and I want no more protests.'

Giddy with exhausted emotion, Misha bit into a peach, unable to settle to the idea of cousins.

'Dear God,' her father said, 'haven't you taught this brat to peel fruit at the table? How old is she? Nearly seventeen and behaving like a twelve year old. That pudding-basin haircut you've given her doesn't help. How will she ever get herself a husband, I ask you, and she'll be good for nothing else.'

Misha ceased to listen, tackling her peach with knife and fork and brooding on shaken foundations. Other people had solid homes, and families they knew about who joined in the rituals, baptism, wedding, funeral. She and her mother sometimes stood on pavements, outsiders, and watched other people belonging. But here they'd begun to have habits; her mother had friends, she went out regularly. Somehow, for both their sakes, she would have to find a way to oppose this man for whom she could never be pretty or sophisticated enough, yet who was capable of throwing such shocks into their lives. But she didn't know how she was going to do it.

Because they were still at their bickering, Misha was permitted to leave the Lipp early. She set off the long way home, crossing the Place St Germain and lingering by the terraces of the Deux Magots and the Café Flore. Here was what she'd yearned to join, the café life. Here Picasso had sat, drawing on napkins, and Hemingway, a big drunken bear, and generations of arguing students, and Philippe. Here she'd dreamed of sitting with him, his sad smile offered to her across the table, the rest of the world shut out.

She stared at the luncheon debris on the tables. The stain of wine in the glasses seemed suddenly like blood. Maybe her father was right, and everyone else, the newspapers, everyone, and there was going to be war. All this would be swept away then, all these people, this world she'd never be able to join because it would no longer exist.

Only she mustn't think of it yet. Forcing her feet onward, she dredged up her dream of being old enough, chic enough, for Philippe, like the woman with the polka-dot ribboned hat, and being with him at one of those very tables, laughing together in the sunshine under the canopy of trees. After all, this new war-talk was just another scare, like the Munich crisis of the year before. Hitler was fooling Europe by going right to the brink again. Where had she read that? Somewhere in the Paris *Daily Mail*, but newspapers fed fear. She must stop reading them. She must continue her education the way she'd begun it, browsing at the bookstalls down by the Seine. For Philippe, she must be able to converse on serious matters.

Shortly she'd reached the river and was sitting on a stool beside her friend and the occupier of the third-floor flat above theirs. He was one of the Seine bookstall owners and months before had begun to pick out from his stock the most significant of the world's classics to fill the gaps in her piecemeal knowledge.

Accepting the slim volume of *Candide* he passed her and turning to her marked place, page twenty, she found herself unable to decipher a line. 'All right then,' she said, startling

9

him, 'if this book is supposed to reveal the truth of human nature and existence, what does it say about someone like Hitler?'

'War is there, my dear child,' Monsieur Steiner replied, pulling his beret down to his eyebrows. 'And fanatical faith and savagery. Why don't you take it home to read tonight? Maybe Voltaire's wisdom will help us understand the upheaval to come.'

'The war won't make any difference to me,' she said. 'I think I'll go on reading a bit at a time, thank you, so you can help explain points. I'm halfway through *The Mill on the Floss* at home and I want to start *Gone with the Wind* again . . .' Refusing also his fond, knowing look, she gazed beyond him to the water and the tourist boats flapping at their moorings. Belonging to Paris as she did, she'd never been sight-seeing and now never would if she were to be banished from it. She'd never walk down there on the embankment either, hand in hand with Philippe, under the bridges of Paris . . .

Jumping up from the stool, she cried, 'Why can't someone assassinate Hitler or something? There'll be just as many of their men killed as ours and he's not even German. How did they let him get into power!'

She began to run and didn't pause until she reached the corner of their street where she waved to Denis, the errand boy from Jubin the grocer's. His wet puppy-eyes followed her to Alibert's, the ironmongery next door. There was hardly anyone else in the street; no shoppers for the brushes and brooms in Alibert's, no housewife prodding the cheese at the grocery's counter whilst Denis watched, breathing heavily in case he wouldn't be allowed to do the weighing himself. At the window over Alibert's shop, his mother was peering from her wheelchair. How would she withstand a war when she couldn't get down the stairs?

The sweet biscuity smell by the baker's reminded her she'd eaten very little lunch so she went in for a slice of apple tart. She'd be hungry later although she wasn't yet and still had to quieten her thumping heart. The antique shop had a poster up: *Closed Until Further Notice*. Why hadn't she given this so much as a second's thought? The

10

family had not gone on holiday, they couldn't afford to, they'd gone south to relations because they thought the war would soon reach Paris. Madame Libaud had told her and she hadn't bothered to listen.

There was Madame Libaud smiling down at her from the window above the entrance to the flats. She and Madame Alibert rivalled each other in spying on street activities but Madame Libaud was the nicer of the two. Misha waved back and held her nose pointedly, turning her head away from the butcher's shop and its hated metallic smell of meat and the red-handed man himself, Lagrue. Cracking bones he was, just at the moment she chose to be going home. He always seemed to be cracking bones, cracking them with an axe.

Turning towards the Bonaparte, she realised she'd made the passing of the shops like a last walk. As if these chairs and these tables set out on the pavement would one day not be there, nor these windows with the brass-rail half-way and the gold lettering against the green stating Café Bonaparte!

Inside, she breathed in the familiar smell: Gauloises, coffee and, faintly, drains, the smell of Paris itself. It had been her first grown-up joy, the place where'd she'd fallen in love with a city and a way of life. The morning of their arrival, she and her mother had sat for breakfast at the table which became hers, in the corner by the left-hand window, where she too spied on street activities. Robert Blanchard, son of the house and ill-tempered reluctant waiter, had slammed bowls and bread before them without in any way acknowledging their order. It was his rudeness that told Yvette Martin she was back home and she'd given Misha a rare smile. 'You can dip the bread in, darling,' she'd said. Always before there'd been a sharp frown meaning: Elbows off the table, sit up straight. Misha hadn't had to sit up; it was elbows on the table and big bites of coffee-soaked bread, melting butter around your mouth and a spoon to collect the warm crumbs at the bottom of the bowl. She hadn't hesitated over this extraordinary freedom.

It was still an enchantment and mustn't be taken away. Robert put pomegranate syrup in front of her without her

11

having asked for it, as if her world were not at risk. It wasn't obvious to him of course; he hadn't heard her father's voice shaking foundations. He looked gloomy, but then he always did. She doubted he ever glanced about him, as she did now, at the poster darkened by years of tobacco smoke – RICARD, LE VRAI PASTIS, at the bottle green tiles, the black stove that huffed out smoke. It was Robert's prison; he wanted Sundays and evenings off like other people but dared not free himself from the family business. Maybe he was wishing there would be a war; that would get him away from home fast enough. He was due to be called up in the first group of men. If he were killed, his mother would die of grief.

Misha suddenly couldn't face the syrup. The chicken lay nauseous and solid in her stomach. She wanted to live on things that didn't have to be slaughtered, bright clean fruits, coffee, bread, cream, sweet-smelling things. She wanted to be free and independent and two years older. She shouldn't have to think of Robert dying. There shouldn't be this threat of war. Everyone knew Hitler was a madman.

'Our girl is sad,' called Monsieur Jules, Robert's father, rubbing the dish of the day, rabbit in mustard sauce, off the blackboard on the counter. Madame Florence, his wife, stood at his shoulder mindlessly wiping salt cellars, brooding gaze fixed upon Robert who was snatching the cloth from the last table. 'Like us all,' she said, 'why should Mademoiselle Misha be any different?'

Misha kept her gaze and her thoughts away from the immense sorrow she had just seen in Madame Florence's face. 'Is Reine down yet?' she said. She must think of something cheerful. Reine wouldn't be worrying about war. She only worried about earning enough money to have her little girl raised in a convent.

'Reine is not down,' Madame Florence called, stirring herself. 'And if you were my daughter, I'd have something to say about you taking your coffee with a lady of the street. One of these days I'm going to tell your mother exactly who you're mixing with. Haven't you met any nice girls at your typing classes...' She began clattering saucers, muttering.

12

Misha didn't feel well enough for this familiar disagreement with Madame Florence. Her heart had given another violent lurch. 'That reminds me,' she said. 'School! I'm to be sent to England to some awful school. And I've got cousins I don't know about!'

The three Blanchards seemed pleased on all counts, pointing out the safety of England, families and the need for proper education in the modern world, which wasn't what she wanted to hear. She wanted someone to scoff away the chill of fear that made her shiver on the hottest of August days.

She couldn't settle to her afternoon contentment as she often did. Why hadn't she noticed before this unhealthy preoccupation of theirs with some war that might not come to pass? She got up and pushed across her sous. They only let her pay half-price for drinks, arguing with true French logic that she couldn't afford more. Sometimes, when they were busy, she helped Madame Florence with the washing up.

'I'll see you at breakfast if not this evening,' she said, trailing back out again and turning towards the apartment. It was four o'clock. If her father had left at the time he said he would, her mother would be free of him and changing to go out. She was never there on weekday evenings until about eight. On Sundays they went out together, for an English tea at Smith's in the rue de Rivoli or to stroll along the boulevards, window-shopping. They were sometimes spectators at the political demonstrations because there was often some protest in Paris, with the Left-wing demanding more for the people, holidays, wages, or freedoms, the Right-wing claiming the people already had too much and would shortly be bringing the country down with a Communist revolution. She and her mother understood little but Misha would repeat Philippe's explanations that in repression and oppression Left and Right wings had disagreeable meeting points. He understood everything.

The Jaguar was gone, Misha saw with relief, and her mother already in the doorway dressed for her outing. She had on her new costume in ivory printed silk crêpe, the print a mere shadow of blue and the jacket very tight-

13

waisted with square shoulders. It was that summer's outfit. She made a principle one each season, choosing pattern, cloth, buttons and trims with precision. 'You don't think I should have bought that beige crêpe instead of the ivory, Misha?' she began. 'How does it look?'

Misha had spent too many hours of her life in the haberdashery departments of Galeries Lafayette or Le Printemps to fall into this trap. 'You did say beige was a made-up colour,' she said, 'that upstart woman, Chanel, invented it. It's not classic enough for a lady, and a lady . . .' She stopped. What did she care if a lady should only wear the classic neutrals with possibly a touch of blue or navy in the summer? How could anyone, even her mother, spend another second on frivolities when the ground beneath their feet was being dragged at?

Her mother wasn't listening. Maybe she was trying to cling on to what she had. 'But isn't this ivory glaring. It suddenly seems somehow . . . and what about the pleat just here?' She picked at the stuff with red nails. 'Be careful with that apple tart, please.'

'It's nice,' Misha muttered, peering at the perfection of pleating at the waistband. 'Look, *Maman*, can't you persuade him to let me stay? He can't mean it, it'll cost him too much. And we were all right, weren't we?' She gazed into the still mask of her mother's face. How could she herself have been born with such a turmoil of longing to a mother so different?

'Don't start worrying yet, darling, please, you'll come out in a rash and for nothing. Maybe the war'll be called off. There are plenty of diplomats and politicians flying all over Europe. It's still being talked through. You'll see, Hitler'll give in, he won't want France and Britain against him. America might join in like last time.'

'I don't care about last time.' Misha wandered into the kitchen to put her slice of apple tart beside her supper on the table, half a baguette, two tomatoes, the morsel of Brie. 'It's now that matters, *Maman*. Please try to persuade him. I can get a job the way we talked about, with the typing lessons you let me start. I might as well get some result out of the expense . . .'

14

'Yes. Maybe you won't need to be like me, married to a man like your father, Misha.' Her mother had followed her. Misha turned and stared. She had never before admitted so much, even when Misha used to shout at her, 'I don't want to be trapped like you!' It was of course rare for a woman to work once safely married but her mother had never seemed to understand how cravenly she was bound. 'Perhaps we can both get a job, Misha, and be modern working women together. It'd be an adventure, wouldn't it!' She leaned up to kiss her daughter's cheek. 'We'll see. I may be a little late this evening, don't wait up.'

'I won't,' Misha said, bending to place a kiss in return, feeling at her most ungainly, as she always did beside her mother, being so much taller. 'You will think about it, won't you, because if my father says I've got to go and I refuse, I say I can't and I hide or something, what'll happen?'

'We'll see,' her mother said, drawing on cream kid gloves.

Misha didn't know until much later that her mother did try, that afternoon to make arrangements for her to stay in Paris outside her father's control. She watched her trot off on her slender legs towards the corner of the street and the boulevard beyond. On cue, Alibert and the butcher Lagrue appeared in their doorways, also to watch Yvette Martin's high heels negotiating the cobblestones.

Now, warm silence, routine, her haven. She mustn't let any of it be spoiled. She must keep this evening intact, make it the same, because there might not be many left.

She did her usual things therefore, putting a spoonful of the Brie on a saucer and moving to the special place which had seemed to be her first haven.

The heat still lingered from the long humid day in this gloomy room which never had much light, facing as it did the inner courtyard. Here were the principal treasures of her childhood, mostly novels that had helped her live her interior life during their travels. Few children were considered good enough to play with the daughter of Michael Martin. There were two dolls with floppy heads, a stuffed dog without ears, and the base of a broken lamp. She'd kept it for its elegant shape, a ballerina with one slender arm outstretched. She'd wanted to be a dancer once but was already too tall by the age of seven or eight. Lessons were therefore a waste of money. Beside the lamp was the photograph of her brother Félix aged about six, taken at their grandparents' farm in the Languedoc where their father had sent him when it became evident his mind wasn't growing normally.

Misha picked this up in her passage across the room. Félix looked solemn in it, and proud, because a dog had consented to be held in his arms. Animals were his only interest. Their lack of speech suited him because he didn't use words either. He'd need his sister if there were to be bombs and guns. Noise made him scream and in the past she'd been the only one who could soothe him. Could this be the way to stay in France? It'd only take a few days to go down to fetch him and bring him back by train. If her father went off again, he'd never know. Félix and she and her mother could be a proper family again, looking after each other. But where would they find enough money for the train fare, even if her mother agreed?

She replaced the photograph and looked across the court-yard to the apartment at right angles to their own. There was the chestnut tree set in flagstones at the centre. If this had grown outwards instead of upwards to the sky, she'd never have caught sight of the fat little tabby waiting with desolate dignity on Philippe's window-sill for his return home.

She sat down in her blue plush chair with the broken spring, put saucer and elbows on the ledge and looked across to Frou on hers. She knew the cat had seen her for she broke out of her trance-like state and began a casual washing of one paw.

Misha smiled. Frou always made her smile and she'd loved Frou before she loved her master. Soon the cat abandoned pretence and jumped heavily down to the flagstones, making her stately way across on slim little legs like a fat woman, all bosom and barrel body, who teeters on the finest of heels. Misha leaned down to help her on to the sill. Her exquisite triangle of tabby face looked up and a violent purr greeted the morsel of Brie.

The two then settled for their next wait, contented and

16

comfortable together. They glanced about them in recognition of usual courtyard evening activities and finally fixed their eyes upon the window opposite for the arrival of Philippe David Constantin. Darkly handsome, clever, at thirty already a professor, he was absent-minded, distant, pre-occupied and yet often chose to bestow on the two of them half an hour of his time.

Frou had begun to stir, ear pricked, a low purr rumbling. Was he coming? Yes, there he was, leaning from his window and smiling, she could see, the rare wide smile that made her heart thud. It didn't matter that the smile might be for the pleasure of watching his very fat little cat in matronly flight across the courtyard, at her impetuous leap upward that almost failed. It might be for her too, and please God, she thought, let this not be nearly the last evening.

Next came the sound of his voice calling, 'Good evening!' His arms were full of hot tabby and she wanted to weep. Her news and her need that evening certainly couldn't wait for his invitation to join him for an aperitif. She didn't therefore bother to go the long way round, using doors, but sat on the window ledge and swung her too-thin legs to the ground, as ungraceful, she knew, as Frou, but if he were to hold her against him where Frou now lay basking . . .

He showed no surprise to see her running across. 'Do you intend to come in the same way as our cat?' he enquired mildly.

The usual absurd blush spread to her ears but Philippe's manners were as perfect as everything else about him. He wouldn't mock her as her father did. He was now so close she could see the thick line of black lashes framing eyes that were hazel with darker flecks. The skin around was always shadowed with tiredness. He often sat up late talking with friends at restaurant tables, or working here where she could see him from her hiding place in her own room, the lamp light outlining the shape of his head as he wrote.

He was still smiling, his usual grave air transformed into lightness with a suggestion of humour in it, almost teasing, that Misha dared think sometimes was especially for her.

17

She looked at his long tanned fingers wrapped about Frou and at Frou with her gaze of joy behind half-closed eyes. The same joy threatened to spread through her but today was different. The thought itself, I am full of joy because he is here, contained a stab of terror and nothing could be the same.

'Would you like lemonade or some of my wine with water, Misha?' He waited for no answer but went into the kitchen, leaving her to climb the ledge. 'I'll offer this prima donna her supper,' he called, 'I didn't stop for fish again this evening, it's still so hot none of it was fresh. The butcher minced up some beefsteak for her. What's to happen to food supplies when war is finally declared, I cannot imagine.'

War! Misha landed with a thump because her clumsiness didn't matter today. The evening before, it had seemed a huge obstacle between her and Philippe. She'd knocked over the lamp on his desk and he'd smiled so sweetly, she'd longed to die of shame. Now there was the word 'war' on his lips and she must face it, find a way to escape from her father's control and help with the war, not run away from it. She'd learn first-aid, roll bandages, wash wounds. Philippe would be proud of her. She'd be proud of herself and she'd be useful, needed for the first time since her father had banished Félix from his sight.

She moved about the untidy room just the same, in case, taking in the familiar images, the shelves of books jumbled anyhow, the volumes on the floor by his desk, the desk itself and the lamp she hadn't broken which gave the light for her to see him from her window. The shade was a pretty blue but there was no other colour in the room, no vase or ornament, only a pot stuffed with pencils and a print of a Paris street near the fireplace. This fact had pleased her for it meant no woman had ever had the right to put her touch there as she longed to do. She'd gone so far as to feel grateful to her mother for forcing her to learn needlework and had been picturing herself kneeling in front of the two English armchairs by the hearth with tape measure and sample book! Misha gave a gasp of pity for herself, remembering how she'd been prepared to be housewifely, for Philippe, and how even this potential sacrifice was to be denied her! She put a hand on the jacket he'd worn, a finger on the button of his lamp, fearing she was doing these things for very nearly the last time.

From the kitchen came Frou's little squeaks of pleasure. This meant her supper had been placed on the kitchen table which was hers because Philippe never ate at home. And then came his voice, low in pitch but strong, breaking into her fantasy that she'd be the one receiving Frou's ecstatic thanks as she went on to prepare their meal, her own and Philippe's after she'd spent a happy day tidying his papers, typing out his research work with skill and speed.

He came towards her carrying the atlas he used as a tray. 'I saw you this morning helping the Widow Libaud back from the market again. How sweet you are, Misha, to spend time on someone no one else bothers with, though she's a bright woman with a lot to say.'

Misha sat down in her usual chair. 'It's only because I haven't enough to do, that's all,' she said. She could hear her own voice sounding ungracious. She didn't want to be sweet.

'It's quite unusual, you know, for someone as young as you to give up your time. She says you listen to her stories about the past and are such a nice girl . . .'

I don't want to be nice, Misha thought, I want to be clever and sophisticated, all the things I'm not.

'My father came back today and said I've got to go to England for the war, to some proper school,' she said.

He had pulled aside his tie and rolled up his sleeves. She could almost feel the warmth of his body and this dreamed-of, dreaded intimacy unnerved her. 'I shan't mind about the danger if only everything can go on being the same,' she cried. 'If only I can stay here with Frou . . .' It was her silliest voice. She'd almost betrayed herself. He must have been able to feel the burning heat of her body as the usual shaming blush spread into her hair.

'Ah,' he said, placing the atlas with precision on the desk and staring at it. 'So.' Misha thought she could hear her watch ticking an entire minute away. 'Yes. If only. What very sad words. What despair they hold in them, Misha.' He didn't turn to look at her. She wondered if he hadn't

19

begun to think of something else, the way he often seemed to do when they sat together. She saw his hand on her glass, his fingers holding it. 'If only,' he said suddenly, startling her, and finally offering the glass. 'I thought it wouldn't be long before your father made some such decision.'

She took the lemonade, careful not to touch him, and watched as he took up his usual place opposite her across the hearth where she'd dream of him being for infinite days to come. 'Let's drink,' he said, 'to your safety in England and to our poor Frou having the supper she demands. When the war's here, she'll be lucky to have horsemeat and you'll be lucky to be in England.'

'To Frou,' Misha said, raising her glass and pushing aside the image of slaughtered horses and her vague knowledge of some past war when the people of Paris had eaten rats and zoo animals to survive. 'But I could just stay here, it'll be safe enough, and who can say that England will be safer? I must stay, you see. I never felt at home anywhere before, my father has trailed us around Europe, but I've grown to love Paris, Frou . . . the Bonaparte. I can't bear to think of leaving anything.' She gave a girlish sniff and was ashamed.

'Oh, Misha!' He put his glass down and she could see his face had taken on such a look of sadness, she thought, He's going to tell me he knows I love him, but I'm just a friend and he loves someone else, the lady with the glossy hair. She heard herself gasp, waiting.

'If only I had the choice,' he said, 'I should like things to go on being the same, I should like to go on looking after my two . . . but if your father has decided upon this for you, before it is too late, I'm glad. I don't want to think of you here when war is finally declared. You could be in serious danger – and, anyway, nothing here will be the same. I shan't be in Paris. I'll be called up.'

For a moment, Misha was flooded with relief that he hadn't spoken of love but then the horror moved up from her stomach to her throat: he was going to war.

'Shortly, I presume,' he went on, 'I'll be on some battle line with many other thousands of men from all over Europe and the colonies too.'

Misha felt giddy. Why hadn't she realised he might go to

20

war? 'But you don't have to go surely, you're not a soldier,' she said, her voice rising. She'd seen the newspaper headlines, heard the news bulletins, and shut her mind to the truth the way she always did.

'I shall have to become one. It will be my duty to go to war, my dear Misha,' he said gravely. 'An easy duty if I remember what I have to defend.' He leaned across and put out a hand as if to touch her. 'You are about to break one of my mother's glasses.' He took it from her fingers and placed it on the arm of the frayed armchair which had seemed hers.

Misha sat carefully back in it and let the routine resume, for Frou had finished her post-supper wash on the atlas. She came to perch on the chair by his left arm. Philippe began to talk about Hitler and his mad brutal boasts of ruling the whole of Europe.

Misha didn't want to listen. 'Why can't Hitler just be grateful for Poland? Isn't one entire country enough extra land for the Germans? Why do they need more? Oh, if you go away, who'll look after Frou? People ate cats in the Great War, I read about it.' Her heart gave an involuntary thud of distress. 'And isn't France supposed to be unconquerable with the Maginot Line round it? I'll stay here and keep Frou with me . . .' Making an immense effort, she refused the impulse to cry because her tears would embarrass him.

Philippe left his chair and moved to the window. 'The Maginot Line is a folly, Misha,' he said. 'Half-built, out-of-date already, and giving grounds for many people to be confident it'll prevent invasion, when it won't. It might conceivably have been some use in the kind of trench warfare we suffered before, but now the Germans have tanks and air power. We've bought horses, you know, fifty thousand cavalry horses! The enemy hasn't bothered to buy in horses for their army and they'll come here in their tanks and their aeroplanes and take what is ours, our land, our food, our industry. They'll call it their New Order for Europe and will commit brutal theft and slaughter on their march through other people's towns and countryside, laying waste as they go on and on . . .'

21

'Yes, to England,' she cried, wanting him to continue for the pleasure of his voice telling her how things really were, wanting him to stop because she didn't want to know the truth.

'No!' he cried back. 'England will have time yet. You'll be all right there, safe. And think of it, Misha, a proper training for your lively mind so it won't be wasted on shopping and housework. Isn't that what you want? It's what you deserve.' She thought he'd turned back to her. She too turned her stiff body towards his silhouette at the window. She couldn't see his face, only the dark shadow of it.

Outside in the courtyard a boy playing with a toy aeroplane shrieked with excitement. This made Frou stir from her doze and waddle across the room to check on the intrusion.

Philippe picked her up. 'As for our little cat,' he said, 'we cannot risk her being pursued by a starving mob, can we? I've already decided to take her to live with my mother in the country where she'll be well fed and kept as safe as can be . . .'

He was trying to joke though there couldn't be jokes any more. 'But Frou's heart will break if you banish her!' cried Misha.

'Oh, I think girls are usually fickle and soon find another attachment that suits them so well, they easily forget their first love.'

She nodded dumbly, unable to reply even in defence of Frou, the incriminating blush spreading up from her toes. Neither of them would ever forget!

'Once Frou has scent of my mother's dairy and the cream churn, she won't want to come back to Paris. And she's certainly young enough to settle elsewhere.'

Misha said, 'No, Frou won't ever settle, she'll be waiting for you to come back from the war.' As I shall be waiting, she thought, a sudden feeling of anguish taking away her breath. Frou and she would be waiting for him together, whatever else happened. She was gazing at the dark silhouette of Frou in Philippe's arms and telling herself she would make sure of it, when she heard him say something extraordinary.

'I wonder if you'd like to join me? We could make a day of it, have lunch there. You could see where I was brought up.'

To this also, Misha was unable to reply. He was offering what she'd longed for, a glimpse into his life, his family, and his past, but the joy of whole hours in his presence was going to be tainted with fear. War was coming and nothing was going to stop it. She was going to lose these precious evening times, and Frou, and then she'd have to begin being really afraid. She'd have to let fear seep into her in place of dreams, because Philippe was going into battle.

Chapter 2

'You mean, poor child, that you never had a real home you could feel sure of?' Philippe's mother asked, her plump cheeks drawn in at the thought of it.

'Yes, and my mother certainly never cooked pancakes like yours.' Misha, recklessly disloyal, tucked into black cherry clafoutis, juice on her chin and two pairs of gentle eyes facing her across the table. She felt warmed through, and not from the August heat that was doubled here in this happy kitchen where Philippe must have eaten countless times.

She put a hot hand on the scrubbed wood. This was where he must have spread out his homework, talked of his school day, the prizes he'd won, perhaps his first girl. She'd have liked to remain here a week to learn the things Philippe wouldn't tell her himself. Suddenly she couldn't take another spoonful because a profound joy filled her and the weight of his gaze was too much to bear.

'Eat!' commanded Madame Constantin. 'Or my goats will be spoiled for their supper.' She wore a faded black cotton dress like most French countrywomen. Anyone could see she was Philippe's mother from the set of her shoulders and a way of holding her head that was the same as his. Her eyes were like his too, hazel with darker flecks. In fact, she was altogether motherly in a way her own mother was not, being mostly occupied in attending to the needs of her son and his guest rather than her own. She hadn't served herself with pancake but was already busy back at the stove putting on water for coffee.

Misha tried to imagine her mother transported to this kitchen where a stove had to be kept up and cleaned out, poultry plucked, vegetables peeled. She said, stifling because his eyes wouldn't leave her in peace, 'If you ever need help with the harvest or anything.' And what foolishness this was! Philippe was smiling at her now because of course there was no harvest. It was a dairy farm, with cows, goats, and fruit orchards. She'd been shown all round it and seen no wheat or corn fields. Embarrassment and heat now coloured pink every inch of her skin. Her hands were pink and covered in cherry juice and she couldn't look beyond her plate.

'With the apples, dear child? Of course I'd like your help if you can spare the time.' Bustling back to the table, Madame Constantin sat down at the table next to her son. 'In fact, if you find yourself in need of refuge during this terrible war to come, I would welcome your company as well as your young strength. That's if you wouldn't mind staying with a lonely old widow . . .'

'Oh, I prefer older people,' Misha said, and stopped at once. She was going to get herself further tangled up in embarrassing conversation. But it didn't matter. Everything was all right. She'd been welcomed here, in Philippe's childhood home, and his mother liked her and she could never have dreamed this day would come.

Leaving Philippe and his mother to say their goodbyes, Misha stood outside on the dusty gateless path where Philippe must have scuffed his boots coming home from school. She was trying to take it all in for the less privileged days to come, the indifferent yet friendly chickens scavenging at her feet, the cottagey house with its faded red roof, the ancient twisted apple trees massed behind it. She could smell fruit scents, and dust. The day had gone too fast, had given her too many images and scents to remember, but she must remember.

She gazed on and finally let herself look up to the first floor window on the left where the shutters of the spare room had been closed. Frou had been locked in so she wouldn't see them leave and set off to follow. Her last view of the tabby was a stiff rump under the bed where she was hiding her head and thus her indignation and her hurt.

Her own hurt was only in abeyance, she knew that. Frou was probably the first of many losses to come. She'd like to run back into the house and hold her one last time.

The day, their day together, was nearly over. Glued to her seat beside Philippe, watching his fingers on gear lever and steering wheel, Misha was too hot, too near him. They'd talked through her entire childhood and some of his and now they'd reached her happiest year, when her father had brought her to Paris. The discussion, or rather his announcement in the Lipp, had also been talked through once more and there was still no solution possible to the bare facts: war was coming, it was coming soon, and her father was sending her to England. And she couldn't stay without a job though she had no training for one, not even a typing certificate. Desperate, she said, 'I might do war work. Women did in 1914. They had men's jobs, running the buses, making ammunition whilst the men got on with their own horrors, rape, pillage, murder, war, just as they've nearly always done.' Now, she thought, a flush of embarrassment making her over-heated skin redder than ever, now he will laugh at me.

Her adolescent discoveries about male aggression were hardly new.

Philippe didn't laugh. 'They're men's crimes, yes, Misha. And the best way for you to be safe from the misery they'll bring is to go to England. I shall like to think of you joining those wonderful English charity workers who make tea and are endlessly resourceful and cheerful. They won't give in to Hitler. Some of the French, you know, are prepared to welcome the German Army if, or when it comes. They imagine it'll bring with it German culture, order and discipline, which we poor grubby French with our love of life and our decadence sorely need. They see the clean, swept streets of German towns and don't choose to notice the bloodstains where for years past Nazis mobs have been committing rape, pillage and murder. But Germany is now a place of desolation, a shameful, degraded place where the sick are not cared for, where gypsies, dissidents of any kind, foreigners, socialists, the Jewish people – all are persecuted, imprisoned, chased out. One day, France might find itself in the same state and not just because the German Army occupies it and rules by SS and Gestapo terror. To take over a country as big as France, they'll need French collusion and they may well get it. So Misha, please do as your father says this last time.' He turned towards her and changed gear with an awkward jarring movement, having to slow down for a stream of lorries to pass. 'You do understand me?'

Misha nodded, knowing he spoke the truth. But she didn't want truth. 'Even so,' she said, 'even if Paris is taken over, I ought to stay and help. I could do first aid and things.' This was her most foolish suggestion because she couldn't bear the sight of blood. 'Like Melanie and Scarlett in *Gone with the Wind*, helping with amputations,' she cried, her voice rising. The rumbling noise of the lorries filled his car through the open windows. 'Writing last letters to loved ones.' Exhilarated, full of anguish, she went further, because she knew he couldn't hear her. 'Or manning the barricaded Paris streets as women did in the French Revolution, risking their life . . .' She'd have liked to begin crying. She'd be helpless in the face of suffering, blood, war, and this would the last time she ever sat beside Philippe.

'Misha!' He'd turned a sharp corner and brought the car to a stop. 'Listen to me. Please go to this Bournemouth. This place which is so quiet and sunny no bomb can ever fall on it.' There were dark lines under his eyes she hadn't seen before, and a new hollowness around his cheeks. The thought came from nowhere that she might lay her lips there. Her head swam.

'And you must stay stout and true as many of your countrymen and women will do. They'll just get on with the task of repelling the enemy. Good against evil, straight-forward. D'you hear me, Misha? Will you promise me that?' He was leaning towards her, his voice urgent. She saw the flecks in his eyes were so dark they were black and there was a black shadow round his chin he'd soon have to shave. She'd never see him shave. She'd never put her lips to his face. She couldn't answer because she couldn't speak. Every moment was bringing the end nearer.

'And when it is over, you must come back to Frou and me. We'll be watching the courtyard for you.'

No, she thought, the time cannot be here yet, and anyway, war isn't certain, he must know that.

He'd shut himself away again, starting up and reaching into the glove compartment. 'Look,' he said, 'I asked Monsieur Steiner to take this photograph of Frou for you. There she is, on the window ledge. I couldn't take it myself. She'd have come to see what I was up to.'

A horn sounded behind them. Misha took the square of shiny paper. This then. He'd thought of this for her days, perhaps weeks before. He'd known she'd be forced to leave Paris. There had been a conspiracy. Everyone had realised it, her mother, the Blanchards, because they'd accepted war was coming. Only she'd been drifting along in her dream world. Here was reality, this goodbye present, this souvenir, and this, her father's vulgar new Jaguar in front of their apartment. Beside it, her father with his driving cap on. This meant he'd soon be leaving. And he meant her to go with him. She saw his heavy face, florid in a last beam of sunlight, looking beyond her as her tired body tried to organise itself to leave the car. She hadn't even noticed they were so near the boulevard St Germain. Her legs were made of jelly.

'Get inside, young lady,' she heard him say. She heard Philippe open his door and say something polite. She wanted to thank him for a lovely day but couldn't move her jelly legs.

Chapter 3

Her mother was hovering by the bathroom door. 'I've put out my new ivory crêpe for you to wear in England, Misha, though it may be a bit short. You've grown so tall. You're still growing! I don't want you going shabby to your English relations. They'll expect you to be wearing something French and chic, won't they? And your cousins will introduce you to some nice English boys. They'll be queuing up for the honour of escorting you to those quaint dances of theirs. In fact, I might get in some nice taffeta silk and make a dress for you.'

'You mean I'm to go now, *Maman*? How can that be? He said a few days. Haven't you tried to persuade him? Isn't there any hope?'

'No, darling, he's sure it's for the best and maybe this time he's right. Quite honestly, Misha, I'd like you to make a fresh start. It's not healthy, mooning over that professor the way you do . . .'

As if in a dream, Misha saw her trot busily away into the bathroom where her own feet followed and took her to the edge of the bath. Here she found herself sitting down with every appearance of unbuttoning her dress. It was a conspiracy, to send her away in a rush. Vaguely, she registered the patch of grey at the crown of her mother's red sheen of hair as she bent to turn off the taps. It was dyed then? And for how long past without telling her daughter? There'd been pretence. Underneath her dream-world, sham. And nothing of her life under her own control. It was her own fault. She'd been blindly letting herself get to this

29

point. Perhaps her father wanted her to show him how independent she could be. He'd be laughing at her more than ever now, because she was a coward, afraid to run away. Where would she go, how would she live?

'I'll be lonely without you, Mish,' her mother said, testing the bathwater. 'It won't be for long, you'll see. You'll hardly have learned how to hold one of those hockey sticks! The war'll soon be over. I've packed all your sets of lingerie, the three lawn ones. D'you remember how I made you unpick those straps a dozen times? And I've put in one of my best black silk in case you should be living the high life over there. How clumsy you used to be with your needle, but you'll thank me one day, it's one area your poor mother's made you independent . . .' She poured in her own Chanel No 5 bath salts as if Misha had them every day instead of once, after she'd had her tonsils out. Stepping mechanically into the water, Misha hardly noticed. She had only one thought: she didn't want to leave.

She refused her mother's suit. The ivory shade made her look shinier and gawkier than ever. But she went so far as to stand in front of her mother's wardrobe discussing the matter sensibly. There was no bickering. They settled on a dove-grey crêpe dress of her mother's from two summers before and a straw hat with a grey ribbon round it. The dress was only a little tight on the shoulders. Misha saw the grey became her, complementing her flush of colour, and the hat balanced her height. She looked more grown-up, as was appropriate.

'Perfect.' Her mother clapped her hands. 'Now don't get creased before you leave. I'm just going down to the cellar to look in our trunks. I've a feeling your bodices from last winter might still fit, and you never know, the war might drag on until Christmas.'

Misha decided she wouldn't say goodbye. She'd write it later instead. It wouldn't be fair to let her mother worry. She'd put a note through the window for her mother to keep secret until her father had given up the search and left. Then everything could be open between them, the dyed hair, everything. Her mother must have had dreams once.

Perhaps her dreams had been of Paris; she had left her home in the south to work in a Paris store.

Philippe's mother would understand as well and she'd welcome her help. They'd produce food together. There couldn't be a more noble kind of war work.

It would be sinful to hide a healthy body in sunny Bournemouth when she could help keep the army on the march.

Philippe was there. She could see his shadow behind the panes of his window and she paused, because the shadow was like a ghost. Perhaps this was a presentiment. He was going to die in battle and she'd one day knock on the glass again, calling his name when he was dead like the traveller in the poem who cries, 'Is there anybody there?' and no one answers. They are long since in their grave. Her legs had turned to lead. But Philippe appeared and threw up the window frame. Misha then saw another shadow behind him, a woman's shadow, throwing off a hat. Heat seemed to swirl about her body because she also saw a polka-dot ribbon land near his pencils on the desk and a voice, not Philippe's, high and sharp, said, 'My God, who's that at the window, darling? One of the concierge's brats again?'

Philippe didn't answer this voice. He said, 'Misha, how smart you look.' And, moving closer to the sill, 'I have a friend here, she's just back from America and some course she's been on. Is your father to leave today?' He reached out to take both her hands in his. For the first time, Misha felt the skin of his fingers on hers and it was too late. Because of the woman, she was already stunned with shock. 'Yes, and I cannot bear to go,' she began and stopped.

What foolishness had brought her here? How much too far she'd gone. He'd guessed, of course, and that was why he was being so kind. She dared not look up into the sweet sadness of his face that would tell her he knew she loved him and didn't want to leave him. She gazed instead at the line of buttons on his shirt. Just an hour before, she'd been near enough to touch them. The middle ones were loose. It was surprising his mother hadn't insisted on sewing them on properly. She'd reached the last one where the skin of

31

his neck seemed so vulnerable when the woman's voice broke in on them again.

'Who is it, Philippe? Hurry up, I must have a bath. That ghastly journey! I don't know why you couldn't bring the car over to Calais to fetch me.'

All the heat in Misha's body vanished. She thought that even her hands, held so tight, had grown cold, like the cold space in her chest. This woman was to stay with him. It would be she who stood behind him whilst he hummed, shaving; she who one day organised new covers for his frayed armchairs.

Philippe leaned forward, his voice urgent, his grip harder. 'Remember, Misha my dear, whatever happens, I'll be here if you need me. I promise.'

He was being so kind. Like his mother, who'd taught him to be kind.

Misha jerked her hands from his. She must get away, as far as she could. England would barely be far enough. He pitied her.

No one noticed her unseemly return. Her mother was busy being a mother at last, fussing over the suitcase. Her father, too big and ungainly for the hallway, shouted out his impatience: 'Come NOW!' I want to catch the late ferry and I've got an appointment in London after I've put you on the Bournemouth train.'

Soon Misha found herself seated in his new and vulgar Jaguar, scrabbling about in the holdall where she'd thrown her most precious things, her favourite books and the shiny square of cardboard with Frou's image on it. This Philippe had given her, in friendship.

Her father's voice reached her. He said, laughing, 'I've told that bloke of yours what I think of him, consorting with a girl of sixteen. Typical bloody Frenchie! Good job I'm getting you away from here . . .'

She shut out the humiliation of his sullying voice and sat carefully still beside him. He revved his engine and set off with an explosion of noise that brought the errand boy, Denis, the butcher and the baker's wife to their shop doorways. I shall never again wave at Denis, she thought, or

32

walk this street, or sit at my place in the Bonaparte. Because she could never return. Not even when the war was over. And more, she must wipe out her memories, all of the precious times, the waiting hour, hide them as Frou had hidden her head. She mustn't think of Frou either, with her pain disguised as pride, or the most recent matter of a black polka-dot ribbon. She must find another dream, somehow. She deserved to be banished, and welcomed banishment.

Her father didn't speak to her again, indulging instead in his usual habit of trying to pass everyone else, gesturing out of the window to indicate his contempt for fools who shouldn't be allowed behind a wheel. In this he was rather French, Misha had always thought. She didn't care now because he too would soon be a part of her past.

On the ferryboat, she saw other people leaving their past behind. It was packed with elderly English couples of the kind living genteel retirements in the south of France, preferring sun to fog and damp. Her father, in the bar, seemed to stand out amongst them, louder, taller. She found she had a glass of lemonade she hadn't asked for and was jammed against his gingery tweed opposite an elderly pair he was being polite to. 'You see, with my secret war work, my aunt, who thinks of me as her own, might well worry herself into the grave. I wouldn't like that on my conscience. Of course, my duty lies with my country . . .'

Misha stared at the couple, at their papery old skin, at their blue-veined hands trembling over their whisky glasses, their shaky earnest nods of agreement.

'What war work?' she asked, waking up. He'd never mentioned 'work' before, being apparently too grand for it. 'You said you had deals to make, you were going to acquire some money at last, you deserved it.' She sat up, making herself comfortable on the stool. She could say anything she liked. She was free.

He took a gulp of whisky. 'That's my cover, child,' he said, winking at the couple. Misha could see they were seduced by his heavy charm. 'But from the moment war's declared, I'll disappear more or less, with a different identity, until it's over. And I can say no more than that.'

33

Misha felt her hand hesitate near her glass. Did he mean he was to be a spy? 'D'you mean . . .' she began. But her father hadn't finished. 'Now I will emphasise this, Michèle. Once you reach your aunt's, don't mention me. Say if you have to that I'm well and have gone abroad. My company's sent me to Africa, say. She'll see that as safer than home. I'll be in touch when I can. Soon as the war's done with and that won't be long.'

'But you don't have a company, Dad, you've always said you wouldn't kowtow to anyone.' She knew he didn't want this kind of reply and that's why she gave it. She wanted to punish him.

Eventually, the three of them learned from his hints that he had some vital role in the war plans of Downing Street, the Ministry of Defence or M15. He'd be required to lead a lonely and dangerous life his family must never know about, especially if Germany did invade Britain. 'I don't mind telling you, Misha, I'm almost certainly on the German hit list and if they get to the families . . .' He shook his head and the old woman stared, hand to her mouth. 'So it's essential, dear girl, you forget you've got a father.'

Misha thought she'd be very glad to find herself without one and very shortly would be old enough and strong enough for him not to matter. If she could be bothered, she'd write about these extraordinary revelations to her mother. When had they ever learned so much about his activities? Her mother had a right to know what he did and maybe would be interested.

She found they were soon dining with the old couple, at their invitation, and the three of them talked long and loudly about The Last Lot, the 1914 war. She watched the man perk up and grow lyrical about the millions of deaths in the trenches, the British spirit and the Golden Youth who'd died. She realised she didn't know how old her father was, or whether he'd been in The Last Lot. He went on playing a part and she kept silent, heart throbbing with the beat of the ship's engine dragging her away to exile. What about This Lot? she thought. And Philippe lying in the trenches covered in mud? How would she be able to bear it when she learned he was dead?

*

Chapter 4

'Oh, *là, là!*' shrieked Misha's cousin Janet. 'I thought you were sixteen, not twenty-six. I say, French knickers! Golly! Wait till I tell them at school. Black silk underwear, tee hee . . .'

Misha looked down at the English plaits on Janet's trim shoulders. 'It's my mother's really,' she said, because she had to say something to this stranger. Strangers should be easy to talk to but Janet was not.

Janet looked up, properly attired for English girlhood in an Aertex shirt and grey worsted divided skirt. 'You won't be needing them at Beaufort House School,' she said, a grin closing her small pale eyes and emphasising the freckles on her cheeks. 'That dress hers too?' she enquired, pausing in her task of helping Misha unpack. She seemed to have laid out most of Misha's life with her possessions on the floor of the attic bedroom she was to occupy.

'Yes,' Misha said, prepared to explain her mother's perfections in detail, the choosing of the cloth, the buttons. If there were money enough, she'd ask her great-aunt if she could have a sporting outfit like Janet's, so she could begin her new life properly. Here was, she supposed, as good as anywhere.

'Thought so!' Janet jumped up, sniffing. 'Come on, time for tea with the grandparents – great-aunt and uncle to you!' She thundered off down the stairs, her sandy-coloured plaits bobbing.

They'd get used to each other, become friends, Misha thought. She'd learn friendship during this war-limbo period and be like other people. Perhaps one day she and Janet'd laugh about these first hours together and the oddness of sudden relations. And she'd belong. Now, first, family tea. She'd be glad she came. She'd be comforted by her aunt, the way she'd been by Madame Constantin. An aunt would be sure to be sad, hearing about her lonely childhood.

Step by step down the stairs after her cousin, Misha felt weaker and weaker. Self-pity was going to make her cry on her Great-aunt Maud's shoulder, on her shawl. There'd be a shawl, a cameo brooch, the scent of lavender, kindly old eyes, a tut-tutting. Even her father would feel a twinge of guilt when he heard about it.

There were several shawls wrapped about Great-aunt Maud, Misha could see that much in the dim-cornered room Janet had burst into, though she wasn't to learn whether her eyes were kindly for they never seemed to be looking her way. There might have been a brooch, but no comforting shoulder. Her aunt sat in a rocking chair by the empty hearth, gently squeaking.

'Golly, Grandma,' Janet said, 'you should see her under-wear! Black silk it is. Wait till I tell them at BH.'

'Ah, yes, your school, my dear.' The voice was no more than a whisper. 'Janet will take you to Daniel Neal's where you'll be fitted with a winter uniform. There'll be so few warm days left, summer dress could not be justified ... the expense ... Would you be so kind to take a cup of tea to your Uncle Harold?'

Misha edged round some ornaments. 'Of course, aunt,' she said, dutifully polite. 'He's in his bedroom?'

Janet fell on the sofa, shaking with silent laughter. 'He's over there, idiot,' she said.

An elderly man was also rocking gently in a chair by the window, so colourless himself, Misha hadn't seen him. She nevertheless sat beside him with her own cup and waited to be asked for the story of her journey and thus on to her childhood and the release of a few tears.

'Right, we're off now then, Grandma. Better get her gasmask fitted,' Janet shouted almost at once, leaping up and clattering china on a tray.

38

'Very well,' the old lady replied, with a squeak of her chair.

Afterwards, Misha learned this was one of the few sounds of the household, with the shuffle and tap of her great-uncle's stick as he made his way along the carpet strip at the centre of the hallway and stairs. Shuffle, shuffle, his slippers went, and tap, tap his stick. They'd all listen to it, she and Janet and presumably his wife, and the servant Joanie in the basement, who had fits and burned everything. And at first she thought that 'Very well, dear' were the only words she'd ever hear her great-aunt pronounce.

'But my baby will die if I've been killed first!' the woman screamed. The air-raid warden patiently replaced the baby-sized anti-gas container on the trestle table in the church hall where the last of the stock was scattered. He tried to take the bundle of wailing infant from its mother for a second demonstration.

Misha, swaying from heat and the smell of rubber, let her breath out in one long 'phut' of rude noises and tore at her own mask, rubber and Perspex squeaking.

'How will my baby live if the gas had already poisoned me and I can't keep pumping that thing?' the mother asked.

'It'll die, of course,' Janet whispered, smirking. 'Shouldn't have had a baby with war coming, should she? Come on, looks as if that one fits you.' She tossed the sandy-coloured plaits over her Aertex shoulders and strode across the hall on games-playing legs.

Misha struggled to pack her mask into its cardboard holder.

'All right, love?' the warden asked. 'Want me to show you again?'

Misha shook her head, face sweating from heat and rubber. 'Is it true, about the baby?' she whispered. The warden nodded grimly. 'But don't you worry your pretty little head,' he said. 'It's just precautions. Hitler's a great bully, that's all, typical short man. We'll see him off.' He winked a kind brown eye and drew himself up to his full six feet. 'You'll see.'

The new mother hadn't heard this. She stood transfixed

with horror, the baby held to her breast. Much later, Misha saw a mother with the same deathly skin. Her child had been sprayed with machine-gun bullets and she held a bundle of red shawls. The war had started by then because no one had seen off Hitler.

Janet was standing in the doorway. 'Better not make blowing off noises with that thing, by the way, not when you're in air-raid practice at Beaufort House. The Rack'll kill you. It'll be bad enough your standing out like a sore thumb in assembly when the rest of us'll be in summer gear. She does like things neat. And maybe we'd better ask my grandmother for more money to get you some sort of reasonable outfit to go about in at weekends.'

'There's nothing wrong with my grey dress, is there?' Misha trailed after her as Janet sprang off again. If only Janet would stay still long enough, she'd like to tell her how strange everything seemed, how she'd never been in a church hall or even a proper ordinary house and that though she was glad to find some family, they were strange too. Such a conversation might ease her bewilderment. What was she doing here watching this Janet do practice long-jumps down the pavement? Her watch told her it was twenty-four hours since she'd stood outside a certain window and heard a voice telling her he'd always be her friend. He'd pitied her because he'd guessed. 'This grey dress is all right?' she cried, exhausted feet taking her after the leaping Janet who'd never be a friend.

'Hardly!' Janet shouted. 'Come on, suppertime.'

Misha had stuffed a Bourbon biscuit into her mouth before she'd taken her bearings afresh in the basement kitchen where Janet had ordered her to sit at the table and shut up because Joanie was listening to Children's Hour. She understood that this was the routine, for Janet and the servant, that they led their own life in it. A biscuit tin was placed between them, there was more milky tea and a story on the wireless about a lamb with a croaking voice. Joanie nodded and smiled at the set on the dresser. For someone eating so many pink wafers just before supper, she was very thin. She wore an overall and a cotton turban and big round blank glasses.

'Goodnight, children, everywhere,' the wireless voice said.

'Goodnight, Uncle Mac,' Joanie cried, head nodding. Misha saw she was well past childhood and might be as much as fifty. More pink wafers disappeared into her mouth as Janet sniggered, 'Supper's burning again, Joanie.'

Joanie screamed, scrambling from her chair with disjointed movements Misha would soon find normal. Grabbing a saucepan from the stove, she threw it into the sink. Steam hissed and a smell of scorched vegetables came from it.

'Look out, old girl!' Janet slammed the lid on the biscuit tin. 'Isn't that a German soldier crouched by our window? I can see his bayonet glinting. He's coming to slice your head off.'

A saucepan lid rattled across the floor, following by a serving dish. Joanie didn't scream again. Misha saw she couldn't. Her body jerked, her mouth open in an O of terror.

'She thinks the German hordes'll soon be streaming across our clifftop to cut her into pieces, don't you, Joanie?'

Misha felt a tremor of feeling in the square of something cold that was her chest. She got up. 'But they won't, will they? She's only teasing, Joanie.' Her face was stiff but the words sounded normal enough. 'I come from France,' she said, and 'I know a lot about the war. There may not even be one.' Joanie rushed round the table and gripped her hand with her own bony one. 'Is it true?' she whispered.

'You're not to pander to her,' Janet shouted, thundering back up the stairs. 'She's only a servant and she gets silly.'

'I'll rinse off the cauliflower,' Misha said. 'If you like, Joanie, we can try putting a piece of bread into the saucepan with it to take the scorched taste out. It works with rice.'

Joanie nodded, still dumb, but by the time the six o'clock pips sounded, Misha knew she had a friend, albeit a mostly silent one, Joanie not being used to conversation.

It was finally to her that she recounted an edited version of her last twenty-four hours. She even managed a brief reference to life before exile. 'If this were, say, three days ago, Joanie, I'd be sitting in my bedroom with a fat little

41

cat called Frou watching the courtyard for people coming home from work.'

She felt a temporary ease with Joanie's rapt interest.

Five blank days. Misha, sitting in her new haven, the basement kitchen, turned the pages of her diary, once the receptacle for the account of her watching and waiting times. She could no longer remember why she'd watched and waited. She couldn't remember the feel of a hot tabby body anymore or the exact details of anyone's face. 'I've written nothing about my new life, Joanie,' she said, 'or about the day they made me leave home.' It was easy. After all, that was all that had happened. And she'd survived for a number of days she couldn't be bothered with.

'Better get on with writing about it then, Mish.' This was Joanie's usual sort of answer which made replying easy.

'There's a lot to describe. My new uncle nearly falling down the stairs at air-raid drill . . . Janet's friends inspecting me . . . going for an interview with Miss Rackman at Beaufort House School.' It was an honour to go to BH, the headmistress had said, and she intended to drag up an interest in the matter, in deference to her former self who'd longed for an education.

'Make it like a story,' Joanie said. She was sitting across the table, a long strip of potato peel winding into a bowl.

'I'll put in how hot and dark it gets in our attic rooms because my aunt makes us have the blackout.'

'And that once when I heard you crying I went in and you hadn't put the curtain down, and what if the German planes saw your light?'

'They aren't coming yet, Joanie, remember. I have promised to tell you when we've got to be really frightened.'

Joanie's knife jerked. 'Oh, here's the pips. Turn the wireless up, the man'll tell us.'

Because Big Ben was striking six, Misha didn't hear the commotion at the front door and was therefore startled to realise that a male voice was calling out to her from the bottom of the stairs: 'This is my *cousin*?'

A naval officer strode in and didn't wait for an answer, taking her hands and kissing her on both cheeks, French-

42

style. She hadn't been kissed by a man before. Her father had never kissed her, much less given her a comforting embrace. But her cousin Peter had charm, she recognised that at once. He stood close enough for her to see his tanned healthy skin, the perfect sharp line of his moustache and very blue eyes shining with good humour. This in itself was astonishing because no one in the house was good-humoured. He looked more than the nineteen or twenty she knew him to be and seemed not to match the sparse, neat bedroom she'd caught sight of from the landing. She'd thought he would be like his sister, short and sandy-haired, no more than a cadet just out of short trousers.

From behind him came Janet's sour voice. 'She's not like our side of the family, is she? Not that we really know where she comes from.'

Peter stood back for an inspection. Misha didn't mind this, and the fact she didn't mind was also astonishing. She felt suddenly pretty, even in her old pink cotton schoolgirl dress with the pique collar. She almost felt that one of her old silly embarrassed grins had appeared. 'Our noses are the same,' he announced, 'and our hair, though mine's thicker. Of course, little sister, she hasn't got your freckles.' He pulled her plaits affectionately and hugged her, striding round the table to hug Joanie too.

'She doesn't like meat unless it's inside tabby fur and cat-shape,' Janet said. 'She's got a photo of her pet left behind. That'll be eaten before the war's over, won't it?' She started looking in cupboards. 'We'll get some of Grandma's war hoard out and have a proper tea now you're here. You didn't say you had a twelve-hour leave coming up.'

Great-aunt Maud appeared at the top of the stairs and told Janet to run to the grocer's for Dundee cake, a tin of peaches and a pound of ham off the bone, so the war hoard was left alone, and Misha finally found herself at a family tea in the unused dining-room where dead flies lay in a rose bowl and the line of dark photographs on the mantelpiece didn't include one of her father. Joanie, scrabbling for the best china in the sideboard, dropped a saucer. No one drew a gasp of breath, probably because Peter leaped up and

43

cried, 'Lucky it's nothing important, Joanie dear, like a bit of you smashed up.'

Misha hadn't seen Joanie blossom before, and if you could say an old man blossomed, her uncle did that teatime. Peter let him ramble on about the kind of horror he remembered from The Last Lot. This usually made Janet snigger but all she did today was kick her legs beneath the table, waiting to tell her brother about her exploits on the tennis court with a former girlfriend of his. 'Rosemary's still in love with you, Peter,' she kept saying, 'she only plays me to hear news of you. I've almost promised her you'll come to the tennis clube fête on Saturday.'

'Can't do that, old girl,' Peter said finally, cutting shocking slices of fruit cake for everyone and actually putting them on their plates so they couldn't be saved for another day. Great-uncle Harold choked trying to get his swallowed before he felt his wife's disapproval across the damask cloth. 'Shan't be able to get down, the Fleet'll be on its special Review, for the King. He'll be taking the salute. It's been frantic, getting everything ready. There'll never be anything like it again – a naval review just before war cranks up. I thought I might ask Misha to come along. She could get the train down to Weymouth like you did when you came in the spring. I do think it's something our French cousin should see . . .' And if this were not enough to bring the munching to a halt, he added, 'Pity you won't be able to miss the fête.' He pulled her plait and grinned at his sister who was crossly hunched over her cake. ''Course, if the committee can spare you, we'd like you to come, wouldn't we, Michèle?'

Misha knew her mouth was open. To be so suddenly accepted! It was probably normal behaviour in ordinary families but it brought a flush to her skin without affecting the square of ice in her chest. She took in the details of Peter's face, the clear frank blueness of his eyes, a tiny mole at the corner of the left one. His teeth had a touching gap in the middle like a little boy's but his shoulders were solidly set under the remarkable burnishings of his jacket with its buttons and bits of metal. She'd have been enchanted to discover this cousin, what, perhaps six days before, to have family, someone to be proud of, and one of the fighting forces keen to defend his country. 'I don't mind telling you, Mish,' he was saying, 'if the French Navy's as prepared as we are to fight off the Hun . . .'

'Shan't need the French Navy,' Janet cried. 'We'll blow them out of the Channel ourselves, won't we, Grandpa?'

Sitting on a wall in Weymouth harbour, Misha shaded her eyes and tried to count the lines of ships cradled in the glassy sea. Fourteen lines of them, Peter had said there'd be, each four miles long. 'And look out for me, I'll be on the one nearest the King's barge.' She could hear the high sound of the crowds waiting for His Majesty and, faintly, the water flip-flapping round the ships, all as smart as paint as Peter had said they'd be, with their cargoes of sailors and officers in full white-dress.

She wasn't looking for Peter. She couldn't somehow get used to him. Perhaps it was his brotherliness. It had been so unexpected. She'd need time. He'd taken up too much space beside her in his sports car when he'd collected her from the station, and he'd drawn too many stares. He was so impossibly polished and handsome, he didn't seem quite real.

She hadn't wanted him to take the risk of being caught out, leaving his ship as he had, and she'd waited too long for him on the platform. Her wait here was too long and she was too hot. Her eyes hurt. Why hadn't her perfect cousin thought to buy her sunglasses? Her ears hurt now, there were guns booming. She'd never asked for a cousin.

But there he was, the King, a small, shy, earnest figure taking the salute, swaying in his barge, rock-solid just the same. Misha felt a sudden swelling of emotion. She stood up. Oh, the small King and the great lines of swaying ships, the hundreds of men lined up to salute! They'd win the war, they'd see off Hitler; it would be real war once these men set out to sea. The British Navy would win the war, and she was British. She was proud of it. This was her place.

In the silence when the guns stopped, she heard a pitter-pattering of rain falling on the polished decks and the dress caps, the Admiral's pips. No one moved, not the merest

45

cadet. No one seemed to blink an eyelid. The crowd gave out a communal sigh and Misha let go of her breath. This was what she was here for. She remembered. War work. Stout war work. Philippe had known it would be right for her. He knew everything. Her Frenchness had after all never quite fitted. This was where she belonged, with these stout and true men, this earnest King, so touching he'd make Janet weep.

When the time came to be able to meet Philippe again, adult to adult, she'd have something to tell him about her war after they'd talked about his. She wanted the war to last a long time, years, so that window episode on the final day would be quite forgotten.

Misha thought, Here it is, at last. War. And I have willed it and afterwards, this moment on Sunday 3 September 1939, sitting at the table with Janet and Joanie, will be written in my memory. 'I'd have thought we should be going to church today of all days,' she said. 'Other people are and why didn't you say earlier so I didn't put on my uniform?'

Janet swung her legs, cool enough in her BH summer dress and white socks. 'God hasn't listened to the millions praying for peace as far as I know,' she said. 'Anyway, what's the point of singing hymns when history's being made before our very ears?'

'How would you like to be stifling in winter clothes on a day like this?' Misha argued for the sake of it, because bickering had become part of their uneasy relationship. She had wickedly willed war to start and here it was. Philippe would be killed in it.

'Don't have to be, do I?' Janet poured herself another cup of Camp coffee. 'Shut up, do, and turn the volume up, we won't hear the Prime Minister.'

Misha watched Joanie scatter salt and pepper on a nasty piece of red meat. She must think of nothing but the itchy feel of the lisle stockings and the heat of her body in navy blue knickers. There seemed to be some music jangling on the wireless. How was she going to be able to bear having nothing left? She wouldn't care now if the first bomb exploded here on the table and bits of ceiling spattered her navy blue serge and the last thing she ever knew was Joanie's mouth open in a silent scream.

'Not Sandy Macpherson and his blasted theatre organ again!' Janet said. 'Maybe, with a bit of luck, he'll be blown up first.'

'Your grandma'll wash your mouth out with soap, saying a word like that.' Joanie's fingers shook. She couldn't get the peapods to open.

Misha brushed biscuit crumbs from the black and red striped tie that was strangling her. How well she'd borne her pain until now! She thought, I have carried this square of coldness in my chest without complaint. I haven't screamed or wept at my exile. Let there be no war. Let Philippe not die. I accept that he is to marry the woman who's so glossy and sophisticated, and I give up my need to see him just once more in the years to come.

She leaned her gas mask against the back of her chair, full of nausea and dread, holding her breath to stave off the smell of warm animal flesh. She'd stuff part of this poor slaughtered cow into her mouth and swallow it if the war were to be deferred another day, another week.

'. . . and so I am sorry to have to tell you . . .' the Prime Minister sounded tired, '. . . that we are at war with Germany.'

It had come. All the waiting was over, and the hope. She'd never see him again, not in friendship, not in love. He'd die. Millions of men were going to die and he'd be one of them and she'd helped will it.

'We stand up for *God Save the King*,' Janet shouted. 'Oh dear, she's crying for her mummy!'

47

Chapter 5

I wish, Misha thought, that bombs had begun to fall on sunny Bournemouth, and in particular on this changing-room in this hateful school. She gritted her teeth. Yes, there it was again. 'Oh, *là, là. Black silk!*' whispered over by the footbaths.

'Let's see if she's got it on now.'

It wasn't fair. She wanted to belong. She wanted to do war work, and where was the war? Hitler was still playing games with people's fears and so far there was no whiff of poison gas, no dead, no wounded to write letters for. And now no proper education for her, after all, that might have helped to pass the time.

'Go and look, Fiona, I dare you.'

Appalled, Misha stared down at the new plimsolls lying at her feet. It was going to be the same here as it was with Janet and she was never going to fit in. It served her right. Looking forward to her first games lesson had been another trap she'd set herself. Because she had thought games would make her like Janet, that her own skinny legs would become sturdy, like hers, and she'd then be able to stride with the same confident air through this new English world that was freshly alien.

The superior blonde girl called Fiona pushed into her. She felt a dozen pairs of gleeful eyes waiting. 'Anyway, where d'you come from?' Fiona's sharp voice enquired.

Misha hesitated over the magical word that was her own. Paris. 'What's it to you?' she snapped. She'd learned the art of the retort from Janet.

48

After that it was too late. She was labelled as 'foreign' and classed with the refugee girls from Hitler's Germany and the scholarship pupils receiving free dinner tickets. Her sole friend was Olga Schneider whose English was so poor she could only sit in the back row of needlework and art lessons. Misha noticed her own English accent slipping into some kind of vague European sound and was glad, glad to be different, that her exile was thus so soundly confirmed. She even found herself refusing to show the sewing skills her mother had forced on her and fiddled about with her patch of black velvet intended to become a gasmask holder.

Sometimes a voice would penetrate her lethargy. 'Michèle Martin, stand out here. Did your Swiss school not introduce you to the Theorem of Pythagoras?'

They offered her Maths with the Lower Third, but how to sit in their tiny desks if you were five feet eight in your lisle stockings? How to do Latin when you barely know French or English grammar? Once an ancient English mistress found her deep in the Essays of Montaigne when she should have been doing a précis. 'This is far too advanced for you Michèle. Return it to the library at lunchtime. One of the Upper Sixth may be in need of it.'

Misha stared at Miss Mason's pale dry skin, at the obligatory frown between her brows. Monsieur Steiner had chosen to start her with Montaigne for his extraordinary insights into the human mind, its weaknesses and its variety. What better way, after all, to begin an education? 'D'you think so, miss?' she asked eagerly, and was ashamed because after all Miss Mason wasn't Janet or Fiona or Susan. She was nice.

'Oh, I'd say *Lorna Doone*, dear. That's an exciting tale for a reluctant reader. Come and see me in the staffroom at four o'clock.'

Misha read *Lorna Doone* again and followed it up with most of the school's fiction: *Vanity Fair*, *The Woman in White*, *Moonfleet*. Most were already on her bookshelf in what had been her home, but they helped stir her from lethargy and stave off the immense boredom of the hours after assembly. It was the routine of the timetable that carried her along, the Monday to Friday, Children's Hour (homework stared at), supper and bed, the blank of the weekends slipping away with a novel read out to Joanie at the kitchen table.

It grew colder. She wore half-gloves and a woollen hat in bed. There were no bombs, only shortages. Aunt Maud reduced the grocery list to save the merchant seamen having to carry inessential produce over the high seas. Janet added to it, thrilled by the thought of the ships zigzagging across the Atlantic, defying destruction by enemy submarine to bring her tinned fruit and cocoa. There was Miss Rackman too, setting an example by not having a fire in her study, and everyone shivering through *Santa Lucia* sung endlessly with complicated descants in the air-raid shelters during drill.

It was only Peter who broke into this routine, insisting on driving her around on borrowed petrol in his sports car. She must get to know, he said, the place that was to be her home for the duration of the silent war people called the Great Bore, so distant and unlikely did it seem. Peter loved to listen to her tales of woe about her restricted life and journeyings from country to country. Her father sounded, he said, a 'cad', but she mustn't worry about him. She was free and a whole rosy future lay ahead.

Peter was easy company. He didn't think any the less of her for failing in war work, finding the first-aid classes revolting, the practice plastic limbs too gruesome with their daubed red paint. There were also too many jolly girls in the BH mould leaping about being cheerful and resourceful in them. She could never be like them and no longed wanted to try.

Peter laughed about war work and laughed about her days at BH, wasting her chance of an education. 'A pretty girl like you doesn't need an education,' he said once, leaning across the table at Fuller's where they often had tea after the pictures on a Saturday. 'It's for blue stockings who won't get a man.'

Misha concentrated on walnut cake in case the merchant ships were blown up and there'd be no more. She ordered a second slice and spat crumbs. Peter laughed at the mess she made, and old ladies at the other tables smiled. She didn't mind about the crumbs with Peter and didn't bother to answer him. She didn't care what his opinion was on education for women. He was, of course, rigidly conventional. She often thought, watching his entrance in the teashop and the way he flashed charm, bowing at the be-hatted ladies as if he were giving them something they lacked, that it was Peter who'd get by on his appearance.

It was too much trouble to argue with him. She had wanted an education in order to be worthy of a certain friendship she'd ceased to think about. And she still wanted it. It was just that she was too tired at present. After Christmas, she'd make a resolution and a fresh start. She'd one day, years hence, be able to say casually, 'Yes, I got my higher Matric that year. Thought I might as well. Then of course they suggested I try for Oxford . . .' She'd give a light laugh and never let Philippe see the years were ashes.

'I say, Michèle! Over here!' It was Peter calling, outside the school.

There was a rustle amongst the girls tramping down to the bus stop. Misha saw a dark mass of hats flood towards and away from him as he was inspected. He did look handsome, standing by the forbidden headlamps of his sports car. 'Golly!' she heard, but barely felt a touch of triumph. She slowed her cold feet, trailing them in fact on the cold lumpy ground beneath the pine trees at the school gates. Oh, not the cinema again! She wanted to go home. She wanted to be with Joanie and Uncle Mac with nothing being expected of her.

'Thought we'd have tea over in Swanage, watch the moonlight on the sea and have a stroll out to Old Harry Rocks . . .'

Misha climbed into the car because she didn't know how to do otherwise and off they sped, bitter wind whipping at her hat and giving her toothache.

By the time they reached his landmark rocks, she was shivering and Peter had to take her hands, putting one in his pocket and holding her by the waist because negotiating the pathway was difficult. The moon was covered by cloud. He tried to talk into her cold ear. 'Did you like the look of that place Swanage? Some nice officers' wives have put up there. It's so near the base, you see, you'd soon . . .'

Misha couldn't listen. A piece of bramble had caught under her tunic. She knew it had torn her stocking and she'd have to mend it. She said, 'I'm frozen, Peter, I want to run.'

Both stockings were no more than holes by the time she reached the glimmer of light on his car. She was panting, feeling an overwhelming need to be at the house with the lights on and Joanie burning the supper.

Peter shouted after her, 'Mish . . . Misha darling!' But she just wanted to be away from there and wouldn't speak until they were back on the cliff road to Bournemouth.

She didn't let herself wonder why she'd panicked. Peter thought it was the dense darkness without the moon and he'd laughed, of course, rubbing her hands and trying to wrap her in his overcoat.

In the house, her Great-aunt Maud was waiting behind the door. At first Misha thought she'd been worried about her, and so did Peter. 'Grandma, I'm most truly sorry to have kept Misha out. You know I wouldn't upset you for the world,' he cried, enclosing her in his rather displeasing embrace. One didn't always want it and Aunt Maud appeared not to then.

'I am concerned that Michèle is taking you away from your duties,' she said.

Misha ran downstairs. It wasn't her fault. Joanie and she were inspecting the torn lisle of the stockings and wondering if they could be saved when they heard him call goodnight and roar away into the night.

'I'll get that new thread out and have a go, you've got no clean ones,' Joanie said. 'And you read me out that poem you're learning. Such a lovely sad story about the poor lady . . .'

'Don't remind me, Joanie.' Misha put a mock schoolgirl groan into her voice. ' "Discuss the narrative power of *The Lady of Shalott*." Heck! What do I know about narrative power! And The Rack gave me such a grilling about it yesterday. Disappointed in me, that's what she said, Joanie, and it isn't fair. No one's shown me anything in that place,

I did want to try . . .' She put her bare feet into the slippers Joanie had warming and sank into her chair. It didn't matter. After Christmas, she'd make a wonderful spurt in everything, astonishing the entire school. 'Smashing cup of cocoa, Joanie,' she said.

'Read out the story,' said Joanie, passing her the book of poetry.

' "Till her blood was frozen slowly," ' Misha read, ' "And her eyes were darkened holy . . . !" I don't think I'll go out in my cousin's car again, Joanie, not before the summer anyway.'

'All right, dear.'

The next day, Misha was so full of feverish cold, her Aunt Maud was called to inspect her swollen eyes and nose. She seemed as vague as ever but some decision was made that Misha should stay in bed and she remained there all week. She had colourful dreams of the Lady of Shalott floating down to Camelot, her face white and dead, until she felt well enough to finish *War and Peace*, when she dreamed instead of horses, sabres and frozen earth.

At teatime on Sunday Peter appeared in the house on another twelve-hour leave. Misha heard him pounding up the stairs. She hoped vaguely he'd brought her chocolates or even a fruit cake in a tin because she'd begun to feel hungry again. She sat up in bed and he strode across the room towards her. 'Darling Mish, what's all this?' She let him hold her and began to weep. She'd had too many dreams. 'I can't do my essay,' she sobbed, 'and The Rack's called me in about my poor work but it's not my fault, is it?'

'There'll be no more school, not if you don't want it.' Peter kissed her gently on her hot forehead and wiped her face with his handkerchief. She knew she was ugly in her woollen hat and reminded herself again how fortunate she was to have a cousin like Peter to offer her comfort and not mind how she looked.

Then the door flew open; Janet flew in with it. 'There you are, Grandma, I told you,' she cried, and thumped back down the stairs. Aunt Maud appeared and everything really began.

At first, Misha didn't understand but she heard Aunt Maud saying, '. . . it is because you are brother and sister. Your father has found himself with two wives.'

Peter leaped from Misha's bed. All the healthy colour drained from his face. His skin took on the grey tinge of ashes. He stared down at Misha with this ashen skin, his mouth drawn back, a dark empty space. She supposed he recognised the same horror in her.

He said nothing. He reached the door in a few strides, pushing past his grandmother. They heard him take the stairs, two flights. There were some slams, the front door, the car door.

Her Great-Aunt Maud, her grandmother, seemed unable to utter another word, gazing round the room as if seeing it for the first time. Her tremor had worsened. Her hands worked as she fiddled with her shawls, and her head nodded, hair standing out. Suddenly she spoke and Misha jumped. She said, her voice thin and faint, 'I'm afraid you have to leave.'

'I'm to go home?' Joy lifted Misha from the bed. 'I'll go now, this minute . . .'

'Would that you could, but that is hardly possible, the war . . .'

'There are still ferries, I've kept a check.' Misha was panting slightly, kneeling on the floor, dragging out a suitcase. She heard herself laugh. She was to go home! Nothing else mattered because she was to go home and one day, soon, she'd be sitting in her haven, remembering, forgetting, home from the war that never was.

'As usual, you are being rather foolhardy. Perhaps it is your French blood. Janet tried to warn us of course, that you would not fit in here but I had promised your father I would do my best for you whilst he carried out his vital duties, his obligations to his country. You have repaid us by turning Peter's head, dragging both of you into . . . decadence.'

Misha cried out, clutching her arms around her in dis-

54

belief. 'Decadence?' Her voice rose as she searched for meaning. The French were decadent, people said, in jokes. 'I don't know what it means. I've never been to the Folies Bergère and it was my mother's black silk camisole set. She says I'm almost a woman now but I've never worn it . . .'

Aunt Maud went on looking round the room, not at Misha. All her body shook, as Misha's did. 'Your own brother!' she said, and stepped backwards as if the space between them were not enough. She closed the door behind her.

Misha didn't leave that day. She was allowed to pack up her possessions properly. The next, Joanie came in with meals and hot tea, whispering and anxious. They didn't speak of her departure because it distressed Joanie too much to have her only friend sent away. Misha ate and drank with appetite, stuffing everything in and staring blankly round the room. She didn't think of much except listing the things she'd never see again. Her mind and body seemed to be shut down.

Janet didn't go near her and she didn't hear her voice shouting about hockey matches. She decided she'd been sent away for a few days until she herself had left, perhaps to her mother's flat in the women's military camp where she was a colonel or something perfectly ridiculous for a woman to be. Maybe she was ridiculous in other ways and that was why her husband needed a second wife.

In the afternoon, she heard her grandfather come tap-tapping up, his stick pausing outside the door, and an envelope appearing with a pound note inside. Misha didn't ponder on this astonishment either.

Aunt Maud returned when everyone else had gone to bed and gave her another envelope containing money, two keys, her ration card and a train ticket. She was to go to the address written inside, apparently her father's most recent London home, and wait there for him to take charge of her.

Misha didn't call her 'Grandma' and didn't ask her if Janet knew she was her sister, that their father had had two wives, and was a bigamist, a cheat and a liar.

55

Chapter 6

The address was in the Soho district and the apartment block one that might have been grand but was no longer. By the front door was a row of six bells. One had 'Martin Enterprises' written in ink by the side of it. This Misha pressed.

There was, of course, no reply, but then she couldn't expect her father to be in the right place at the right time, so sensibly used the larger of the keys she'd been given to open this and follow a further label up to the first floor where she found another: 'Martin Enterprises'. Her heart leaped wildly at the sighing breathing sound the door gave out. She hadn't realised she was afraid, and had been buoyant throughout her journey for she'd soon be home. Her ordeal was over. Fate had sent it to make her stronger, worthier of friendship, mature without the passing of the years. She was even prepared to forgive her father, or to pretend she would in order to ease matters for him. She'd be home faster that way.

A heap of letters had been the cause of her fright. Some were addressed to her father so she called 'Dad!' several times, stupidly; he couldn't be there if he'd failed to pick up his post. Mail to him meant deals, manoeuvring, money.

Inside, the flat had the same relentless chill as the outside air. Her cold hands struggled with her case and the letters which, dutiful daughter still, she sorted mechanically into piles on the kitchen table beyond the hall. There were other names on the envelopes besides his, variations of Michael Henry Martin, even Martin Michael Henery Esquire, as well as the Martin Enterprises of the doorbell. Her mother's name was there too, Yvette Marie Martin, Mrs, and that of his other wife, Gwendolyn Violet Martin, Mrs.

There were no signs of habitation in the kitchen, nothing but a kettle and four teacups, not a sardine tin, or any hard green crumbs from an eaten loaf, not even a coffee grain. She wasn't frightened yet. This was obviously a rented flat. Her father ate out, it was simple, and anyway she didn't care. He would shortly turn up, summoned by his mother. He'd breathe fury and impatience and send her home where she belonged.

One day Philippe would return from the war and probably call out to her across the courtyard that he was fetching Frou home and would she care to come along? It could be almost the same.

Apart from a gingery silk tie in a wardrobe, there was no trace of her father in either of the two bedrooms of the flat, though the beds had linen and blankets folded at their foot. The sitting-room had chairs many people must have sat upon but they seemed to carry no history, no coins or pencil stubs, no hair stain on the antimacassars. There was a sideboard with in it no personal paper, no old photograph of someone on a beach, not even a new leaflet with 'LOOK OUT for the BLACKOUT' on the front. Misha wondered if her father had even bothered to fill in the form for his ration card as the rest of the country had had to do.

She decided she was too weary to care, and too cold, so sat down at the kitchen table to wait. Across the alleyway was another block of flats with a notice on a window: HOT LIPS, TOP OF STAIRS. She could hear the muffled sounds of buses rumbling along the Charing Cross Road. She didn't trouble to take off her BH gabardine overcoat, scarves or hat. Shortly her father would thunder up to fetch her, snorting impatience to be off, and they'd be at Victoria Station for the ferry train the quicker. She had only to endure a few more hours, and she'd be back looking across the courtyard. She'd put everything aside, the events since August, exile, loneliness. Shame too. Philippe had always known she loved him. He'd teased her, gently, the way he teased Frou whose heart was as full of passion for him as her own. They'd have that again, she and Frou; it was better than nothing.

Her father didn't arrive that day. From the table, Misha watched the sudden winter night fall, really night because of the blackout. She hadn't thought in time to go out for tea and buns in a café somewhere, but felt a little comfort to know she would have been able to. She even thought she might one day return to discover London properly and grow fond of it. She'd been too young to appreciate a city on their last stays, but could remember having tea with her mother in the Joe Lyons teashops around the Strand and Piccadilly Circus. She'd spent many an hour in Galeries Lafayette in Regent Street watching her mother pick her way through the fabrics and silks but they'd done that in all their places, even if it was only a village shop that sold everything.

She brought back these few memories of London as she sensibly made herself a bed in one of the rooms with the chill damp sheets. Eventually she went to sleep in it, lulled by the faint sound of swing music from the flat overhead which meant other people were near and she wasn't entirely alone. But she didn't feel quite so buoyant.

Five days later, Misha's father still hadn't come for her. She thought there must be a straightforward reason why this was. She counted the money she had. She bought two stamps and a packet of Basildon Bond writing paper costing one shilling and eightpence in the Charing Cross Road and then sat hesitating between writing to her mother or her grandmother. Finally, she sent a brief note to her mother. Of course, she herself would almost certainly arrive before it did, but she viewed the sending of it as a sign of normality in her life. She had written so many letters of complaint to her during the exile in Bournemouth, the act was natural.

It wasn't in fact easy to write because of the cold. There was no gas supply to the fire in the sitting-room. Her first task each morning was to put on the kettle for her worst ordeal, washing herself after leaving the bed with its mountain of blankets. She ceased to bother with the bathroom, making the matter more endurable by staying in the kitchen where steam gave a hint of cosiness if not warmth. She bared a little of herself for each kettleful of water, finally reaching her feet which she lifted into the sink with her top clothes in place vest, bodice, BH pullover, the blue tweed jacket her mother had made and sent her in October, already too small. She felt cursed by the nasty gap left at the top of her leg by a missing button on her suspender belt and by the fast-dissolving sliver of soap left to her.

She hadn't gone so far as to buy the Sunlight for washing underclothes. She'd be home shortly and looked forward to her mother's scream when she got hold of them. If there were funds enough, she'd set her heart on new sets of shop-bought yellow woollen ones. The knickers would have legs – she wanted yellow legs down to her knees, with elastic for stopping the draughts. She'd seen some in Marks and Spencer.

She'd known all the Paris stores and now knew the London ones along Regent Street and Oxford Street: Galeries Lafayette, Dickens and Jones, Liberty, Peter Robinson, John Lewis, Marshall and Snelgrove, ugly and dark with sandbagging outside but a haven of warmth to her. She'd developed a London walk by this time, which ended in the Strand at the Joe Lyons where she basked in comfort and paid a shilling from her precious stock for tea, egg and chips. Once she almost ordered a sausage. On someone else's plate, they looked so fat and inviting.

By the time she was searching through the daily letters to her father's various aliases to find the reply from her mother, she was still making the best of it. Her British side came out, she felt, as she saw the Londoners making the best of waiting for war in a limbo of cold and bitter darkness, their streets shut down from dusk, without light or heat, the barrage balloons overhead shadowy ghosts more fearsome than protective. She spent her days amongst them, scurrying as they did, slipping about on the icy paths under the starkly frozen trees of Hyde Park. She tried to pretend she was going somewhere urgent too, working in some Ministry with urgent war business to attend to, unable to fraternise because 'Careless Talk Costs Lives'. Sometimes she'd pretend to be a housewife and pick up the leaflet on

'How to Reconstitute Dried Egg'. She was fond of the one which asked: 'What are the Housewife's War Aims on the Home Front this Winter?' because it gave its own reply – 'To Safeguard the Family against Ills and Chills and to Build up Strong Nerves and to Maintain Energy for Work!'

And if her father hadn't been coming for her, she'd have found a place for herself somewhere. There was a canteen run by volunteer ladies near Waterloo Bridge, serving soldiers on leave from France where there was a front but no battles, and those on anti-aircraft gun duty to protect London from the air-raids that never came.

Only she dared not go in and offer to wash up for what if her hands were deep in warm water and grease and her father was stamping around the flat, waiting for her?

She found she had to return there every two hours or so because a certainty that he was would overwhelm her and drive her back.

The evenings and nights were the worst because her father had not of course organised blackout curtains for the windows and if she heard him thundering and snorting up the stairs, she might forgive him everything.

But there was never any sound on the stairs except from the comings and goings of the two girls who lived overhead and played blues music that helped lull her to sleep. They'd shout to each other about forgotten keys and bottles of gin and rendezvous for lunch at the Savoy Grill, and when there were parties there'd be officers whistling and laughing.

One day, she was going to approach one of the girls and ask if she could possibly borrow a pound with a watch as security. If they didn't seem to be in so much of a hurry all the time, she would have done it already. It would only be until her father came, she'd say, and had there been a Mr Martin about lately?

Chapter 7

2 Stacey Street,
Soho

9 December 1939

Dear *Maman*,

I write again because perhaps you did not understand my last letter? My aunt is not my aunt but my grandmother and she doesn't want me in Bournemouth, she's sent me to London for my father to take charge of. Only he hasn't come. I don't know what to do.

Here Misha paused to take off her gloves, brooding on her anger against her mother. She could hurt her for her extraordinary negligence by telling her she wasn't married to Michael Martin! What would she do if she were not a married woman, if she had given birth to two illegitimate children and had lived a falsehood as he had? But if Philippe were ever to learn she'd been base, like her father . . . She recounted the money she'd laid on the table and took up her pen again.

The trouble is, I've only three and elevenpence left and I do need some more money, please. I can just manage on about two shillings a day if I refuse to be hungry. I have to have a penny for a newspaper because I want to follow the war news. There's no wireless here. I don't know how I'm expected to pass the time.

61

I need soap and shampoo, that's fivepence, and my stockings are in holes. I'll have to have a new suspender belt and some needles and thread for the hem of the blue tweed skirt you made me. It seems funny to think you don't know what size I am anymore because the jacket was too small to start with. Also I'll have to have my hair cut, it's in my eyes. That costs a shilling. But if you can very quickly send me three pounds and your passport, I can come home at once and shall need none of these things. That's what the train and ferry fares cost. I must be on your passport as well as my father's. Can you send me a telegram? At once, if possible?

Soon she'd rushed off down the stairs and was passing her letter through the icy gap at the Post Office. Now a whole day loomed before her as arid as the others so she ran off again across the Charing Cross Road, working her way up into Regent Street, past Dickens and Jones, into Haberdashery at Marshall and Snelgrove, Oxford Street, to pick wildly amongst the ribbons and laces as if her mother had sent her to find an exact tint of honey-coloured grosgrain that she must have and she couldn't go home until she'd found it.

On then to John Lewis's and into Ladies Hats, sitting there on a stool and trying on horrors, breathless, exhausted, looking ridiculous and plainer than ever. Once, Peter had insisted on taking her into the hat department of Bournemouth's most select store. It was after her mother had sent her a parcel of warm clothing including the blue tweed suit. And he'd stood there, looking impossibly, unpleasantly handsome, picking out a felt boater in a misty shade of lavender-blue he'd decided was an exact match for her eyes. She'd said, 'My eyes are grey, not blue,' and let him pay two and elevenpence for it.

Snatching off a veiled cocktail hat in black, she couldn't remember wearing the boater. She'd lost it somewhere. She sat trying to remember where with an ugly rust-coloured monstrosity on her head and her hands shaking, eyes as red as her cheeks because she was frightened, frightened to be so absolutely alone in the world. She'd wanted to lose the blue felt. She'd stuffed it down the back of a chair in the sitting-room in Bournemouth.

She'd never wanted a cousin and didn't want any kind of a brother.

2 Stacey Street
Soho

13 December 1939

Tellier, Madame Hortense
Domaine Tellier,
Hérault,
France

Ma chère Mémé,
Do you know where my mother is? I write to the old Paris address and there is no answer. I am stuck in London by some terrible mistake about passports, you know what my father's like, and I haven't any money. He told her to come down to you if the war worsened and I wonder if she has anyway? Or maybe she has gone to Aunt Yvonne. Has she written as usual to Félix?

I wish I could be with you in the Mediterranean sunshine.

Kisses to Félix, and please reply by return, *chère Mémé*.

2 Stacey Street,
Soho

19 December 1939

Dear Grandfather,
Please do not show this letter to Grandma. I don't want her to worry. There has been some misunderstanding between her and my father. He hasn't come for me yet and the flat is empty. I'm sorry I didn't have time to thank you for the pound note you so kindly thought to give me. It's been most useful. I wonder if you could

63

send me another? I have to buy food for myself. I'll
return it as soon as my father comes. He did once tell
me he was going to do some secret war work and I
hope it's not so secret Grandma won't be able to get
in touch with him!

My best wishes to you and Grandma for Christmas
and the New Year.

2 Stacey Street,
Soho

22 December 1939

Dear Joanie,

I hope you're keeping well and not doing too much.
London is quite nice but cold, of course. The trees in
the parks are stiff and white, it's like a Christmas card,
and children are skating on the ponds. There are lots
of accidents here with so much traffic in the blackout.
I can hear swearing when I'm in bed.

Is your cooking getting more difficult with the
rationing? Sometimes I long to be back with you,
supper in the oven, Children's Hour on the wireless. It
was so cosy.

Joanie, I wonder if you might be able to take a pound
from your Post Office savings to lend me? I had to
buy Christmas presents and daren't tell my father I've
overspent. Ask the man at the Post Office, he'll see to
it for you. I'll pay you back next week. Please send it
urgently, Joanie. Don't tell Janet. I'm so glad the
Germans haven't invaded Bournemouth. I told you
they wouldn't!

Misha had the last letter stamped ready to give to the
postman when he called the next day. He always called.
Then she would not have to venture out. She had half a
loaf, some cocoa and milk left.

She was watching for him when the doorbell rang, and
its ring was shock enough. She clattered down the stairs.
Here he was, at last, her father, key forgotten of course. He
needed two wives to be organised.

It wasn't her father. It was a telegraph boy, handing her a telegram. He was swiftly joined on the doorstep by the postman offering her a parcel.

She didn't take much notice of the telegram. It was addressed to her father so she put it on his heap of envelopes. He'd see it first when he did come. He'd come by Christmas Day, probably on the day itself, as a present; he liked surprises.

Tackling the parcel with the beginnings of excitement, she thought, Janet has sent me something for Christmas, she is sorry I've left, she knows we are sisters, she's sorry, she misses me. She had time to wonder what Janet's message would be. This seemed more important than her choice of gift.

There was no present. The parcel contained messages for her, though; it held envelopes, all the letters she'd written to Bournemouth since her banishment, to her grandparents and Joanie. They were still sealed. It also contained letters to her from her mother.

Misha looked carefully at the dates stamped on the front of these and opened each one in sequence.

I am so glad, Misha dear, that you are at last at a good school and doing steady work . . .

Of course dear, it cannot be nice to be playing games out on a cold field, but think how sturdy and strong you'll be . . .

I do hope you will be taking that examination – Higher Matric, is it called, Misha? It could help you get into the Sorbonne after the war . . .

Nowhere in them could she find a trace of a reply of any kind or any acknowledgement of the information she'd sent about BH or the house in Bournemouth. And nowhere of course, was there mention of her presence in London.

It took Misha some minutes to realise that her mother had been sending her a weekly letter that was mechanical, like the one she had always sent her son, Félix.

Then she had to suppose her mother had not received hers, that she no longed lived at their Paris flat because surely she wouldn't have ignored her last call for help? And so she lived a secret life, just as her husband did.

Misha had left until last the envelope with her name, just 'Michèle', written on it by Janet. Inside were only a few lines.

I suppose you know you have killed Peter? Because of the shame you brought on him, he volunteered for manoeuvres in the Baltic Sea and fell overboard during a storm. No one could reach him. He died of cold. You have broken my mother's and my grandparents' hearts. I hope you are satisfied and will leave us alone now.

She folded this carefully and wondered if she should bother to boil the water for her tin bottle before she returned to bed. She had sevenpence ha'penny in her purse.

Chapter 8

Misha stared at the lampshade over her head. It was almost black with dirt. A spider that hadn't died from the cold had hung a few wisps of web there. She supposed she should have done some cleaning.

It was afternoon, she thought. She'd better get up, refill the bottle and let its warmth help her to sleep again.

To this end, she moved a stiff leg into the wilderness of cold beyond the coffin-like shape she lay in, muffled in mouldy blanket. If her father didn't come today, she'd probably not manage the effort again.

How could this be – that she had not a single member of her family to care about her? That she had not a single friend, though she'd been so willing to offer her friendship to Janet and all those girls in the English school with their games-playing and their hymn-singing? Why hadn't she ever belonged there? She'd tried. Her tunic hem had been no longer than the back of her calf when kneeling. Her hair hadn't touched her collar. She'd washed her hands before luncheon without fail and had never forgotten to use her napkin. She'd even tried to put others before herself, though no one had welcomed this gesture.

In fact, the only person who'd ever held out his hand in friendship to her was far away on the front line, waiting to die as she was.

Misha sprang up, pushing off the damp blanket. Philippe's face had come to her in her sleep. It had been so clear. He'd smiled his rare smile, the one he used to give her when she ran across the courtyard and arrived at his window, looking foolish but not feeling it. In the dream, she'd felt suffused with joy, and it seemed to her she'd heard his voice reminding her he'd always be her friend. And she'd felt warm. She still felt warm. Stumbling into the kitchen, too hot in fact in her stockings and socks, her cardigan and the layers of scarf, she switched on the kettle. Today she was going to wash, properly, because she had something to celebrate.

Yesterday's absolute despair had given her the dream, and the reminder. Philippe. She did have a friend. He'd promised her he'd always be her friend. So she was going to spend her last sixpenny piece on a telegram. She'd send it to Philippe at his mother's farm. He'd find a way, somehow, to get her out of this place. Friends were supposed to help you out of trouble, and she was in trouble.

And then she'd see him again. Paris would be full of officers on leave, like London, and one day one of them would be Philippe and she'd run along the boulevard to where he was, waiting to make sure she was safe, and she'd thank him.

She was imagining her first sight of his dark head raised towards her, when she heard a shout coming through the letterbox. 'Bailiffs, Mr Martin!'

This was startling in itself, a voice through the door, but Misha knew at once she wasn't going to answer it. She was aware of bailiffs. Some had come to their cottage in Ireland and they'd had to creep out the back way. She very calmly finished washing her second foot and dressed in most of her wardrobe. She boiled up water to pour over a spoonful of cocoa, leaving enough for two more cups. Into this, she dipped the rest of her loaf of bread and, sitting down, settled herself to wait until it might be safe to run to the Post Office.

An hour might have passed when the bell rang again. Misha didn't even turn her head. But this time it was a woman's voice, shrieking through the door. 'Michael! For God's sake, what are you up to? Answer this door at once.'

And the woman didn't go away. In the end, Misha

couldn't bear not knowing who it was so got up and answered the door.

A woman stood there, a smart woman. She said, 'Where's your mother? I suppose my husband's gone off somewhere again. Did he leave a forwarding address? Go and ask her, please, I'm in a hurry.'

She had red hair, like Misha's mother, but her eyes were sharp and she had an air of briskness. She seemed to have the same build, however, and she was as slim. Her uniform had a gloss to it, although Misha's mother would never have contemplated a uniform. She supposed that was the main difference between her father's French wife and this English one. Misha knew at once it was she, however slow her muddled brain. 'He's not here,' she said.

'I can see that. I need to find him at once. I have to tell him his son has been killed. We have to arrange a funeral.'

Misha's gaze travelled up from the black armband around her khaki sleeve she'd first thought was part of the array of badges and stripes, past her rigid jaw to her sharp eyes that were no longer sharp, having tears in them.

'If your mother is not here, could you tell me where she is? Doing war work? I'll go and see her. She'll understand how important it is that I have my husband's forwarding address.' She waited for an answer; she probably thought Misha simple. Misha couldn't reply, she hadn't the words. 'A telegram was sent here,' the woman went on. She seemed to want to take out a handkerchief but couldn't allow herself so took off her cap instead. She looked older without it. There was a touch of grey at her brow and her forehead was lined. But Misha could see she'd been pretty, like her mother, once. 'And I've got to get down to Bournemouth this afternoon.'

Misha finally managed to say what she had to say. 'My father has disappeared. There's a lot of post for him if you want to see it. Some of it's addressed to you. It's in the kitchen.' She had to admit the woman didn't look stunned, though she surely must have been. Her mouth drew down rather; perhaps it was her stiff upper lip at work.

Misha stood back to let her pass and followed her into

the kitchen where the correspondence sat in untidy heaps. 'I have sorted them,' she said, 'but they keep falling over. There's so many. That's your pile.' She indicated a dozen or so envelopes by the tin of cocoa.

The woman didn't go through them with any interest. She flicked them about and picked up some that had 'Yvette Martin' on the front. These she stared at. Misha said, 'That's my mother,' and to help added, 'She lives in Paris now, with me, but she comes from the south. My little brother lives in the south, though, with our grandparents.'

'Absolutely fascinating,' murmured Gwendolyn Violet Martin. 'I must hear all about it one day, but for the moment I have to get down to Bournemouth.'

'My cousin Janet knows she's my sister,' Misha said. 'And my cousin Peter was very kind to me. Please accept my condolences.' There was no reason to spare her. They contemplated each other. For the first time, Gwendolyn took in everything about Misha, her grubbiness, her uncut hair, her deathly face, her skinny body wrapped about in near-rags. Misha saw she didn't have her mother's prettiness, had never had it. She had the same small pale eyes as Janet, sharp and cold, as if she played tennis with the fierce desire to win, as Janet did. She couldn't bring herself to ask Misha anymore. Her mind seemed to be ticking over, assessing new matters. Misha waited. Let her reveal something.

But she didn't. She said, 'Do you have a bag or a holdall, for me to put my husband's correspondence in? I'll take it with me down to Bournemouth.'

'I've got some string,' Misha said, 'you can tie it up, if you like.' She wouldn't help the woman any more; she was Janet's mother.

'Never mind, I'll send someone for it,' she said, walking past Misha to the hallway. 'Will you still be here next week?'

'Dunno,' Misha said, reverting to the state of adolescent simpleton.

The woman closed the door very quietly behind her.

Afterwards, Misha decided she could admire Gwendolyn Violet Martin. To have been presented with the actual evidence of her husband's treachery without so much as a gasp of surprise was rather admirable, she thought. And she must

70

have been surprised to find Janet's half-sister answering the door, whatever Janet had warned her to expect.

In a way, she was quite sorry to see her leave. She'd been company of a kind for a minute or two.

She'd settled to mull over the visit when she heard the call of the bailiffs again. Before long, they'd broken down the door. With them was a man to cut off the electricity.

They found nothing they wanted in the flat. There were only the heaps of bills, and her sitting at the kitchen table, wrapped about in clothing like a tramp, dirty and starving, a spectre.

She stared at the three men staring at her, asking her questions, until Georgiana came in and saved her. Georgiana was the vision of blonde chic who shared the upstairs flat with her friend Patch. The two of them and their parties with the blues music had already saved something in her because they'd represented normality, though they led a life she'd never known. The men must have asked Georgiana for help and she'd given it instantly, warmly, because that was the sort of person she was. The first thing she said was, 'Come on, old love,' in ringing aristocratic tones Misha obeyed. She got up and began to babble excuses, apologies.

Georgiana wasn't listening. She said something decisive to the men and half-pushed her up the stairs that Misha had seen as a pathway to normal life.

The second-floor flat bore no resemblance to her own prison. She felt heat from a wonderful fireplace. There were photographs about, books, newspapers, and a gleaming piano holding a pot of violets and Christmas cards.

Georgiana offered a man's dressing-gown and said, 'Think you can stand a bath?'

There was steam and something perfumed in the water and her limbs became pink instead of blue. Afterwards she was ordered to sit by the fire and she scoffed a kind of stew Georgiana said was rabbit. She didn't care what it was, mopping up the sauce with doorstep pieces of bread, crumbs and gravy all over the tray.

Georgiana watched, seated opposite in the ski suit she'd been wearing that winter against the cold. She had an air of relaxation and contentment that the French call feeling good in one's skin. Misha thought she'd never seen anyone so justly matching this expression. She was smoking. Cigarettes weren't rationed.

Misha stopped halfway through some pudding, nauseously satisfied. 'I'll pay you back with coupons,' she said, 'I haven't used mine.' Her voice sounded odd, but then it had been unused for weeks.

'Want to talk?' Georgiana said. Smoke drifted round her porcelain skin and swathe of light hair like Rita Hayworth's, though blonde rather than red. She had the same manner of walking, easy and somehow majestic, as if life's problems could be sailed over.

Misha began to babble about mistakes and misdirected letters, even about her father's abandonment though not his bigamy. That meant so much else, lying and cheating and strangeness. 'I haven't even got my own passport, I'm on his,' she finished with a wail. 'I can't get myself home even if I find the money.'

'First thing,' Georgiana said, asking for no finer details, 'is the French Embassy. We'll try and persuade them to let you travel with a visa and no passport. I think you've a right to be helped back if you lived in France before the war. Meanwhile you need some money. Got any talents?'

'Absolutely none,' Misha burst out, eager to prove her incapacity.

'Can't cook by any chance?'

'Oh, I ran our flat in Paris, my mother didn't care for housekeeping.'

'Righto, you've got a job. You can cook for me and Edwina, that's my flatmate. Everyone calls her Patch because she used to look like her first pony. We loathe cooking and we're lazy. You can do the shopping, the queuing, organise the coupons and so on, till we get things worked out for you. Think you can manage that?'

'I'll start as soon as I've sent a telegram,' Misha said.

Georgiana never told Misha why she trusted her, and why indeed she had taken charge. No one would think, to see her, that she would bother. She was so glamorous to begin

72

with. Not just the hair and the ski suit, that wasn't of course English, but the perfect bones of her face and that skin, transparent at forehead and neck, showing its blue veins. She had a great shout of a laugh, like Patch. They came from the same place in Dorset and had ridden together as girls. Patch worked on the fringes of the film world, making propaganda shorts for the cinemas, and Georgiana was a model for a fashion house that was still creating evening wear in sequins and velvet as if there were no real war. It was almost possible to believe it would never come and life had always held this struggle with shortages of food and coal. They only talked about the war to curse it. All the men they knew were officers at the front line or in some training camp or other. There was much to-ing and fro-ing on leaves and at weekends, and then of course there were the parties.

Misha's frantic walks came in useful in her new role because she knew all the places that had been offering unlikely items. Dressed in a pair of Patch's old jodhpurs, some fur boots of hers, an enormous man's pullover stuffed under her blue tweed, itself squeezed under her BH gabardine, she didn't even mind the cold when queuing. Sometimes she got offal this way. She didn't actually handle it, Patch did, because as she said she was used to skinning hares at home. Once it was part-cooked, Misha put it into a pot and threw in whatever else seemed hearty: beans, potatoes, lentils from the dark little shops in Old Compton Street. It made stews she was proud of. Finally she was useful and needed. She belonged.

Neither of her new friends ever mentioned she'd once been starving but there was much talk, all of it light and bantering, of chaps and new songs and home (the country), or darling Freddie (a dress designer) and the divine bloke Susannah had brought the night before. Misha listened and laughed, suspending thought, waiting for a telegram.

She didn't always stay up for their parties; tiredness had become a habit. She'd hand round the first drinks and slip away as the cigarette smoke formed a hazy layer over their heads and they wound up the gramophone, someone singing with it. They adored Jelly Roll Morton, all the American

73

crooners, the Andrews Sisters. The music grew softer as the night wore on and she drifted to sleep on the camp bed in Georgiana's room to the sound of Patch singing *I'll See You Again*.

She learned how easy it can be to pass the days if you fill them with chores. She became busy, rising earliest in the mornings for a proper wash and to make the first pot of tea for the others. She made a routine, sorting the laundry on Thursdays to be despatched on Fridays, and wondered without much interest why she hadn't been capable of doing such things for herself. There was her shopping list to draw up, her walk to plan each day: Post Office for stamps for Patch's correspondence with four brothers on various parts of the front line, Berwick Market for a new zip for Georgiana's ski suit, brown, 19 inches, before Old Compton Street and half a pound of lentils. Rationing had increased in December and they each had only four ounces of ham and bacon a week and the same of butter, though sugar was still at a generous twelve ounces.

Afterwards she thought she hadn't even remembered Frou and had certainly stopped waiting for a telegram. She no longer looked at the door to her father's flat when she passed it and didn't enquire about the bailiffs or all that mail piled on the kitchen table.

Then Georgiana dropped her bombshell. Over breakfast one morning, she said, 'Chap called Jeffrey came last night. Says he can push through that visa for France. He knows someone in the Embassy.' She took a healthy bite of toast with the marmalade her mother's cook had sent them, and winked at Misha.

Misha stared back in horror. She didn't want to go back home now. She was comfortable, almost happy, with a job to do. She didn't want to start thinking. Even her French grandparents hadn't replied to her letter. Why? And that sixpence for a telegram had been wasted.

Georgiana must have read something in her face because she winked again. 'And I'm coming with you,' she said. 'Always loved Paris. Like to see it again before the Hun bombs it to smithereens.'

74

'Always loved Theo, she means,' Patch said. 'Have you scoffed all that marmalade? Any dripping left, Mish?'

'Butcher wouldn't let me have any on Tuesday,' Misha said, 'I'll try again this morning.' She had her day planned. She hadn't expected anything to disturb her.

'Love of her life,' Patch was saying. 'Poor, of course, an artist, but charming, my dear. Oh, yes, especially when he can see a few hundred francs' loan coming towards him.'

Misha thought, I shall run along the boulevard St Germain and into the square and on one of the café terraces will be Philippe, on leave. I shall see his dark head above all the others at some table and it will be as if there is only him there. I shall sit down casually beside him and we shall have a talk and I shall hear him say he didn't receive the telegram from me, but if he had, how quickly he would have sent help!

But first she would run home to her mother. Her mother would explain why she'd had to abandon her and they'd make everything right between them. She stood up and threw back her chair. Her head was pounding. 'Will one of you lend me another three pounds?' she said.

Chapter 9

They hadn't planned on arriving Paris in a howler of a snowstorm, only in cold and war, the same as they lived through in London. Georgiana shrieked, 'It's the end of the bloody world, it must be!'

Misha could hardly hear her. She peered out at the Place Roubaix from wrappings of scarf and velvet beret. Snow lay thick and solid halfway up the sandbagging around the newspaper kiosks. It had buried a solitary taxi. Hurricane winds were heaving clouds of it up and over the Gare du Nord, washing off soot, and there were sheets of ice between their miserable hotel entrance and the café where they wanted to take their Parisian breakfast. How was she to get home?

'Won't let it stop us,' Georgie shrieked again, and set off, hunched into her best squirrel coat and hat. Misha's fur boots, once Patch's, were instantly edged in snow and she was senseless, battered by bitter wind at her ears and mouth. She held hard to her beret, staggering after a Georgie growing more white than red, her squirrel fur succumbing to the snow.

The waiter regarded them without much interest though they were the only customers. 'It's the end,' he shouted simply, and perhaps he didn't care.

'*Oui*,' Georgie yelled back, giving out melted snow and the smell of wet fur.

Misha trembled over a bowl of coffee as if she had not longed for this moment, as if she had not seen it as her first step home.

'This is good, old love,' Georgie said, her ringing tones almost at normal pitch. Melted snow dripped from her hat on to the perfect porcelain skin and into her clear English eyes. She hardly blinked. 'Even if it's our last.'

And it was good. Misha drank the scented stuff, symbol of her first happiness, and dipped in strips of bread and butter. The crumbs lay at the bottom, the way they always had, but she didn't spoon them up; she couldn't find the strength.

Georgie soon called for seconds and they consumed these, each silent. 'Think you can stick to our plan?' she finally asked. She'd been watching Misha.

''Course,' she said.

'Right, rendezvous at this Café Bonaparte of yours, 'round teatime?'

'Right,' Misha shouted.

At the doorway they parted, Georgiana to stagger off to the street where her boyfriend lived, Misha to cross the river to whatever was left.

Nothing seemed familiar to her, no buses hooted, no drivers cursed, no workers streamed up and down the gaping metro steps; they were stuffed with snow instead, and over the river the Eiffel Tower was a mere black shadow, Notre Dame a giant pillar of snow. Nothing moved but white whirlwinds. Was this cataclysmic storm some portent for her return? Sliding one boot in front of the other, she felt only indifference. Here, after all, was just one more hurdle and she was used to hurdles. She must shut out the edge of dread and pretend she was running for home and her mother, who would ease her long pain by explaining her abandonment.

There was sandbagging along the shops that had seemed hers. In front of Jubin's, Denis the errand boy was fighting to get the shutters up, snow on his beret and overalls, too preoccupied to notice her. Good. She wanted to see no one because this homecoming was not how it was meant to be, and anyway she was too cold to speak. The ironmonger's was dark, and the baker's too, though she thought she caught a faint yeasty drift. If it was a bread day, she'd run across later so she and her mother could breakfast quietly together. Her mother would recount the street gossip after the explanations. Offering a wave to the door of the Bonaparte, in case her friends the Blanchards should see her and be hurt by her passing by, she managed to get the key from her wet pocket. How many times she had repacked it when sorting out her suitcases! It had meant that one day she'd turn it in their door and her old life would be there, the same. The key turned easily enough and she shouted, '*Maman!*' using her body as battering ram to defy the wind.

Her mother was not inside. Misha leaned, breathless and gasping, against a door that hid no one. The sewing machine was on the sideboard and the pile of *Marie-Claire* sat damply in its place. But no one sat in the chairs and hadn't for a long time. She knew this. It was like the London flat. But she went on into the main bedroom where the wardrobe held clothes she remembered. She made the black suit with the astrakhan collar quite wet until she remembered she needn't search for her mother's latest outfit. She didn't know what it was. A winter had passed between them. The bedside table had nothing on it, not her mother's hand cream or manicure set or the photograph of Félix, nor the one of herself aged eight with plaits.

In the kitchen where she went in her squelching boots, Misha knew at once the stove was long cold. She put a wet glove on to its coldness and moved into her own room. Everything was as she'd left it. She picked up her dog with the torn ear and finally allowed herself to look across, past the snow-laden tree, to the blank shutters opposite.

Had she expected them to be open? Yes. Yet she knew he'd been mobilised like everyone else. He was somewhere far from Paris, near Belgium or the Ardennes, on the battle lines. She needn't struggle from her window across to his calling, 'Is there anybody there?' like the returning traveller in the poem. There was no ghost. Philippe was alive, on some frozen defensive position, waiting for the enemy. He'd never received her telegram.

And her mother had never received her letters. Without needing to go round to the concierge's entrance, she knew Madame Bassas had been removing them from their letter box outside the main lobby. How the woman would love to pass them over – and with what a furtive grin! Well, she must avoid the concierge.

A sense of desolation enveloped her with the cold and the wet. She could hear water dripping from her BH overcoat. Perhaps my mother is dead, she thought, without further emotion. What other explanation could there be? Her mother first went mad and wrote those mechanical letters and then committed suicide because she'd learned of her husband's betrayal.

Accepting the fact she had no mother, she went out again, turning into the storm towards the Café Bonaparte and the Blanchards who'd try and make everything better. They were going to put a bowl of coffee, her bowl with the green and gold line around it, on her table in the corner, saying nothing until she'd drunk it, taking no money. They'd wait for her to tell them about her exile but first they'd tell her how her mother had killed herself.

The Blanchards hadn't seen Misha's mother since the day a few months before when they'd watched her go off with a suitcase after finishing her sewing job, the Sunday dress for Madame Florence, grey with pleated bust, the second of the two she'd ordered to give her work.

Misha sat with her bowl at her place by the window. Snow battered against the panes and the wind went on howling as she and the Blanchards shouted their way through the niceties about Misha's stay in England and Robert Blanchard's time at the Front. They'd each been as miserable, she and Robert, it was agreed, and might just as well have been at home where they belonged.

Then Reine staggered in as the only other customer, her housecoat in guise of mackintosh and her working boots spoiled by the snow. As tactful as the Blanchards, she threw herself down at Misha's table, offering up a wet red boot to show her where the stains would be later. 'And the drying!' she cried. 'Two nights' work these cost me, Misha, and my darling daughter needing shoes too. If they weren't the tools of my trade, no one realises!' Her face, pale without its makeup, mouth different but still generously wide though lacking its crimson, she leaned companionably

79

forward and recounted some items of street gossip to which Misha barely listened. She had seen nothing of her mother, Reine said, and her sympathy lay in the air as heavy as the Blanchards'.

Finally, Misha stood up. 'I'll see you all later, about three o'clock,' she announced, trailing her damp clothes back to the door. They'd been pleased to see her, and when she'd found her mother or discovered what her end had been, she'd be pleased to see them.

First she'd begin her search, starting in the boulevard St Germain. She knew it was pointless, that even her mother wouldn't have gone shopping on such a day. She also knew an immense weariness was seeping into her with the cold, and it was only the image of Georgie waiting at the Bonaparte that drove her back there at the appointed time. Without Georgie, she felt she might have sat just down somewhere and stayed put.

It was Georgie who decided they should set up a temporary home in Misha's old flat until the storm sensibly gave up and let them get on with looking for her mother. Misha found herself making up beds again, one for herself in her old room, one for Georgie on a camp bed in her mother's, for the sake of decency in case she should be dead. The word came quite easily to her mind, and came without emotion.

There was money. Georgie's grandmother had sent her a five-pound note to enjoy herself with in Paris because she wished she herself was a modern girl and hadn't wasted her youth in corsets, chaperoned. Georgie always enjoyed herself, of course, but it meant they had enough for food, drink and coal. Rationing had begun in Paris by then but the best shops had plenty. They stoked the stove with fuel and had comfortable mornings over a late breakfast at the Bonaparte, and evenings at the other cafés with Georgie's friend Theo and his côterie.

Misha found she had finally joined Parisian café life as the group moved from the Dôme to the Select, to the Flore or the Lipp on a whim and there was talk, always talk, about music and painting and love affairs as the saucers from their glasses piled up and someone eventually had to pay. No one referred to the war or the bad weather. The only restriction apparent to them was the dim blue light inside the cafés and the blackness of the streets outside as they strolled from one to another, still talking, the leader in charge of the torch.

If only, Misha occasionally let herself think, if only her exile hadn't happened and there'd simply been this. It was too late. She would brood on her day's search for news of her mother as she drank cheap, warming crème de menthe, sitting like a spectre at the gaiety of the tables. With the velvet beret Georgie had given her and her inflated BH gabardine, she looked much more exotic than they. She half listened, wreathed about in their smoke, to talk of art and cinema and wondered why other people didn't have to live in a state of limbo, waiting.

One evening, Georgie told her she had to go back to work in London. 'You going to come, Mish?' They were in the Dôme ringed about by the usual crowd. 'Might as well, you know.'

'No,' Misha said. She'd been expecting this. Perhaps she'd been staving off her decision until it came. 'No, I think I need to find out about my mother first.' She thought, And if she is dead, then perhaps it will be easier to let the stove grow cold and give in. It'd be long time before Georgie got to hear of it. 'Deaths have to be registered, don't they? I'll try the police too. Maybe she's moved to one of the hotels I haven't tried yet. She's as likely to have chosen a hotel. She so hated housework, even shopping for food, let alone cooking. Madame Libaud reckons she left soon after me then came back for a bit to pack properly and finish her sewing jobs.'

Georgie nodded and lifted her glass. 'I'll be able to give you a quid or two.'

'No more, George, thanks.' The police, coming for her body, would pocket Georgie's money. 'I'm going to get a job.'

Theo said something to Georgie. Misha gazed blindly at Blanche beside her, who was really a chap called Bernard. She always wore a long silver lamé dress beneath a rabbit fur coat which shed hair over the table tops. Misha thought, I don't want to die.

'Do not cry, *chérie*,' murmured Blanche, putting out a workman's rough fingers to stroke her cheek.

'Don't *touch*!' Someone called Toutou who worked the cabarets and might have been female slapped Blanche's wrist. 'And look at you, dear.' Blanche took out a powder puff and, sobbing, dabbed at the blue shadow of beard on her chin.

Misha thought, Even these people had proper mothers and a home. Smoke and heat made her head swim. Ten o'clock, the clock behind the bar said. Another hour of cosiness, false friendship, refuge. Tomorrow she would start at the local police station. Her mother's new residence or her death had to be registered somewhere.

If not, perhaps she'd gone to her parents in the south, in which case she'd be tucked up in feather down, comfortably fed with duck and sausage cassoulet, the dog on guard against prowler or enemy. And she herself was just as much orphan. More so, for her French grandparents had also abandoned her. What sin had she committed to be so roundly rejected by all who knew her?

Georgie pushed across a third crème de menthe and Misha saw her mother coming through the door.

Chapter 10

Philippe Constantin had promised himself that one day he'd sit inside a Joe Lyons teashop as Misha had done as a child, and here he was. It was Sunday. London was as cold and dreary as all of Europe. He stared at his plate where some chipped potatoes lay soggy and white and a fried egg had a film of fat over it.

What had she eaten those long months alone? The telegram was dated in December, weeks before, and had gone to and fro between his postings. He felt as cold and empty now as Misha must have felt, waiting for a sign from him. He watched a layer of milk settle on the tea he wouldn't drink. Three days he himself had hung about the entrance of that place until the tubby cheerful girl with the strange name had arrived, bundling herself from a taxi with a whole chicken and other good things she'd brought with her from the country. She had firewatching duties to get to and had dashed about, stowing sausages and a dead hare, and clucking with sympathy over his concern for Misha.

She'd called from the kitchen that he wasn't to worry anymore – George was looking after her. Philippe's heart had lurched and he cursed himself for a fool. And then the girl had flown back into the room to point out a photograph on the piano. 'There's Mish with me and George,' she'd said.

His heart had resumed a sensible rhythm and he'd stared at the black and white image of Misha standing between two girls called Georgie and Patch. Her face looked older and sadder, her eyes huge and desolate as they'd seemed to him that afternoon when she'd heard Eveline's voice and had thought too far. He picked up the frame and held it to the window, imagining late nights and drinking she wasn't used to. He called out then about her father.

'Oh, that pig!' Patch had yelled, emerging freshly enveloped in a ski suit, looking even plumper. 'All those bills and Misha was dying of cold and hunger. If it hadn't been for George and me!'

So he learned there'd been no drinking, and he couldn't take back the suffering, couldn't take back the time and choose to open his window that hot August day to let her in.

Chapter 11

Misha's mother was not dead. She was alive and wearing the fur coat she'd always wanted. It was the same rust colour as her hair and this had a new unfamiliar style, fluffed out around the fur toque. There was of course no other sign of the weather, no scarf or old jumper like everyone else. On her delicate feet she wore chic little boots.

Misha had time to take it all in, her mother's new clothes and her old expression, both sulky and blank. She gave one of her glances about the Dôme, searching for someone, and went out again.

There was crème de menthe around Misha's mouth. She couldn't swallow it and couldn't move. Georgie said, 'What's up, old love?' Misha managed to shake her head and smile.

She wanted to move, wanted to think, to understand that her mother *had* simply abandoned her. She had been living in Paris then, in this, their district, writing her letters in advance because she couldn't be bothered with real correspondence and didn't care how her daughter bore her banishment. Like her husband, she had another secret life. Misha thought, That is why the two of them chose each other. It had always seemed strange and now she knew. This tiny satisfaction soothed her. She swallowed the green stuff. Theo grinned through his sandy beard. He fancied he looked like Van Gogh and Misha could never understand why beautiful Georgiana was so taken with him. He couldn't paint either, if his portrait of Georgie was anything to go by. He'd given her pink and gold swirls for a face. 'You've had one too many, little girl,' he said, 'time for the sandman.'

But it was time for truth and Misha didn't want it.

Blanche put a hefty arm around her shoulders. 'What's the cruel man saying, *chérie*? Tell Blanchette.' Misha struggled to free herself. Toutou pushed past her knees because it was her turn to go and sing at the Jockey night-club along the boulevard. Everyone shuffled round and Misha was able to shout to Georgie: 'I've just seen my mother look in here.'

Darling Georgie didn't hesitate. She got up, dragged Misha out and they were both in the doorway before the beret was jammed back on Misha's head.

Left to herself, Misha might have sat helplessly on. Who would want to recognise abandonment by two living parents, separate rejection, each on their own side? As it was, she was sure they were too late, but Georgie decided her mother had been looking for Misha and they must simply follow the boulevard to the flat to catch her up.

Misha recognised the shape of her mother at the door of the Bonaparte, outlined by the feeble blue light as someone left. When they reached the café, she was already seated at a table by the stove. Misha couldn't get herself into the room but Georgie took an arm and steered her towards her mother, crying in her most ringing tones, '*Bonsoir, Madame Martin, je suis une amie de Misha.*'

Misha's mother lost her blank look and one of distaste crossed her face, because of Georgie's terrible accent. 'I speak English,' she said coldly, getting up and putting her arms around Misha.

Misha felt damp fur and her mother's icy skin and sat down beside her, wordless. If before she thought her mind had been whirling, it hadn't, until then. She watched Georgie and her mother, their voices coming from a long way away, being carefully polite, Georgie talking about the flat in London as if all that had been ordinary. Misha's mother had abandoned her; she hadn't been caught up in some disaster, no accident had claimed her life, she hadn't jumped into the River Seine from loneliness or poverty.

She let the two of them be wonderful with each other, as her mother inspected Georgie's squirrel coat considered the fine aristocratic skin of her face, the blue veins, the cheekbones. She didn't entirely disapprove, Misha could see, once Georgie had stopped trying to speak French.

Monsieur Jules put hot lemon in front of Misha without her having ordered it and finally in front of the other two because no one answered him when he asked what they'd like. Then Georgie shrieked, 'Right, shall I come and say goodnight to Mish in an hour or two?' because she always knew what to do.

'Very well,' Yvette Martin said. Georgie strode off and there they were, Misha and her mother, who had spent seventeen years together, unable to speak. Monsieur Jules, having observed the drama, came across carrying a tray of soup and bread.

'I'm so happy to see you here, Madame. It's like old times,' he said, putting it carefully on the table. Alibert and the awful butcher Lagrue paused in their game of dominoes, listening.

It was only after her mother had touched her lips to the first spoonful that she was able to utter her first words. 'What is that on your head? And please take off those English scarves,' she said, and began to cry. Now the whole room was staring, the old man no one spoke to, Picot the journalist, the two domino players. Misha didn't care. She removed the beret, gone grey with the velvet rubbed away, the BH navy blue scarf, Georgie's red one. Off too came the BH gabardine and there she was in her full misery, the jacket made too small and sent on bursting from the jumper underneath, dirty, her hair chopped about with scissors, her face paler than ever, plainer, with its two bright patches because she was crying too. She said, 'Are you still sending me letters to Bournemouth?'

Her mother tried to blow on her soup but had to wipe her eyes with the napkin instead. Misha broke off pieces of bread and sucked up liquid too hot. Her teeth hurt. 'I need to go to the dentist,' she said, 'and the hairdresser, look at my hair and what about my clothes?' She had to stop to rub tears, soup, crumbs, from her fingers.

'I had to go away for a while.'

'What, a holiday in the middle of a war, in the middle of winter?' Misha cried, removing a piece of something nasty from her mouth. 'You know I don't like meat,' she said with adolescent petulance, feeling herself regress with the need to feel she had a mother who cared about her.

'You must eat it,' her mother said, finding some of her old authority. 'There's a war on, isn't that what you British are saying all the time?' Here was one of the resentments she'd been in the habit of using against Misha and her father: they were British. 'He was looking after you over there. I thought you didn't need me anymore.'

'Of course I still need a mother!' Misha cried. But she didn't, she mustn't. 'Did you know those people in Bournemouth were my grandparents? Did you know they didn't want me?' She was about to shout something about her father's second wife but stopped; her mother's face was suddenly a tight mask. She was clearing her bowl of soup, the sharp line between her eyebrows deepening the way it used to do. She was very pale and didn't look as if she'd had a holiday. Misha thought, But I won't spare her everything, she doesn't deserve to be spared. 'I spent weeks absolutely alone in my father's flat in London because they sent me there. He's disappeared, did you know that? I wrote to you, I begged for your help, and if it hadn't been for George . . .'

'I am very sorry, Misha. I didn't know I couldn't trust your father with responsibility for you. He was the one who wanted to take you away. I said we could go down south to my parents for the war. He didn't want that, he said the bloody French wouldn't fight, he said you'd be safer in England with your aunt and uncle.' Finally she looked up at her daughter and her eyes were full of angry tears she somehow kept from falling.

'My French grandparents,' Misha hissed, wanting to shout, wanting to hurt her, 'that's another thing, I wrote to them in despair, begging them to help me, they didn't so much as bother to reply and I was starving at the time.'

She thought, It doesn't really matter anymore. Her mother wasn't dead. Was she glad? Yes, but what mysteries to unravel now? Mechanical letters to offspring living abroad could not be viewed as normal.

The stove beside them spluttered. Yvette Martin eased

off her fur coat and opened the bag on her lap. 'I've had a very anxious letter, two in fact, from your grandparents,' she said. 'They had yours asking about me but you hadn't put your full address on it, Soho was all you wrote at the top of the paper, and even peasants can see that's not enough. In the end Pépé sent a few hundred francs to the Bournemouth address, how they scraped it up I don't know. Mémé can't sleep for worrying, as if she didn't have enough to keep her awake with the war coming. At her age, with Félix too, look, you can read it for yourself.'

Misha ignored the proffered letter. 'So you haven't been on holiday with them then?' She spooned up soup fast. Madame Florence was peering at her over the cashtill but she didn't mind. There wasn't much they didn't know about her last months. She might have embroidered the facts a little but facts were facts; she'd had sevenpence ha'penny left when the bailiffs came and Georgie and Patch saved her.

'Your hair looks as if it's been chopped off with a knife,' her mother said. 'Go on, read what Mémé says.'

'I believe you, they were worried. And if I didn't reply to their replies, I didn't get them. That Janet kept all my correspondence until Christmas and sent it on to me for a Christmas present...' She let her voice tail off, exhausted. Should she tell her mother Michael Henry Martin Esquire was a bigamist and she had no right to the ring on her finger? Or to her name, Yvette Marie Martin, Mrs?

'We'll see if Boris is in Paris, you can have it cut tomorrow if he is, and we'll try and find you something to wear.'

Misha watched her mother put fingers through the new fluffed out coiffure and take out a compact, powdering her face without looking at it. If she'd given her eyes a glance, she might have seen the tears behind them, as Misha did. If she felt like her she'd be afraid she'd burst with them. 'We got enough money then?'

And suddenly, she had wiped away the months of separation as if they had never been. She had her old life back, complete with resentment, petulance, bickering. There'd always been this matter of money.

'Money isn't a problem.' Yvette Martin snapped her bag shut.

Misha stared. Old times hadn't included that statement. 'What?'

'We've got money,' her mother said, adjusting her hat. 'This girl'll keep you company tonight? Here's a few francs for your breakfast, if you're not too proud to take them.' She pushed several notes under Misha's soup bowl. 'I'll come and collect you around eleven tomorrow morning.'

'But aren't you coming home with me? Where're your suitcases?'

'Don't ask me any more questions, darling. I'm tired now. Trust me. I'd glad you're home. Goodnight.'

Misha's mouth was open as she gazed after her mother in her rusty fur coat disappearing through the door of the Bonaparte.

Madame Florence murmured, 'Poor lady, poor lady . . .'

Misha said, 'What about me?' to her mother's departing back, and began to weep openly in spite of the stares of Alibert and Lagrue and the seedy journalist Picot, all obviously fascinated by this evening's home-grown drama.

She wept so much that Madame Florence offered her a plump shouder and she wept on that, then Georgie put her head round the door so Misha wept on her squirrel coat. She could hear herself sobbing and couldn't stop. An immense flood of tears seemed to have been waiting to flow and she couldn't stop them. 'My father, my sister,' she heard herself repeating, 'my mother . . .'

They gave her whisky and she felt better, able to totter down the street with Georgie to the flat where she'd packed up her things in Yvette Martin's room, in case of her return that night. 'I had a feeling she might not be coming back, actually,' said Georgie, restocking the stove with the coal her grandmother's money had paid for and putting on milk to boil for cocoa.

'But where was she and where is she now?' Misha wailed from her room. 'She's supposed to be looking after me, I am only seventeen.' She thought, Now it must be over. I'm being silly. I'll expect nothing from anyone. It's safer.

'Well, she's not been starved of finery wherever she's

been.' Georgie clattered cups on to a tray with the jug of milk and the biscuits they'd bought in the rue Madeleine. 'She always have that diamond, did she?'

'What diamond? She always said her engagement ring was glass and typical of my father.' Misha struggled to put on her nightdress and smooth out a place on her bed for the tray. 'Are these the last of the gingernuts?' She needed the comfort of sweet nursery food.

'The diamond on her right hand wasn't glass,' murmured Georgie, 'and the fur wasn't squirrel. Maybe she had something to sell and ran off with the proceeds to have one final glorious fling before the bombs come to wipe us out,' She sat on the end of the bed and handed Misha a steaming cup.

Misha fell against the pillows arranged as for an invalid and dunked biscuit.

Georgie was particularly soothing, telling her funny stories about an aunt of hers who went endlessly round the world on cruises to use up her money before she died. Misha thought, My father, my sister, my mother, all mysteries, secrets, shutting me out.

She said, 'I think I'll go down to my grandparents in the Languedoc, Georgie, and look after Félix. They care about me.'

'OK, old love,' Georgie said. She'd allow a little self-pity.

Chapter 12

Misha was dry-eyed by the time her mother was due the next day. Georgie had advised giving her a proper chance to explain herself and Misha intended to. Nonetheless, her first thought on forcing herself awake had been that she was somehow going to crawl out of the difficult age she was trapped in, not quite adult, and take charge of herself, depending on no one, expecting nothing.

Georgie pointed out she'd have to get a job for that. Misha was going to start looking for one as soon as her mother had recounted her winter. She wanted everything to be clear so she could make her mother part of the past, along with her father and the family she hadn't known about. She mustn't need any of the people she'd called on for help, not even Philippe. Especially not Philippe.

And no one must ever help her again. When they'd packed up Georgie's things for her return, Misha held out the rest of her grandmother's money that Georgie had tried to hide under the cocoa tin. 'No more, George, thanks,' she said. 'Just me now remember.'

'It's Paris money,' Georgie said, sitting on her suitcase to close it, 'and you're having it until you've found a job, so shut up.' Her heavenly blonde swathe of hair shone in the dingy winter light of the room. Misha felt a little pain around her heart; she would miss Georgie more than anything. She was so whole. She'd never lie or let anyone down, certainly not her family or friends.

They were both startled to hear Yvette Martin unlock

the front door and call out her daughter's name in a tone as light and easy as if there had been no parting, no pretence.

'She doesn't realise, George,' Misha said.

'Give her a chance, Mish. She's had a hard time maybe. I mean, married to your father, and he's not her fault.'

'No!' Misha felt she might have been able to laugh. 'I shall miss you,' she said.

'Patch and I'll always be at the flat whenever you need us, and if they do bomb poor old London, you've got the Dorset address.'

Then Yvette Martin stood in the doorway, dressed in another fur coat of the darkest, silkiest brown. 'Isn't your nice friend leaving?' she asked.

This was almost too much for Georgie's pride to bear but she swallowed her retort, accepted the envelope Yvette Martin held out to her as repayment of her daughter's debt, counted it carefully, and in a whirl of activity kissed Misha goodbye and was gone.

'Get your coat, darling, the taxi's waiting.'

Stunned by the speed of George's departure, Misha trailed round the room picking up scarves and the wretched BH gabardine. It seemed to her the air was colder than ever and would go on being colder without her friend.

'Is that your only coat?' her mother asked.

'Are you ashamed to be seen out with me?' Misha shouted. 'How could I have another one, for heaven's sake! My father paid for this, I suppose, then he disappeared and when I came home you had disappeared too. You're supposed to look after me, but you won't have to anymore!' She saw her shouting face as she peered into a looking-glass to put on the beret. She was going to weep again and didn't want to. She must tell her mother she was going to get a job. 'Just pay for one outfit and I shall ask for no more.' She would scrub floors; it wouldn't matter.

'Wipe your face, Misha,' her mother said.

A surge of unwonted fury made Misha swing round on her. 'Don't you feel anything?' she shrieked. 'Aren't you sorry? Aren't you ashamed? Where were you!'

Her mother had the same look on her face as when Misha's father hurt her with words. A vein throbbed at her temple by eyes that had been pretty and were now desolate, looking up at her daughter. 'One day, when you are old enough, you will understand and perhaps will forgive me. Remember, please, that I thought your father was looking after you. I don't know where he is now. He has paid the rent to the end of the lease, the landlord has informed me. He stopped sending me his paltry money orders after he took you away with him.'

There was nothing more to be said after that. Misha had nowhere to vent her anger and no more tears to shed, so she followed her mother into the taxi and out of it again by a clothes shop in the rue de Rivoli.

They had forced her into a woollen dress, dark blue with stiff square shoulders and a belt with a buckle. It was long, down to her calves, and the sleeves were so tight she could barely get her skinny arms into them. She stared at her reflection with huge shadowed eyes. Her body was no more than a skeleton and when had she begun to have this ghost-like pallor, this air of a sick dog or a street beggar?

'Take off those boots, *chérie*,' her mother said, Misha's old rags a disgraceful heap at her delicate feet. 'My daughter's been living on her own in London,' she informed the saleswoman.

'Ah, the English!' The woman held up her hands in wordless comprehension. All was clear to her. She brightened. This poor creature, Misha, had been amongst the worst dressed in the world. She flew into action, bringing in more things for Yvette Martin's approval, a coat with a fur trim, a speckled grey and white tailor-made.

Misha didn't protest much. Her skin was itching with unaccustomed heat, irritation, shame. Her mother's choices grew, draped across a chair. She hissed suddenly, 'But where are we to get this much money?'

'Never mind,' her mother said, a flush on her cheeks, eyes lively, holding a pair of thick stockings up to the suit.

Misha thought, They have been together, in a conspiracy. 'Is it my father's money? Have you been living here with him all the time, hoping I'd stay away?' She tore at the buttons of the rose pink silk blouse she was trying on. Now

94

it was clear. The two of them, both her parents, wanted her so little they'd hoped she'd never return.

'Don't be silly, Misha,' her mother said, absorbed in shades of grey.

Misha rebuttoned the blouse, heart and head thumping. The shop doorbell pinged. 'Madame's Monsieur is here,' the sales woman whispered, looking round the curtain.

'Ah. Thank you,' Yvette Martin said 'Just the right moment. Will you have these items here packed for me and sent to this address? And perhaps my daughter may keep on that suit with the pink blouse, we're going out to lunch. Hurry up, darling.'

'Which Monsieur?' Misha asked, fingers poised on the buttons. 'Can I go to lunch with Patch's boots on?'

'Come and see, Misha, he wants to meet you.'

She didn't realise at once. She thought, This must be the man friend from the old days. She'd suspected there'd been one her mother saw during her afternoon and evening absences. Four o'clock was when she left the flat, all dressed up. She met women friends she'd known from her Galeries Lafayette days; they'd take tea and sometimes go to the cinema. Misha hadn't minded that she almost certainly had a beau also. She needed to be admired, with a husband who never said a nice word. Finishing the buttons, Misha shrugged on the jacket. Her mother could divorce her husband who wasn't legally one and marry this chap.

Right boot on, she pulled aside an inch of curtain. The man stood by the counter, ushering her mother into a chair. They looked cosy together. He was short, not much taller than her. He had one of those camel hair coats over a full body and very shiny shoes. And a ring. Misha saw it glinting as he got out a cheque book and began to write.

He must have caught sight of her one eye peering at him. Bright little button eyes twinkled back at the curtain, plump paunchy cheeks aglow. He was nearly bald. He said, 'And am I to see the charming girl in all her glory?'

Then Misha understood.

She took off the pinky brown jacket, laying it carefully over the chair, following it with the rose silk blouse, unbuttoned also with care, to avoid snags, for it wasn't hers. Pinky

95

brown skirt next. She'd quite liked that. It had a nice kick pleat at the back.

Her mother called to her as she was replacing the dirty velvet beret and the BH gabardine that was more grime than cloth. 'Pierre wants to meet you, *chérie*. He's a busy man, don't keep him waiting.'

As she approached him, Misha saw he was even older than she'd first thought. He was at least sixty-five. She'd never know exactly because she didn't intend to see him again.

He tried to take her hand. She thought he was going to kiss it. She'd known he was that sort.

'Goodbye, *Maman*,' she said.

Chapter 13

Misha walked fast home in Patch's boots, along the rue de Rivoli, trying to turn her head away from the sparkling windows with their jewels and fine silks, their hide bags and crocodile shoes. One had a monstrous notice up: 'Madame has a Duty to be Elegant'.

No more dreams now of elegance and chic, of becoming a woman of the world fit to hold Philippe's arm. Even if she earned such things with honest toil, she'd yearn for them no more. They were for women like her mother, earned by women the way she had earned them. She was going to return to where she belonged across the River Seine, to her own quarter where the air was darker, the buildings more sandbagged, dingier, waiting properly for war like honest people were.

Hesitating in front of the Bonaparte, she realised she wouldn't be able to have meals until she got work; Georgie's two pounds would have to be eked out. But she didn't want lunch. Rationing, meatless days, cakeless days, how well they'd suit her.

And now she knew everything she needed to know. Decadence, she thought, is my mother. And it is me. I killed Peter with it.

Skirting the café and going home the courtyard way (not looking at windows, refusing memory), she picked up a letter from the postbox, and climbed into her room.

Very well then. No father, no mother, no sister, no brother. Nothing now but herself and past dreams and this cold and this emptiness.

She didn't read the letter at once but wandered about chewing on biscuits. She tidied things, looked in cupboards for edible remains, and decided she was grateful for her London experiences. They'd taught her how to endure many things.

She was cleaning the bath when she thought of the letter. It was from Patch and would be full of London gossip, no longer of any concern to her. It was nice of her to write, though.

Keeping it as a reward, she polished mirrors with pages from *Marie-Claire*, and postponed what she most wanted to do – go into her mother's room and bundle up her clothes ready for removal.

Tomorrow she'd approach the Blanchards about their letting her have one meal a day in return for washing up or serving at table. She'd manage on that until she found other work. Maybe the war would finally begin and she'd be needed. She could do first-aid.

She pushed aside unbidden images of herself as heroine, clambering through ruins like the ones seen of the bombing in Poland, dragging out the wounded. No more dreams now. She didn't want them.

Patch's letter didn't have London gossip in it. It had gossip about Philippe. Philippe had been to London on an aeroplane, to find her, to help her, because he'd had her telegram.

I think he risked court-martial, coming over here in a war for you, old love. Where've you been hiding *him*, you devil? Tall, dark, brooding, *gorgeous*. He can share my bread and dripping any time! Tell him my daddy's rich, Misha, if you don't want him. No chance, I suppose, but God, how I longed to be as thin as you when I saw him standing outside our door! Been waiting there three days.

I'd been home for more grub (got two hares, a whole chicken, loads of sausages off Cook, gin off Pa). I now demand to know what happened next. See what a loyal friend I was though, Mish, sent him straight back to you, honest. Fretting something terrible, he was, to think of you starving all winter. Said it took the telegram weeks to reach him and him weeks to get a mate to fly him over. I tell you, I'd starve for months if he came to find me in a great white flying machine. Write AT ONCE to let me know the next episode.

Misha spent most of the afternoon in the bath, grooming herself and weeping. She had, of course, to change now. She had to have clean clothes and shining hair because she was going to see her friend Philippe David Constantin, who was a true one. He wanted to see her, to know she was safe. He'd almost found her in London and he'd find her in Paris soon, or she'd find him. Her long, long torment was over. Exile, banishment, were sent by Fate to make her stronger, worthier of his friendship. Nothing would ever seem so precious, nothing in her life to come but that. Her dream of seeing his dark head there on some café terrace was going to come true, and he'd look up and there she'd be, his friend, grateful forever because he'd known how much she needed him.

Gasping with joy, sobbing, Misha scrubbed her grey winter skin with something scented Georgie had left, and in the re-run of her dreams was transformed into a well-groomed woman he'd be proud to hold out his hand to. Only she wasn't, her face was a skeleton's and her body too, except when it was wrapped about in old clothes. Then she looked like the Michelin Man.

She'd reached her skinny knees when she heard a key turn in the lock and her mother call: 'Misha, what on earth are you doing with that ghastly suit and my shoes?' She'd dragged them out of the wardrobe, in fact, to find something to look human in for her friend Philippe. They were draped around the stove on chairs to get the mould out, though some of it was in the lining and wouldn't show. She couldn't get her feet into any of the shoes but had tried them all on nonetheless. A dream couldn't include running towards anyone in steel-tipped laceups or ancient fur boots, even in wartime.

'Darling!' Her mother was behind her in the doorway of

the bathroom. Misha's bare back was exposed but she wouldn't turn round. She stopped soaping herself and picked up the hand-mirror and scissors. She intended to cut her hair in the bath to save mess. 'You're too young for pride. Please, Michèle.'

'Don't call me that. Age has nothing to do with it. I'm old enough for anything, not that you'd know. I've lived half a year with no parents, banished and abandoned by both of you, that's what's made me grow up. If I hadn't had dear friends! My father's a cheat and a liar, and my mother . . .' She dropped the scissors in the water and fished about for them.

'Pierre loves me,' Yvette Martin said. Misha could hear her fumbling with coat and gloves.

'You needn't take anything off, I don't want you to stay. He'd marry you, I suppose, if you weren't married already. What a joke!' She wouldn't say the truth. It didn't matter now. 'I don't want you to stay,' she repeated, 'I'm going to manage on my own. I've got true friends. I'm all right.'

'Pierre wants to help you.'

'I'll vomit if you say his name once more. A horrible dirty old man . . .' She couldn't see her own spiteful face for steam on the glass. 'How long were you on holiday with him, forgetting me!' She didn't need to be spiteful now, didn't want to be; the words kept coming by themselves, like the tears.

'He's charming and treats me like a queen, Misha.' Her mother came up behind her and took the mirror from her hand. 'Unlike your father,' she said. 'If you knew what I'd suffered!'

'I know what you've suffered,' she said. 'I was there, remember? You should have left him years ago and got a job. We'd have managed, and better.'

'What could I do? I've no training for anything. I was only waiting for you to be old enough, and I thought you were, you see . . . I didn't forget you. I was ill all those months, in a nursing home. Pierre paid for everything and sent the letters off to you every week so you wouldn't worry about me. He's a good man.'

And her father wasn't. But Misha couldn't make herself

forgive her mother yet; she couldn't bring out the phrases and refused to turn round. 'This water's cold,' she said.

Her mother handed her a towel the way she'd been used to do. 'I needed someone to love me. If I'd waited any longer, I'd have been too old. Please don't cry anymore.'

'To sell yourself, yes, you would have been,' Misha shouted, spattering water in her haste to cover her nakedness. She dropped the scissors and yelped. 'Now you've made me lose the scissors.'

'If you wish, I'll write to Bournemouth for you, to see if those relations of his know where he is. If you won't take my money, or Pierre's, yes, it is his and I'm not ashamed of it, if you won't take that, your father must make you a proper allowance.'

'Don't you dare write to them!' Misha cried. 'I don't want any of you.' More especially, she didn't want to think about them. She didn't need to now. She wanted to think about Philippe and herself, not a fat little man who was good to her mother, or about her mother being ill without her.

Or about a forgotten woman called Eveline, who'd probably gone back to America.

They managed to get themselves into a calmer state to discuss Misha's wardrobe sensibly. They went through the garments in Yvette Martin's room that Misha had already thrown about. She sat on the bed and her mother knelt on the floor turning over skirts. She didn't allow herself to ask what her mother's illness had been or to soften at the sight of the line of grey hair at the crown of her head. She remembered how touched she'd been on seeing it that other bath day before England. It had been the first intimation of any secrecy between them. Now she knew how much had been hidden – and it was too much to forgive though her heart kept singing out. *He'd* been to London and stood in that flat entrance, waiting, waiting... 'Where is my father?' she asked. If she knew about her father, even as much as she knew about her mother's last months, she could put them to the back of her mind and accept that they hadn't been perfect parents. Perhaps she'd been unlucky, but it had toughened her and she wasn't truly unlucky because there was Philippe. 'Has he been doing some kind of war work? He hinted something about M15 . . .'

Yvette Martin burst out laughing. 'Who knows, Misha, with your father? I think we should assume we shan't see him for a while. He disappeared once before when you were three and gave me no explanation when he turned up again. Or, at least, not one I could believe in. And I don't care anymore.'

By the time they'd sorted out suitable clothes and put them around the stove, they'd resolved nothing. Her mother left again as Misha dressed in her old underclothes and the tailor-made she'd chosen. She was back with the scissors in the bathroom when her mother returned, followed by a taxi driver staggering under a box of groceries. 'I hope you won't refuse to eat, Misha,' she said, 'I'll see you tomorrow.'

Stacking tins of soup and caramel desserts in her own kitchen, Misha, suddenly exhausted, couldn't stop obsessive, resentful thoughts going round in her mind as if there had been no letter. Her mother was once more abandoning her. Where were her tears, her regrets? The too-short, too-heavy tweed of the suit, the stockings that didn't fit, made her breathless with irritation as she prepared herself a feast she didn't want. Even the sizzle of the frying potatoes, the prettily peppered egg, weren't soothing. Her mother didn't know that her own daughter could make a meal out of half a pound of lentils and an onion!

And when Philippe saw her again, this handed-down outfit on her skeleton body, he'd be sorry he'd gone to London to help her. He was used to women like Eveline. He just pitied her, being naturally kind, like his mother, because she'd sent him a call for help. He saw her as a child. And he probably knew about her mother.

There was egg around her chin. Her tongue burned. She looked down at her oily fingers and the frying pan set on the table because there was no point in using plates, not for one, and began to cry. Patch must have had an hallucination from war-hunger. How could it be true that Philippe had gone to London to fetch her?

She had dragged herself to the Bonaparte in her old clothes

for breakfast when her mother's head appeared over the brass rail. She stayed long enough for coffee, watching Misha dip her bread. 'Do you remember, darling, I let you spoon up the crumbs on our first day in Paris because in France it's not bad manners? How pleased you were then! And you had it all down your new jumper, blue it was.'

'I do remember,' she said sourly, refusing to spoon up any crumbs. 'Doesn't that Pierre have breakfast?'

'Not with me. He has it with his wife. He takes his aperitif with me and often his supper, sometimes his lunch if he's not too busy.'

'Wonderful!' Misha said. 'He has a wife so he won't even marry you decently.' She heard a spiteful note in her voice like her half-sister Janet's, and was ashamed. There was no need to have learned her spite, her malice, her quick retorts. If it could be true that Philippe had stood for three days outside that flat in London, she must unlearn them. She must unlearn them now, at once, because it must have been true even if no one else thought she was worthy of such an extraordinary effort, crossing the Channel in wartime.

'Marriage is not always decent,' her mother said, pushing aside her coffee bowl and taking up a crocodile handbag.

Misha stared at the indecent thing and into the face that had the blank look she knew so well. An unwanted pain gripped her chest and her old pity welled up as strong as before. 'No,' she said. 'Please tell me . . .' She thought, I want to hear my mother tell me of her misery with my father and she'll be unburdened. I shall forgive her for her treatment of me and we'll become friends.

But her mother was handing her an envelope. 'You'll find a few thousand francs in there, Michèle. It's clean money. Your father's. I've sold his rings, the engagement and the gold band. The diamond wasn't worth much but I think you can call that the allowance you'll need for the time being. I don't know where your father is. Neither do I care.' She wasn't looking at her daughter. 'I've put my address inside too, the apartment Pierre has rented for me. It has a telephone. The number's there. All I want is for you to promise me you'll come to me, you'll swallow that pride and come to me if you're in trouble? Will you do that?'

'*Maman*,' Misha heard herself cry, 'you like your rings. I'm sorry, please try to understand.'

'Yes, Misha, I will try, if you'll try to understand me. Perhaps when you are older we can be friends again.' She got to her feet before Misha could reply, and was gone.

Misha stared at the yellow poster on the opposite wall. RICARD, LE VRAI PASTIS it said, the same as it always had since her first day in the Bonaarte, spooning up crumbs with her mother. She had sent her mother away. She deserved this cold space around her. She was no better than her father; she took after him as Janet did, being self-centred, unloving, unlovable. No one needed her, no one wanted her company and it wasn't surprising.

She'd reached the stage of letting tears of self-pity fall down her cheeks when she suddenly gave a gasp at her own silliness. Of course she wasn't alone in the world because someone did need her and would welcome her company. She got to her feet and stuffed her mother's money into a pocket. There was enough for the train fare, more than enough. Oh heavens, she thought, I'll hold Frou again and she'll sleep on my pillow snuggled into my shoulder and I shall fall asleep to the sound of her little snore and Madame Constantin's louder one coming from the next room.

Why hadn't she thought of this before?

She mustn't be too forward of course. She'd go for the day, to make sure everything was the same at the farm, that his mother hadn't arranged other help. They'd exchange news. His mother would see she'd grown up and could be very useful as an extra pair of hands. She'd tell her son this in the next letter and he'd learn that she might still need him as a friend because she had no one left but a part-time mother.

Then they'd make arrangements for her to move in.

Chapter 14

Frou was sitting in the path where the gate had once been. Tabby fur gleaming, as plump as ever, she turned a vague indifferent eye towards Misha as she heard her name called. Misha jumped from the farm cart that had given her a lift and gathered her up. How many months she'd spent without this warm silky weight in her arms! Her squeaks of protest were the best sound she'd heard for a very long time. She buried her face in fur, laughing with pleasure, and shortly Madame Constantin came out to gather them both up.

They were soon all at the kitchen table. There was something on the stove, smelling good, home-baked bread, soft cheese and butter that was pale the way Misha liked it. She was ravenous, but not in a hurry.

'My poor son,' Madame Constantin said, 'sitting in that chair where you are, brooding on his worries, drinking too much of our precious Calvados . . .'

'What was he worrying about?' Misha ventured, her voice weak from emotion. She was here, in Philippe's home, where he'd sat, taking in his mother's tired face as he must have done and Frou's cross little triangle of perfect tabbiness. It'd been eight months since she'd last sat there, and apart from that plan of her father's to send her away – so easy to scoff at then – she'd been happy. She'd had Frou, Paris, the waiting hour. Since that time, she'd learned great chasms can open up at your feet if you're not in charge of yourself. She'd had sevenpence ha'penny left, and if Madame Constantin knew that, she'd have something to say.

'The war,' Madame Constantin muttered, 'the Army being unprepared, and he had trouble with some generals over writing reports they didn't want to read. Then that lady of his arriving at the farm when he wanted peace, after all his worrying about the Army buying 50,000 horses for the war and no tanks like the Germans have.'

Misha heard the words through a hollowed space in her head. 'What lady?' she said calmly, grabbing Frou and laying her face in fur. Beautiful Eveline, of course. Patch must have made a mistake. Philippe had simply been in London on some war mission for a general and had thought to call and see his old friend, having received her girlish cry for help. He felt sorry for her because of her awful father.

'The Parisian,' Madame Constantin said, getting up and stirring at the pot on the stove. 'This is only potatoes, my dear, and stock with a few vegetables in it.'

'I don't like meat,' Misha said, holding on hard to Frou who'd consented to lodge against her shoulder. What could he have thought of her, expecting him, a near stranger, to get her out of a flat in London in time of war? The same, she supposed, breathing in the fur smell, that he'd thought of her before: just a girl, young and rather silly, who needed a friend.

Her grown-up tweed was suddenly stifling. She wouldn't wear it again. She put Frou carefully on the table and laid her head beside the cat. Her tail, a joke tail which didn't match her queenly plumpness, draped itself over Misha's arm.

'A sharp little Parisian,' Madame Constantin went on, 'with designs on my boy, though I know I mustn't interfere. Naturally it has to be his choice.' She waved a spoonful of soup about to cool it for tasting. 'Pah!' Misha couldn't tell whether her disgust was for the *potage* or the image of the Parisian lady. It didn't matter. She had come for news. She had it. Here was Frou, in good health, the same cool gaze, the privileged acceptance; she had put out a delicate paw to touch her skin. And there, back on the front line after a number of leaves, one of them in London on some mission, was Philippe, in good health too evidently. In Paris was Eveline, who was going to be his wife although Madame

106

Constantin did not approve. Mothers didn't, usually, of women with designs on their son.

'Then there was some telegram his headquarters had mislaid . . .' Madame Constantin began to ladle soup into two bowls. Misha almost said, I know about the telegram; it wasn't important. She looked up into the old lady's face that had a shadow of his in it, the same hazel eyes and thick brows as he had and the same strong growth of hair. She had a fixed line between her eyes whereas his came and went as he thought. It had shown that August day he had sent her away from his window. She seemed weary too, as he had that day. 'I couldn't help him. It hadn't come here, his telegram, though he came looking for it and then afterwards wrote to me about it. Was I sure it hadn't come, a telegram from England? Someone had told him about it but it had been sent on to some other place. He kept asking, as if I am so foolish as to have been unaware of the telegraph boy, and in a war too. What mother could fail to dread the telegraph boy? Is there enough salt in this soup, my dear?'

'It's wonderful,' Misha said, 'just right.' She expected it was but didn't remember having swallowed any. Everything was ashes now and she wanted to go away again, back to Paris, to begin her new life, a job and independence.

They were dipping sugar lumps into plum brandy and it was almost time for Misha to start walking back to the station when Madame Constantin said, 'And he once wrote asking me to have a bed made up in the spare room to shelter a friend for the war, if the enemy doesn't come this way.'

'He meant the Parisian?' Misha asked, to be sure of more pain.

'Mademoiselle Eveline!' she snorted. 'I presume. As if she and I could bear each other for more than an hour.' She scraped sugar grains from her glass and poured herself another drop of brandy. 'Or,' she said, 'as if I dare leave Frou alone with her. The woman pushed her most brutally off this table, yes, and she says to me, "I've always thought of cats as vermin, Madame." Well, my dear, I never knew until then how much I loved having cat hair in my food!'

She laughed like a young woman and Misha laughed, laying her face against Frou's belly fur. She was snoring and they were tipsy.

'Not a clean woman,' Madame Constantin said, wiping off sugar with the back of her hand.

'Not clean?' Misha said, astonished, delighted.

'Not a clean soul,' she said. 'Then, just last week, he writes wanting me to make arrangements for me and this friend to travel further south together. Have I kept the basket for Frou? he asks. Well, I've told him, I'm going nowhere, however much that Hitler madman goes on blustering. Does he think he can invade France and half Europe without our fighting back? Last time the Germans came here, it took us four years to drive them out and they lost their youth over it same as we did, so it gained them nothing but suffering. Wickedness always turns round and destroys the perpetrator, my dear, though it may come through strange and hidden ways and hardly ever soon enough.' She slammed her glass on the table and sighed. 'Anyway, I'm too old to be going anywhere and I've no heart for sending animals to the slaughterhouse or for that matter to be setting off to Tours with a Parisian.'

Misha kept her face buried in Frou's fur and went on listening, entirely uncomforted by the fact that Philippe's mother so disliked his choice of Eveline. In this, after all, she was only being a mother.

Chapter 15

Misha thought she couldn't forgive her mother because she'd come from the bed of that man. Perhaps it was because she couldn't bear the thought that Philippe was going to share his, probably had shared it, with Eveline. Because the facts were plain: Philippe loved Eveline.

She had long nights to brood about it in the chill emptiness of the flat with her loneliness growing more certain, stretching ahead for weeks, months, years. She knew she craved most a second letter from Patch for confirmation of the visit, and then next her mother's silent presence.

Of course, she could make no choices. She couldn't decide to try for the Sorbonne one day and start studying immediately, because the war might suddenly burst into life and it would have been for nothing.

And it was easier to put off decision, to guard against forgiveness now that she had too much time to turn her hurts, her resentments, her unfounded glimpse of joy, around and around in her mind.

She didn't tell her mother how she missed her though Yvette Martin took to calling in at the flat in the mornings at around eleven o'clock. That happened to be the moment she chose to be leaving for her morning task at the Bonaparte, earning her lunch. Her mother appeared not to find this abnormal; she'd made her own decision – to clothe her daughter. She said she'd sold her old watch to buy materials and patterns, and installed herself at the kitchen table with the sewing machine, where she'd been used to sitting. Misha would stare at her head bowed over the machine, dump a

109

cup of coffee amongst the braids and cottons, and struggle with the desire to make everything the same between them.

She even liked what her mother had chosen, silky cotton in a hyacinth shade for one summer dress and navy blue with white flowers for the other. But she wasn't generous enough to admit it and chose to watch her mother from the distance of her own superiority. Her mother had failed her as a mother, she was a victim and nothing was going to be right in her life ever again.

Soon her days began to take on an aspect that was hardly more cheerful than the nights. She took up her old roaming habits when not at the Bonaparte, wandering about until she decided to force a purpose on herself. This was to buy a suitable outfit to see out the last of the cool days.

Her mother was actually unable to speak when she saw what she'd chosen. It was a green and red checked jacket worn with a green skirt and red beret, the essence of bad taste and still her mother said no word of reproach.

Not knowing why she'd bought it, Misha went on clattering about looking for shoes to go with this colourful ensemble. Here she met the difficulty she deserved. What accessories could go with red and green? Even she could not contemplate green shoes. She'd look like a clown. She understood why her mother had kept to neutral shades, but failed to tell her she'd learned a lesson.

And she wasn't in a hurry. She had no one to dress for now but herself; it was an empty victory. She left the outfit hanging up and wandered the boulevards in her rag-bag stuff, looking at black, grey, brown, beige shoes. She wasn't really looking, she was trailing about her old haunts, trying to recapture old dreams, sitting in cafés, searching for Philippe although his mother said he had no leave due. She went on watching for him, in case.

When she heard his voice calling her, she thought it was in her mind. She was sitting on the edge of the terrace of the Deux Magots in the Place St Germain. The square was bathed in spring sunshine, there were sticky green buds on the trees. She was staring at the Brasserie Lipp opposite, where her father liked to lunch, where they were lunching that day he'd said she must go away. Her mother had ignored his usual barb about wiping her plate with bread. She was remembering the very look, set and without expression, her mother had in his presence and how she herself had tried to cover the too-red bones of her own chicken so she shouldn't have some such barb thrust at her. She thought, My mother must have been very ill to have written those automatic letters and not want replies. I must forgive her soon. Savouring the memory all the same, because there'd since been so many painful things to forget, she thought she could hear his voice, calling her, the way he had from his window the last evening, on the Saturday after the Lipp luncheon. It had been very hot. She hadn't known it would be the last evening.

'Misha.' Again. Just like his voice. And into her vision came the hand she knew so well, with the long, tanned fingers and the tanned wrist. His khaki army shirtcuff was frayed. His voice said, 'Misha, Misha,' two or three times more. She looked up past the jacket sleeve on to the gold pieces near the epaulettes. He sat down next to her. She turned towards him slowly as if still in a dream, and like a dream there seemed to be only his face there, and her, with sunlight around them. She couldn't speak. Her face was stiff and she couldn't turn her head towards him. She saw his fingers lightly touching her glass of pomegranate juice, which would remind him she wasn't a chic woman of the world. She thought, If he'd move his hand closer, I'd dare reach out and touch it. For he'd gone to London in search of her and she had a right to be grateful.

He said, 'I came to London to find you but you'd left. I had gin and sausages with your jolly friend.'

Misha said, 'I thought you weren't coming, so I travelled to Paris with Georgie. She saved me.'

'I'd have saved you,' said Philippe gravely. 'I went there to save you.'

Misha watched his hand edge towards hers, and saw a still life on the cold marble table-top, the hands almost touching, the edge of her disgraceful jacket, her skinny wrist, alien khaki on his skin, the glass of pink sweet stuff and the saucer with a scrap of bill on it. Beyond, as if

111

behind a glass door, the rest of the world. 'I wish I'd been there to welcome you with Patch and the gin and sausages,' she said. Her hand was trembling, or perhaps it was his.

'It doesn't matter now.'

'No.'

'Your mother's here? I called at the flat but there was no one at home.'

'Some of the time, I'm really on my own now. I'm searching for a job, actually.'

'Yes, my mother told me all about that.'

She forced herself to look up again at his face, the weight of his gaze stifling her. She'd dreamed she'd see him on a terrace in the sunlight, and here he was. She said, 'I didn't do any stout war work and I haven't been brave.'

'I think you've been brave enough,' he said, and a voice broke in on them, a high sharp voice. Eveline's.

'Philippe! Thank God I've found you. Your concierge, that Madame Bassas, said you had unexpected leave and had gone out to supper, so I've trailed round all the terraces. What on earth's happening?'

Misha heard the words in a sudden burst of sound that was the world coming back. Of course, she'd been too hasty, letting joy stifle her just feeling his gaze upon her. And though she hadn't known there was any thought in her mind beyond that, there was Eveline. There'd always been Eveline.

Philippe seemed to hesitate before getting to his feet. 'Ah, Eveline,' he said, 'I was on my way to see you. The leave was quite unexpected and it's short, but if you didn't know about it, what were you doing at my apartment block?'

'I need to borrow your place for a while, mine's been requisitioned of all things. The whole building's being taken over for more civil servants and it's not as if there's going to be any war now . . .' She was irritable, ready to list all the explanations, but Philippe interrupted her. 'This is Eveline, Misha,' he said, 'Eveline Leclerc. And, Eveline, this is my old friend Michèle Martin.'

There was a grating of chairs as Misha got up. She shook Eveline's cold hand, sat down again, and there was more talk between them about his sudden unexpected leave. Eveline was argumentative, fretful, and Misha had time to look at her properly, having only glimpsed her before. She had fine high cheekbones, a perfect matt olive skin like her mother's. Her hair was a rare blue-black, and rarer still she had enormous blue eyes ringed with dark lashes, perfect eyes, perfect prettiness, and her hair was a gleam of jet curved below ears which were no doubt perfect too. A little hat in mustard silk was perched on top of this perfection and she wore a yellow silk suit to match, with a fur cape.

Misha cringed back into her rag-bag clothes and endured the cool stare Eveline threw her between cross looks at Philippe. It had disdain in it, and irritation, but that may have been because Philippe had displeased her and was continuing to do so. He hadn't told her he was coming to Paris and he obviously didn't want to lend her his flat. Why didn't she take a hotel room?

An order was placed for two whiskies and more pome-granate syrup and another still life was set up for Misha to gaze at, three glasses and three saucers, a second bill and his hand. The background was mustard silk and glossiness. She thought, sensibly, He is silently showing me his friend-ship, that he is glad I am safe and soon he must be gone again. There was nothing to stop her taking in every part of his face, after Eveline's. It was just as she remembered it, but paler, surely, and tireder? His hair was different from the weight of his cap, a touching line where it had sat on his forehead. She could see the twitch at the corner of his right eye as he spoke calmly to Eveline, disputing her claim to his flat. His collar was looser than it should have been. He had lost weight.

When she really understood he was near her, sitting on the café terrace, she could only think of laying her head on his shoulder. She felt almost that she was leaning drunk-enly towards him, Eveline being in another world that was not theirs. She wanted to say, I had sevenpence ha'penny left, the sentence that was the symbol of her endurance, and, They say I killed my cousin Peter who wasn't my cousin but my brother. She wanted to lean her head on his shoulder, to relieve herself of the burden of it, but the

113

woman was saying something. And he replied, 'Michèle is going to join us for supper, my dear,' so there was still time left for her.

Philippe asked many questions in a distant voice about her months in Bournemouth and London. They shared an omelette and a plate of hors d'oeuvres and retained an air of three strangers though Eveline kept on a bickering about the apartment.

'Very well, Eveline. It won't be too much trouble for me to stay in a hotel on my brief leaves in Paris. Let us say I do you this good turn and by way of thanks you help my friend Michèle here, by trying to get her work in the fashion house?'

Eveline did not appear stunned by this offer request though Misha felt her mouth drop open in the old childish way.

Eveline said, 'That's all very well, but I don't know how long we can keep going at Maison Schwarz. I've got my own job to worry about as well. Who's going to need a dress designer if this damnable war does get going? We've sold the summer collection, of course, but autumn sales are no more than doubtful.'

'You'll do your best, my dear? Michèle's father will be most grateful to you if we can do anything to help her during this difficult time. He's an officer with the Allied Forces at the front who got a nasty back injury on manoeuvres and its prostrate in England at the moment. I was his liaison officer, he telegraphed asking me to get in touch with Michèle and see what I could do . . .'

Misha heard this calm lie with surprise but didn't realise then how much it must mean about the distance between them. Eveline gushed a bit, powdered her nose with pretty hands that had bright red nails, perfect like the rest of her, and it was all over. They were going to fetch her bags and take them to his old apartment. He helped her on with her fur cape and admitted his surprise she had her bags ready behind the counter at the Lipp. 'I assumed your concierge would let me in. We must do what we can to help each other in wartime, mustn't we?' she said.

114

Misha gazed up into his face and saw the movements he made, storing them with the tone of his voice and the feel of his hand formally shaking hers, betraying nothing. She heard Eveline laugh and didn't care. Her heart was light because although he was leaving again for the front, he was not staying with Eveline and he had crossed the sea to her. She would have to brood on the matter, weighing these two factors against their long association.

Chapter 16

Eveline's eyes were the most unimaginable blue, hugely perfect and blank. Standing beside the owner of Maison Schwarz, Fashion Wholesaler, Monsieur Schwarz himself, she also seemed impossibly slender and chic. 'She can sew, her mother taught her, so I thought if we could take her on just whilst Solange is pregnant . . . I mean, the buttonholes have got to be finished, war or no war, and none of the girls is good at buttonholing. I just hope she won't let me down . . .'

'I don't let people down,' Misha said. 'And it's really nice of you to go to so much trouble, Eveline.' A swell of hatred rose in her throat against the beautiful eyes and cool beautiful skin Philippe must once have touched in love. 'And I'm sorry I'm late. I couldn't find the rue des Rosiers. It's much farther over the river than I thought.' Overheated from running and from fear of this, her first job interview, she stood in the doorway of the workroom and let herself be surveyed by all eyes. She'd like to turn round and leave. Even her mother couldn't have imagined she would begin her working life as a seamstress. But she would not make Philippe look foolish.

'Sit down, dear,' Monsieur Schwarz said. Plump, dark, bespectacled, he had an air of preoccupation Misha was soon to find normal. 'Give her a strip of flannel and a trial buttonhole, Marcelle. If she's good enough, she might as well start today.'

Seated at the big workroom table between Roseline, the apprentice, and Berthe, the finisher, Misha realised her

116

arrival had been no more than a brief interruption in their talk of war. As she struggled over a perfect invisible stitch with grey thread on the grey cloth, Roseline leaned towards Marcelle, head of the workroom. 'According to my dad's paper,' she said, 'they rounded up all those poor Polish soldiers trying to resist the invasion and put them in railway carriages with gas sent in that killed them. They died of asphyxiation and our boys'll get the same, you see!'

'It wasn't gas, my girl, it was lime. They put lime in and the fumes spread and killed them that way.' Marcelle, authoritative, comforting, inspected Misha's first buttonhole. 'Not bad,' she said. 'Do me one in that silk, and do stop frightening Michèle, everyone. Look, her mouth's open. If she can cope with silk, she'll be joining us.'

'I didn't know anything about them killing soldiers,' Misha said, gazing beyond Marcelle to the adjoining room where she could see Eveline drawing on a board. 'Not like that.'

'Rumours, dear child,' Dimitri the toile-maker said from a corner. 'And anyway, they won't gas civilians, so you're all safe.'

'Monsieur Schwarz doesn't think he's safe,' Marcelle said grimly, tacking a piece of grey flannel. 'Nor the kids. What's to happen to them and Madame if the Germans close this place down because it's owned by a Jewish family?'

'It's his living here, or his life and the lives of his family. I told him that last year,' said Dimitri, slipping pins into the waistline of something brown on the dummy.

'If he'd listened to us and started making military uniforms the Army'd have looked after him and sent him south anyway, though it's hardly likely Hitler's going to come as far as Paris. The Germans didn't last time . . .'

'Oh, he is,' Misha burst out. Why had she forgotten? How had she? There *was* this war, the Germans were already starting on Norway and Denmark, and if Philippe was defending the borders of France . . . *Lime*? 'He *is* coming here, he said so, a friend told me ages ago. Hitler's written about it. After the last war when he was put in prison, he wrote a book and said he'd invade France and get to Paris and conquer it and the French people . . .'

Roseline gave another little scream, a hand clasped to

117

her mouth. 'My dad says he'll come here too. Whatever shall we do?'

Misha stared across at Eveline. Did she know about lime and railway carriages?

Berthe, the finisher, nudged her elbow. 'Don't think she's designing anything,' she said. 'She's probably writing to her lover on the front line, a major or something high up, he is, and ever so handsome, much too nice for her . . .'

Misha rocked in her chair, fingers unable to hold needle and silk. How could she have allowed herself these light days, this lull in her fears, this contentment because Philippe had sat beside her at a cafe?

She ran home across the bridge that evening because she was going to make Monsieur Steiner sit down beside her for his aperitif and ask him to tell her the truth about German methods of slaughter with lime fumes.

But first the concierge handed her a letter. And by the time she had read it through until she knew it almost by heart, Monsieur Steiner had gone home for his supper.

My dear Misha,
Imagine a slow-flowing river, with the sun on it. Meadows leading down, marshy, with fat yellow flowers I don't know the name of, bullrushes, some very busy ducks sculling around with their young, moorhens diving. When the village children are let out of school, they go to the banks to play, in and out amongst the gun emplacements they accept as normal. They smell hot metal and river water, catch baby fish that quickly expire and get their feet wet.

I'm billeted in the priest's house. I sit in his parlour now, writing on his green plush tablecloth. The house-keeper has just come in with my first glass of red of the morning. Later there'll be a meagre luncheon, later still a hearty supper and talk, avoiding God, about which we have argued with some warmth. In his guest room where I sleep, he has left me a bible, a row of religious works I shan't open, a chest of long winter undergarments, hard white collars and a black hat.

118

The village has been my main base for some months and I know it well. There are three cafés, two butchers, four bakers, the church and the two schools this side of the river, and on the other mostly houses, one other café, a hotel perched up in the gorge where it offers good clean air, fishing, peace. The three bridges across the water are mined, of course, but the enemy is not expected this way. On the strip of sandy beach over there, sappers are at present at work relaying mines that were dug up against winter damp. I can see them from the window, distant toy figures in the sunshine, and can see too some outside contractors down by the machine-gun emplacement near the churchyard. When they built these last winter, they were foolish enough to place the gun-slits facing the wrong way and now have to rectify the matter.

You can tell, Misha, how little the enemy is expected here, can't you? So you need have no fear for me. It's, only that the area is part of our border – we're in place as a precaution and the usual military tasks go on because that's the way it is in the Army. The British are doing exactly the same in their positions. They are more at risk that we are – I cannot tell you exactly where I am, of course, but be assured that if or when the enemy decide to attack, it will not be through the gorges that protect this village.

Have you a picture of the little place, its river and its banks, its three bridges, the sandy soil opposite? Now then, imagine from the sand steep cliffs rising (the hotel perched there), narrow rifts where water has worked its way through, on and up to woods so dense they seem almost black to me as I glance up. I know there's oak there, beech, undisturbed wild green raspberries and wild strawberries that are never picked.

A single road has been driven through but is not much used. These villages stay isolated more or less, and if I tell you, Misha, that beyond the oaks, the pastures of the next have been planted with corn as usual this year, you can see that the enemy is not expected.

However, I do want you to recognise that matters in Norway are serious, and might be likely to escalate the war in the rest of Europe. I'd like to come to Paris to impress this on you myself. Will you speak to your mother as soon as you can? I believe you said her parents are in the Languedoc and I count on her being able to help you get down there, travel with you herself perhaps. Just in case she has gone away, I am sending you enough money for your train fare. Please don't be proud about this. You'll be able to reimburse me when you are earning, after the war.

Was Eveline able to find you a job in her workroom? I hope so, she did assure me she would try in return for the favour I offered her. But that job doesn't matter for the moment.

I'm also asking my mother to leave the farm with Frou and get on down to her sister in Tours. I arranged some time ago for a neighbour to help with the slaughter of her animals so there will nothing to keep her there. I once thought the enemy would not travel the same way as they did twenty-six years ago, but I was almost certainly mistaken. I went so far as to ask my mother to prepare the spare room for you when I first had your telegram. She thought it was for Eveline and wasn't pleased because she dislikes her. They are very different. My mother has the warmest of hearts.

The motorcyclist has roared up to collect my letters, Misha, so I can write no more. Reply to me immediately, please.

Putting this precious envelope in the pocket of her dress with the white flowers, Misha thought about cold hearts and Eveline and Philippe's sparing time to write to her. Did he realise how warm her heart was? Or that his letter had made it impossible for her to leave Paris yet? If he had sent one, he might send another. She'd ask for another. She wanted to go on knowing he was safe. If he learned she hadn't left, perhaps he would come himself?

First, she'd have to look up the French for 'kingcups', for her reply, then she'd have to look at the map of France to work out where he was in the village by the gorge that was never going to be touched by war.

She ate a distracted supper at the Bonaparte, refusing to let her eyes linger on the headlines in Monsieur Jules's newspaper: NORWAY FIASCO, BRITISH TROOPS WITHDRAWING. This was another scare. Warmongering.

And she had so much else to think about. Lime fumes instead of proper battles, and a cool, dark parlour looking out on to a sunlit river with ducks and children rippling the water.

Chapter 17

'All right, let's ask the English girl,' Alibert the ironmonger called from his corner in the Bonaparte opposite Misha's where he was playing dominoes with Lagrue.

Misha jumped. She was so tired of Alibert! She held up the Paris *Daily Mail* which had already told her too much about the disaster in Norway, but it didn't make any difference. Here it came: 'Mademoiselle!' in the oily voice which matched his sallow skin and the too shiny moustache like one of his own brushes. 'Mademoiselle, maybe you can tell us why those aristocratic generals of yours sent British boys to fight in the snows of Norway with rusty rifles they didn't know how to use and no overcoats on their backs!'

'And no transport or air support.' Lagrue moved a domino with his fat red butcher's hand and snorted. 'This is supposed to be modern warfare not something out of the past.'

Misha offered Alibert the longest stare she could maintain, taking in the grubby beret on his head, the slightly menacing chisel in the pocket of his overalls. Robert Blanchard had told her the inside pockets held dirty photographs and she hoped her glance conveyed she knew it. She would like to inform his poor widowed mother who crouched in the window of their flat above the shop that her son was worse than Lagrue who belonged to some right-wing group more fascist than the Nazis. 'I am not the Minister in charge of Britain's war effort, Monsieur Alibert,' she said in her calmest tone, affecting an English accent for good measure.

122

'But if I were, I should certainly have ordered coats for the fighting in Norway.'

It snows in the Ardennes, she thought, where Philippe probably is. She and Mr Steiner had worked this out. But it's spring there now, with kingcups and baby ducks, and I needn't worry.

'My contacts say half those poor devils have been lost in the snow already, they fell in and couldn't get up,' sniggered Picot from a table near the stove. He started scribbling in his notebook because he was supposed to be a journalist. 'Too late there for a woman's touch,' he said. 'Maybe all war ministers should have a mistress interfering in a country's affairs just like our own dear Prime Minister. Only Reynaud's bitch would be more interested in buying herself diamonds with our taxes to stash away in Switzerland than seeing our boys had overcoats.'

Misha spared him one of her cool looks, pretending to take in afresh the hunched shoulders in his mackintosh and muffler of no colour that he never took off. She'd seen panic in his foxy face once, when a police inspector had appeared in the doorway of the Bonaparte. Madame Florence said he was some kind of spy but spies were known to be all over Paris lately.

A sudden and overwhelming need to cry made her grip her newspaper. What would Philippe think if he knew she was trapped here, having to defend her entire country? The dark green walls, the crowd of café regulars, seemed to close in around her. I wish, she thought, I were back in the Bournemouth basement with Joanie. How straightforward her life had been then! If only Philippe would write another long letter, she wouldn't feel so unutterably alone. But she managed another retort. 'If there were women ministers running matters, there wouldn't be any war,' she said.

Reine, on her way out to begin the night's work on the corner of the next street, hooted with laughter, her crimson generous mouth open wide. 'And I tell you what, my little *chou*,' she said, teetering over to Misha's table in something tight and shiny, 'we'd do a better job of it than this lot of assholes!'

Misha watched Reine disappear through the doorway and

123

grinned to herself, smoothing out the *Daily Mail*. If Reine didn't lie in bed all morning, she'd have liked to see more of her in spite of Madame Florence's disapproval.

'That Churchill with the cigar, he'll sort matters out,' Monsieur Jules, faithful as always, called across the counter. 'He's somehow so British, isn't he, Mademoiselle?'

Misha felt a burst of grateful pride that gave her the spirit to call back: 'A British bulldog, that's what he is, and that's what we'll all be when the time comes. No one need worry about the British.'

She chewed on a radish and tried to sound at ease when she wasn't. What if French battalions were withdrawn from the safe place by the river and sent out to stifle in snow without guns or overcoats? What if Philippe lay there in the snow, rigid, dead, one hand held up? Her own hand with a blood-red radish in it wouldn't move beyond her plate.

Around her, the conversation degenerated further with the matter of the Duke of Windsor choosing to live in the south of France instead of his own country, thereby proving which was the superior. It was a wonder no one accused her of being Jewish or a freemason's daughter as well as Anglo-Saxon. She fixed her eyes again on the headline article in her paper. There it was in print, a barely believable story: 1,500 raw British recruits, no more than cadets, thrown into the snow without one piece of equipment to fight crack German troops. Why had this happened when half the men of England had been in and out of training camps since the summer of 1939? And the entire country had been put to work, raising money, knitting balaclavas and thick socks! What had it all been for?

She couldn't help a heavier dread settling around her. If the British, with their months of preparation, hadn't been ready for the fight when it finally came, how could the French be with their state of unreadiness? Everyone knew about it. Rumour said the officers wore open-necked shirts on parade and smoked, and the men didn't bother to salute. It was said most of them wouldn't be able to fire a rifle if they had one. They'd had too much time to wait and too much red wine in their daily rations. The railway stations near the front line had become drying-out centres!

If she weren't careful, she'd weep now, and the ghastly Alibert, and Lagrue with the metallic smell of blood on his clothes, would see it and snigger all the more. Which, she wondered, clutching the radish, would be worse? To drown in churning seas like the half-brother she must never think about, to freeze in snow or stifle from lime fumes deliberately placed in railway carriages? Who had thought of such a sinister method of slaughter? Who bought the lime and who had locked the carriage doors and heard the screams and not torn them open again? War was supposed to be matched fighting, hand to hand, bayonet to bayonet, each man having his chance.

'Are you going to eat that radish or not?' Monsieur Steiner's kind low voice asked. He took it from her fingers and smiled, putting his glass of red wine opposite her and sitting down as he often did.

'If only it were proper war,' Misha heard herself say, 'and we could be sure our soldiers were seeing the same sky as we are, there over Jubin's shop – look, pale blue it is – even if they were dying, to be seeing that and not . . .' Her eyes, startlingly, met a pair of big blank blue ones. Eveline's. Eveline was looking back at her over the brass rail and she was smiling. What could she want in a common café, where she never even took her breakfast as so many of the tenants of the apartments did?

'Is that you, Misha dear?' She'd come through the doorway and was standing by the table, as sleek as always in her mustard-coloured outfit. 'Let me introduce my cousin to you, he's from Switzerland.'

Misha closed her open mouth and found herself shaking the hand of a tall man of twenty-two or so. He had the same blue eyes as Eveline and bore some resemblance to her. She recognised that at once, though he was blond and tanned and looked as if he had just been doing something sporty.

'Eric Rous,' Eveline said, sitting down beside Monsieur Steiner as if this were also her second home. 'A distant cousin. I'm putting him up at the flat whilst he's on an engineering course here for a few months. Eric, this is my friend Michèle Martin, from the fashion house.'

'How do you do?' said Eric, snapping his heels together and bowing. He said it with an almost perfect English accent. 'I am hoping we may have a little English conversation together, Miss Martin.'

'Yes, Misha,' Eveline said, her remarkable eyes fixed on Misha as if they were affectionate sisters. 'Eric does need to meet some young people so I thought of you. Can you tell him a bit about London? He wants to go there next if the war doesn't start up.'

'Of course,' Misha said. But she wouldn't. She hated anyone to practise English on her. 'If you'll excuse me, I'll let you both have a chat with Monsieur Steiner here. If Mr Rous wants to know anything about Paris, he's the one.' She turned her own charming smile on Eveline's cousin, so as not to let herself down. He had the same perfect high-cheeked face as she had, the same gloss that had something to do with grooming, perfect skin, perfect hair. She was not going to like him. In fact, she disliked him already. 'I have to go and see an elderly widow, Madame Libaud. I usually do about this time of day.'

Glad to be in the open air, she ran across to the baker's. Often she used the old lady as excuse to leave the Bonaparte early, supper half-eaten, because even Madame Florence's kindly worrying about her was more than she wanted. Being with the Widow Libaud was almost like being alone without the emptiness of her own flat. Accepting two broken biscuits offered by Madame Doucet, the baker's wife, she passed on the gossip about Eveline's cousin, bought the hard, dark bread now part of Parisian life, and went back into the flats to climb the stairs.

The old lady never seemed either pleased or surprised to see her but always offered a second chair beside her own in kitchen or parlour, wherever she herself was sitting to watch courtyard or street. She'd watched Misha from the days of her impetuous dash across to a certain other window but didn't often mention the very recent past.

A stove still burned in the kitchen. There was a cup of

126

tepid soup for Misha to dunk her bread in and a not unkindly gaze from Madame Libaud herself who had suffered in her eighty-nine years, which included the siege of Paris in 1871 when rats had been the last food.

Misha recounted the evening's snapping over the war news and made them both hot chocolate. 'At least no one in England made me feel I shouldn't be there,' she said, forgetting Janet's hostility and watching the lights go on in the sitting-room of the flat below them to the right. She mustn't look, mustn't think about Eveline there. And how strange for her to have a cousin. She didn't seem a family person. You couldn't imagine her caring for a grandmother or taking a baby niece to the Luxembourg gardens for the air. 'Eveline Leclerc's got some cousin, a Swiss chap called Eric, staying with her,' she said, by way of finishing the day's events.

'I thought he looked like her,' Madame Libaud said, leaning forward from her chair to peer down. 'He'll be as unpleasant, I should think.'

'What way unpleasant?' Misha asked companionably.

'Not in a way a girl your age should know about.' In the gloom, her old face took on the look of an owl's. 'I wonder the professor let her back into his life once he'd managed to get free of her clutches. Though I never did think she'd lead him as far as the marriage certificate. Then after what happened!'

Misha sat up. 'What happened?'

'Never you mind.'

There'd be no more information. Misha knew she'd have to start questioning the girls at the Maison Schwarz. Yet all they seemed to know of Eveline was what she was able to recognise herself – her irritable nature, her sharpness, the fact that she often wasn't drawing but writing, and behind a closed door. They said she didn't understand the cut of a cloth either.

'Not that she wouldn't look very nice on a gentleman's arm,' Madame Libaud added.

'Yes!' Misha laughed. 'But being pretty isn't always what counts, is it?'

She tried to settle to mulling over the familiar subject of

Eveline but the images of soldiers lying dead in snow were far too intrusive.

Chapter 18

Misha woke up with a start, heart and head thumping. She'd been dreaming she was back in Bournemouth with the air-raid siren howling. But the howl was real. She sat up. So the enemy had come. It was still night. They always came at night.

She lay listening. Another noise. Someone was rattling her shutters and shouting. It was a foreign voice.

They had come this close. They were in the courtyard, defiling it, and she must get up and face them. They'd be worse, like dogs, if you tried to hide or run.

Struggling to free herself from a damp bed, she opened one shutter by a centimetre and peered through the crack. She was prepared. She'd face the green uniform, the helmet, the rifle, the cruel slit of eyes. She was glad they'd come. The fear of them, the waiting, had gone on too long.

There was no green uniform. She saw Eric Rous dashing to the next ground-floor flat, banging on their shutters. Who did he think he was?

The thrill of urgency left her. Eric of all people had set himself up as hero to warn everyone of the coming enemy. The policeman and the schoolteacher, Vautrin, had put their heads out and were also following his movements in disbelief, as if stunned by noise and the sight of him being ridiculous in a manner not suitable for Parisians. And for a mere air-raid siren howl! She herself felt so calm now, she was almost cold. Eric had calmed her in a way he hadn't meant. How silly he looked as the noise stopped so suddenly it was like the sun coming out. A clutch of birds flew from the tree and he grinned, putting fingers to his ears as a few faint feathers floated around him. 'No bombs!' she heard him cry. 'Everything all right this time!'

She had time to wish it were later and the Bonaparte open for coffee when a frantic clattering sound made her freeze with terror. Tanks. There were actually tanks on their cobbles. Where was her mother? She couldn't face tanks.

Forcing herself on stiff legs to go to the front door and edge it open, because not being able to see was worse, there were no murky green turrets aimed along the street.

Instead, she saw the wonderful brown nodding heads of the milkman's dray horses and the milkman himself smiling at her because she wore a nightdress. Misha stepped out and leaned weakly against a warm flank. 'I can't tell you how pleased I am to see these creatures, Monsieur. Have you spotted anything coming here, any enemy planes getting through?'

'Our anti-aircraft fire has held them off,' the milkman said calmly, shifting his Gitane to the other side of his mouth. He might have been reporting the weather forecast.

'But the sirens and the guns this time!' Misha cried. She'd been shamefully afraid, briefly. She wasn't the stuff of heroines. This was going to be hard to forget. 'We've often had guns,' she said.

The milkman shrugged. 'You'll still be needing your litre of milk, child, and my beasts aren't frightened yet, so you've no need to be. They'll know. Go and get your jug, I'm late as it is.'

Misha watched them rattle off and shivered again. Her mother should be here with her, someone, anyone.

'Hello! Don't be afraid!' It was Eric.

'I wasn't afraid,' Misha said sourly. He wore a silk dressing-gown over flannel trousers and gave off the same air of chic as Eveline. How displeasing this was, in a man. His teeth were too bright as well, and too small, pointed, like a girl's. She wasn't afraid anymore. She'd forget, easily, that she had been. Eric was ridiculous.

'Next time, do please go down to the safe place you have allocated to you. One day, it will perhaps be the enemy.' He shone the teeth at her and Misha scowled.

'I know the drill perfectly well,' she said. 'We all do.'

'Ah, but you did not follow it. Naughty!' Eric wagged a playful finger at her. He had manicured nails. 'Remember, the enemy will come one day,' he said.

'No, they won't,' Misha said, avoiding his approach and stepping into the stepping into the street in order to make a show of waving to the baker. He was coming up his basement steps and had a floury air about him, even in the gloom. 'Good morning, Monsieur,' she called. 'Bit early, that air-raid siren, wasn't it!'

'We'll hold 'em off!' Doucet replied. 'We're ready for any of their tricks!'

'We certainly are,' shouted Misha. She felt better.

Misha couldn't swallow her breakfast coffee in the Bonaparte, even though Monsieur Jules had warned her stocks were getting low. She had just seen a soldier with full backpack practically running past the café.

'Isn't that Jubin the grocer's son?' called Monsieur Jules from behind the counter. 'I thought he came home on leave two days ago.'

'He did,' Misha replied. 'He showed me some pictures of German planes. They're supposed to be able to recognise them.'

Monsieur Doucet downed his breakfast beer and stood up, flour from his apron drifting onto the table. 'If he's been recalled already, then our boy won't get his leave this week. And look,' he said, already in the doorway, 'there's two more passing. It'll break his mother's heart if Joseph doesn't have that leave . . .'

Monsieur Jules mechanically put out coffee cups but his mind wasn't on the task. 'And we don't know where our Robert is, but if there's a recall, Misha, how shall I keep it from my wife?'

The elderly workmen taking a break from repairing sandbagging on the corner of the street confirmed the bad news over their white wine. There were notices up everywhere. All military leave was cancelled and the stations were already packed with soldiers getting back to their camps.

'And I can't say I'm sorry,' one said. 'The waiting's been getting on my nerves. Let's get it over and done with.'

Misha couldn't finish the coffee. Her heart appeared to be sitting somewhere in her throat. She'd woken too early every day since the sirens had so frightened the city. There was no night anymore without anti-aircraft fire rat-tatting into the skies. And now the general recall of troops. This meant an escalation of the war, perhaps the true beginning of it. She got up. She had no words to comfort Madame Florence. Hitler wanted France, he wanted Paris, and he was coming for it.

Running down to the boulevard to look for one of the notices, she didn't need the confirmation of the written word. There was so much khaki and so many green buses full of khaki making for the bridges to cross the river for the stations, it seemed like a march of giants ant. And with the soldiers on foot, there were wives and mothers who knew as she did that it was time for war.

She felt sorry for them. One day some would get a telegram and their lives would be changed forever. The Ardennes was safe, of course. None of these men would be going there. It was barely protected. Philippe had said so. Uneasy just the same, she put out a hand to a passing corporal. 'Is anyone being recalled to the Ardennes front, please, Monsieur?' He stopped and grinned. 'Top Secret, that is, my lovely, but never you mind, we'll send your boyfriend back to you all in one piece, eh?' He winked and clattered off towards the river.

Please, Misha thought, do send him back, although he isn't my boyfriend. What a silly, inadequate word! She'd never wanted a boyfriend. She wanted Philippe.

At Maison Schwarz, they had to wait for the afternoon papers to learn the real and fearful news laid out in black headlines: HOLLAND LUXEMBOURG BELGIUM ATTACKED BY FURY OF FORCES, DEAD NOT YET COUNTED.

This, then, the reason for the general recall of troops made plain. Sinister in the spring night, parachutists had floated down to cut lines of communication at airports and

132

military posts so help couldn't be called for. First after that came the extraordinary shock of tanks rumbling through the streets and lorries packed with soldiers and in the night skies hundreds of aeroplanes appeared, to shoot down fire on the sleeping Dutch and Belgian people.

Marcelle, as head of the workroom, read out the news slowly. Monsieur Schwarz and his son Bernard, sixteen years old, who would too soon have to become a man, paced about by the windows. Misha, trying to read the words upside down, thought about villages near gorges. Please, she thought, say nothing about the Ardennes and please repeat that France is safely defended along the length of her borders. Then he and I will keep safe for each other and one day sit on a terrace together with the rest of the world shut away.

'Entire districts have been wiped out,' Marcelle said, 'like us here, say, in the Jewish quarter, or Misha over in St Germain, all the streets and buildings crushed to nothing and the people in them, the grannies, the babies, the pets . . .'

Roseline gave a scream. 'But they won't come here, will they? We're safe. They're shooting off the German planes every night, it's ages since we slept like we used to. I mean, the bombers won't get here?'

'Nothing to stop them, girl,' Monsieur Schwarz said harshly, 'and they get far enough to take their photographs, that's the preliminary stage. They take pictures of where they'll bomb and then one day that's it, like those poor devils!'

'But Holland and Belgium had guns fighting them off too!' Misha cried, staring down at the damp flannel she'd been messing about with. There was a spot of blood on the grey cotton thread but it didn't matter. The Dutch and Belgians had lost more blood the night before than she could ever imagine and one day this cloth might be covered in hers. Her fingers were cramped so tight she'd never release the needle. 'Must we just wait here for them to come?'

'There'll be announcements,' Monsieur Schwarz said. 'We'll have to listen to the wireless. And keep calm.' Pacing to and fro across the window, he and his son took up their muttering. No one else spoke. In the hot dusty air of the room, there was only the rustling of the newspaper as Dimitri turned the pages again.

They all started as a voice called up the stairway: 'I'm looking for Mademoiselle Michèle Martin?'

Misha felt a flood of warmth. Her mother, at last, had come to be a mother to her and there'd be an easing of her loneliness. And there she was, slim and chic in a new fawn-coloured suit and hat with fur trim, come to take her away because the war was creeping closer and she cared enough after all.

Yvette Martin placed a quick cool kiss on her daughter's cheek and dashed about the room being polite; even my mother, Misha thought with gratitude, knows it is not the done thing to burst into workplaces about family matters. She sat back in her chair to wait. This was her mother's social mode; she'd missed it.

' . . . and I said to your dear wife, Monsieur Schwarz, I knew she'd understand. She's a mother herself with three still at school . . .'

Madame Schwarz, so dark and plump beside Yvette Martin, seemed seduced enough by her charm to wipe her eyes, red from the morning's weeping, and bring in a tray of tiny glasses. They were all to have schnapps. No work would be done that day, any more than it had been done the preceding ones. Who would want grey flannel suits when nothing would count except surviving? And if you were a Jewish mother, with the Nazis coming, survival would be the sole aim.

'What's this shouting about?' Eveline came in from the design room but only Misha seemed to notice her.

Marcelle and Berthe were regarding Yvette Martin's fur-trimmed hat. 'Sable?' Misha heard Berthe whisper. 'Mink!' Marcelle replied. She remembered past shame, watching her mother sit at the table amongst the cloth she was turning over with the merest flicker of distaste. The fawn shade of her suit matched her eyes exactly. Was her mother too going to die? It wouldn't matter how she'd earned her mink then. It mustn't matter to her, Misha, now. With a flash of horror she'd seen an image of her mother lying dead with the

134

petals of the cream-coloured camelia she wore on her lapel covered in blood and soot. Her mother had come because she cared enough to take her away from Paris to safety. Of course, she'd refuse. But she was proud, after all; no one else's mother had rushed up to demand her daughter be given leave from work.

She was watching Eveline taking in every detail of her mother's perfect grooming, and so took a second to hear what her mother was finally saying.

'I've had a telephone call, darling, from the front itself. Yes, you wouldn't believe the crackling, it made my ears ache . . .'

Heat spread up from her toes, filling her body, stifling the beat of her heart.

' . . . says I've got to see you leave Paris at once. The impudence, my dear Madame Schwarz! As if I, her mother, the one who weaned the child, was not in torment during these difficult times . . .'

A priest's parlour, Misha thought, heat swirling in her head. A cool dark parlour with a glass of red wine in it, and there in a corner a telephone . . .

And now everything is almost all right. He's thought of me and soon he will be home to see I am well for himself.

'Perhaps we should go down to Mémé's?' she said dreamily. 'Lots of people from the Bonaparte are leaving Paris, and people from around here, aren't they, Madame Schwarz?' She thought, I don't want to go before I've seen Philippe again, once more.

'I hate the country, you know I do. Mémé fussing, all that emptiness, nothing to do.' Yvette Martin's lovely fox-eyes sparkled at her own frivolous nature.

'In a war, Madame,' said Madame Schwarz, her glass of schnapps untouched, 'in this kind of war, maybe nothing to do would mean we were safe. Just think of the poor Poles. So many hanged, they say, and for a rude word to a German!'

'Who was the telephone call from?' Eveline had sat down and accepted a schnapps. 'Is your husband back from England, Madame Martin?'

Misha smiled. She felt the smile spread from her chest

and take over her face. 'I suppose your cousin Eric'll be there soon,' she said. 'That's if the Swiss are going to fight this time, for a change.' How worthy of Janet and how satisfying this spiteful remark! Janet had taught her much.

' . . . for all I know it could have been from my husband, though we are separated, you know. I really couldn't say. It was from a military area, I could hear planes, honestly I could, Madame Schwarz, and this voice saying he was speaking on behalf of someone, I couldn't hear who, such a line it was! I must send my daughter south, that was the instruction. I ask you, as I hadn't been begging her to go myself!'

Misha found herself taking in some schnapps. She choked. Eveline's big blank eyes gazed at her. 'My father's dead, I hope,' she said. 'because if he isn't, he should be.' Everyone was staring at her but she didn't care. War should mean wiping away pretence and convention because only life itself could matter, and death. 'Being a father doesn't mean you change into a saint and can be allowed anything. The German bomber pilots must some of them be fathers and it hasn't stopped them killing children in Poland and Holland and Belgium, or grannies or mothers, or pet dogs and cats just like their own at home.' Pausing, breathless, exhilarated, she smiled at Madame Schwarz's horrified face. 'I do hope my father's dead because if he isn't, he'd just left me to starve in London, and not many fathers would do that, would they?' This had all tripped out by itself and she laughed at the sudden unexpected exposure of a truth she'd buried well down in her mind. I want, she thought, I want the telephone call to be from a priest's house and not from my father, and soon I shall find out that it was, and one day Frou and I will be at the window waiting for him to come home.

The conversation went on without her, her mother drawing it back to her own world and the new spring fashions on display in the rue de Rivoli. She asked that Misha be allowed to leave early and they went together to the Luxembourg gardens to sit in the sun on the hard chairs by the icecream seller. She didn't mention Misha's outburst.

'Pierre says there's nothing to worry my head about over

136

the new happenings,' she began, settling herself and crossing one fine silk-clad knee over the other. 'They won't get to France. Anyway, the call wasn't from that father of yours, I think it was on behalf of the professor you're so fond of. Who else do we know at the Front? He kept on at me after you'd left for London, that if ever you had to come back here, you were to go straight down south to be safe until the war was finished. He doesn't know how stubborn you are. Still, I'm glad you've been meeting some people your own age in England. That Georgie! I suppose she does have style. Has she any brothers, d'you know? I wonder she didn't invite you for one of those country weekends. You did say she lived in a manor house? When this is all over, a nice visit to Dorset'll do you good.' She took out her compact and began to powder her nose.

Misha squinted down at her mother in the sunshine and grinned. She'd have liked to kiss her. This was the mother she knew. 'I had a letter from Georgie a few weeks ago,' she said. 'She and her friend Patch have joined an ambulance unit. They'll have to ferry the wounded to hospital when the bombing starts on London. I wish I could do something like that.' This she added from habit. Mostly she wanted to go on waiting.

'Well, if the call was from your professor, I wonder who gave him my telephone number? Those Blanchards, I expect. That street is no better than a village. There's none of that kind of thing in my apartment block, I can tell you.' She adjusted her veil and handed some francs to Misha. 'Look, go and buy us an icecream.'

'Which flavour? I thought you didn't like icecream.'

'Strawberry,' her mother said. 'That's Félix's favourite, isn't it. You know, I thought we might go up to the station later and get you a ticket for Montpellier. Félix'd love you to be with him, he was so attached to you. He used to follow you about like a little dog.'

Misha laughed. 'It's no good you trying to make me leave in that roundabout way,' she said. 'I shan't go, not yet. If your Pierre says you've got nothing to worry about, the same applies to me.'

And it suddenly seemed to her that she was full of

strength and could face anything the Germans cared to
send.

Chapter 19

In a village by a gorge in the Ardennes forest, Captain Philippe Constantin had been instructed to have the church bells rung.

Being half-expected, it was an orderly evacuation. The Captain himself stood by the roadway beside the priest, watching his men help ferry out the elderly with their sad bundles, fruits of a lifetime's toil. What could he see in the eyes of the old lady offering the sign of the cross to the priest? Pity for him, perhaps, and contempt, because he and his army had let her down.

The housekeeper had left him supper but he couldn't turn away from this weary village procession. A soft summer night was falling, sweetly scented from the garden flowers. If he lifted his head, he could smell the river water, cool and muddy, but if he lifted his head, he would have to watch the girl coming towards him, a child clinging to one hand, a grandfather supported by her shoulder. Oh, the dignity of her, the grace of her slender limbs! She wouldn't look at him. Of course, she would not have Misha's eyes, huge and desolate... 'Bring that lorry in closer, Corporal,' he shouted. 'Can't you see these people have too far to walk!'

Maybe Misha too was being herded into some departing vehicle. He could only hope she was if she hadn't left for the south as he'd begged her to do. And begged that mother! Communiques hadn't yet reported that Paris was taken but with the lines cut, who could say what was happening anywhere beyond this ancient place which might soon be in the hands of the enemy, or worse?

139

Nearly done now.

It had been almost silent, the evacuation, apart from the sound of the revving engines, the slam of truck doors, boots on the cobbles. 'You're not leaving, Padre? he said.

'My duty is here, my son.'

'We won't be able to offer you any protection.'

'Ah.' The priest wrapped a hand about his crucifix. 'Maybe my time has come too. Has your colleague returned from that little reconnaisance trip you plotted together?'

'Not yet, Padre. And I can't hear his engine.'

'Does he feel, as you do, that unreasoning sense in his bones that the enemy will come, how did you say, blasting their way through here?'

'He does, sir.'

'And you do not withdraw your company? Or ask for reinforcements?'

'Both refused. High Command believe strategic defence lies north.'

'Refused,' the priest repeated. 'And so we wait, hoping you are wrong, my son.'

'I want you to take the keys I have left in your parlour. They belong to my car, you know where I leave it. If necessary, use it please, get away. You see, I can tell you now. Lemaire went up yesterday – remember you said you could hear a light plane? Well, it was him and he saw them, the enemy. Fifteen miles of them, he thought, columns and columns of men, with tanks, whole armoured divisions, engineers, all without any pretence of camouflage, marching through the forest roads in the sunlight. They know we've seen them and they don't care. Lemaire put in his report. Three official planes were sent up last evening, but they were thrown back 30 miles off by an entire squadron of Stukas supported by Messerschmitts. I was ordered to evacuate the village. That was the result and I think the enemy has been devilish clever. So I stand beside you, wishing too that what Lemaire saw was a kind of mirage caused by the sun as someone from HQ suggested. There are apparently several divisions in reserve somewhere, two or three days' march away. They may be sent up, but it'll be too late. And there'll be no air support.'

140

'God protect you, poor boy,' the priest said, 'and these men. Listen, they are singing. I shall go and join them. It may be they'll want to confess.'

'Don't let them know . . .' Philippe watched the priest he had grown to respect trail his black skirts off along the cobbles which might soon be shattered into splinters. 'I will leave also a letter,' he called after him, 'and a report of the events of the last two days which I should like you to take charge of if you are able to in time . . .'

The priest turned to nod and wave, disappearing into the soft darkness of the night.

Philippe Constantin hummed the chorus tune of the old drinking song he could hear coming from the barracks and turned towards the river bank. He wanted to stand there, listening for the rumble of tanks. Because he thought they were very near.

'You girls had better work out your prices in German,' sniggered Picot in the Bonaparte.

Reine, standing by the counter with her friend Juliette, flashed him a crimson and white smile. 'Well, at least the Krauts'll be men, little friend, and that's more than you can say.'

Juliette, whose pimp had finally had to let himself be called up like every other man, didn't bother with Picot. 'I can't stand not knowing how bad things are,' she said. 'Damn' newspapers, what do they tell? My poor Gran's in Le Havre. I'll kill the first German I see if they bomb her, I warn you. Ask the schoolteacher, Reine, he should know.'

But Vautrin didn't. 'All I know, girls,' he said, 'is that I'm thinking of sending my wife into the country though the train fare will make us short till the end of the month and there's our fifth child on the way. I must stay. My pupils have their finals coming up and I shan't let them down.' His pale eyes peered short-sightedly at the evening newspaper Reine had spread out on the counter between the Byrhh ashtrays. 'Most of this'll be out-of-date already and I imagine any really bad news'll be heavily censored. They don't want to create a panic.'

'Ah, but the French Army will hold, won't it, Monsieur?'

Eric's too-bright voice called. 'The French Army, the best in the world, the most valiant, the stoutest-hearted!' His pointed teeth bit precisely into a piece of raw carrot.

'We've been on a precipice before,' offered Monsieur Jules, pouring Vautrin his pastis.

'Only now Holland and Belgium have started slipping over,' suggested Picot, pleased at this cleverness and looking foxier than ever with his sandy hair standing up. He stared into Reine's full bosom as she leaned across the newspaper.

'What I can't understand, Monsieur Vautrin,' Juliette said, lighting a Gauloise from the butt of her last, 'is why Holland's only got one aeroplane left. I mean, an entire country has one aeroplane? I thought the Dutch were rich.'

'They are rich,' the schoolteacher said. 'They wanted to leave their wealth in the Indies instead of spending it on defence. They had fifty aeroplanes to start with – a few days ago, imagine! – and the Nazis had hundreds because they've been starving their people for years in order to build them.'

Please, thought Misha, sitting tight back against her part of the wall in the corner, please stop talking about it because I can't stand it anymore. That morning Marcelle had reported seeing refugees streaming down the avenue Clichy. Belgian refugees in carts and the Dutch in their fat black cars stuffed to the roof with most of their household goods. Half the people of Holland and Belgium had decided to leave their homes to the German troops and the world was a different place. Because Hitler had begun the way he had planned all those years ago. And he wanted France next, and Paris too as the brightest star in his New Order for Europe. If his slaughtering troops were not held off on the Belgian borders, it wouldn't be long.

Sometimes they'd bombed the Belgian towns with the stubborn ones still thinking their houses would protect them.

But there'd be hope if they could be held off at the borders. Or perhaps a false peace could be signed to keep them away.

How sickly the scent of the chestnut blossom along the boulevards that afternoon! Funerals, that's what the blossom smelled of.

'Misha!' called Monsieur Jules. 'What if we turn to the BBC news and you translate it for us?'

She heard his words but felt too tired to move from her seat.

'Pah!' she heard Alibert shout, sucking at the last drops of his Pernod. 'As if we Frenchmen want to hear the voice of British capitalism.'

'I do think, my poor Alibert,' said Monsieur Jules, 'that the BBC is accepted world-wide as giving the most frank and unbiased news service, and I would like our dear Mademoiselle Michèle to act as interpreter for us this evening. These are not normal times, and if I choose to have my wireless tuned to the BBC, it's my right, I presume?'

Misha stirred herself enough to walk to the counter. Adjusting the dial, she heard the familiar comforting voice of the announcer. 'Here is the BBC Home Service,' she translated, and had a vivid picture of Joanie standing over a bowl, shelling peas. She could smell cabbage and pink wafers and cocoa. How easy her life had been then, in that limbo! This was reality, this reporter shouting from some roadside in Belgium: 'The Germans have been bombing in Belgium today'.

She interpreted as fast as she could. 'Mainly roads and aerodromes and refugees. Their latest trick, one which goes on top of shooting and bombing the ever-increasing stream of refugees, is to machine-gun the cattle in the fields and lots of these have been seen lying about dead.' She had to shout, like the journalist, because of the noise of people crying and the violent rat-tat of the guns. She saw open mouths all around her, Picot, Lagrue, Alibert, all the boasters. Poor Juliette was sobbing for her grandmother; Reine, an image of terror, realising her daughter might not be safe in the convent which cost her so much.

Everything was worse, for all of them, because they'd heard the screams and the guns and would never be able to forget. Newsprint was easy to forget, maps with arrows of armies on the move were too. But not these sounds. In the silence when the report was finished Monsieur Jules offered brandy and they drank a toast to the refugees whose very personal bombs they'd heard with their own ears. How many survived that onslaught? It didn't matter. There'd be more. Misha said quietly to Madame Florence, 'Don't worry if I'm not here for breakfast. I think I'll take another trip into the country to see a few things, cows and fields. I need some air.' For the cows exposed to machine-guns, helpless in Belgian fields, might soon, in a few days, be Madame Constantin's. And sunning herself on an apple branch, watching the gateway with no gate, might be a fat little cat called Frou. Who had thought she'd be safe in the country? Philippe. But he had not known this, could not have known it. He'd spoken of death and destruction but he hadn't known about bombers machine-gunning people as they ran. No one could have imagined that. Some special minds must have plotted it. Perhaps the same ones who'd ordered the buying of the lime and the careful placing of it in locked railway carriages in Poland.

She was going to ask Madame Constantin if she would come to Paris with her. The cows would have to be properly slaughtered first, to save them suffering.

Frou wouldn't mind being put in the basket if she knew she was going home.

And if she couldn't soon hold hot tabby in her arms again, she'd lie down and weep.

'Oh, my dear child, don't cry, you'll set me off, and we've got more than cows to worry about.' Madame Florence put both hands up to her once-plump face and the reddened eyes that no longer had the sharpness of the cash-taker.

'You see, our friends the Belgians haven't been able to put up much of a fight,' cried Eric. 'Not very much use as allies eh?' He held up a manicured finger and wagged it.

No one so much as gave him a glance, not even Picot. The drinkers held out their glass for another drop of best brandy and gathered into a tighter knot.

Chapter 20

The clerk at the railway station didn't want to sell Misha a ticket. Did her mother, he enquired, know she was taking a frivolous trip northwards in a time of war when everyone else was fleeing south? 'Look about you, Mademoiselle,' he shouted, 'look at the poor devils crammed into this place. Do you see anyone waiting to leave? You do not, they are all arrivals, and if we don't get extra staff to help us very shortly, there'll be a strike.' Misha put on her English accent and the sweating man shrugged, passing a ticket across.

She was glad to be the only person in her carriage. She took off her sunhat, opened the windows wide and sat down to enjoy an English draught. The French, she'd learned, always shut windows. They'd have preferred the smell of *saucisson* and wine from the litter on the floor, left by the last lot of refugees; they wouldn't have minded the heat either or the stuffiness. Smoothing out the cloth of the blue dress her mother had made – this was its first outing – Misha edged her sandals into the mess of sausage rind, bottles, and things more doubtful still. What did litter count for now? There were already complaints in Paris about the casual untidiness of the refugees streaming into it. But the street cleansing department should be glad to clear it up; in Rotterdam and Brussels there were bits of human bodies.

At the village stop, there were none of the farm carts about to give her a lift and no one in the village street to help her. Going into the café to ask the way to the

Constantins', she saw the proprietor sitting alone in a drunken stupor, flies on the remains of his lunch.

Back in the street, she stood listening. Heat pressed on her sun hat and burned the skin of her wrists. No sound now but the flies buzzing, no child laughing, no mother calling, no aircraft rumbling.

Recognising the road leading out of the village as the one which would take her past the lane for the farm, she set off. If Madame Constantin had left with the rest of the inhabitants, she'd be satisfied that Frou was safe.

In the church crypt, Captain Philippe Constantin took out his fountain pen and notebook and, sitting with his back to cold stone, began writing:

This is to serve as testimony to events of the past hours. Few will survive to tell of them. They came at dawn, infiltrating through the woods under cover of dark with devilish speed and cunning. They had rubber boats, their own bridges, bridge builders, and though we blew ours, it was too late. Our guns too late also though by heaven some men did their best. All lost. Volunteers crawled down, lost too. Squadrons of enemy overhead, 3, 6, 9, Stukas in formation, hell of shrieking, 80 Messerschmitts as support. Our sole 3 plus 12 RAF bombers sent up. None returned. Have seen troops on back road, some on horseback, beasts trying to get home to die, mad with fear, all in retreat. Officers without radio contact. I saw a gunner dash screaming at major and shoot him, yelling Traitor! These men have been betrayed. I saw the General on back road sobbing and was glad. His adjutant shouted at me that no wireless in operation and we couldn't see each other for smoke and noise.

I should like to tell the priest I have known hell on earth. No sign of him here, hope he survived. I work on a radio to try for help but doubt there is help to be had.

In last hour, I have seen the rest of the entire division turn and flee, on foot, truck, lorry, hanging on. They'd

146

thrown down their rifles. I have a sapper with me, he and I found each other, being the only ones facing the right way. If I fail with radio, we intend to go back out and between Stuka attacks, which we can time, will make one positive act, useless though it will be.

I didn't know such noise could exist.

The sapper says the river was on fire.

Later: I have lost the sapper. He crawled outside to see if he might set something up. I followed after I'd heard another attack pass. I saw his leg lying where I think the road was. It was next to a body I think was Lemaire's. Perhaps the General will be pleased if he lives to learn Lemaire cannot make formal report of reconnaissance trip he made. He saw them coming. Fifteen miles of them, marching in sunlight, happy, everything planned years since, and we knew it and did nothing but set up a few guns without protection or ammunition, gun slits facing wrong way. We bought 50,000 horses. They won't make horse meat now.

Later: I have crawled from hole by crypt. Fountain pen grit in it, using pencil. Half church gone. Must be day but air black, smoke, dust, debris. Something burning on river, all gone opposite bank, rubble hot beneath me. Edged down to water. A straggler of the 2nd lying there with barrel of wine, drunk. Ease him away from machine-gun. Gunner body with shell in hand in way. Lie down for roar of another attack, must be last because all gone here. I scribble blind, notebook nearly used. Can see glimmer of tank movement across by bridge they made. Will settle here and wait. Found some shells not blown.

Wait. If smoke will clear, see better.

Later: Am folding this last page into tunic and if found want it to bear witness to tragic consequence of inaction, incompetence blindness useless defensive positions must never defend again always attack first I

147

suppose now Paris will fall like other cities M and I will never know of each other's death.

Misha caught sight of Madame Constantin in the dusty lane leading to her property. She was standing beyond a gate in a field with cows grazing. She didn't ask why Misha had come but held out her arms in an embrace. She had other things on her mind which apparently did not include flight.

Introduced to Marguerite, Misha put a hand on her heavy golden flank to feel the life in there. The cow considered her touch gravely, head turned, slow jaws moving. Misha laid her face against the hot skin and pictured machine-guns thudding, this swollen belly split open.

Madame Constantin said, 'What shall I do with her? I can't take her to the slaughterhouse – if anyone should be left there! Two will die, but which first?'

Misha thought, She does not know yet and I shan't tell her. But she did know. She said, 'Those wicked ones have been working on new weapons, guns in aeroplanes so they can send their bullets down on women and children along the roads and beasts in their pastures.'

'Yes,' Misha said, 'I heard it on the BBC.' She could smell honeysuckle. She took off her hat to fan the flies away from the cow's tail.

'Maybe they don't kill them properly, that's the worry of it. They'll lie suffering, thirsty, vermin at their wounds...'

'I've come to see if you're going to take Frou down to your sister's, now the fighting has begun,' Misha said. 'Your son, won't he be worrying?'

'I shall go nowhere,' Madame Constantin replied, 'and there's little chance he'll know. He'll have no need to learn of my end, nor I of his. That's how war works. I just hope they come together.'

Misha watched an insect buzz around Marguerite's ears and saw her belly split open, the wet calf struggling for breath in its mother's blood and she saw Madame Constantin dead, and Philippe, and she herself knowing it before she too died.

Madame Constantin said, 'I have my rifle ready and if that riff-raff come here, I shall shoot this Marguerite first, then her calf, two shots that'll be, then Pompon and my old Juliette, seven years she's been with me, and I'll go down into the cellar with that little cat after I've shot the goats. If they come with their boots and their wickedness into my house, I shall do what must be done. Knowing women and children and innocent animals have been mown down from the sky, I feel I've lived long enough.' She wasn't crying. Misha could see her face, older, hard and set under her hat. A bee crawled in and out of a cornflower in the brim though honeysuckle was tangled up with the dog roses in the hedge and there was blossom to spare, today.

Heat pinned her into the grass and there was whirring and buzzing in her head. She said nothing. When you recognise true grief, you have nothing to say.

Afterwards, Madame Constantin agreed Misha should take Frou. She had the basket ready lined with muslin from the dairy. Perhaps she'd been planning to take her somewhere once. She wrapped up two fat *saucissons* for her, pointing out that even Frou would be glad of common meat if there were nothing else. She filled an enamel jug with water, reminding Misha that milk is not a natural element for cats and they cannot digest it. She didn't seem to want to talk about anything though she went through some niceties about Misha's own and her mother's health, and food supplies in Paris. She didn't mention her son. Misha didn't ask about the Ardennes. His mother thought Philippe was going to be killed and she must begin to be really afraid.

They walked together to the station, Madame Constantin carrying the basket, she with a clattering bag of Frou's supplies. The train was in, already packed with those escaping farther into France with most of their household goods. This sight had become ordinary. There were chickens in boxes, hot children wailing, stoical grandmothers. Misha saw a bright green parrot in a cage on a luggage rack and a bucketful of soiled nappies. Nobody bothered to glance at her with a cat. Madame Constantin gave Frou one furious awful look she knew would be her last and couldn't speak to say goodbye until they were about to move off. Then she said, 'Try and keep safe for my son, dear girl, in case he should come through.'

Misha couldn't see her to wave goodbye; she was weeping too much. She supposed his mother had guessed she loved him.

Frou stared at the windows of her old home. Her eyes barely left them. She seemed neither to blink nor to turn her head. When Eric or Eveline came to close or open the shutters, she took no notice; they were not her master. She was waiting for her master and he didn't come. Misha, watching her stiff rump, felt another little edge of desolation creep into her heart. Sometimes she would go across to take the cat in her arms and sit under the tree with her. Frou remained stiff and ready, in case his face should appear. Misha grew dizzy, staring with her, as if the old days were back, and had to keep the comfort of the hot tabby body for the nights when the persistent, urgent rat-tat of anti-aircraft fire around the city kept them awake.

Then Robert Blanchard came home from the front, limping along the street towards the Bonaparte one Sunday at the dead time, four o'clock in the afternoon. Misha was at her table with a pomegranate juice, Monsieur Jules was dozing over his newspapers behind the counter, his wife having a nap upstairs.

Misha gasped aloud when she caught sight of Robert. He was very nearly at the end of his tether, half his uniform torn off, a bandage of sorts around his head, one arm hanging useless. He had neither cap nor belt nor rifle. She thought he had deserted and would be shot. She whispered across to his father, 'Robert's come home,' not wanting anyone else to hear. His mother had sensed something because she opened the shutters and gave a mother's frantic scream.

Robert didn't show he'd heard his mother screaming or reveal any sign of being glad to be home. He didn't get as far as the door but sat at a table outside. His father sat opposite, staring at his son with a face as white as his moustache, fearing perhaps that Robert would have to be hidden.

150

Madame Florence was not allowed to smother him. She managed to restrain herself somehow. A child could have seen Robert was beyond embraces. If his mother had begun on him, Misha felt he would have fought her off like a caged beast. He needed brandy first and then the doctor.

And not a word about his arrival had to be said in the Bonaparte. It was lucky he'd trailed along the street on a Sunday afternoon when the shopkeepers were taking a nap behind closed shutters. You couldn't trust Lagrue, for one, or Picot, not to report it to someone in authority, and there was always the poor bewildered policeman Chartier. There was also the newcomer, Eric, his bright eyes flashing into every corner.

Later, though, Misha began the habit of watching over Robert during the same dead time, four o'clock, when the world always seemed tireder. The workshop did its pretence work only in the mornings by them.

She made him a cup of real English tea bought in the chemist's shop and sat by his bed, where he lay staring into space. Opening the shutters a crack, she'd watch the sunlight move across the floor until it reached his bedside table and the glass beside the medicines. The doctor had asked no questions. She kept very quiet, murmuring to him about her days at the fashion house and the new Eric. One day she edged towards the question that lay between them. 'I suppose you weren't anywhere near the professor's battalion, Robert? He's been in the Ardennes for months.' She couldn't wait any longer.

'No, I was in the Reserves,' he said. He didn't look at her. He had his face turned to the crack of sunlight but perhaps didn't see it because he suddenly burst out, 'If we hadn't had those two days marching up there, Michèle. We'd had no rest. But it was so quiet at first, the sweetest summer air, we could hear the water slapping against the river bank. We wondered if we'd be able to bathe in it the next day. We could hear planes but then there've been aircraft buzzing about for months. We were fools. We were glad not to be sent to the Albert Canal, knowing we'd be in for it there . . .'

The hot room seemed to grow chilly. Misha watched Robert's face, dreading the truth to come. If she got up

151

now and rushed to some other task, shopping for Madame Libaud, anything, she need never hear it.

'God, though, the cunning of them, Misha! They'd planned it, you see, knew everyone would be looking to the other borders. Dawn it was when they came, and they had rubber boats with them to cross the river, their own bridges. Can you imagine? Bridge builders, the lot. And they started sending hell over before our artillery could get going.' Breathless, he sat up and took a sip of tea. 'God,' he said again, 'you should have seen the planes, perfect formation they came in, three, six, nine, pretty, until the smoke came and we couldn't see them anymore. We couldn't see anything, our platoon, we hadn't got our orders to move up so we just covered our heads as best we could. And the shelling! I think some of our planes went up there but the enemy had fighters, Messerschmitts. If you can imagine hell as noise, you can imagine the whole sky filled with shrieking . . . You're senseless from it and when the limbs of your mates are blown into your face . . .' He began to weep silently, without sobs. 'And the horses gone mad, screaming screaming . . .'

Misha wrapped her arms about her chilled body and wept with him, hell as noise in her head and flying limbs seen as clearly as Robert had seen them.

'They'd got their tanks over the bridges and when we saw them coming, frightful you know, monsters out of the smoke, you couldn't hear for the planes and our officer appeared then, I saw his gun and his white hand raised up, he ordered us on but our corporal, he wouldn't have it, I was right behind him, I heard him shout, "No, Sir, I'm not sending my men into that!" He shot the officer so the officer wouldn't shoot us, I think he got him in the knee, he went down anyway, I saw that, then me and the corporal started to run because the tanks were coming and we hadn't any tanks . . . And if anyone from High Command is left, I'll be shot as a deserter, Misha.'

And so she learned that the unimaginable had come to pass: the Germans had broken through at the place thought to be impregnable, the Ardennes with its slow-moving rivers, its gorges, its villages perched high up. She had fool-

152

ishly misled herself, living on the dream of the priest's house and the baby ducks.

She must straight away start walking the boulevards in case Philippe should come limping home like Robert, shot in the knee by his own men but alive.

There was still a little hope left to her, and she must hold on to it.

Chapter 21

'How very clever,' observed Monsieur Steiner. 'The newspapers make it all seem like a victory. Look here, very neatly put.' He placed his glass of red wine on the counter and read it out: ' "French and British armies are smashing their way to the sea, in the most glorious rearguard action of any war." '

'Well, now we know where we are,' said Monsieur Jules sadly, pouring out Alibert's pastis. 'We can't count any longer on the Belgian Army. It's simpler with the Allies under one command.'

'Never trust a Belgian,' said Alibert with satisfaction. 'At least the Dutch monarch did the decent thing and left the country rather than kowtow to the enemy after they'd given in.'

'I think we are better off,' Doucet the baker, a gentle man, said in his quiet voice. 'We know where we are, the two of us. We managed it before in the Great War. You'll see, our boys will take fresh courage, they'll make that glorious stand.' Everyone knew his son was still part of it; even Alibert couldn't mock the baker.

Misha peered at the map the Blanchards had fixed to the wall. There, in the north and not so far away, the allied armies were being driven towards the Channel. Oh, send in the British Navy, she thought. She wanted to burst out again about her day at Weymouth, but the regulars around her had heard it before. She'd spent the entire afternoon here again; company was better than solitude for hearing worsening war news and studying maps of the enemy

154

advance. She no longer looked at the words 'Ardennes Forest' spread across a green patch. The war was finished with there. Philippe was probably on his way home already.

'Old Pétain'll see us through,' suggested the old man no one ever spoke to.

'Field-Marshal Pétain?' spluttered Jubin the grocer. 'Pétain waved on hundreds and thousands of us to death at Verdun! That was supposed to be a last stand and there were two more years of it.' He swung his wooden leg and kicked at the counter in a rare show of feeling. No one protested. It was said a broken heart lay inside his thin chest; his wife had died in childbirth just before Verdun and now that child, a strapping lad he'd raised himself, was somewhere in the rearguard action.

'Heard the latest joke?' sniggered Picot. 'There he is, Field-Marshal Pétain, hero of Verdun, called into the War Cabinet to give it an air of knowing what it's doing. He dozes off in his old-age fog and suddenly wakes up, asking, all querulous, "Why aren't we making more use of the carrier pigeon?"'

'Carrier pigeon,' Eric called from his side of the stove, 'what is this, please?' No one bothered to answer him so he was obliged to take his copy of the evening paper up to the counter and shine his perfect teeth at the company for elucidation.

'Doesn't that course you're on teach you anything?' Alibert said sourly, and for once was supported.

'We're listening to the BBC news now,' said Doucet kindly, 'if you don't mind?'

'Ah, the truth,' smiled Eric, always undefeated by the air of chilliness which greeted him in the Bonaparte. 'You and your BBC truth, Mademoiselle Michèle. Maybe one day there will be no more BBC and then what will you do for truth?'

Monsieur Jules turned the volume louder and Misha feverishly listened and translated the confirmation of what they had already half-learned from the newspapers. ' ... under the fierce onslaught of the enemy bombers, the trapped remains of the British and French armies has been driven to the coast ... for days and nights now ships of

155

every kind have plied to and fro across the Channel in response to a call sent out by the British Navy to help them take the British and French troops off the beaches where they've been forced by a furious and unequal attack by Panzer tanks.' Her body an empty space, with her heart still frantically beating, she tried to spill out the words fast enough. 'The men stand in the black sea water amongst their dead holding up rifles to shoot uselessly back at the Stukas screaming across.'

They could hear the screaming. Eric's teeth shone. 'It seems the German Army has superior forces and courage,' he said. 'What a very great pity for France and England, isn't it?'

'You will be quiet please, Monsieur.' For once, Monsieur Jules showed his distress. 'Our grocer here and the baker, they both have sons at the Front. You are hardly discreet.'

The report was finished, but it was enough. Misha edged away from Eric. She was going to be very sick. She felt dizzy. Hundreds of them, thousands of men, helpless, knee-deep in bloody water with the planes coming over to mow them down as they stood. She went to sit at the nearest table opposite Jubin who had raised his head to listen to her translation. He looked as white as she felt, his eyes as mournful as a dumb animal's; he feared he was going to lose his son, and his son was all he had. His evening glass of red stood untouched and his arthritic hands lay still on the tabletop. Like the clumsy leg he had to swing awkwardly to walk, his head lay to one side. His look at her said he would cease to have any reason to live if his son were shot down in that dirty sea.

'We'll get another report later this evening, will you come in and hear it?' Misha asked him. 'You know, if the Navy's there, it'll be all right. If you'd seen them saluting the King as I did once.'

Jubin shook his head. 'I can't trust Denis to close up properly,' he said.

'I don't think it matters about closed shutters anymore,' Misha suggested. And it didn't because half the fighting men of Britain and France had been chased into the sea.

'You say the ships are saving them, taking them across the Channel?' Jubin asked.

'A great armada of ships, the man said, and boats, pleasure boats, you know, those big steamers that take tourists up and down coasts. Well, they do in England. They make a lot of noise. I used to live in a place called Bournemouth. I saw them in August last year, sweet they were, sort of important and puffy, like fat people, and children would wave to you from them if you stood on the clifftop. You felt silly waving back but always did so as not to disappoint the kids. You could see the bunches of sunhats and brown skinny legs . . .' She was crying a little but so was Jubin and they sat as if alone within the dark green walls of the Bonaparte, each with their imagination and their fear. Her fear was as great as his, and like his, was muddled up with hope. She knew very well though that no one from the Ardennes could have been saved on the beaches of Dunkirk. They were at opposite ends of the country with hundreds of tank divisions and thousands of enemy soldiers in between.

Vaguely, she looked out into the street where the Vautrin family were piling into a taxi. With four children under ten and another on the way, the teacher had persuaded his wife to set off for the country where her parents lived. 'The Vautrin family are leaving then,' she whispered.

Jubin nodded, wiping his face with a handkerchief. 'She wanted to buy extra sugar and flour. I let her have a bit. What else could I do, poor woman but if anyone finds out, I'll have a queue out there.'

'Chief!' Jubin's errand boy Denis suddenly appeared in the doorway. 'What am I to do?' He too whispered, in the theatrical manner he had adopted since he'd learned about parachutists dropping from the sky over Rotterdam. 'The policeman's wife wants some tinned stuff, you know. She's going, her duty's to her children, she says, before her husband and he won't leave the force.' He tried a wink before turning his brown puppy-eyes upon Misha.

'I should think not, if the police depart . . .' Jubin got to his feet, dragging his artificial leg around the table. He shook Misha's hand. 'Thank you, Mademoiselle,' he said, 'I shall call back after I've closed the shop, if you'll still be here?'

'I always do the nine o'clock news as well,' she said. How else could she pass the evenings?

'Many boats and ships coming across the Channel?' he asked.

'And many men being saved in spite of them, in spite of the bombers tipping out their bombs, and the fighters machine-gunning all along the beaches and into the sea,' she said, fresh tears threatening, because in her mind, she'd seen them and was now as weak as a kitten. She really had to hope that Philippe was at Dunkirk because the onslaught against the Ardennes front was barely being mentioned by the news services; it wasn't therefore a glorious rearguard action or a pretend victory in the Ardennes. She'd rather he be saved by one of the stout-hearted men she'd seen in Weymouth harbour, in one of those glorious ships, than by anyone else.

'He's saved, our boy, he's alive!' Madame Doucet, the baker's wife, rushed into the café. She'd been running along the street. Everyone must know at once. 'Yes, the telegraph boy came just as I was making my husband's first cup of coffe. Oh my heart! It leaped right into my mouth and I screamed because of course I thought...' She leaned against the counter and Madame Florence, beaming, poured her a tot of brandy. 'Oh, I thought my Joseph... oh, I did, Madame Florence... where's Mademoiselle Michèle? I must tell her...'

Misha extricated herself from her corner, swallowing her second cup of coffee, from hunger. She'd had no supper the night before; she'd forgotten to eat because Jubin's fear had reached into her more than the news report. Her heart though, now, was leaping with pleasure because someone had been saved and so it was true, about the boats and the ships crossing the Channel.

'This place where he is,' cried Madame Doucet, her pink plump face suffused with tears of joy, 'look, Mademoiselle, an English name. Say it out for me!'

'Worthing, it's Worthing,' laughed Misha. 'A place by the

sea. Joseph's in an English seaside town, can you imagine!'
She waved the telegram like a flag.

'I shall, my dear, if you'll be kind enough to tell me a
little about it? If we could work out how he got there!'
Madame Doucet couldn't get her breath.

'It's the ships like they've been saying, the naval and the
pleasure boats. I think your husband heard the translation
last night, they've been sending everything that floats across
the Channel from England to get our men off the French
coast, and they've taken them home.' She ran across to the
counter. 'Let's look at the map.'

On the map spread out beside the coffee bowls, Misha
found Worthing and described it for Joseph Doucet's loving
and sobbing mother. 'Cliffs, I suppose,' she said, 'white, with
green grass on the top, and a beach below with deckchairs
and people in sun hats, safe people, women knitting and
men being stout and tall enough to see off Hitler.' Letting
the tears fall because the Blanchard and Doucet mothers
were weeping, Misha's voice shook. 'Maybe some of the
boats have left Bournemouth where I lived once and maybe
someone we know is in Bournemouth this very minute.'
Giddy, she could see it clear as the light over Bournemouth
bay, a paddle boat coming back from the Isle of Wight with
SS Belinda on its side and Philippe standing on deck in a
mess of khaki and oil and blood, shading his eyes to see
where she had once stood. There were a few safe cuts on
his left arm, the one he didn't need so much, but enough
so he couldn't be sent back.

The excitement of the telegram spread along the street
and the Bonaparte did a good trade in celebratory drinks
all day. But the reread and refolded telegram didn't stop
Chartier, the policeman, from announcing his wife's departure further south. Unpompous for a policeman, and fearful
for his role if the enemy should take over the city, they had
decided Tours was far enough south to be safe now that the
enemy was likely to turn back from its conquering journey
to the coast and look towards its finest prize, Paris.

The happy baker, Doucet, didn't agree with him. 'They
won't get to Paris, they didn't last time.'

'But what have the Allies left to fight on with?' Chartier

159

said. He'd just come off day-duty and was exhausted because he'd had to spend it trying to keep the hundreds of refugees from blocking the streets around the main-line stations. 'As I see it, no matter how many thousands of men have been saved, their equipment hasn't. How could they take off our tanks, our lorries, our machine-guns? Life has had to come first but it stands to reason a retreating army driven into the sea under a storm of shelling can take nothing with it.' He removed his casque and wiped the blond hair from his forehead. He looked too young to be a policeman.

'Perhaps the six o'clock news will tell us more?' Jules Blanchard said, turning up the volume on his wireless. 'Mademoiselle!'

Here was the evening ritual begun. Misha got wearily to her feet. She felt as tired as Chartier looked but she didn't let a single broadcast slip by now.

The main report was from Dover, not from the French coast. And there were cheering sounds instead of the shriek of aircraft. She felt herself smile. Around her the usual crowd smiled too. Even Picot let his foxy face ease into a grin; the weary Chartier's face was transformed. 'They're dirty, these men,' she translated, 'dirty, yes, exhausted, yes, but in their eyes is their joyful, irrepressible spirit. They cheer as they come slowly down the gangplanks to be welcomed with tea and buns. Soon they'll be packed off again into trains for Hove or Poole, even Dorchester because there are too many to be helped here . . . all along the line the local people, overjoyed at their safe arrival home, hand up chocolate and cigarettes. The sun is shining and there is this: that hundreds and thousands of men have been brought back and are still being brought back from the hell that is Dunkirk harbour . . .'

'Hundreds of thousands,' she repeated, her flushed face in a silly grin because everyone else was smiling. 'And look, there's another telegraph boy going past. I bet it's a telegram for Jubin, saying his son's been saved and is having to eat an English bun. When he gets back I shan't hear anything else but how it tasted like a floury brick or something, as if I were responsible for English baking.'

160

'I think I'll get a bottle of champagne up,' Monsieur Blanchard said. 'If there's one person who deserves a toast from us all, it's poor Jubin.'

'Here's Jubin's boy now,' Misha said. 'Denis, was it . . .'

Denis wasn't smiling or laughing. His beret was pulled right down to his eyes. A cut was bleeding on one of his big clumsy hands. 'Telegram's come,' he announced. 'Marius.'

Everyone could see then that Marius hadn't been safe in Worthing. Marius Jubin was dead. Denis had cut his hand pulling down the shutters.

'Did you hear it, Mish, the bombing last night?' Roseline, standing in the doorway of Maison Schwarz, was whispering as if the enemy could hear.

Misha nodded. 'They say it's the Citroën factory over on the outskirts.'

'Yes, well, it's not far enough away for us. My dad says we're going. We're packed and everything. He's got a cart from somewhere and we're setting off just as soon as I've got my wages and my mother's got hers from the warehouse. My grandma in Orléans is going to take us in but I don't know how her and my dad'll get on.' Shivering in the morning air, pale face pinched, Roseline sniffed back tears. 'My baby brother's sobbing fit to burst because dad says we've got to leave Rex behind.'

'People are taking their dogs with them, I've seen it,' Misha said. 'Yesterday I saw an old man sitting in one of those open vans and he was hugging two little terriers.'

'Yes, but my dad never liked Rex, 'cos Rex never liked him and used to snap back at his boots when Dad kicked out at him of a night when he'd had a glass too many.'

Misha, glimpsing a world she didn't want to have to worry about, put aside the image of an abandoned dog she'd never met rushing around the streets in search of his departed family. 'The anti-aircraft fire did hold them off more or less,' she said. 'Why's your dad deciding now?'

'He says they're coming nearer by the minute. My mother says the lazy devil might have to work if the Germans come here and that's why he wants to go and if he doesn't settle down in Orléans and not cause Mémé any trouble, she'll send him back on his own to get a job working in one of their barracks. At least there'll be work, that's what she says.'

Marcelle came striding next along the street with a smile on her face. 'Held 'em off, didn't we?' she called. 'They say those Citroën factory girls got straight back to work like nothing happened, sweeping up the glass and getting on with making shells. That'll show 'em, won't it?'

Only, Misha thought, if the enemy gets to hear of it which was unlikely since most of its army was on the move, with two great claws stretching across France and towards Paris.

'I'm thinking I might ask to get taken on there. At least I'll feel I'll be doing something, what I wouldn't do to get a gun in my hands!' Marcelle, a rare smoking Frenchwomen, had lit a cigarette and was puffing angrily on it when the workroom door opened suddenly and Monsieur Schwarz himself appeared. 'We're closing, girls,' he announced. 'Come on up quickly, I've got your wages ready and a little extra as holiday money.'

All the brown stuff and grey flannel had been packed out of sight. Cloth dust lay on empty shelves.

'You've sent the kids away?' Marcelle asked.

Monsieur Schwarz nodded but it was clear he wanted to say no more. Misha waited only as long as it took the rest of the girls to come up, in order to say goodbye to them. Berthe was on her way to the Gare du Nord; she too had only called in for her wages. 'It's the waiting my mum can't stand,' she said. 'And with Dad being in the army, we don't know where, there's no reason to hang around.'

The closure was expected, but Misha lingered with an odd feeling of shock. She'd belonged here, briefly. She'd once made a perfect buttonhole in a gold velvet jacket to Marcelle's complete satisfaction.

Trailing out into the street with her, Misha saw bunches of workers standing around outside their doors. Some of the shutters in the once-busy place had not been opened. No one sat in the café next to the horse butcher's. There'd always been a collection of elderly men there, hunched over ancient chessboards, playing day-long games. 'It's different,' she said, 'like everything's slipping away.'

162

'Wasn't hardly anyone in the markets this morning,' Marcelle said, 'but come on, let's have a last fling. We'll do the boulevards, the posh ones, and then have a glass of champagne together.'

'But are you going to stay, Marcelle? Or shall you wait to hear news of your husband? Perhaps he's even now in some English seaside place.'

'Pah, my old man got back weeks since!' She trotted fast in her high heels, past the closed laundry, the cobbler still at work, and the picture of a leaping horse under the notice 'Horse Meat Bought'. 'I didn't want the girls to start spilling the beans everywhere, and I wasn't exactly proud of him. He deserted.'

Misha, trotting fast to keep up, said, 'I know a deserter. I actually saw him come home. I do think there ought to be a different name for them, less shaming, because it wasn't their fault they were forced to run. No point in letting a tank mow you down, especially if you've got nothing to fight back with.'

'And you've got a wife and two kids back at home, right?' said Marcelle. 'That's his argument but somehow, you know . . .' She was breathless but didn't seem to want to slow down. 'I dunno, it just sticks in my craw. And I know they were sent out there ill-equipped, I know they had all that waiting time for getting drunk in, but if you can't trust the men to protect the wives and kids! Ought to put some of us in, wouldn't take me five minutes to get rat-tatting with a machine-gun.'

Out in the broader sweep of the rue de Rivoli, Marcelle pointed out the windows of the famous shops. 'Look at that stuff,' she said. 'Crocodile handbags, gold, diamonds. "Madame has a Duty to be Elegant"! Who are they kidding? A few chosen tarts in this world can be elegant, and that won't change, war or no war, never does.'

'Maybe those things'll be smashed anyway, the window glass splintered by bombs and thrown all over the street with the diamonds so no one'll know which is which,' Misha said, panting slightly. Marcelle walked too fast for her keep up. 'And maybe the Eiffel Tower will be blown up and iron

163

splinters strewn over the city.' She gazed across at the familiar silhouette against the sky. 'I've always thought it ugly but somehow it's part of what I want to keep and I don't care if I am half-English, looking at it now, there's a funny pain around my heart.'

Pausing to gaze too, Marcelle sniffed. 'Well, they'd better not touch our cathedral, that's all I say. Imagine this place without Notre Dame and the Eiffel, eh? Oh God, Misha, I don't feel like spending money on a drink, do you? Whatever is to become of us?'

'I don't know, Marcelle, but perhaps you'd better save your sous for the moment and I suppose I had better had . . .' She paused, and stared at nothing.

'Boots, that's what we ought to buy, if anything,' Marcelle said. 'Boots for the kids and warm clothes for everyone, because there might not be anymore coming . . .'

'Yes. Or food, Marcelle, food that keeps?' Not wanting or needing boots or warm clothes, Misha thought of food for Frou. 'I'll stop at all the grocers on the way home.'

Marcelle sighed. 'Yes. Come on, Misha, we won't have the champagne now. We'll drink it at the end of this bloody war, not the start of it.

Misha nodded, her mouth dry.

'I'd better get on home. You coming in the Metro with me? I'll hold your hand and pretend you're one of my kids.'

'I can't go down there, you know I can't. And anyway, what if the enemy arrives when we're trapped in some tunnel?' She wasn't joking.

'God, you're giving me the creeps! I'm off, Mish. I'll see you soon. Whatever happens, it won't last long.'

Misha watched Marcelle disappear down the steps of the Metro, a dark cavern suddenly more menacing without the usual mass of bodies struggling in and out. I want everything the same, she thought, all the irritable smelly Parisians going about their usual cross business. I want the swish café terraces I feel too poorly groomed to sit at; I even want glittery windows back, for the rich and decadent. I want Paris whole, and not this chill around my spine and images of iron splinters crashing through the air.

Making her way into the humbler side streets to find a

164

place to buy a sandwich for her lunch, she found none not packed with people. Refugees, of course, she realised. How could she have avoided worrying about them until today? All citizens had learned to recognise refugees by the bewildered look of the dispossessed with no daily routine, no work, no home. If they were lucky, they'd have been found lodgings by the Red Cross. If not, who knew where they slept? Probably in station waiting-rooms. This café looked and sounded like one itself. There were suitcases on the floor and entire families sitting silent over empty cups.

Rag, tag and bobtail of people, Misha thought spitefully. Everything their fault. Foreigners. Why don't they go home. There was a toddler pulling at her skirt, a mess of pap around his mouth. In a moment he would put a grubby finger into her cheese. She edged her foot towards his unsteady ones. She could smell his nappy. Picking up her sandwich, she refused to look down as he fell. He'd be all right. Soft bones. His wailing was no more than the general wail of the room. Her teeth comfortably chewing on thin hard bread and cheese, she felt her eyes meeting a pair across the table, so dark these, immense, taking up the face with its drooping skin. The eyes belonged to one of the foreigners, a grandmother, probably the toddler's and spoke of a despair and a weariness beyond measure. Misha didn't move. She wasn't going to pick up the child. He was a nuisance and should have been kept out of her way.

The toddler himself was climbing up his grandmother's long black skirt, fitting himself somehow between the table and the black breast offering no comfort. Lodged there, minute fingers clutching the marble, he presented his wide open wailing mouth. He knew Misha had kicked him. Looking into the desolation and fear on his young face, Misha thought he'd already grown used to kicks, to this uncomforting bosom that could give him nothing. 'Would the baby like a piece of my cheese?' she said.

The grandmother shrugged. Perhaps he had lost his mother. Perhaps she was one of those bombed down as she ran along the roads of her country. Misha groaned. She didn't want to look into anyone else's pain, she wanted to

165

nurse her own and sit there hugging a bit of Paris in case it should be gone.

It was already gone. Pushing across the entire sandwich, Misha got up. Let the poor little scrap at least fill himself for one meal. His wailing had stopped. Good. She could forget him now and forget the unfathomable weariness in the old woman's face and her own spiteful thoughts.

'A free chair, Susie, over there!' Misha heard an English voice above the café's babble. 'Grab it do, quick!'

'You want this chair?' she said calmly, turning round to meet a blonde English girl wearing a nurse's cap and a grey uniform.

'I say, do you speak English?' It always surprised them.

Misha didn't bother to answer that. 'Hurry and come and get it,' she suggested, 'bit of a crowd in here.'

'Bit of a crowd everywhere, you should see the station!' The girl called Susie sat down and shouted over to her friend: 'Got it, old thing, have to take it in turns.'

'I've heard there's hundreds still arriving on the trains from Belgium and further north from here,' Misha said, jammed up against the English girl's shoulder. She'd be polite; she was well brought-up.

'Thousands actually, and the French troops mixed in with them too now, you know, the ones in the retreating lines, God, what chaos it is and if that wasn't all, there's enormous queues forming for Parisians wanting to go south by train, people who haven't a vehicle to get away in. Thank God, Audrey's managed a couple of sandwiches by the look of it, I'm starving . . .'

'What do you mean, troops?' Misha asked. 'Officers? French officers as well as men?'

'Some I think, yes I've seen one or two officers but mostly they've got all the buttons and so on torn off so as to try and mingle with the locals, don't want to get taken as prisoners-of-war if the Huns do float down in those parachutes, terrifying, isn't it? Aud, old thing, give me my share then you can sit down. This here's an English girl, what's your name? You can come and give us a hand if you like? Feed a few babies. D'you know, there's some stray babies and toddlers just sort of left about, no one knows where the

166

mothers are . . .' She was having to shout louder as the noise around them increased. No customers appeared to leave the café though more were trying to get into it.

Misha felt the stifling panic she had in all enclosed places. 'Sorry,' she said, 'I'd be no good as a nurse.'

'Not nursing, just feeding 'em, holding 'em safe for a bit, staving off the screaming a bit longer . . .'

'Sorry,' Misha repeated, 'I can't.'

Outside, taking deep grateful breaths of air, she thought, Philippe wouldn't be arriving home by *train*.

Nevertheless her feet took her of their own accord right up to the station area well before she had realised it. Getting near the station entrance wasn't possible. The station courtyard, the street leading up to it in each direction, the station cafés, all were packed with people. Some seemed to be hanging on to the railings. Amidst the now-normal mess of suitcases and bags, they seemed to have been waiting a long time. They were almost silent. Only a few very hot policemen were shouting. Edging herself between two pillars on a closed shopfront, Misha decided to wait too. If she could make out any officer khaki amongst the bodies, she'd go on waiting, that day and the next, all week. She had nothing else to do now. And there was still a little hope.

She need never tell Philippe she'd kicked a baby.

If she thought about the baby properly, she'd open her own mouth and howl.

She must have dozed, lodged there. Her back was made of ice, from the stone of the pillar. Her face, she felt it without needing a looking-glass, had taken on the hopeless look of all those people jammed against each other, waiting.

She wouldn't wait any longer. There'd been a glimpse or two of khaki but it wasn't officer-type. Nevertheless, the English girl had told her something. She would return the next day, to lend a hand. Here was her chance after all to do something stout and British, like Susan and Audrey. How stout and British they were, what fine noble self-sacrifice lay waiting for them! She herself would manage something mild enough and so be able to tell Philippe she'd

167

at last fulfilled his expectation of her. Perhaps she wouldn't need to tell him. He would tumble out of a train, weary, bloodied, alive, and he'd look across to where she was, kneeling on the platform, exhausted but struggling on with whimpering wet babies and starving toddlers she'd somehow found milk for and being brave, British, the way he liked her. And she would glance up and there he'd be.

A smell of urine and sweat had mingled in a humid layer over the street. A man was shouting: 'Make way, for God's sake, this woman's having a baby!'

There was some shuffling over by the railings, a dazed turning of heads.

'Can't you see, this woman's going to have a baby, the ambulance has got to get there!' It was one of the policemen shouting.

The mass wanted to move but no one seemed able to get an edge on anyone else and therefore start the space needed.

'How can we call an ambulance if you don't let us pass!'

Behind his shout came the high scream of the woman, and then another call: 'I'm a midwife, let me get through!'

Beside Misha, a middle-aged lady burdened with a winter coat and hat began to sob. 'What's to become of us?' she kept repeating, 'Is this the revolution over again?'

Misha, stifling, shouted, 'Let me get OUT!' Her chilled body had become a tornado of panicky heat. Bending her head, she had to push through people at waist height. They were trying to get forward to see the woman giving birth on the pavement! 'Keep back,' she kept saying, uselessly, because everyone was shouting now and the poor woman still screaming.

Down on the boulevard, it was hard to make her legs work for the trail back home, and if the dog hadn't whimpered she wouldn't have looked up crossing the side street. But he did whimper and she did look up and therefore learned something else she didn't want to know.

A very old lady was holding the dog in her arms. It was much like her, sorry-looking, small, mangey, trembling.

The old lady and the dog were also in a queue, dozens of people long. Each held a dog or a cat, on a lead or in some kind of basket. Misha saw a proud red tabby in a proper wire cage, its mouth open, panting. A terrier was barking, two canaries sweetly singing a song over the head of an enormous bloodhound spread in a miserable heap across someone's feet. And sobbing helplessly a little girl of eight or so leaned against the wall, one bright eye, one black kitten's ear peeping from her cardigan.

At the head of the queue, far down the road, was the sign; Veterinary Surgeon.

Misha began to run. These animals were going to be put to sleep. She didn't want to look upon all that pain. Enough of her own lay waiting. How was she to keep Frou safe? Had the French wireless been shouting out some advice, some *decree*, that animals must be put to sleep? She mustn't lose Frou because she'd made a silent promise: that she and Frou would be there watching the courtyard when Philippe came home from the war.

Chapter 22

There was a hand-painted poster on the door of the Bonaparte: CITIZENS OF PARIS TAKE UP YOUR ARMS PARIS MUST BE DEFENDED, it said.

Misha stared first at this and then at the policeman Chartier who was reading it with an air of disbelief. Joining him outside, Monsieur Jules muttered, 'A young man ran in and asked me to allow it up. But it cannot have come to this. Have the police had their instructions?'

Chartier shook his head. 'The army will defend the city, that's all I know at the moment.'

Misha stumbled inside to her place in the corner. Today she had almost seen a woman giving birth on a pavement and she'd seen dozens of animals queuing up for death. She was beyond feeling and if the errand boy Denis was going to fulfil his dream and be given a gun to kill parachutists, would no longer raise an eyebrow. If she'd got Frou safe, she'd ask for one too. If anything happened to Frou, she'd use it. She'd die using it if she heard the enemy had slaughtered Philippe.

'Pomegranate syrup, please,' she said wearily, 'and if there is any bread, a sandwich would be nice.'

'But where are these arms, where the ammunition stocks?' Monsieur Steiner was unnerved enough to be shouting. 'It's all very well, but the newspaper headlines are saying the same. Fight to the last, they say, but with what?'

'The Paris Radio's been giving rousing talk too, listen.' Monsieur Jules ran behind the counter to turn on his wireless.

'A pomegranate syrup, please, Monsieur Jules,' Misha called. 'And is there anything to eat? I've had no lunch. I can't tell you what a day I've had.'

The radio voice cried, 'Should the Germans reach Paris then we must defend it with every clod of earth rather than have our city razed to the ground and fall into the hands of the Germans.'

'I wonder the authorities allow such talk to go out,' Monsieur Steiner said, 'and I ask again, where are the field hospitals being set up, where the stack of coffins, the fresh burial ground? Because if you've got street fighting, you've got deaths, injuries, you can't order people to take to the street without it being fully thought out.'

'Aren't any authorities anymore, Monsieur,' said Picot, sidling through the doorway in his summer uniform, a crumpled sandy-coloured suit and a very grubby straw panama. 'Haven't you seen the puffs of smoke all around the office blocks of our dear city? It's the civil servants setting fire to their files in the courtyards.'

'What files?' Chartier asked crossly, sinking into a seat by Monsieur Steiner. 'You must refrain from spreading rumours, Monsieur.'

'Any old files, names, addresses, who cares, it's all going now and when the enemy come looking for information, they won't get it. My sources say . . .'

Misha stood up and wandered out into the street. If she could get the the errand boy's attention by calling up to his bedroom over the shop, perhaps he would creep down and open the door. She needed some food for herself. And if there were any tins of anything, meat or fish of any kind, she'd buy them for Frou. She and Madame Libaud had stocked a war-hoard in the cellar for the three of them already but she'd better use her wages to buy more, then find Frou a hiding place. Perhaps behind the tins. After that, she'd put her mind to guns, or broomsticks for that matter, shovels, fire tongs. That's what the local defence volunteers had been armed with in Bournemouth and nobody there thought they were worse than useless. All her British spirit was going to come to the fore very shortly; she could feel it rising. It had started rising some long time before, when she'd had nothing to do with it. Now she had something, plenty; Frou and Paris to fight for, two of her most precious things.

Denis was standing in the doorway; she could see an edge of overall. Good. The shop had re-opened for business after the death of Jubin's son. The shutters weren't open, only the door. Perhaps he was cleaning. 'Denis!' she called in an urgent whisper. 'Any chance of something to eat?'

Denis didn't reply. He was giving little jumps, up and down, and his hands were jamming his beret right on to his nose. 'Have they said you can have a gun, Denis?' She said, without interest; she'd have some persuading to do to get food from him. He wasn't allowed to sell anything.

Denis danced, frantic eyes indicating something behind him. Misha peered into the darkened shop.

Past the counter, beyond the shelves that had once been full, swinging from a rafter in the storeroom, was the body of Jubin. There was only one boot showing; he'd taken off his wooden leg before he hanged himself.

'What papers!' shouted Misha. 'I've had nothing to eat all day and Monsieur Jubin's dead. Is this a time for papers, Madame Bassas?'

The caretaker stood squat and short on the doorstep. 'There is no need to be snappy with me, Mademoiselle. I've got my police reports to fill out the same as always. And it's not as if you're one of us, is it?'

'I've got dual nationality, you know I have, and my mother's as French as anyone else.' Misha leaned wearily against the door jamb. Let the woman see in; she had nothing to hide.

'Then there's the matter of the lease,' the concierge went on. 'You with no parents, maybe the landlord'll be wanting to know who's living here now.'

'What will it matter if Paris is to be razed to the ground? It will be if we don't fight for it, haven't you heard!'

'No, I haven't.' Madame Bassas seemed to smirk. 'But I have heard it's to be left as an open city. That means the enemy will be able to walk in without doing any damage at all, so leases will matter, my dear, you'll see, and I shall still

172

be able to do my job. And I would like you to give me your dear mother's new address so I can complete my files.'

'My mother's just moving again, actually.' Misha managed to be quick enough for this reply though her head hurt so much she could hardly see the woman. It was true then, what they'd been saying in the Bonaparte: the caretakers would be glad to work for the Germans, they'd be their best spies. And they'd be after her mother! Heart thumping with her weak head, Misha gathered her strength. 'I'll let you have a note of the flat she's chosen as soon as I can, Madame Bassas,' she said carefully. 'Of course she's gone to the country for a while, until things settle down. It's best, isn't it?' Janet had taught her the usefulness of the instant lie, and her mother that one must always be polite to caretakers. 'Excuse me, please, Madame,' she said. 'I have to get some supper and with poor Mr Jubin gone . . .' She must manage to be polite.

'That reminds me.' Madame Bassas's tone had sharpened. 'Since you mention the grocer. That cat of yours. If this city becomes short of food or is under siege the same as it was in 1871 there'll be no feeding of cats, you know, and if I see you giving the animal any food, I shall report you.'

Misha, unable to answer, stared back; the woman seemed to be shrinking as she stood there. Oh, yes, a very suitable spy for the enemy, and a very easy first target for the gun she was going to get.

'I'm thinking of reporting that cousin of Mademoiselle Leclerc's. I suppose you don't know where he was born? I need to know for my records and he's not being very helpful . . .'

'He's from Switzerland,' Misha said fast. Easy, it was easy to be a spy; she could be one herself if this woman would now go away and leave her. She wouldn't be able to hide Frou in the cellar, it would be the first place for a caretaker to look. 'Now, he's a foreigner, isn't he, Madame Bassas, and I think I heard him saying he hoped no one would ask for his papers because they were out of date.' An urge to see the woman gone made it hard to stand still. She was no longer tired, no longer hungry.

'Did you indeed?' Madame Bassas sucked at a loose

173

tooth. She didn't appear to remember what she'd come for because she turned and swung off down the street towards the Bonaparte. She was bandy-legged and short of stature but was moving with some speed. Misha watched her pause to wave up to the widow Alibert over the ironmongery. She had, she supposed, thought herself and Frou safe in the flat, in the street itself for that matter. She'd been wrong. How often had she been a little off-hand with this woman? Once or twice. Perhaps more. Now she was to pay for it. There couldn't be any peace for her now. It was lucky she'd asked her mother to fashion a harness for Frou, just in case.

She had barely the strength to open a tin of soup for herself and might not have bothered if Frou hadn't been agitating for her sardines.

She was lying on her bed, the cat curled into her shoulder, planning matters, when the doorbell rang again.

A chauffeur was standing on the doorstep; he had on a black uniform with a cap. Behind him, her mother's man, Pierre someone, came across the cobbles towards Misha, taking small steps like a fussy woman. He dismissed the chauffeur and removed his panama hat but she didn't invite him inside. His face was shiny with sweat and he wiped it, offering Misha a twinkle that wasn't very warm, making an effort though and starting off with polite chat about the hot evening in a Maurice Chevalier accent. She might have guessed he would have English at his disposal and would like showing it.

Without his hat, there were only a few strands of hair on his head. She regarded these with distaste but began to listen when he was over the charming part. 'Please,' he was saying, 'I want you and your delightful mother to travel together, forgetting those little mother and daughter problems, natural at your age, yes, dear me, yes. Use this special pass, I've gone to some trouble to get it for you, it's a government pass, make sure the gentlemen at the station realise you are fortunate enough to be a friend of someone in the government.' He handed her an envelope; he was panting and wiped his face again.

'They say the government's running away too,' Misha

said. There was no reason to be polite to anyone now and the rudeness that Janet had taught her was coming in very useful. He was a blur in the dusk.

'Dear me, no, my child. Rumours . . .' He gave a kind of laugh. She took the envelope mechanically, searching for something else to say about the authorities in general since her mother had been right, he was one of them.

His voice dropped to a whisper though there was nobody but Misha to hear it. 'We mustn't create panic, oh no, we must be sensible and remain calm. I want you to be a good grown-up girl, go across to your mother, take a taxi, there's money, go south at once, you and your mother, go today . . .'

He was already walking off, plump body taking women's steps.

'Take a taxi!' cried Misha, 'we haven't seen taxis for days, taxi drivers were the first to leave Paris, they'd got the petrol but surely the government shouldn't be going, aren't you supposed to be in charge of us, you're paid by the people to look after them!'

He was already squeezing himself into the back seat of a long black car; the chauffeur was sliding it away from the pavement. There were files, boxes heaped up on the two spare seats. Monsieur Pierre of no other name then offered a wave from his safe distance; perhaps he thought he had a cheery goodbye look on his face, but he seemed tired to death without his Maurice Chevalier act.

Misha knew she should have been surprised at his appearance but was not; the most unlikely events were passing into routine. 'I've almost seen a woman giving birth on the pavement!' she shouted in case he could still hear. 'What if they blow up the Eiffel tower, has anyone thought of that?' She would very much have liked to begin crying but she managed to put the envelope, folded, into the cocoa tin with the rest of her money, all she had in the world. There'd probably be a healthy sum if she could be bothered to count it. Thousands of francs with that from the sale of her mother's rings, and what Philippe had sent for her train fare. She had many times the train fare to get to her grandparents. What a pity there were no trains running.

Tomorrow, she would have to think about far too many things.

The telephone behind the counter of the Bonaparte wasn't working. That was her first decision on waking, to telephone her mother and repeat the advice her man had given. 'Can't get through,' she told Monsieur Jules. 'I suppose I'd better walk across the river and bang on her door instead. She won't be awake yet.'

'And you shouldn't be awake either,' he replied, 'and since your father isn't here, I demand you sit down and eat some semblance of breakfast before you go anywhere.'

'My father?' muttered Misha. 'Imagine him worrying about my breakfast!'

'Well, if you were my daughter! Here, eat this very quickly before anyone else sees it.' He passed across a slice of cold omelette. 'Your favourite, look, here's the pepper sprinkled on, be quick.'

Misha put her teeth into something soggy. She felt very sick, beyond hunger. 'Can you keep it for me until I get back? I'll be starving by then.' She was starving now, she thought, and had been for weeks, more.

'But it's hardly light and you look like a ghost, child . . .'

Misha couldn't listen; she set off towards the boulevard because action had to begin somewhere. She hadn't passed poor Jubin's shop before she heard a muffled rumbling sound. Tanks, she thought vaguely, but not clattering enough. Perhaps some more army units moving up to protect Paris from a camp towards the east. If she hadn't had to decide about getting Frou away, she'd have been glad to hear it.

On the corner going down to the boulevard, she had stepped over the cow pat before it occurred to her that she hadn't seen one before, not in Paris.

Then she saw the back of Alibert, pushing a handcart along the cobbles. This was not an unusual sight; he often delivered bundles of wood for firelighting in it. It was just that his mother's crutches were sticking out of the side, and his mother's black elbows in their widow's weeds, and his

176

mother's black button-boots, shiny and unused because she couldn't walk.

She hadn't had time to skirt around them before she caught sight of their postman in a mailvan with mattresses strapped to the roof, and three ladies of the street, rivals of Reine and Juliette, in a Renault being driven by the cheese seller from the Sunday market.

These apparitions, she realised afterwards, were a prelude, a warning, of the sight that met her on the boulevard itself. Carts there were, wheelbarrows, coalmen with their horses, firemen in their trucks, funeral hearses jammed with the living, cows with swollen udders, five goats with the billy leading. Paris's population that hadn't already left, Misha thought, panic rising in her, and some from the villages around, and all the officials, from the postman to the governmental Pierre someone, they'd joined a medieval procession fleeing a plague. Only the enemy was the plague and she had *slept* whilst everyone else had heard there was no time left, not for defending Paris with every clod of earth, not for anything but flight, because they were going to raze it to the ground as they had Rotterdam. Something in the night must have told them to go now, this dawn, this day, and she was going to be left behind and wouldn't be able to save Frou, much less her mother or herself.

It took her two hours to get across the river to her mother; more escapers kept tumbling out of the side streets and joining the creeping procession. Nobody was hurrying but they'd have liked to; she saw it in a kind of frantic look in the eyes of the set blank faces of the old men sitting on piles of bedding, of the children too frightened to cry, of the panting dogs on ropes being dragged amongst the wheels and the carthorse hooves. Where had the carthorses come from? Where this cow swaying her belly behind a blue-painted farm wagon? This was not the country, it just smelled like it, Paris, the most beautiful elegant city in the world, smelled like the country and sounded like it, with ennervating sheep voices over all the rest.

Her mother's maid let Misha into the flat. She was leaving. She held a suitcase and had put on her hat. They

177

didn't speak. The maid simply closed the door behind her. Misha shouted because she'd stifled her panic too long: '*Maman*? Where are you?' She expected her to be in the bathroom, preparing to set off too, but she wasn't. Yvette Martin was still in bed. 'Get dressed quick, *Maman*. Everyone's really leaving now, haven't you heard?' She was panting and sweat had soaked into her blue cotton dress. Her feet were blistered. When it was all over, they'd start hurting.

'Oh, I shan't leave, darling. You know me, I hate travelling and I hate the country. We've been through it all before.' Misha's mother eased herself out of bed and put on a peignoir in peachy silk. She looked pretty, and cool. 'You'll have to change the dress,' she said. 'You can't go like that. But I'm very glad to learn you're going to be sensible and get on down to Mémé's.'

'You mean you'll let me go on my own?' Misha shrieked. Her mother didn't look at her; she was rummaging in a wardrobe.

'I've finished that harness you wanted me to make for your cat, look, here it is. I got some nice soft leather in the Galeries. Though I say again, you shouldn't even consider taking her anywhere, you should have left her safe in the country. Cats can hide, they manage. Now, you'll have to be careful about your money, I've heard there's looting and robbing going on. There were some muslin money belts on display at the Galeries. I did get one for you though I must say I don't think much of the workmanship. I've re-done the stitching, of course . . .'

'Your man's been to see me,' Misha interrupted, half laughing, crying. This recounting of a morning's shopping could last an hour. 'He's given me a pass so we can get away easily. People do assume you'll be worried for me, and please try to understand, people are taking their *cows* with them.'

'He's so sweet, I told you he was, I suppose he was on his way somewhere and thought of you, he doesn't expect me to go.'

'He does, he wants you to leave, now, today.' She had to sit down. She thought how strange her mother's capacity

178

not to be surprised was. '*Maman*,' she said, 'clothes do not matter. Please close your wardrobe door, I don't need anything and nor do you. It's life now, and death.' Exhaustion and heat had reduced her will to argue. 'The rest of Paris knows we're going to be bombed shortly. They must have heard something in the night. People are saying Paris will be defended if the enemy attacks, but it's possible it'll be declared an open city. That can be done. Then it won't be bombed, they'll just walk in here with their tanks and their uniforms. Let's go and and find a little hotel in the country for a while, somewhere that'll take Frou, and wait there. You can wait to hear from your Pierre.'

And I, she thought, I shall wait and wait and keep his cat safe for him, and one day there we'll be, me and Frou, watching at the window for him to come home from work. 'The British and the French will recoup and drive them out, it won't be long, but surely you don't want to stay here with German soldiers walking the streets?' Sweat was glueing her to the fancy bedroom chair.

'Misha, look at me.' Yvette Martin crossed the room and put one cool hand on her daughter's hot arm. 'I hate the country. I am a city person, I hate travelling, I hate noise and heat and dirt. I shall stay here until Pierre comes back to fetch me. He says I'm not to worry and I shan't. You must go right down to Mémé's. Go as far as you can. You have your whole life ahead of you, you are not like me. Do you remember, how much you wanted not to be like me? Well, you aren't. You're brave and stout and British. You have fine moral feelings about love and war, grand things. I haven't. I just survive. I'll survive here with the Germans in the city. If they do come, you'll see, nothing much will change for ordinary people, and maybe they'll do some good. Pierre says there's been too much laxity and selfishness in this country, too much high-living, people have grown lazy, they want holidays and big wages and that's socialism, the country can't afford it. Pierre'll look after me anyway.'

She was smiling, calm, beautiful in her peachy silk with her fox-eyes and her red hair. 'The only time he let me down was the day I wanted to ask him if he'd find us a place to live, you and me, when your father said you must go to Bournemouth.'

'This is the second time he's let you down,' Misha said, 'because he's gone now.' She eased her damp back from the chair and looked down at her blistered heel. This wasn't a good start to a journey. Why hadn't she thought harder and not let so much warning time slip by? She wasn't ready for a journey; leaving, staying, it had all been talk of some indefinite future.

Her mother shrugged. 'I don't think it was his fault, it was only his wife that other time, she made a fuss. The first telephone call I'd ever made to his apartment and it was for your sake, Misha, but he wouldn't desert me. He's just got war things to see to, he's an important man, he doesn't want me to concern my pretty little head with all that.' She sat down at her dressing-table and fluffed out her hair. 'I mean, he really looked after me for the abortion, some men wouldn't, and he paid all the fees at the nursing home, God knows how much it cost and he sent those letters on to you. He knew I didn't want you to worry.' Dropping the brush, she leaned back. 'Oh, it's so hot already,' she said. 'Are people really going off in carts and wheelbarrows?'

Misha considered. What abortion? And then everything became clear. She knew, at last. She could go now. 'Thanks for the harness,' she said. 'I'll take a sunhat and a couple of dresses. I don't know how many I'll be able to carry.'

'That friend of your professor, Eveline someone, she was in the clinic too. Same as me, I heard.' She tied a brown ribbon around her hair and got up. 'She's not a lady anymore than I am, my darling. Come and give me a hug, will you, I shall miss you because I do love you, however rotten a mother I've been.' There was a film of tears over the amber eyes.

Misha stared hard at her. 'You mean Eveline Leclerc had an abortion?'

'She did, so don't let her put on any airs and graces after you get back to work at the fashion house when this is all over. You give her a few cool little looks, you know, so she'll wonder and be forced to be nice to you.' She was very serious with her motherly advice and held out her arms.

Misha's head throbbed. It was her own fault. She'd forgotten. She'd let impossible dreams slip in. But it mustn't matter. She mustn't let it. He was still the most wonderful friend anyone could have. She was still sick with longing just to hear his voice calling to Frou.

'Angel, don't cry, we mustn't either of us cry, you know, we must be glad because now it's started, it'll be over the sooner and you and me'll be together again, we'll find you a nice husband and I'll sew you a dream of a dress. I could start looking for a pattern soon, couldn't I? It would give me something to do. I wish you'd let Pierre help us. I mean, the best silks, I could get them now, before it's all sold in the shops.' She got to her feet because Misha hadn't wanted her embrace. 'I wish you weren't so proud. Most women wouldn't be. Look at that Eveline woman for one. She wasn't too proud to let that Swiss chap pay her bills at the clinic. And, anyway, what else can one do without one's own money . . .'

Misha's heart burst back into her throat. It was all right! Eric. The loose ends tied up. She'd go now. And her head was as clear as day. She had a lot to do yet. But it was going to be easy.

There was no one but the Blanchards at the Bonaparte when Misha finally fought her way back there. She'd noticed a thinning out in the procession, but crossing the river it had seemed to her the old stone was ready to crack from the weight it had to bear. This would, she reflected, make it easier for the enemy to blow it up. She felt quite calm. Because very nearly the worst had already happened: the enemy was well on its way and she knew what she must do.

'Robert's heard there's going to be an armistice,' Monsieur Jules told her after she had recounted her morning, from stepping over the cow pat to the creaking bridge that might not hold. He took out a handkerchief and wiped his face. Madame Florence slammed saucers about.

Misha asked, 'They're giving in?' But this possibility could no longer matter. The worst *had* come about; the citizens

181

of Paris were abandoning their city, giving it up to Hitler, and it was no more than a matter of time before Nazi jackboots would be stamping up this very street. They'd be carrying little whips and would push old ladies on to the street holding the whip around their throat, the way they had in Poland. She'd seen this on newsreels long before, going to the cinema with Georgie, and she'd shut the images away like everyone else. 'I shan't be able to worry about Madame Libaud,' she said, 'but we did put a stock of food in the cellars for us and Frou, ages ago. D'you think she'll be able to get down there on her own?'

The Blanchards weren't listening. 'Better our giving in than everyone dead,' Madame Florence shouted. 'It'll be declared an open city and we'll live instead.'

'Well, I shan't live here, not with Madame Bassas saying I can't feed Frou. Anyway, I don't want to anymore. I'll vomit if I see one of their uniforms.' She heard her voice rise. She didn't feel calm; she wanted to start running at once. She'd stayed too long already. Taking ravenous bites of her slice of cold omelette, barely able to sit up at the counter, she said, 'I'll come back home after I've managed to keep Frou safe and the Germans have gone. The British'll get them out, you'll see.'

'And how will you manage to leave today with no trains at all, according to Picot? You think you can walk a thousand kilometres down to your grandparents?' Madame Florence stopped slamming saucers about and went into the kitchen for more omelette. 'You'll have to eat as much as you can before you set off, you won't be able to carry a lot with that fat little cat dragging down one arm. Though she'll soon be losing weight!'

They packed her a hamper of food that lasted, cheese, *saucisson* from their larder, bread in a cloth. Misha was refilling the enamel jugs for Frou when the telephone rang, making them all jump. 'I thought the lines were cut,' she said, arranging her things on the counter. 'I'll run back for these when I've changed and collected her ladyship. Oh, if it weren't so hot . . .'

Monsieur Jules was promising to look in the cellar for

Robert's old haversack, for they'd seen she wouldn't be able to take clothes with Frou's basket to carry as well as the hamper, when Madame Florence gave one of her shrieks. 'It's the professor, oh, the dear man, he's alive, just in time, she was leaving us, Monsieur . . .' The receiver was wet, she was sobbing over it.

Misha took the wet receiver and heard his voice speaking to her. He sounded far away but it didn't matter how far he was because he was alive.

He said, 'Misha, don't stay in Paris any longer. Go now and keep safe for me. Don't do anything brave and foolish, forget you are British, forget that especially, please. One day we shall meet again, I promise, and . . .'

The line was cut. Misha held the wet receiver a little while longer but knew there'd be nothing else. That didn't matter either. She'd had more than she could have expected, except in her dreams. This crackling noise with his voice coming through it was far more precious than any dream. Because it meant he was somewhere, not far away, alive, and one day, there they'd be, she and Frou, watching the window.

There was no time for proper goodbyes to the Blanchards or Madame Libaud but she knew the war couldn't last long now it had finally begun. The British and French were on the side of right and right must prevail. They'd regroup, somehow, and send the enemy whimpering back to their own country.

Soon she set off walking down the boulevard with Frou and their supplies. They were only leaving to be sure of keeping safe. And it wouldn't be long before they were walking up it towards home.

Chapter 23

The family with the farm wagon pulled by a carthorse were very kind. They'd had to stop to adjust the reins round the horse's sweating neck and said they could see Misha was faltering. They had room enough for her inside, being only three adults and a baby. She had been faltering. This was because of an injury to her leg. She couldn't remember what had caused it. But it was so full of dirt, it had ceased to bleed. She hadn't had time to inspect it; the place called safety was still distant and maybe she and Frou would never reach it. The farther they travelled, the farther came the planes, strafing and shelling. They carried machine-guns and had black crosses on their bellies. If you looked up, you might see the black cross and the pilot guiding his aircraft along the line of refugees. They also aimed at the villages, the fields, the crops, and anything that still had life to flee.

Stroking the old animal and letting Frou sniff at it through the wire door of the basket, she struggled up into the back of the wagon. This was as hot and sooty as the air outside but had an added welcome smell of manure, hay, people. It sheltered the grandmother, the daughter-in-law and her child. It was the grandfather trying to cajole the animal onward, she was told, and the son was at the war. There couldn't be much polite conversation because of the rattle of their household goods added to the road noise of beasts and people on the move.

'It's a wonder your horse hasn't bolted!' Misha shouted.

The grandmother shrugged and gave a sign of the cross. 'If he wasn't stone deaf!'

Lodged on the bench beside the baby's cradle, Misha held on to Frou's basket. It was a miracle Frou hadn't died of terror and she herself too. How many more miles and days to go? How many days got through already? She couldn't remember and now her feet were trapped between a cooking cauldron and a sack of potatoes and if the planes came shrieking back, she'd have to throw herself out with Frou still held tight. She felt that if she managed to keep Frou safe and the haversack on her shoulders, nothing else would matter. She had long before abandoned the hamper somewhere and only carried the essentials, Frou's water jug, her *saucisson*, a very wet piece of cheese, some rock-hard bread and a change of dress.

Shortly it was necessary to rest the horse. The grandfather stopped in a field that was empty of other travellers and almost untouched. A whole tree stood in it, its bright green leaves something of a shock. They'd seen so many burned ones on their journey, and burned crops, burned gardens, houses, churches, people. Misha helped down the grandmother and the woman with the baby and was invited to join them for supper. There'd even be soup warmed up, they said, if they could get a fire started. A nursing mother needed proper nourishment.

She offered to look for twigs for it on her way back after letting Frou out on her harness to pass water, and had reached the corner where the hawthorn hedge grew thick when she heard the first warning sound. She'd never been quite sure whether this distant high-pitched whine came from the mass of other refugees on the roads or from the approaching engines of Stuka or Messerschmitt. She had time to grab Frou and jam the basket against her waist, falling to her knees, the fastest way to the ground. She had time also to look for the family. The grandfather was getting out the cauldron, the mother standing by the gate, rocking her baby. A thin wail was coming from it. Misha shouted, 'Look out, get down, the planes are coming!' before she shoved Frou's basket into the hawthorn, and followed it with her own head and shoulders. Why had the woman gone so near the road?

She wouldn't hear her scream. And Stukas, Messersch-

185

mitts, they all shrieked the same. Some people knew the difference between them but to her, fighters, bombers, what did it matter?

Then the guns came thudding and rat-tatting. Hell is noise, Robert Blanchard had said, and it was, and heat too, and maybe Frou wouldn't live through this hell of noise and heat any longer. She edged her face hard against the basket. The earth beneath them throbbed. The basket shook, but perhaps it was Frou shaking it. They should be used to hell as noise, but they weren't. She thought she could feel the touch of a nose on her ear. It was the closest she could get. 'Hold on, darling, hold on, nearly over!' she yelled.

The planes never stayed long. Everyone had a chance. And there were plenty of other refugees on the roads of France for the enemy to aim at. They were trying to get away and in fact were leaving themselves open to the bullets and bombs. The Germans couldn't have planned it better – women, children, babies to shoot at, household goods in wheelbarrows and carts laid out for them to destroy from the sky. Perhaps they didn't stay long because there were so many more roads with easy targets on them. Someone had said there were millions of people on the roads south. But the enemy had killed so many already, that might have been an exaggeration.

She lifted her head a fraction, moving a cautious hand to free her hair. Yes, there the woman was, over by the gate, her mouth open in a silent scream. There was always silence after an attack, heavier, more silent than before. You'd have to know hell as noise to really learn what silence was. She was holding her baby. The white shawl was red now.

'The woman's baby is gone, Frou,' she said for herself and the cat to hear her voice. 'She wasn't careful. She shouldn't have stood by the gate.' The basket was shaking. Misha lowered her head towards the dark space that held Frou and edged a finger through the wire door. They were both whole, she supposed, and that was all she could worry about. The woman with the red shawl was not her first mother holding death in her arms. Anyway, she'd known about it in Bournemouth. Bournemouth had warned her about all this and toughened her. She was grateful. Maybe

186

otherwise she wouldn't have been able to survive this other endurance test. Refusing the immense weariness that threatened from somewhere in the pit of her stomach to force her to lay her head into the warm damp earth, she crawled backwards into the field. She couldn't afford to lie there.

The woman with the baby was still standing by the gate, half her skirt blown off and her thighs black with smoke. She stood in the black grass with her black legs like a statue and in her arms the red shawl and the rest of her baby. Her face was as white as a shroud with her baby's blood spattered on it.

Misha didn't go across to help. The father-in-law was lying down, perhaps dead. It would be best if they all died, there and then. She couldn't see the horse and would be better off assuming it was standing behind the wagon in the silence that was always silence to him, munching soot-free grass. She'd leave them because she'd seen too much already. And these people had been real to her, sensibly running away to safety with everything they needed or wanted, each other and sustenance, because the son was at the war. They couldn't have known they were going into the war too. She didn't want their pain loaded on to her own. Anyway, the whole world was beginning to scream.

A long black snake. The enemy, advancing. A river, moving onwards, its bed other people's roads.

Philippe Constantin, from his hiding place in the bedroom of an empty house in a village in its path, watched the snaking river glide round the hillside he'd left an hour or so before. He'd had fuel for the truck then.

He couldn't remember where he must be but this was one of the richest, greenest of valleys. He'd seen pastureland, buttercups, butterflies for that matter. How had they survived? The pigs had not, or the cows. They were lying dead in the ditches with half the army. The bodies he'd seen during this, his own very personal and solitary flight had quickly rotted in the heat.

He was hot now.

If the café across the road hadn't had its heart spilled

187

over the cobbles, he'd have risked a trip over for a drink. The tin plating below its sign CAFE ROUTIER had been torn off and was perched on an upturned chair. RICARD, LE VRAI PASTIS, it read. He'd stared at one like it before. The Bonaparte, that was where. He'd stared at it when foolishly sitting at Misha's place in the corner by the window, because she must have stared at it, and then he'd stared at the bowl of coffee Madame Blanchard'd served him though he usually took his breakfast in the Flore.

Silence outside now but for the very distant hum of the snake and some insects buzzing, the silence of a Sunday afternoon when everyone had comfortably eaten and was sleeping in cool bedrooms like this one, the shutters closed, the children sent to play in the fields. There might never be any such Sunday afternoons in this village again. If they hadn't bombed it, they might be planning to use it for a garrison of their troops.

How hot it was! He must ease off his jacket. The blood had dried to powder. If the village well hadn't been contaminated, he'd draw water to cleanse the wound. Perhaps he had time for that.

As he turned, he heard a sound that was familiar: the click of the safety catch on a rifle.

'The town's burning!' the man shouted, trying to run in and out of the straggling procession, round the half-dozen sheep, the overturned Citroën with its wheels up, the dustcart, a clutch of cyclists whose tyres hadn't burst yet, and the wheelbarrow with a sleeping child in it.

Of course his town's burning, Misha thought. The whole of France is burning, surely, and Paris was going to be razed to the ground with her mother in it, the Blanchards, Madame Libaud, Monsieur Steiner and all his books. *Candide*, the tale that was going to teach her the truth of human existence, must be no more than a few floating pages on the dirty Seine. It wouldn't matter now because truth was this soot-filled air, this filthy road strewn with her fellow travellers' belongings, their baggage and sometimes their bodies or their children's bodies.

Desperate to change Frou's basket from her left to her

right hand, she thought no more of the city she had left with such joy in her heart. The simple task required some planning. Where, for instance, could she find a patch of grass verge or foot of ditch that didn't have a grave in it? Kneeling between the wheels of the overturned Citroën, her eyes met the sight of the small fresh one edged behind some twisted bicycle frames and a box with copper sauce-pans spilling from it. This grave had a cross. A makeshift one, of course. It was made from a walking-stick broken in half and on the top of it a doll had been tied with a ribbon that had once been pink. It wasn't her first child's grave. She'd seen child bodies too. This was just her first doll and now she couldn't get up again. 'All right, Frou darling, nearly there,' she said pointlessly, leaning her sweating face against the wicker basket. Frou wouldn't hear her. The sheep were making too much noise.

A dusty grey Renault ground to a halt near her Citroën and a door flew open, knocking her backwards. 'They're coming!' a voice yelled. A wild-eyed woman with a baby got out, dragging a toddler. An old man followed and pushed them to the ground beside Misha. She watched vaguely as they crawled past her and settled by the nearside of her own shelter. 'I think you'll find it's only a rumour,' she shouted, lodging her head with its filthy sunhat on a very gritty tyre. She'd have liked to stay there for a long time. It'd be easy. If it were not so noisy, she might sleep.

Other people had begun to shout too. A nice woman in a turban took the trouble to try and disentangle herself from a couple of sheep and call out to her from the other side of the road: 'Get behind that car, dear, they say the German tanks are coming.'

But she didn't have the strength to get up. Perhaps she was just too tired. She knew she was sitting there in a haze of sooty heat, that Frou's basket was riven to her right hand and the German tanks were coming, if it wasn't another rumour. It didn't seem to matter much. It might be true. There was a kind of extra rumbling beneath her, a more urgent sound somehow. 'Tanks, tanks!' A high-pitched cry was travelling down the road, a despairing keening sound which was quite understandable. They'd already endured several attacks that day. During one, she'd managed to bury herself and Frou in a haystack and once had crawled under a Paris-by-Night tourist bus with some people being driven from an asylum in it, but if the tanks came now, she wouldn't be able to move.

She might have fallen into one of her sudden dozes when her heart and body lurched awake. She knew at once. 'The tanks have come, Frou,' she shouted, 'but they won't hurt us.'

Then there was only noise, filling the air like the soot, getting into every part of her, her mouth, her nose, her chest. If she didn't open her eyes, someone would bury her, the Germans would bury her and Frou with everyone else. They were such a clean people, Philippe had said. They liked clean streets. They'd tidy up once they'd finished, sweep up with their giant tanks that had crushed Poland and Belgium and Holland. All the children would go, the animals, those poor awful sheep making their noise, the women holding their babies safe, the Sunday drivers, the twisted bicycles, the villagers selling water at ten centimes a glass when it should be free. And that priest she'd seen throw himself over a perambulator jammed with a granny and a toddler, thus saving two lives and losing his own.

She was trying to open her stuck-together eyelids to prove she wasn't a corpse and to see Frou wasn't one either when she heard the woman behind the Citroën shouting something terrible. 'Take my baby, please!' She forced them open then to see the woman who'd gone mad and was offering her child to the enemy.

There she was, standing in dirty grass, her silk stockings torn and nothing on her feet, her skirt flapping from the swish of the enemy tanks speeding onwards, a clattering filthy green disjointed monster, and, yes, holding up her baby. Misha opened her mouth and tried to shout, chin numb from the vibration. 'Stop, I'll hold the baby for you!' The poor woman must be having an hallucination caused by fear and heat.

'Cowards! Cowards! Save my baby!'

And the old man, her father probably, shouted, 'Where's the bloody front line!' He was shaking his fist and Misha

190

'Heard about them cardboard coffins they got stacked up in London, dear?'

Misha shook her head in answer to the woman beside her in the train from Southampton. She'd somehow got herself into this though she couldn't remember leaving the ship.

'Thousands of them, there is,' the woman said, her knitting needle tapping busily against Misha's arm.

'And most of 'em's small,' the younger lady opposite mouthed, indicating her several children in the carriage with them. These were climbing about the seats and the youngest, a pasty three or four year old, had a trail of green stickiness on her chin that was about to transfer itself to Misha's grey crêpe dress.

'That Hitler'll target schools special.' Misha's companion went on knitting. 'And the orphans there'll be from the drowned sailors! This here's a cot blanket, it's my fourth so far . . .'

'I've not had no time for no knitting,' the mother said, 'what with getting our stuff packed up. I had to give my second set of saucepans to my neighbour, she's not going anywhere, she says, but my old man says they'll bomb the ports first so's to stop our ships and submarines fighting back . . .'

Out in the mild morning sky over the sea, silvery barrage balloons were floating. Misha watched them bob and sway like giant sausages. There was this here in England, this protective layer in the sky itself, and this readiness, this preparation, coffins and talk of orphans. Her father must have been mistaken. He'd sent her to the wrong place. England was far more at risk than France. Good. A dull satisfaction made her settle back into her seat. She'd be in danger – she welcomed danger – and he'd be sorry. One of the coffins would be for her. She'd be buried in a cardboard coffin and have no grave because the whole of England was to be razed to the ground.

She was so occupied with listening to her companions' gossip about death, she gave no thought to her destination and was startled to find herself on the platform of Bournemouth station. What did she do now? Shouldn't there be someone to meet her? She might as well be a war-orphan already but if her knees would stop shaking, she'd find her old spirit that had demanded independence and hadn't been allowed it. She had money, all her worldly goods in a suit-case, a photograph that was precious and a flattened pack of Gitanes with three cigarettes in it, once stolen from someone's study.

'You all right, love?' a porter asked. How far she'd come! No French porter would have been so nice.

'I've just travelled from France,' she said.

'Refugee, eh? Well, you're safe here, my lovely. Safe as houses, Bournemouth. We'll look after you. Come on, what's the address?'

'Thank you so much,' said Misha. 'I'm lucky to be here, aren't I, safe as houses?' Except that she didn't want to be safe. She had no one to be safe for.

The taxi driver was nice too. There was a non-urgent conversation between him and the porter. She told herself it was pleasant to be amongst comforting people who didn't jabber and curse at each other, who weren't rendered ill-tempered by life itself as the French so often seemed to be. Though she liked jabbering, as a matter of fact. She remembered then how much she liked noisy people. Her father said they drank too much ennervating coffee, but he was hardly fit to judge. In a brief resurgence of feeling, she was filled with sudden fury against him as she watched the safe, solid houses of the town pass, the sea, the cliffs and the open sky. When had he last seen these? She didn't know whether he'd ever paddled in this misty blue water or built castles in the sand. She should know. This should already be part of her own past too.

And it was alien. She'd never belong, or want to. What was she doing in front of this shut-up house with a clumsy criss-cross of tape over its windows and blackout curtains drawn as if war had already started? The porch smelled of hot paint and dust and the bell echoed as if the place were empty. She had time to fear it was.

heard jeering from other people beyond her Citroën. 'Yes,' she cried, 'Get out, all of you, go home!' She rolled on to her feet. She must take her part, show them they wouldn't be staying long. 'Cowards!' she yelled. 'Murderers!' And saw a French soldier's arm waving from the back of a truck.

The truck was full of grubby French soldiers, laughing and waving. And following it was a French officer's car with some officers in it. Without their caps, covered with soot, their teeth showing white, French officers were speeding along the road.

'Bloody cowards!' the old man shouted again. 'What about us?'

'Get back to the front line!' someone else cried.

Misha held on to Frou's basket and stood beside the woman who'd hoped her own army might keep her baby safe. Philippe wouldn't hear her shouting, or perhaps see it was her beneath all her dirt. But he'd recognise a tall, too-thin girl, and then the shape of a cat's basket, and he'd order his car to stop and the entire convoy too . . .

'Our beloved France is lost,' the old man said.

Misha took off her sunhat to give Philippe a better chance of seeing her.

Chapter 24

Philippe looked into the barrel of the rifle held at the level of his heart. This must, he thought calmly, be something from the 1870 Prussian war. But it had been cared for. No rust. Polished, wood and metal. And heavy. There'd be no finesse in a shot from this thing. It'd blow a head off. 'Good afternoon, Monsieur,' he said, and looked up from the barrel across a row of military medals on an old man's chest. His face was all nose, and there were sharp little eyes looking at him from thick white eyebrows matching his moustache.

'Pierre-Marie Pavin, Corporal, 18th Hussars,' the ancient said. 'I require the use of the window. I've been obliged to watch the enemy invading our land before, and this time I intend to save the honour of my country. Since you and your fellow officers haven't been able to do so.' He shifted the rifle in order to spit on the floor. 'Captain,' he said.

'You're going to make some gesture, shoot from this window, at the enemy's front column?' Philippe asked, moving to put his back against the wardrobe. He didn't think it appropriate to smile, nor did he want to.

'I do. Be so good as to descend my staircase. If you wish, you may leave and run off after the rest. You'll find petrol in my shed at the back. It might be enough to get that truck of yours started up. I've no desire to see you slaughtered or made prisoner-of-war, since your task remains – to remove the enemy from our soil. For myself, I'll have done my part before I die.'

He stood ramrod straight in his denim overalls as if he

were twenty again. Philippe saw this and heard the hum of the snake coming nearer. 'Perhaps,' he said, 'I can be of service here. Let me take the rifle. My aim might be surer. My training is more recent, perhaps.' If he weren't so weary, he'd have liked to sit down over a glass of the old man's wine and talk about the days when the blunderbuss had been carried into battle.

'If you don't go down those stairs, Captain, you may be the first to discover how sure my aim is. Go!' He made a gesture that had no aggression in it.

From weariness rather than fear, Philippe turned on his heel and went down into the kitchen where he intended to find the household's wine. His body called out for a drink, long and strengthening, and his mind called out for it because if the rifle in the bedroom was blasted into the street as the snake's head curled into it, then a strengthening glass of wine'd be the last thing he'd know.

He'd most of all have liked to see Misha's face once more and the joy in her eyes if he were suddenly to appear beside her. Where was she now in all this? Shoot, old man, he thought, reaching under the sink. Shoot and finish it for me because I'm a fool and if I weren't, I'd have told her and we'd have had a few days together. And that pride of yours, old man, is beyond price.

Misha stood beside the woman with her baby held up to the retreating French army, its juddering noise throbbing up from her feet to the arms that held onto Frou's basket. The baby was crying, probably. Its mouth was open very wide. There was soot around it. Its face was very red with effort. Lorries kept on swishing past and none of them stopped. Nor did any of the cars stop. The tanks were such monstrous beasts, they wouldn't be able to stop without good warning.

Her eyes stinging with the effort to see through the flashing filthy green of everything clattering past, Misha spotted something white. Ambulances. There was a red cross showing on some of them.

If she hadn't been looking so hard, she would have seen Georgie's hair, its blonde intact, a swathe tied back under

193

a very funny cap. Georgie was wearing a cap, a uniform, khaki with sleeves rolled up on her wonderful, strong, healthy arms and Georgie was driving an ambulance. She felt her own arms, jammed tight around Frou's basket, begin to tremble with the effort she was making to shout, shout at Georgie to stop and save her. Georgie was going to save her again if she could just shout loud enough.

'Captain!' The old man was clattering down the stairs with his blunderbuss, eyes wild.

Philippe placed his empty glass on the kitchen table and refilled it. The wine had been as he'd expected, thin, acid, but how good. And how good life had been, could have been!

'They're detonating the bridge, we must get on down there, they need our help.' He grabbed his beret from the back of the door and Philippe found himself outside in the hazy heat before he could gather his thoughts.

'You mean there's some unit of our own still down there?'

'They'll have arms to spare,' the former corporal shouted. 'There's only a few of 'em, come on.' He was sprinting round the corner of his house like a twenty-year old, denim flapping on his thin legs.

And after all, why not? Philippe felt the hot sun of life on his head and found his own legs running too after a proud, foolish old man. I shall not, he thought, die ignobly, and if ever anyone afterwards should learn of it, let it be said that Captain Philippe Constantin did his duty to his country, to his battalion, to a slender girl with huge desolate eyes who'd expect it of him. Where was she now? He'd never know. The worst pain would be to know she was suffering and never be able to get to her.

Round past the café, there was indeed a bridge. He hadn't thought to look as far. The long black snake had been coming the other way, was indeed still coming. It wasn't much of a bridge or much of a river but nonetheless, blocked, it might retard the enemy's advance an hour or two.

A colonel of the sappers was emerging from the river bank with two or three of his men. He showed no surprise

to see him. 'Get across to the stables,' he said, 'take command of my chaps in there. And do what you can when I give the order. When the bridge blows, we'll wipe out as many as possible.'

Silence. Dust swirling. Misha watched the third or fourth ambulance and Georgie disappear past her upturned Citroën, the now-dead sheep and the body of a man who'd been pushing a bicycle.

'The bastards!' someone said.

'Why don't they make a stand, Papa?' The woman who'd offered her baby to the army, held it against her shoulder. It wasn't crying anymore. 'Where can we get milk? Who will save the children?'

'We'll make camp somewhere,' the father said. He put his arm around his daughter's shoulders and she began to sob.

The road noises began again, survivors gathering their strength to stumble on, past the dead sheep and the new humps that might be abandoned bundles of clothes or bodies.

Misha looked down at the burning coals of her feet. She must get these moving again. It was all right. She'd start them moving and keep on and on until she caught up with Georgie's ambulance.

Philippe offered a second salute to the three men stationed in the hayloft of the stables a few yards from the river. He felt obliged to asked the gunner dragging his machine into place, 'How many rounds, corporal?' But of course, it was folly.

'Not enough, Captain.' There was sweat on his capless brow and horseflies buzzed around his ears.

'What does it matter, we'll see nothing but the first few of 'em and that'll be the end of us, won't it, Sarge?' The sergeant, seated on a saddle beside the gunner, chewed on a straw and spat it out. He had no answer and took no more notice of the old man with the blunderbuss running up to join them than he did of the flies crawling over the stains on his jacket.

195

'I'll take up my position to the right of the gunner.' The old man didn't wait for orders.

'What ammunition can he have?' Philippe murmured. Light-headed from heat and wine, he calculated the length of the path between stable door and bridge. Insects were thick on the dried horse manure, fresh nettles were spreading. Beyond, heat danced over a very small river. He could hear its little swirling noise. Soon it would be dammed with broken stone and would find its own new way, in and out, just the same, with tiny splashes, after the merest pause. A new river would then run under the wheels of the oncoming mechanical poisonous snake and have no more effect on it than fire from an ancient rifle and a machine-gun which might get in one round or perhaps two.

Now it was coming. He could feel its vibration beneath his boots. And so he turned and saw the black snake reach the end of the street. It began to break up into its true shape, a nose of steel, dusty steel and metal, dark rumbling metal, coming very slowly. It wasn't in a hurry. Inside, there were rows of coloured shoulders, all the same, and above, identical bronzed faces, slits for watching eyes, and glinting steel helmets. The shape spread out over the upturned chair and the painted words RICARD LE VRAI PASTIS. He could see a casual elbow at ease on a car windowsill and then couldn't see it.

'Get ready, men,' he said. 'As soon as the bridge blows . . . And pass me that rifle, Sergeant.'

Painful against his wounded shoulder, the rifle gave a little click that was familiar.

The sergeant yelled, 'Get down, Captain!'

It was perhaps night already. Misha, leaning against the tree by the stream, couldn't tell. All the days were dark now, from smoke. The enemy did seem to like blowing things up, and when they'd blown them up, sending in more shells to make sure everything was dead and if not dead, then burning.

Her throat hurt. She could smell the stream water through the dirty air. A cool sort of smell with mud in it. She'd peeled off her sensible brown shoes and the socks she'd put over her blister that last day in Paris. All the skin was blistered now and some of it had peeled off with the socks. In a moment she'd go and put everything in the water. Perhaps she'd fill the enamel jug first, in case.

It would have been worth going on if she hadn't lost Frou, but she'd never have to tell Philippe that his cat had escaped from the tiny safety of her basket; that her plump little body was lying injured somewhere with neither of them to comfort her.

Chapter 25

Misha shrieked. Something, someone, had touched her. And she couldn't move, couldn't get away. Her leaden body was riven to the earth, glued against the trunk of the tree. She must have fallen asleep and should have known better. This could be anyone. Lurching forward, haversack askew, she forced herself on to her knees. Her knees and her feet were burning coals and she'd never be able to run. She could smell soil. She'd give in. Without Frou, it didn't matter. 'Frou!' she shouted. A low wailing moan answered, making her hair stand on end. Oh, God, she thought, it's someone dying and far too close. May they die quickly! It was the best one could hope for.

Peering downwards, she saw the slope she'd climbed the evening before. It was a desert. Green grass with dew on it, buttercups, daisies, and no Frou. There was even a hedge she'd scrabbled about in because she'd heard a rustling sound. But it must have come from mice, voles, not Frou. There'd been ragged robin, ghostly pink in the moonlight, and dull green nettles, dock leaves. The enemy hadn't been there.

What time was it? It didn't matter. 'Frou!' she called again. The moaning answered, louder than before, braying. She would not look round. She wouldn't be able to help, much less save them. She probably wouldn't be able to save herself or Frou. Upturning the cat's basket, she put in it her shoes, the bloodied socks, the sardine tin and the harness the tabby had slipped from. She hadn't tried to. She'd just got thinner. She wouldn't want to be lost somewhere.

If her mother could see the fine soft leather she'd chosen for Frou's harness, the minute stitches glued in with dirt! But her mother would never see it. Paris was burning and everything in it, someone on the road had reported. Her mother would have been trapped in her apartment, burned to death in her peachy silk peignoir, her fluffed-out red hair all singed. The café'd be burned with the Blanchards inside, Robert, who didn't want to die, and his mother, who wouldn't have time to grieve. Madame Libaud wouldn't have got down to the cellars without Misha to guide her and so would have burned to death at the parlour table with the green plush tablecloth and the glass of red wine covered in ash. Perhaps she'd have decided to stay there and die. You died quicker if you gave in. Give in now, she thought, not looking round at the dying person behind her tree. But Frou, don't give in yet. I'm coming. Listen, and you'll hear me calling.

She was buckling the wire door shut when the high distant whine sounded. This was a pity. She might have reached the hedge if she'd been quicker. Perhaps it would be better to make for the shelter of the tree? No. Only ten feet to go, for the hedge. She must do it. She'd managed to get to her feet when she felt something hot behind her knock her down and she went rolling down the slope, screaming, her hand gripped on the basket because she must get Frou back into it. She'd promised.

Misha laughed. Her body crammed into a hawthorn bush, hugging Frou's empty basket, she shouted, 'No room for two!' The cow moved its head to and fro with a terrible urgent rhythm. Saliva dripped in long trails from its mouth and all over her and the basket, but she didn't mind. She supposed it was still moaning but she couldn't hear it for the planes. Huge brown eyes with the longest lashes looked into hers. Hot breath, a strange hot rough tongue, snuffled over her face and dragged off her sunhat. There were oozing scratches over its head and the udders were crimson bloated balloons.

There was not room for two. She could feel the bones of its lumbering, desperate body. How to make it understand it would have to move backwards? She was trapped between a cow and hell as noise, and if the planes didn't pass over quickly, she'd start keening and moaning like the animal until she had no breath left.

It seemed to her that in the sudden silence after they'd gone, the cow paused. She had time anyway to make a frantic manoeuvre sideways in order to crawl under its belly. With space and air to breathe again, she lay full-length to survey her slope. The navy dress now had a shredded skirt and only one sleeve but her mother would never see it.

There were trees at the bottom, in a line. These seemed to suggest a road. Beyond that was a second wooded hill with smoke billowing out. Good, she thought, the planes missed me and the cow and Frou and got an empty wood instead. She was about to laugh but struggled to stand up instead. 'Frou!' she called as loud as she could, her voice tiny after the plane noise. 'Sardines, come on, come on!' This was her mealtime call at home. Frou always answered. Picking up the cat's basket, she checked that the sardine tin remained in it and stood stock-still, listening for Frou's answering squeak. She could hear her own blood throbbing, and insects. And the cow, braying. An echo seemed to drift down into the valley and across to the other hill.

She had to set off again, stumbling down the hill, because she couldn't bear it. 'Frou!' she called again, because she couldn't stay there and couldn't go without her. Fresh blood had appeared on her feet. She'd like to wash them after she found Frou. If the cow would just stop moaning, Frou might hear.

It didn't stop. The braying came louder than before. Her filthy hair stood on end. Had the cow freed itself and was stumbling down the hill too? She made herself stop and turn round. The animal heaved towards her, covered in blood. They were both covered in blood and it was so close, she could feel its saliva on her arm. She thrust the basket into its bloody chest. 'Get away!' she shrieked. 'I can't milk you, I don't know how!' The cow lifted its head and Misha looked into eyes mad with fear and pain. She'd known, months before, that she wouldn't be able to bear it. And she'd boasted she'd do first-aid!

The wound in his left shoulder had begun to bleed again. It's fortunate, thought Philippe, that the shard of glass is also on that hand. Being right-handed, I shall manage very well. He lifted his head inch by inch until it was at the level of the shattered window and then raised his good arm to inch away the rubble covering it. Still there, on the other side of the river, was the burying party. They were leaving the Colonel's body until last, but were well advanced with their own dead. There was even a cross-maker down there, hammering. Well, old man, he thought, we got a few, me and you and the Colonel, and they're being buried now without military honours. You'd have been pleased to know that. Pity the rest of our little troop put up its arms and the white flag. But it's been worth it. He could see the old man's body in the gloom, the blunderbuss in its home-made harness, lodged against a bloodied chest. He'd fallen very neatly and died without a murmur, but as he'd wished, with honour.

I shan't fail you, old man, he thought as he began to drag himself across the planks, and if you hadn't made that last gesture towards me ... ! This former corporal of some ancient campaign decades before the Great War, had had quicker reflexes than he himself. He'd heard the boots reach the bottom of the hayloft steps and he'd taken over the machine-gun himself, knocking Philippe aside and somehow kicking a bale of straw in front of him. And he'd managed to blast the first one off the steps. So that had meant one less enemy soldier to rejoin the conquering snake and one more, himself, to continue the struggle to destroy it. By the time the burying party had put the Colonel under the earth in a no-doubt inferior grave, he'd have removed his saviour's blue denim overalls. He could then watch them set off again after the snake's tail, over the bridge their sappers had repaired and onward. He'd set off too, to honour the old man, his country and a promise. 'I shall remember what I have to defend,' he'd told her.

*

Misha looked into the extraordinary lash-fringed eyes and wanted to weep. 'I just don't know what do,' she said, and put her free, dirty arm about its neck. She was ready to burst with shame. For an animal lover and someone Philippe had such touching faith in, she was useless. Go and work with those English charity women, he'd said. They'll get on with things. A sort of symbol of plain goodness, that's how he'd seen them.

She hadn't even managed to join the Girl Guides! She hadn't liked all those girls leaping about, or their mothers, the jumblesalers, the knitters. She expected some of them had rushed to Dover harbour to help the wounded soldiers from Dunkirk. They'd have made tea, huge urns of it, persuaded dozens of bakers to turn out extra buns, forced people to give up their cigarettes.

All right. She was going to milk the cow. Any Girl Guide could turn herself to that. She even had a jug, and somewhere a cat for the cream. Sweating in every part of her, she released the cow and knelt down beside it. 'You'll have to try and keep still,' she said. 'Marguerite.' She'd call it that in memory of another cow, another time, long before. Undoing the buckle of Frou's basket, she took out the jug, settled it into the grass somehow and seized a swollen fleshy teat. Marguerite kicked a back leg, overturned the jug and heaved herself further down the slope.

Misha knew she would never be able to keep her still. But she herself could be resourceful. She'd more than proved that on the journey. The cow needed to be tied to something firm. And she had a tie. She took off the haversack, removed from it the belt of the blue dress she'd never changed into, got to her feet once more and carefully stepped after Marguerite with replaced haversack, jug and basket.

Marguerite was beyond further protest at feeling the belt around her neck. Perhaps she thought that here at last was her milker, because she responded to Misha's pulling as well as she could.

It was in making for the bottom of the slope and a possible gatepost that Misha spotted more than a gate. She saw smoke. Ordinary smoke. It was coming from a chimney nestled on a rooftop down in her valley. A smoking chimney meant a fire, a hearth, perhaps food. And perhaps someone to milk a cow.

The rooftop belonged to a convent. Misha knew this from her first sight of a living person since she'd left the main roads. This was a nun and the nun was drawing water from a well in a courtyard. Scrambling down past some outhouses and through an entrance, she called out, 'Sister, sister, I need help, please!'

She didn't wait to be asked inside, dragging the cow past the gate. 'Does anyone know how to milk this poor creature? I can't manage it, you see, and I think she's going to die.'

She might once have been the kind of nun to smile sweetly on the poor. But this one wasn't smiling. She was weeping. She'd been weeping for a long time, Misha thought, as she'd been herself. She was plump, with a pale face, swollen, and red-rimmed eyes. Seeing Misha, she put her hands up to her mouth as if to stop a scream. But it must have been all right because she pulled herself together and rushed to close the gate behind her and the cow. 'Oh, you poor beast,' she said to Marguerite, and began to wipe its head with her cloak-like garment. 'Did you see who left this creature behind to suffer like this unmilked?' She'd stopped crying and her eyes were sharp enough, looking at Misha.

Misha shook her head. 'I'm from Paris,' she said.

'Only a number of our villagers have seen fit to abandon beasts who've given them a living. We've collected seven so far to join our own dear Flora, and good butter and cheese they'll supply. Animals aren't the only ones abandoned. We've a number of elderly and disabled to feed down in the village, and we didn't think we'd live to see this day.' Her arthritic hands moved fast along Marguerite's back, picking out burrs. 'But the good Lord provides . . .'

'I'm from Paris,' Misha said again, 'and I'm very tired.' She searched for the right words for people of the faith. 'And I'm asking for succour,' she said. She sat down on the edge of the well because she couldn't stand any longer.

*

With the light of a new day, Philippe thought he'd achieved much. There was a note he'd written and put under the door of the Mayor's office, informing him that the body of one Corporal Pierre-Marie Pavin lay in a hayloft by the river, killed in action after an heroic final act to save the life of a captain of the . . .th.

He'd written this with the old man's pencil and paper. He'd had the old man's stale bread, a good quantity of his cheese and half a bottle of wine. In a housewife's string bag, he'd stowed a chunk of ham, a tin of petits pois, one of caramel dessert and another bottle of wine. It was a pity French women only cared to use fresh produce and kept so little in store. He'd taken the half-packet of coffee sealed with a peg too. There'd been no water to make any and most of all he longed for a cup of the strongest, most perfumed brew. He'd have liked to cleanse his wounds, his hands, his face. But the pipes must've been cut by the shelling for there wasn't a drop from the tap in the kitchen and he could find no well. He'd done all these things painfully, little by little, with one hand. The moonlight had helped him. There'd been stars and a great calm. He couldn't hear the enemy advance rumbling beneath him anymore. And it all seemed very far away. He was almost rested.

There were only a couple of hours to wait. If he was to pretend to be a simple countryman with nothing better to do than shop for his wife, he'd have to wait a bit. No one shopped at dawn. He'd find no difficulty in appearing a little half-witted, as he intended. In fact, his head felt lighter than a balloon. He could make himself dribble. Perhaps it had better be shopping for his mother. No woman would take on the village idiot. And he'd prefer not to have a wife, even a pretend one. Not yet.

He stood out in the street beside the crushed tin poster: RICARD LE VRAI PASTIS. He was listening in a sweet cool dawn, alone in the world, and the world a desert. Only the birds sang, full-throated, as if to remind him he must live. Almost mid-summer now, he remembered. The sun would be very high. It was a perfect time to be existing on what could be foraged from the land. And he'd play a sharp game with a lead-coloured snake that brought with it its own burial squad.

Very shortly he'd be back home, in Paris, and possibly before the snake reached it.

'No, I won't come in, thank you,' Misha said. 'If you don't mind me sitting here to rest for a while?' She put Frou's basket carefully beside her feet. 'If there is milk, please, I should like to take some with me, if you can spare it. I've got a jug. Perhaps with a few crumbs of bread in it, she'd find that easier to digest and I'm afraid she'd be sick if she had anything too creamy. I know milk can be difficult to digest . . .' She was rambling to herself because her nun had disappeared with the cow.

Three or four other nuns came out to gaze at her. She saw round, clean faces, wrapped about in veiling, brown eyes, concerned, and one pair of blue. They'd brought her a bowl of warm water, for her hands, and a bucket for her feet. They didn't say much, but seemed to communicate with a private muttering of their own. She put her feet into the wonderful water in the bucket, instantly dark brown with bits floating on top, lodging the bowl on her knees to soak her hands. Every inch of her burned. She was peering down at the outsize calf of her left leg, the one she'd thought healed by dirt, when the cobblestones flew up and hit her.

If he hadn't decided to rest, and just where he had! Philippe stared feverishly at the flapping tarpaulin over his head. Now where were they taking him? Edging sideways along the bench towards the back of the ambulance, he tried to look out of a grimy window. Fast, they were travelling fast, he could tell that from the flash of trees disappearing quicker than he could count. Another ambulance behind this one, of course. The snake necessarily travelled with its own ambulances. French units had been lucky to get charity ones driven by women!

God, if he hadn't let himself fall asleep, and in such a place! A wood. Any army would camp in a wood for shelter, cover, easy protection. Had his wits really deserted him? And he'd left the bicycle against a tree, of all the follies.

That's what had caught a sentry's eye. And then he'd caught it and his idiot-act hadn't convinced them. They wanted his papers.

'We shall be better able to help you when we reach the hospital.' The orderly finished attending to one of their own privates on the opposite seat and came to look at his hand. 'And where did you get the injury, please?' He had very adequate French.

Philippe shrugged. 'Broken glass,' he said. 'I was on my way into the town. If you'd be kind enough to drop me off as you pass? I know where our hospital is.' That would be the last place to go.

The orderly laughed. He was astonishingly clean, with a white armband and cool skilled movements. 'All your doctors have fled,' he said, 'No one there, no nurse, no doctor, no medicines!' He shook his head playfully. 'But we shall see to you, oh, yes, and to all your people. No one has anything to fear from us. This evening we set up on outskirts Paris, yes, and then we do everything.' He waved an arm and set to work with a bottle of spirit and a pair of scissors.

Because Philippe couldn't pull away fast enough, the scissors sped through the cloth of the denim shirt and revealed the old wound.

'Ah!' the orderly said, smiling.

Philippe looked down at what he didn't want to see, a piece of his khaki shirt stuck down with blood. He'd cut away as much as he could, but it hadn't been enough.

'Ah!' the orderly said again.

Chapter 26

The nuns were very kind. They helped her up from the cobbles and sat her gently down on the bucket she'd over-turned. She refused to go inside because she was still dirtier than the dirtiest tramp and they were pre-war clean.

They had pre-war hearing too. She was on her wet feet and making for the outbuildings, yelling, 'Planes!' before they'd so much as lifted the hem of their robes. Slamming a rickety door behind her, she realised at once she'd have been better following them into the convent. They probably had a cellar, whereas the barn seemed to be held together with string and was rattling. Nearby, a shell or two had fallen already.

Pausing for her eyes to get used to the gloom, she edged her way to the hot comfort of a cowstall where Marguerite was shaking too. She fell to her knees from habit and crawled in beside her, keeping her head down in some very smelly straw. She waited. Hell is noise and heat and waiting it for it to be your turn, she thought. Somewhere another shell must have dropped. She felt it through the ground.

It wasn't their turn. The planes had veered off and the sudden silence came, sweeter than ever. She put out her hand and reached up to stroke Marguerite's flank. 'I'm sorry,' she said. 'Tried to milk you. You'll be all right here.' She'd have liked to lie down beside her and sleep for a long time. In fact, she needed to sleep very badly. Her head swam and she gave in, lying back in the straw. Just a few minutes and then she'd return to the strangeness of company, conversation, washing. 'You've even got friendly mice in here,' she said. 'I can hear them rustling about.' She could hear Marguerite's snuffling breath too and her own, deep and welcome. She'd give in. She had to.

Then she sneezed, the sneeze woke her, she opened her eyes and saw a pair of eyes watching her. These eyes were huge, very round, set in a perfect triangle of tabbiness stuck all about with straw. And from this, Frou gave a little squeak of crossness and relief.

Misha ate a piece of ham. Hidden amongst three poached eggs, it hardly noticed. And Frou was gobbling hers. She had to eat with one hand. The other had Frou's harness tied round it twice. This didn't allow much freedom of movement so she kept it lodged on Frou who was crouched on the bench beside her.

'And all the time, that little creature here with us,' said the cooking nun, Prudence, 'refusing to come into the house even for the cream.'

'Sorry she won't be able to take the place of your tom who ran off last week.' Misha was dribbling egg yolk but no one seemed to mind.

'I don't think she could tackle a rat. Once or twice she's caught a bird by its feathers, but they've always got away. Her mouth's too small to get in the killer bite.' For the hundredth time, she looked down at Frou and edged her fingers under the leather. Tight enough, too tight perhaps, but the cat'd have to put up with it.

The nuns were eating plain bread and milk, whispering and muttering in the way she'd guessed was normal to them. Their kitchen was like Madame Constantin's, with a tiled floor, ancient copper pans, bread rising under a cloth. A crystal wireless set sat clumsy and out of place on a dresser amongst old plates and a vase with daisies in it, but she'd mopped up the egg before she realised its portent. 'News?' she asked. 'You've got real news? The wireless stations aren't blown up?' The questions came out very fast. 'Is Paris burned to the ground?' And then, 'Is the French Army beaten?'

After the feast, they persuaded her into a cell-like room

208

where she washed all over from a succession of refilled china bowls whilst Frou lay on the bed watching. She discarded every item of her clothing, applying spirit to most parts of her body, but couldn't deal with the long cut in her left leg. This, she decided, was still better left alone. It hurt more than the rest of her and was puffily swollen. She covered it with one of the cotton stockings Sister Estelle brought her, rolling it down to the knee. She covered the other leg with the second, pulled on a pair of their charity-school knickers and covered herself with a charity-school dress in stiff grey calico.

Then finally Sister Estelle was satisfied she had all she needed and they were alone, she and her cat. She lay on the very clean sheets in her clean clothes, skin burning all over, throbbing, her left leg throbbing, and her heart calm enough. She was ready, though. Also ready beside the bed were the clogs they'd given her and Frou's basket, scrubbed out by Sister Honorine and lined with clean muslin. Frou herself, thoroughly wiped with a damp cloth, lay under her left armpit, rigid and snuffling, tightly held by the harness and her left hand. They'd had a little conversation and if they could allow themselves, they'd have a little nap. Paris, home, wasn't burning. It had been declared an open city. It was untouched.

The French Army was almost untouched also, being in retreat, and no doubt planning to regroup elsewhere. Everything was going to be all right. The money belt, filthy, with damp notes and her identity card in it, was safely back in its place under the dress. She had Frou, her basket. They were all she needed to restart her journey south. Soon she and Frou'd be sleeping in another bedroom with a red-tiled floor and mosquito netting over the window. Her grandmother would waken them with a huge bowl of coffee, steaming, new bread to dip in it. For Frou, perhaps minced rabbit. There were too many rabbits in the Languedoc. They wouldn't starve whilst they were waiting to go home.

He'd have liked to pace about. He didn't want to sit still. Philippe felt around the door of the ambulance again. Nothing to give him leverage to get it open. Yet with all that bustle outside in the hospital yard, he'd pass unnoticed almost, especially with his fellow wounded removed from his company. Again, he peered through the window. There were a number of trucks more or less in a semi-circle, dozens and dozens of men in uniforms of all ranks, each with their prescribed tasks. This was what was remarkable. It was as if an entire army's arrival in a hospital grounds in someone else's country had been rehearsed over and over again. Perhaps it had.

The door swung open, startling him. 'Supper, Captain.' A tray was thrust at him by an orderly as fit, tanned and healthy looking as all the scurrying rest of them. He sat on the bench, gloomily chewing on fresh French bread made with white flour and an excellent pale cheese. There was good wine to follow. He was glad of it all, yet it stuck in his throat. Requisitioned produce, this must be. They'd have taken over a bakery, and set a local baker to work. If they'd done this . . . He took up his position at the window. A local supplier coming in and out of the gateway was all he needed.

He knocked on the window and his orderly appeared. He put in a request with the return of his supper tray. 'WC, please,' he said. 'And I don't expect to be kept waiting any longer before I see your commanding officer.' This was for the form. He did want to be kept waiting, in fact. He also wanted an instrument of some kind. Anything metal would serve.

'And d'you know, Cap'n, they came into my shop yesterday, they bought up the last of my chocolate, went into the back and got it out, smiling all the time, that was the worst and shaking bank notes at me. Now, that can't be real money, can it? Good French money?' I asks them, great big lads, smart, new cameras they had too, every one. They'd been taking shots of the village square, imagine, and I'm in one or two photos, yes, passing across some butter as if I hadn't a dozen customers begging for it . . .'

Philippe, painfully jolted, lay on the grocer's potato sacks, covered ignobly in empty cartons with '12–250 grammes Café Premier' written across them. 'Did they give you the money? Did you look at it? It could've been false, you see, printed long ago, because this invasion has been very well prepared, my friend.'

The man didn't hear him. He was pushing his delivery van to its limit. 'And then, listen to this, Cap'n, one of them, he opens a bar of Chocolat Menier and he opens his little pat of butter. I'd been cutting it up small, you see, I hadn't many customers left, and most of them old, everyone else'd gone south and I wish I had . . .' Hurtling down a hill, he turned a corner with a screech. 'So this chap opens his pat and he opens his chocolate and he spreads the butter on the chocolate with his fingers and then he stuffs it down his nasty throat and d'you know, I made up my mind there and then I wouldn't be able to stand 'em, not in my own shop. So when this commanding officer bloke comes in and gives me a form and says I've got to deliver all my stocks to the hospital, I takes his money, I delivers the stuff fair and square, and blow me if I don't find a stowaway . . .'

He could smell the tyres burning. Philippe closed his eyes. He must rest. Another half an hour, the grocer had said, and if his petrol lasted, they'd be in Paris by three a.m., still night. Paris wasn't razed to the ground, he'd said. It had been declared an open city. It was untouched.

He himself had already made his plans, but wanted first to learn that the two people precious to him were also untouched.

He'd have preferred a few smouldering ruins, the fire engines, anything to tell him Paris was not lost, was not dead. He'd seen enough. He began to hurry because crossing the dead city was taking too long. The silence was more than he could bear. How could he have imagined Paris empty? A city, empty, silent! Yet if it had been declared officially open to the enemy, a kind of life would have continued. And there'd certainly have been the street women, the tramps, drifters from the nightclubs, traders setting up at the markets.

Where were they, and where the enemy sentries, the patrols, the marching boots, the shouted orders?

His own boots seemed to echo round the street corners

211

and bring the stray dogs snuffling at his trousers, and every shutter was tight shut.

Aiming for the river, he was far enough to make out the sandbagging reaching half way up the cathedral when he heard them. Here they were! Motorcycles in front, with that particular spurting, powerful noise made by all young men with their first machines. These were young men coming with many machines. Pausing on the corner of the boulevard, he saw them. They were four-abreast, in perfect order, rows and rows of them with perfect lead-coloured shoulders and coal-scuttle helmets that should be comic. They were all the same size, like toys, factory-made.

He had no need to hide. Paris was expecting them, silent, empty, open.

But he had to wait for the infantry. These came goose-stepping along behind the motorcycles, too many, every inch of them the colour of lead in the early-morning sky. Then came their tanks, filling his silent, empty city with noise.

He had to wait a long time before he could make his way down to his own river and cross it, an escaped prisoner-of-war, a criminal.

The Widow Libaud showed no surprise to see him at her door and he hadn't needed to bother with preliminaries. She'd understood and had soon rummaged in her trunks, finding there a linen suit of her husband's, two shirts and a brown tie, all so well folded they were barely creased. 'You'd better have the waistcoat too,' she said to him, her old eyes hooded, blank, because she'd seen other wars. 'It won't always be summer where you're going. D'you want a straw or a felt hat, and what about shoes? The boots don't match a fine suit like that.'

Enclosing himself in her bedroom to avoid her fussing over his wounds, he'd shortly kitted himself out in the excellent cloth and was regarding himself in the glass. Not bad, he decided. Different anyway and clean, respectable. It must do.

An immense weariness made him long to lie down on the feather down of the marital bed. How sweet rest would be there, in lavender scent, mothballs, gloom! But he hadn't time for rest. 'Madame,' he called, 'may I trouble you also for writing paper and pen? And some kind of small case or bag that'll give me an air of going about my normal business?'

She had it all ready for him on the parlour table: a worn attaché case she said she kept her savings book and family papers in, the second pair of socks, the extra shirt, a comb and the pâté. She'd worked fast, he thought, and saw from the flush on her cheeks and a faint sparkle about her that she'd enjoyed herself. As she packed the items one by one, she kept thinking of others and darting off with a little cry of pleasure. 'Aspirin sachets,' she said once, and then, 'what about a razor?' This was another item from her dead husband's effects and one he appreciated, though he wasn't sure he'd manage such a cut-throat thing with only one hand of any use.

Very quickly, he had written his note, signed and sealed it. She took it away to stow in a drawer in the bedroom and returned to join him in wine and sweet biscuits. She had much to tell him, but made the story brief: about their evenings and the bread and soup they'd shared, and Misha's lonely trail through the days – with evenings spent in a café! 'And that cat,' she said, 'as if it were the most precious thing in the world. I believe she left in the end because the Bassas woman threatened her she wouldn't be able to feed it in a war. And your heart'd break to see her stumbling down the street with the animal in a basket and the hamper for its food.'

Yes, he thought, and got to his feet.

The good woman didn't ask him if he had another note addressed to a Mademoiselle Leclerc, but then, she'd guessed many things.

Not much later, he was walking down the main boulevard and saw the new flag waving over the Eiffel Tower, blood red in the setting sun.

213

Chapter 27

Misha, sore feet awkwardly lodged into the clogs, watched a wonderful dribble of honey curl on to her portion of the supper porridge. She was trying to smile, from politeness, but her face had stiffened from hawthorn scratches. 'May I take porridge up to Frou later?' she asked.

'That's another thing,' plump Sister Prudence said, handing her a dish. 'The little cat. You can't be thinking of taking her journeying again. You will have to leave her with us . . .'

Misha nodded vaguely, indicating absolutely nothing. They were terribly kind, all of them, Prudence, Estelle the laundress, and the elder one, Sister Agathe who was now seated on a stool by the dresser with her face pressed to the crackling wireless, listening for news. And what ease they lived in, she thought, breathing in the smell of honey, what comfort and order. They had proper meals and prayers and bedtimes! But they hadn't seen a red shawl in a mother's arms or a doll fixed to the top of a walking-stick cross. 'I think I'll leave tonight,' she said. 'I don't know why I didn't think of moving on in the dark, when there are no planes. May I borrow a map? I'll send it back when the war's over.' This kitchen built of its massive stone was no safer than anywhere else and just because the enemy had been bombing other areas for a few hours didn't mean they wouldn't return to lay waste here. And they couldn't know she had only one aim: to reach the place Philippe'd said would be safe and wait there with Frou.

Sister Prudence dropped the porridge ladle and put both

214

hands to her cheeks. 'Travelling alone, in the dark, in wartime . . . What about the deserters, the marauders, the dogs gone wild? Do tell our dear refugee, Sister Agathe, how foolhardly . . .'

'She must stay with us until the war's done with,' barked Sister Agathe over the whines and splutters of the priest's wireless. 'Now be quiet, all of you, it's nearly time.'

'What about waiting until the priest comes in for his supper? He'll know what's best,' suggested Sister Estelle. She smelled of soap.

'Where is he now?' Misha asked, as a courtesy, swirling milk into her dish and mixing it well in. The priest would not able to offer her advice. He hadn't seen heaps of bodies lining the roadside, as she had, some of them dead and the rest shrieking as they heard that very particular Stuka whine coming closer, closer.

'He's giving the last rites up in the wood. Some of the poor dear troops camped there, quite defenceless, and the enemy seemed to know it . . .'

Misha dreamily spread the loveliest pale butter she'd ever seen in a thick layer on her crust. Maybe, she thought, we could stay here, me and Frou, and be safe. I could help in the dairy with my Marguerite; I could take bread and milk down to the abandoned sick and elderly in the village. There'd be other animals to save, other cats, dogs. She'd seen plenty frantically rushing about in search of their owner. She could start her own sanctuary. If only the enemy could be finished with it . . .

'The robes will fit her very well. She and Sister Esetelle are about the same size . . .'

'Do be quiet, please,' barked Sister Agathe from her post by the wireless.

'And if the war calms down, I mean if the enemy are to leave us to live our lives . . .'

Sanctuary, thought Misha, what a beautiful word. I will offer sanctuary. She bit into a wonderfully scented piece of crust and butter. There was all this here for her and Frou, porridge, cream, eggs. A whole cellarful of chickens was apparently scrabbling about under the kitchen floor in case their yard was shelled.

215

'It was Georgie-something, I tell you, Sister Prudence,' Sister Honorine said, 'So difficult to pronounce and in the end we called her George.'

'Well, Sister, we did laugh when we decided to call her that, didn't we? Such a beauty yet doing man's work and wearing a man's shirt and tie, a man's cap!'

Misha thought, I shall do women's work, soothing, offering sanctuary, easing the suffering men's war has caused. Philippe had suggested that, women's work, he'd said. She leaped to her feet, knees banging against the table. She'd have knocked over the bench if Sister Estelle hadn't been sitting on it. 'What name did you say? Ambulance drivers, women, and one called George?' She wiped her buttery fingers down the front of the charity dress. 'Quick, oh quick.' She was shouting at the top of her voice. 'Let me get out, show me the way and where are my shoes, I can't run . . .'

'Sit down at once!' Sister Agathe shouted louder. 'It's the Queen, the Queen of England's going to speak on the BBC News, she's sending a message to the women of France . . .'

Misha fell back on to the bench, her mouth open, her heart thudding with a surge of something, some memory, some hope from long ago.

The high sweet voice was suddenly clear, in very slow and careful schoolgirl French. 'And the time will come, I believe wholeheartedly, that after these bad days, the time will come when our two people will by their endurance and hard work be able to say to each other, Now everything is all right . . .'

Blinded with a wash of tears, Misha stood up with the nuns as a band began to play the *Marseillaise*, and then, better, or perhaps worse, *God Save the King*.

They were all weeping. Misha rubbed an arm across her face and said, 'I'm going on. I can't give up yet. I've got to get back home, to England. I sometimes forget I'm British, or half, and when I'm reminded, it sort of spurs me on. And then, you see, George, Georgie's my friend. I've got to catch up with her. She'll drive me back here to pick up Frou and then she'll help us get to England.' She was panting and they were staring. 'It's safe as houses, England is, Hitler'll never

216

cross the Channel. I'll help the war effort somehow and when it's over, I'll come back and thank you properly. Oh, I do wish my shoes weren't ruined. I can't run in these clogs and I must run faster now than I've ever run in my life!'

Part Two

Chapter 28

'Please hurry.' Misha watched Sister Agathe's robes slip through the door of the Mayor's office. If she didn't hurt so much all over, she wouldn't be standing here. She'd have run well ahead of Sister Agathe without waiting for the Mayor to give them the latest information about the French troops in the wood. The priest had said there'd been more wounded and dead from the recent shelling. These were being quietly buried or treated and the rest of the unit intended to lie low. If the enemy had finished bombing their particular patch, they'd go on lying low for as long as they could. Which was all very well, Misha thought, but the seconds were leaping onward. Anything could have happened since the priest's visit up there and Georgie could be moving off without her and Frou.

Resting against the wall, grateful for the cool stone, she shifted the nun's basket of food for the sick to the other hand and gazed across the village square to an elderly invalid gazing back at her from the only unshuttered window. Misha nodded brightly, indicating the basket. Nothing else moved in the still, heavy air with its fine soot on the usual debris. A French Army car had skidded into the village pump at the centre and lay on its roof. Beside it was a huge gun on wheels, a heap of smashed rifles, some twisted bicycles. Trailing along the pavements were beer barrels and a dead sheep with its fleece left in a bloody pile, the flesh cut out for meat. This is litter in the grand style, she thought vaguely. Once people had worried about cigarette packets and crumpled tissue from the morning baguettes.

Otherwise, it was almost like a public holiday in any village square, the red TABAC sign all dusty, the shops and houses shuttered, the flag drooping over the Mayor's office. She could feel a burst of agitation that made her want to drum her heels; she'd have liked to march up and down. Hurry, hurry, she thought, straining for the sound of Sister Agathe's barking voice coming from the office. She could hear something. She was about to knock on the door and call out that she'd start making her way towards the woods when it flew open and a man rushed out, twisting a chain around his shoulders.

'Get inside or leave the square at once, Mademoiselle,' he shouted, and another man followed him carrying a loud hailer. He jammed this against his mouth and began to run round, banging on shutters and yelling, 'Residents of the village, please stay indoors. The enemy is advancing rapidly towards us . . .' With the urgency of his task, he leaped over the bicycles and the dead sheep and on to the invalid's window where he banged on that and cracked it.

Sore feet as if glued into the clogs, Misha made an immense effort to move, holding out the food basket to Sister Agathe who stood behind the Mayor, her face blank. 'Oh, it is not finished, dear child, not finished yet,' she murmured, and didn't see it. Misha herself therefore put it carefully on the ground by the wall and turned her head painfully back to the street she must cross somehow in order to get back up the slope behind the square and thus on to the convent to fetch Frou. Head swimming, she couldn't make her body take the first step. Anyway, should she at once make for the wood, in case Georgie's unit didn't know the enemy was coming and was still there?

The Mayor's man went on shouting: 'The village will be declared open and no damage will be done, no one will be harmed . . .'

'Monsieur le Maire,' she said urgently, 'are our troops still in the woods, please?'

'I want that cannon out of the way,' the Mayor shouted, 'I don't want them thinking anyone's going to make a stand . . .' He had begun to sob, noisily, as if he were a boy

222

again and not old enough to hide it. 'We are lost,' he said, and took out his handkerchief. 'Can't we find a sheet or something, anything, to put over that cannon? We can't have them thinking we're part of the army's last stand!'

'What shall I do, Sister?' Misha called in desperation. 'Which is best, to make for Georgie or Frou? Because, you see, Georgie may be gone . . .' She wanted to move, to make a start on one of these. If she didn't hurt so much, she'd have made a start already.

'Villagers are advised to stay inside,' the loud-hailer man shouted.

The Mayor shouted, 'Here they are,' and stepped out into the street holding up a white cloth which hadn't been his handkerchief. 'Put your jacket over that cannon, man!' he shrieked to his assistant and wiped his face with his sleeve.

Misha turned to look up the street, past the cannon and the well and the invalid's face, a mask of terror behind her cracked window. She saw a clean, shining, silent vehicle slipping along the cobbles towards them and threw herself back against the wall. The man with the hailer disappeared and the Sunday silence fell again as Sister Agathe strolled off the pavement to stand beside the Mayor, a still, calm figure, at ease, out-of-place. Misha started to call her back, and stopped. Of course they wouldn't hurt a nun, or for that matter a man holding a white flag, or her, a charity-school orphan who just wanted to cross the road.

The shining thing came to a stop in front of the Mayor and his guardian and some German officers stepped from the back of it. The Mayor offered them his white flag and they saluted him, bowing to Sister Agathe, heels clicking noisily, disturbing the silence. They began a conversation, as if they were on some formal visit. They were smiling. She heard them say that Monsieur Mayor and the village inhabitants had nothing to fear from them, that indeed they expected village life to continue exactly as before. They had very correct French and she couldn't move because she had the ridiculous clogs on and didn't know which way to go. The chief officer had very clean manicured hands holding black gloves. These hands reminded her of someone else's. She stood stupidly staring at his hands and at his clean jacket, lead-coloured it was, every crease on it perfectly crisp. His boots shone and he had soot-free gaiters. They all had, the three of them standing with the Mayor and the driver of their vehicle. Even the peak of his cap shone and his skin was lightly tanned. He looked healthy. They all did. The car looked as if it had been driven from a showroom in the Champs Elysées.

A chill crept up from the burning flesh of her feet. She should be very afraid. She should scream or spit at them, she thought, nausea edging up from her stomach.

She looked down at herself, at her scratched and puffy legs, at her charity dress already dirty, at the rolled-down charity stocking stuck on the wound. She was trapped in a place she barely knew the name of. She'd crawled there through half of France. This Mayor she didn't know, still sobbing, looked as if he'd slept in his clothes, as he probably had. His village square was decorated with a cannon and a dead sheep and three enemy officers glowing with cleanliness and pride.

And there were more coming to show them up. The motorcycles were very quiet. They hummed along nicely, three abreast, guided carefully by very young men. These seemed to be identical. Their shoulders and their funny helmets matched in size, exactly. They filled up the street.

She pulled herself away from the shelter of the wall, stepped out of the clogs and began to run across in front of the humming machines. She had time. Her feet had made up her mind for her. She'd go for Frou first and when the enemy had slid through this place, she'd return and make for the wood to see if Georgie were still there. It was simple. She wasn't going to panic.

She reached the invalid's window and recognised the look of despair in her eyes. She knew it was the same as her own. Pausing, she was about to step around an empty beer barrel when she took hold of it instead and with a surge of strength, pushed it across the cobbles in front of the humming machines. She saw two drivers lose their stiff, half-smiling gaze. She heard the invalid lady shriek with delight.

There was some clattering and clanging of wheels, a very loud curse and hands came out and caught hold of her.

Chapter 29

She was in a truck. She saw tarpaulin and the moon shining through. It was night then. A shock of pain from her left leg made her cry out and a face appeared above her. Was this the enemy? 'You must leave me alone,' she said quickly. 'I'm British.'

The face disappeared and several others took its place. The rumbling noise stopped and she heard a voice. 'What on earth d'you mean, my man, you've taken another English girl prisoner? You don't take women prisoners at all. What kind of war is this?'

Oh, thought Misha, what a wonderful voice, like everyone's nanny, everyone's teacher. But the reply was in German, harsh, like a command.

She lifted her head and saw through a gap in the tarpaulin a group of soldiers. Now the English voice was speaking in very poor French, slowly, as if the men were deaf and stupid too. 'I am an ambulance driver, do you understand? An ambulance driver. I pick up French wounded, red cross, look here, a red cross, I save the wounded . . .'

Misha cried out. 'Help me, please, English girl! I'm English too.' She rolled off the pallet – what awful hands had lain her there? How and when had she fallen asleep? She couldn't remember, would never remember, but it didn't matter. What she had to do was drag herself across this truck floor.

Panting, Misha inched aside the tarpaulin behind which enemy soldiers and an English girl were shouting at each other. It was going to be all right, there'd be two women at least or perhaps three. She wouldn't be driving alone. Always travel in threes, girls, they told you at BH, and if approached by a male, two stay together and one go for help. No one at BH could have imagined hundreds, thousands of enemy males, though, with guns, and a BH girl their prisoner.

Head swimming, sweat soaked into her calico dress and the cloth someone had put round her left leg, she whispered, 'I say.' Everyone in the group outside the truck was in uniform. There were at least two skirts, some rolled-up khaki sleeves and one girl's arm right in her vision. 'I say,' she whispered again. 'English.'

One of the skirts turned round. Managing to force her head up and look past some sturdy English thighs, a belt, a khaki tie like a man's, she saw a cap like a man's. This had a swathe of blonde hair tied under it. 'Georgie,' she said. 'Can it be you?'

Patch's voice said, 'God, Georgie, I think it's Mish.'

Georgie and Patch managed somehow to lift her into the front seat of their ambulance whilst the German officers were still shouting at them. Oblivious to their shouts, affecting deafness, Georgie was at her most English. 'We're not part of the fighting troops, imbeciles,' she was saying, keeping up a litany of things she wanted to tell them although they weren't listening. 'Whoever heard of women prisoners-of-war? Whoever heard of a girl of seventeen being capable of committing a hostile act against an entire unit of bloody great German soldiers? Little boys, were they, on toy motorcycles?' She lodged Misha up against the gear-change lever and put an army blanket under her head. 'Keep still and shut up, leave everything to me,' she whispered.

'I will, Georgie.' Misha, her body on fire, watched through a haze of sweat as German soldiers leaped about, in and out of vehicles, trucks, tanks. There was half a battalion camped in the fields around them, Patch'd said, and with the dawn, they were off again in pursuit of the French Army in retreat. There wouldn't be any more fighting, she and Georgie were sure of it. The war was lost, they said. This

227

was probably for the best, temporarily. It'd give the Allies a chance to regroup somewhere and buy more tanks. More of everything mechanical was needed, Georgie'd said, and more bloody cunning too. The enemy had too much of both.

'You ought to be Minister of War, in charge.' Misha giggled weakly as Georgie jumped into the driving seat beside her and yelled at Patch to get in quick. 'And you're the only one who'll ever help me go back for Frou.'

'They can't make a decision about us and it's worrying 'em. I mean, a girl criminal and female prisoners-of-war? Not in the rule book – but it may be to our advantage yet.' Georgie started up and put the truck in gear. 'I say we just do what they've ordered, like good little girls, except be separated. For the moment, there's no chance of escape. They're making sure of it.'

Patch, squeezing herself into the passenger seat, gave a cheery wave to a gesticulating officer and pulled on her cap. 'Thing is, Mish,' she said, 'they're robots, see. Look at 'em dashing about at their jobs. We reckon they've rehearsed it. I mean, anyone with any sense could see it'd be best to let us push off and get ourselves back to base, back home for that matter. We're not carrying a 25-pounder, for God's sake, only four French wounded and they're as near death as dammit.'

'Officers?' Misha asked. But she knew Philippe couldn't have come this far south. He was still somewhere in the Ardennes, probably a prisoner-of-war. 'They do look after prisoners, in a sort of way, don't they?'

'It's the planning that's frightened me.' Georgie hunched herself over the steering wheel as their vehicle juddered into place behind a whale-sized tank. 'Everything to the last detail. They cut our telephone lines so none of our troops knew what was happening. They fixed up their own – we saw 'em doing it, Mish. They had telephone engineers with them. Some of the French officers we met weeks ago up near the Belgian border, they said there really have been Fifth Columnists in France for months, years even, pretending to be storemen or office workers. Come the German advance, they put on a Nazi uniform and got to work, knowing all they needed to know about a place for their purposes. We've been trounced from every direction.'

'And they're French speakers, they like, take charge, Mish, stroll into some half-dead town with only the old and the invalids left in it and show how wonderful they are by having the gas and electricity put back. Place we stopped at just before you were brought up to join us, they got the baker out of hiding and gave him flour to start baking bread for everyone. We had some.' Patch grinned.

'So naturally the locals begin to think they're not so bad and their own lot have really done the dirty, setting off south the way most have to save their skins when there was nothing to worry about, the Germans meant to help...' Georgie coughed. 'Bloody diesel fumes!'

Head reeling, Misha half listened. 'I can't believe you're here and I'm with you,' she said. 'If only I had Frou as well. I shouldn't have left her, I knew it as soon as I got into the village street... Am I really a criminal, Georgie? I'm not sure I meant to push that barrel in front of them.' Her words sounded hazy, like the air around the giant tank ahead. 'I think I'm hungry. Pity we haven't got half a pound of lentils to cook up with a few potatoes and an onion. D'you remember? If only I had Frou here, safe in her basket on my lap, I'd be happy again. No one'll rape me, there's three of us, you need three, one to run for help...'

'Pass her that last shot of brandy, Patch,' Georgie said. 'Next stop, I shall demand water, hot water, gallons of it. Remind me not to give in until I get it, they'll have forgotten she's not an ambulance driver by then. Our poor bloody wounded'll get gangrene if they aren't washed and we must get Mish's leg cleaned up.'

'What leg?' Misha said. 'My legs don't hurt anymore, actually.' She felt Patch's hot hand put something to her mouth and a wonderful burning sensation spread through her.

Patch put a finger on the brandy flask and licked it. 'Don't talk about food, Mish, please. Damn' good German sausage we had last night. They've been feeding us better than our own lot could.'

'Wasn't German, it was French, good French sausage it

229

was,' said Georgie, 'same as everything else the Nazi hordes now inhabiting this country are consuming. That's why they're here, remember, to take what is other people's, being superior to the rest of us, needing more world space.' Misha thought she heard Georgie crying. 'And I'd like to find some huge machine-gun as big as the Eiffel tower and mow the lot of 'em down!' Georgie was crying. She banged a fist on the steering wheel to stop herself.

'Calm down, old thing,' Patch said. 'Look, isn't that one of our old field hospitals? I hope we're not going backwards.'

Soldiers were busy in the fields their convoy was passing. There were tents being dismantled and the humps Misha knew to be the dead were stacked up in corners. 'Bodies,' she muttered, 'and more bodies.'

'They must be French ones,' Patch said, 'the German soldiers get proper burials.'

'They like to be clean, don't they?' Misha said, watching two horses in harness with a sort of rake in a pulley behind them. This seemed to collecting broken rifles and other pieces of metal from the farm land. They might have been cutting corn if every stalk of it hadn't been trampled to dust.

'I'd rather be filthy, covered in dirt, not wash for a year, than have their dirty minds, Mish, because there can't be anything dirtier than mass murder from the skies, can there? I mean, babies, toddlers, the elderly with their poor old legs and hearts worn out, we've seen thousands, Mish, it'd make anyone weep . . .' Georgie couldn't stop.

'Anyone but a Nazi,' Patch put in. 'And to think we joined a Mechanised Transport Corps to ferry the wounded of London, and next thing we know they're asking for volunteers 'cos poor little Holland and Belgium's been bombed first, and now here we are, bloody prisoners-of-war! My pa always said never volunteer for anything. I wonder what they'll give us for supper . . .'

Misha woke up with a start. Her head had dropped on to Patch's shoulder. 'The Brits and French'll regroup before long, won't they? And chase the lot of them back home?'

'Yes, love,' Patch said.

'Did I tell you the Queen of England spoke to the women

230

of France on the BBC news?' Misha moved her head, as light as a balloon, from Patch's shoulder and lodged it uneasily against Georgie. If they all weren't so hot, if the sun wasn't now blazing through the windscreen, if there were not so much noise . . . 'Sweet her voice was, really sweet, and the French was like a schoolgirl's, you know, the grammar and the words in the proper order. She told us that one day, we and the French'll be able to say everything's all right again. I cried, of course, and so did the nuns. I wonder if they'll make sure Frou's all right? I must get back to her as quick as I can, I'll never go home without her, they'll free us soon, won't they . . .'

'If those bloody officers don't get a doctor for Mish our next stop, I'm going to kick up quite a stink, Patch.'

'Can't we pretend she's royalty? I mean, we could throw her papers away, burn 'em. We've told 'em she lost 'em, they don't know they're still round her waist. We've said she's a nurse attached to our ambulances who got left behind after the last lot of shelling, but we were quick enough to give her address as our London flat. Good thinking, that was. We could actually make her into anyone.'

'Yes, except that for all we know, old love, they've bombed Buckingham Palace and everyone in it by now and even the King couldn't get us out of this lot.'

Chapter 30

Philippe sat at the table in his mother's house with his left arm and shoulder laid out on some of the muslin cloths from the dairy. Sweat ran down his spine and into the hairs of his bare chest without cooling him, though he had on nothing but a pair of cotton trousers. 'Can you make a start, Mother?' he asked.

'D'you think I bore you nine months for us to come to this?' She'd cried all through the stripping off of his second pair of denim dungarees, given him by a chap cleaning the river banks of the debris of battle. His linen suit had most embarrassingly shrunk. He'd had to spend an hour or two in that river because an entire battalion of enemy artillery had chosen to cross the bridge he'd been intending to pass. He'd had to drop into the water and lie there, his head more or less clear under a willow tree, until they'd roared off. The water had trembled, as the earth always did. It was strange, now, to be so hot. 'Mother,' he said gently, 'I haven't much time left. I believe there're still pockets of fighting in some areas. I shall have to move at night and it's always slower . . .'

'You'll have no time at all left if you leave again so soon, you need to build up your strength. What if this doesn't work and there's no doctor to be had, what then? They're shooting escaped prisoners-of-war, you know, old Vincent down in the village told me . . .' She clattered another pan on to the stove, pouring water into it. 'And I can't get enough heat,' she said. 'D'you think I've a crumb of coal in at this time of year?'

232

'Prisoners-of-war are protected by the Geneva Convention,' he said. She didn't need to know the truth.

'Not escaped ones,' she said, blowing her nose.

'Well,' he said, taking another gulp of Calvados to prepare himself, 'I've managed to remain hidden all the way here on foot from Paris, with the Nazi armoury lining our roads and stacked into our pastureland. They're living in our manor houses, they occupy the hospitals, the schools, the town halls, they buy up our shops with false money, they inspect our gardens and if they see fresh earth, demand that it be dug up again in case some poor devil has decided to bury the family silver out of their sight.'

'You told me,' she said flatly. 'I don't need to know anymore, and how d'you think I'm going to cut into my own flesh and blood? If your father'd lived to see this day!' She took hold of a pair of sugar tongs and lifted the bone parer from the boiling water.

Philippe swallowed more Calvados and watched her come towards him. She'd grown pitifully thin. Her overall, her black dress, were loose at waist and neck. 'I've come to see you're all right before I go,' he said, 'and now I'm ready. Here, sit down with that knife, you'll find it easier. When it's done, I'll rest a bit and you can get on with baking some more bread. Soup'd be nice too. I could carry it in a bottle. It's not far, Mother, and I'm over the worst of it. It won't be long before I've earned the right to sit in my own home again, with the two people I care about most.' He saw his mother's hand with the knife in it approach his left shoulder, shut his eyes, and kept talking. 'It won't be long, you really might as well get the beds made up, and with your old Marguerite still in one piece, why not start making your cheese once more? It'll give you a daily occupation, and feed you. Remember, if Misha does come, she hates meat. The enemy'll leave you alone, you know, if you cause them no problems. With only a few officers installed down in the village, you need never see a uniform. That place I told you about, where the river worker gave me his overalls – and fed me! he said they'd done nothing but get the bakery working again. And perhaps there's more news coming through, put the wireless on.'

233

'D'you think I haven't heard enough news!' His mother tipped the brandy bottle over his shoulder. 'An old man of eighty-four's been put in charge of us. The whole lot of our so-called government have run away from their responsibilities and left us the one who sent all those young men to their deaths at Verdun! I haven't forgotten. He'll send more of you to die in a lost cause, soon as he gets the chance and if he thinks we mothers are going to let a second generation be massacred ... Hold still!'

Fighting nausea, Philippe kept on talking. 'But you said he'd announced he was asking for an armistice, Mother. That can't mean sending thousands to their deaths, can it?' She was making him smile, as she used to do.

'Surrender, that's what it is, why give it another name!' his mother shouted. He heard her drop the knife and go back to the stove for the other. It wasn't finished yet. 'D'you think I can stand either? I might as well be dead here and now because I'll never see you again.'

Philippe didn't raise his head. He wished he'd taken more of the Calvados. When she'd opened the second wound on his hand, he'd reward himself with the rest of the bottle and then he'd sleep a good twenty-four hours. He'd need that. He wished he'd learned a little more of the art of detachment. He must think of Misha walking down the boulevard, overladen, alone, slender in a navy blue dress with white flowers, Madame Libaud had said. And the basket with the fat little tabby crouched there, rigid with fury and fear. He must think of them both still safe, somewhere, or he needn't go on. 'Mother, turn the wireless up, please, there's a lot of interference.'

'It's them,' his mother said. Her warm hands picked up his left one and turned it over. 'They're jamming the BBC French station, and Radio Paris is only giving out their horrible music. How d'you expect me to bear that? Now, keep still!'

'They'll try and fill French heads with propaganda the way they have their own people for years past. How else d'you think young men would be able to slaughter women and children from the skies the way they have?' He felt his left side jerk and glanced up into his mother's face. She'd gone as white as her muslin cloths. She must have almost finished. Yes. She was covering hand and arm with something cool, clean muslin soaked in the *eau de vie*.

'I'm turning that set off,' she said. 'As soon as this is done. You're going to sleep and I want no more of any of it. Hearing our new Prime Minister assuring us his old heart is broken was enough for me. What about our sons' and fathers' and brothers' *lives*, I say, never mind his heart? He'll soon be in his grave anyway, he shouldn't be the one to decide who gives in or who fights on.' She got up and began to clatter about again with knives and bowls.

'Listen,' Philippe said, taking a deep breath and reaching out for his glass with his good arm, 'your heart is broken too, and if I stayed uselessly here and let them trample all over my mother's land, it'd not be likely to mend. I shan't be the only one. It's not some wild idea of my own, though I admit I was planning to go as soon as I knew Paris was lost. The river bank worker said one of our generals had put out a call on the wireless to anyone not taken prisoner to join him in London. The fight'll continue, you see.' He got carefully to his feet. He felt almost strong enough to get up the stairs.

'And how,' his mother said, still clattering, 'will a few of you over there in England end this contamination of our country? What if they get there before you, what then? What if you never get there and I live on, hoping and waiting for nothing?'

'I'll get there,' he said, 'and well before they do.' He thought of the great stretch of water to be crossed and the miles still to go before he reached it. 'And there will be an end to it.'

Chapter 31

It was their third day on the roads. The convoy was coming
to a stop on the edge of a town in which no inhabitants
were visible. The open spaces, however, the football ground,
the school yards, were full of French prisoners-of-war,
standing behind the fencing to watch them pass. They had
no space to sit down. Misha, her balloon-size head seeming
to float up beyond the noise and the fumes of the tanks in
front and behind them, tried to focus on their faces. 'Any
officers?' she asked Patch, who was nearest the verge.

'We told you, that gorgeous bloke of yours isn't likely to
be anywhere in this area. The Ardennes lot were hardly
touched. The enemy went through there like a dose of salts.
He's as likely to be back at home as anywhere. You'll see,
when we get to Paris after they let us go, that's where he'll
be. The first thing we'll do is make him take us out to
dinner.' Face sweating, pink-cheeked and as plump as ever,
Patch sighed and shook the brandy flask in case she should
have missed a drop. It was one of her favourite fantasies,
that Paris remained untouched and its waiters were still
clattering chairs around, and huge dishes of charcuterie,
baskets of bread, entire sides of lamb.

'We're stopping at a hospital this time. Thank God.'
Peering through the windscreen, Georgie slowed her heavy
vehicle and eased it into a courtyard as instructed by the
orderly with his little red baton. 'Heavens, the tanks are
going straight on. Are we to be left in peace?'

'Well, this place looks almost like a hospital,' Patch said,
surveying the building. It had once been white and most of

236

the word HÔPITAL remained over the entrance. 'Not all the windows have been blown out. I can see a few sheets hanging off the sills. There's at least half the roof left. I'd say there might be one or two wards in it. But the shelling was done some time back. Looks sort of settled into its misery somehow.'

'Long as we get our wounded into some kind of beds. How they've stood this juddering hour after hour, I'll never know.' Georgie drove into the rear courtyard and found a place to park near what would once have been the kitchens. The dustbins were still grouped by the basement steps and had been scavenged by rats. A trail of rotted food was mixed with other things on the cobbles under a dark cloud of flies. 'Well,' said Georgie, jumping from the ambulance and easing her stiff back, 'least there might be some disinfectant, d'you think? A few clean bandages?' She ran round to open the vehicle doors as Misha and Patch climbed from their places to join her. They didn't want George to discover one of the wounded had died on her own.

But all four were still breathing. They knew this at once from the low, stifled moans that issued out with the stench of their sweat and the dressings that had been left on too long. 'Tell 'em Patch and me are doing the usual rounds to see what we can cadge,' George instructed Misha. 'And sit there on the floor between the stretchers. Don't move. The one thing we must do is stick together.'

'The others have gone for water and anything else they can get.' Misha waved both arms into the space in a pointless attempt to keep out the flies. 'And this is a hospital. There's going to be disinfectant, doctors, nurses probably. You're going to be treated. You all right, Raymond?' she called. He was the worst case. But she didn't know any more of them than their type of injury and their name. It was best not to let them acquire a personality, a family history. They were almost certainly going to die, George and Patch said. Raymond managed an extra moan. She thought she could see a slight movement in his left hand.

She turned and sat between the stretchers, keeping up a feeble movement of her arms. The flies had plenty of other things to crawl over. A giant heap of soiled bedding was taking up one corner of the yard but the unit's cooks were setting out their field-kitchens not far from it. This was obviously not important. It might have been so once but not any longer, like so much else. Her vision hazy, she watched for Patch's cap and Georgie's blonde hair moving about amongst the trucks. They'd made a number of friends with the nicer soldiers, the ones doing the lowliest jobs, and always managed to bring back something. They did it with charm, because charm was natural to them, and because they had nothing else to use.

She might have fallen into one of her sudden dozes with an arm across her face, for the next thing she was aware of was the approach of a German officer escorting Patch and Georgie back to the ambulance. Georgie was shouting: 'I *demand* treatment for my wounded, Major.' She stopped very close to him. 'I have five, three French privates, a corporal with a very bad chest wound, and our assistant here, Miss Martin. D'you want them to die within thirty metres of hospital wards?'

'It is being arranged, Mademoiselle, please be patient.' The officer clicked his heels and bowed at the three of them. His English was of the academic sort, perfect, and his face of the stern kind, with dead eyes. Misha thought she would rather be on her feet to support Georgie, but Patch indicated she should remain seated.

'I can also smell bread.' Georgie hadn't finished. 'Are we to be patient also whilst your men eat, and we and our wounded do not?'

'I think, Mademoiselle, that the vanquished army has not been so very kind to its prisoners-of-war.' He bowed again.

'Wrong.' Georgie's porcelain skin reddened. 'At the front line we saw German POWs being well-treated. They weren't herded like animals behind barbed wire as ours have been, their dead were not left in heaps whilst our own had proper burials, and what rations there were have been shared out. We've been with Allied troops for some weeks, Major, and shall have much to report to the proper authorities when this is all over, believe me. Allied troops have kept to the Geneva Convention throughout.'

238

The dead eyes snapped. Misha and Patch had the same instinct to reach out and give Georgie's damp shirt a tug. Georgie didn't feel it. 'And I've never heard of any army taking women prisoners-of-war,' she said.

'I have never heard, my dear Mademoiselle, of women wearing war uniforms before.' The boots clicked and he moved several steps away from Georgie. 'Nor of a woman commiting a hostile act against the German Army. May I remind you that such an act is punishable by death? Luncheon will be served to you very shortly. Good day.'

Misha looked carefully down at her feet, alien feet, like someone else's, swollen, scratched, covered in charity-school stockings only partly torn. Her head did not feel like her own either. Or her arms with their burning skin. Georgie'd said this was sunburn. She'd never thought of sunburn. She'd never thought anyone would shoot her. 'Look, you two,' she said, 'just let them arrest me. You go on without me. You'll be freed sooner or later. I'll manage. I'll tell them I didn't mean to do it. I'll tell them I'm sorry.'

Before either of them could answer, an orderly arrived and passed Patch a tray. On it were seven thick slices of baguette with butter on them and a jug of coffee with one cup.

Georgie laid these out carefully on the floor of the ambulance beside Misha. 'God, this butter's melting already,' she said, 'disgusting!' Misha and Patch began to laugh, because Georgie was indomitable. They laughed so much, there were tears in their eyes. The least-wounded soldier called out to demand to know who could be laughing. He was the only one able to accept his bread.

Misha dipped hers into the black liquid that was real coffee and more tears flowed for the yeasty, buttery taste of it all, so long missing.

'Generous of 'em,' Patch said, her chin glistening. 'What they don't know is how much stronger it'll make us feel. Soon get out of this place, we will.'

A crowd of German privates suddenly appeared to be standing around them before she had time to take more than a mouthful. They held shiny cameras and were jostling each other with every appearance of wanting the best viewpoint for a photograph of the rear of an ambulance with its sick and its attendants.

Patch hesitated over her first bread in days. From behind it, she whispered, 'What they up to? Use a bit of pidgin French on 'em, Mish.'

Misha, glad to put down her supper, extracted the answer that the three of them were their first women prisoners and the soldiers wanted to send pictures home.

'We'll be lined up on German mantelpieces. Cheek!' Patch said, waving the men away and putting an arm over her face.

Struggling with the cup at which she had first turn, Misha said, 'Look, I think I'll crumble my bread into this, and you can spoon it to one of your wounded.'

'You mean you can't manage dunked bread, old thing?' Georgie stopped staring blankly at the departing German soldiers.

Misha shook her balloon-like head and put the cup carefully by the feet of the hip case who would keep groaning, who'd been groaning for days. Maybe a little food would ease his pain.

'Mish, you're not to let that damn' officer creature frighten you. Me and Patch are going to sort it out. It'll be easy to fool 'em. If I hadn't gone too far, we'd have managed it already. You're a nurse, right, an English nurse attached to our unit. You got lost. You got frightened. Some nuns helped you and when you heard we were still in the area, you tried to get back to us...' Georgie took an angry mouthful of her bread and butter.

'Then you heard the German saviours coming on their motorbikes and you were confused,' Patch took up the theme. 'You inadvertently kicked into a barrel, and blow me if it didn't roll across the street... I mean, what else is there to say?'

'Plenty about her being English,' Georgie said. 'We must go on repeating it until in the end we wear 'em down...'

'And they let us go or send us home,' Patch finished, wiping a hand across her mouth. 'I mean, who'd want to go on bothering with us? Every place we stop, they have to dig us separate latrines. Bet you there's no water in this place. If there's one thing you can be sure of, if a building's been shelled, the water pipes are gone. Funny, isn't it, how much we've learned about modern German warfare? We'll be able to give lectures on it when we get back to Blighty.'

Misha, giddier than ever, trying not to smell warm butter, leaned against the side of the ambulance. 'Why have I *got* to be English, though?' she said.

''Cos if you're French, you're one of the conquered ones and they can do what they like with you. They'll be wanting to set an example, for a start . . .'

'Leave it to us, old thing,' Patch said. 'Sure you don't want your bread?'

'No. I think I'd like to lie down for a bit.'

Georgie climbed into the vehicle first to see if she could get a little coffee down any of the wounded. Her worst fear was that they'd die of dehydration before she and Patch could finish their responsibility to them by delivering them up to proper medical care. On her knees beside the hip case, the cup to his lips, she said, 'Explain to him, Mish, that no one knows whether the water supply is completely destroyed or not yet, but there are some wards not bashed in. The French doctors have left but the German ones will look at them after they've seen to their own wounded and sick troops. Tell 'em they'll soon be lying in clean sheets with Patch singing a lullaby . . .'

Misha dutifully managed a laugh and called out the translation as Georgie edged herself out backwards. Patch laughed too. She'd taken out the army knife she'd found in the grass at their last halt and was cutting off the hip case's boots. 'Ask 'em who else wants their boots cut off.' she said. 'And I think this is sharp enough to start a cut in the trouser legs so I can tear them off. They'll be so much cooler.'

Crawling on to the ambulance floor, Misha managed this also before she lay down in the dark and foul-smelling space between Raymond and the hip case. Above them, the two leg cases were also somehow still alive. 'How hot it is in here,' she said. 'And so many of these flies! Patch might find one of those flypapers to catch them. They can do anything, you know. They will get you treatment. They'll sort things out.' She closed her eyes. 'It must be very nearly

241

all over,' she murmured, and a hand gently touched hers. It was Raymond.

Misha took hold of his hand. It was very hot, with something dried on it: blood and dirt. Raymond began to cry in the same, stifled way he'd been moaning throughout their journey. She'd never be able to sleep with this sound so close, with such a swimming head and the strange, nauseous lump in her throat. Parts of her were hurting but she wasn't sure which parts. And anyway, she'd become used to pain. How many days into the flight from Paris before her first scratches? She couldn't remember. But Frou was whole. She'd kept Frou whole. It was just that if the nuns didn't remember she was safe in the basket under an iron bedstead, she wouldn't be safe at all. How long before she'd die of dehydration? She squeezed Raymond's comforting hand and began to cry with him. 'They've condemned me to death,' she said.

Chapter 32

She must have slept until she heard Georgie's voice shouting at her to wake up. They'd received orders to go to the Kommandant and two guards were waiting to take them. Somehow, Patch and Georgie got her out of the ambulance, and they made the guards be patient until Patch had wiped her face with rag dipped in the coffee. 'Tell our wounded George is going to demand treatment for 'em while we're there,' Patch instructed, wiping round her eyes because Misha couldn't get them open. 'God, you look awful. You'll have to hold me on to me on one side and George the other.'

'Yes,' Georgie said, taking her by an elbow, 'and whatever else you do, keep quiet.'

Escorted by the guards, they were shortly inside the hospital and in what had been a doctor's office and was now the Kommandant's. He himself stood behind a desk in full lead-coloured regalia which included a cap with a shiny visor. A whip lay with his gloves on the desk beside a silver cigarette box. On a side table were a coffee pot on a tray with china cups and a crystal whisky decanter. He was inspecting the identification papers of Patch and Georgie and Georgie was being very patient, watching him. Misha, propped between her two friends, also watched his manicured hands flick the pages about because she didn't want to look at his face. This had a livid scar on the cheek. She'd seen that, and some very small flat blank eyes, so she looked at the hands instead. She'd seen ones like it before, and heard English spoken with the same stiff correctness he was using. When she was able to lie down again, holding Raymond's dirty, comforting hand, she'd remember where.

'And the passport, the international driving licence . . . Also this certificate enabling you to drive an ambulance attached to a French Army unit – these are all missing in the case of Mademoiselle Martin?' he asked suddenly. He glanced across at Georgie. He'd seen he'd have to deal with her. 'And if she is your associate, Miss Fitzgerald, why . . .?'

'Lady Fitzgerald, please,' said Georgie.

'Lady Fitzgerald? This is not clear on your passport.'

'Certainly not,' Georgie said, helping herself to a cigarette. 'I wouldn't dream of using it. So common now. My pa sits in the House of Lords though. It gives him something to do.' She put down the lighter she'd taken without asking and blew smoke into the Kommandant's face.

He smiled. 'D'you know Oxford at all, Lady Fitzgerald? I spent many happy summers with an aunt there as a youth. Ah, now, what is the line? "Stands the clock at ten to three and is there honey still for tea?"' He tapped his fingers lightly on Patch's papers and smiled again.

'That poem's about Cambridge,' Georgie said. 'And I hope your lot haven't . . .' Misha felt her take a huge breath. Patch's plump arm, on her other side, seemed to grow rigid. Georgie wasn't going to be able to stop herself. From the corner of her eye, she watched Georgie redden and grow pale again as she did stop herself. 'Perhaps one day we might have tea together,' she said, looking at her cigarette and not at him. 'When this is all over. Oxford or Cambridge, it doesn't matter which.'

'Oh, indeed, Lady Fitzgerald. I shall hope to invite you myself, for tea, yes, in one of those little tearooms. It won't be long. I must say we have been surprised how quickly we have been able to take our place in France. We think perhaps a month now before we are in England. So much nicer for us all and there is no point in an unequal struggle.' He bowed and clicked his heels. 'I am very fond of those sandwiches,' he said, 'cucumber, I think, very finely cut.'

'In that case,' Georgie said, her elbows working so fast Misha had to struggle to stay upright, 'in that case . . .' She took in so much smoke from the cigarette that she choked

244

and then she had to spend half a minute removing the tobacco strands from her mouth because she'd bitten into the end. But the Kommandant kept up his smile and Misha and Patch kept still.

'In that case,' Georgie finally said, 'I take it we can expect to be repatriated right away? Will you telephone the British Embassy in Paris, please? If our chaps there have been forced to leave, the American Consulate will be dealing with British affairs since they haven't yet declared war on you.' The words were coming out in a rush. 'They'll get us repatriated from there after our nursing assistant has received treatment for her leg wound.' She couldn't stop now. 'And if you think that your foul, slaughtering troops will be in England *ever*, you are very, very much mistaken. Kommandant.'

She'd lost her advantage. Everyone in the room knew it. Misha, nausea in every part of her, saw the Kommandant lose his smile. He flushed, the scar on his cheek showing livid, the small flat blue eyes growing blanker. He picked up the whip which had lain beside his gloves and slapped it on the desk. 'This is enough! I have been too patient with you!' A little spit sprayed out near Georgie. Misha gasped. Georgie's perfect porcelain skin had almost been contaminated and perhaps in a moment the whip would be curled around the skin of her neck. She'd seen this happen in Poland, on the newsreels. 'You have also lied to us. D'you think we cannot see Mademoiselle Martin is far too young to have been trained as a nurse, and certainly too young to be sent abroad to join fighting units? When our doctors have operated on her leg, we shall have many questions to ask her.'

'Miss Martin is as English as we are. She was actually born not far from our home village, in one of those dull little seaside towns where nothing happens. Father was born there, wasn't he, old thing?' Georgie didn't give Misha time to answer. 'What's more, his parents are still living in the very same house on the top of the cliffs – you know, white cliffs of Dover sort? Pretty.'

Suddenly, her cigarette was of great interest to her. She was studying it from all angles. The Kommandant went on tapping the whip until the coffee cups began to rattle and Georgie said, 'What's more, that's where they'll die. Naturally. Of old age. And absolutely not under a pile of rubble from your bombs or trailing along the roads trying to escape 'em like half the poor devils of France.'

'Enough, I say.' The Kommandant threw down the whip and shouted: 'That's enough! And I repeat, Mademoiselle Martin is a French national who was, in error, brought to join you in the convoy. You decided to befriend her from a foolish sense of womanly solidarity. She has committed a hostile act against the German Army and will be sent to prison to await trial. In the absence of her papers . . .'

'How on earth d'you expect her to have kept her papers? D'you know how many times we've been shelled? Your aeroplanes with their nasty black crosses have been slaughtering the wounded and the charity workers, Kommandant, never mind the babies and their mothers, the elderly, the animals. D'you know how many agonising deaths we've seen? Can you tell me how your pilots sleep at night? Because I'd really like to know.' She was still calm. She dropped the cigarette on the floor and put her shoe on it.

'Enough! Do you hear me?' he shouted, and Misha shouted, 'All right!' Georgie had gone too far and it was her fault. She'd tell them the truth. She was born near Montpellier. She had dual nationality but was born in France and mustn't let George go on fighting for her. The lies would be found out and George was getting herself into trouble.

'Oh, dear, Kommandant.' Patch's whisper was as clear as the shouts. She began to sway in a most effective manner. 'Oh, I feel faint. I need air. I'm going to fall, help me . . .'

'Leave her!' the Kommandant ordered, and gave an instruction in German to the guards in the doorway. Patch was manhandled upright and the three of them pushed back into their row in front of the desk.

'Now,' the Kommandant said quietly, 'I am very glad we have had this little contretemps. It has helped me make a decision. You'll get your wish. You will be kept together.'

'It'll be easier for you, sir, really,' Patch said. She drew herself up to her full, plump height as if she had never

246

fainted in her life, and used her most regal tone. 'It is terribly kind of you. We are most grateful.'

'Do not bother with your play-acting anymore, Miss Montgomery.' He picked up one of his own cigarettes and took his time in lighting it, gazing out of the window. 'You are right in supposing Paris is now a German city,' he said. 'And your wish to be taken there will also be granted. The Cherche-Midi prison happens to be in the capital.' Idly picking up the whip and slapping its against the lead-coloured cloth of his breeches, he went on: 'Mademoiselle Michèle Martin will await trial there on a charge of committing a hostile act against the German troops. You, Miss Georgiana Constance Fitzgerald, will be tried on a charge of making inappropriate and untruthful statements about the German nation.' He looked straight at her but Georgie wouldn't look at him. He must have tired of his game because he began to hurry, to have finished with it. 'Miss Penelope Alice Montgomery will be charged with failing to point out the error of these statements. Before you leave, Mademoiselle Martin's leg wound will be operated on by our army doctors. We do not neglect our prisoners-of-war, unlike the British, Miss Fitzgerald. Good day to you all.'

Chapter 33

'They won't get away with it,' Georgie hissed as the soldiers led them up to the first floor and into a room with six hospital beds in it. Some were made up with linen but the bolsters bore an imprint of the last sick person's head. It must have been evacuated in a hurry when the shelling started. Most of the window panes were broken and there were few signs that medical treatment had once taken place there except for bedpans in a corner and a solitary temperature chart fluttering across the floor.

'We'll escape somehow,' Patch said, surveying the disorder without distaste. 'Beds here, good. How long since we slept on one, George? How long since we slept? Wow, I enjoyed that ladyship bit though! Wish it'd worked. Still, we learned something we didn't know. Paris is taken for a start, but they haven't got to England yet.'

Georgie held Misha's arm and led her to the bed next to the one Patch was inspecting. 'Lie down there,' she said, 'you were practically fainting for real unlike our actress friend here.' She groaned and eased a hand into her back. 'They'd better not start on England. Imagine them ploughing through dear old Dorset ...'

Patch giggled and eased herself on to her chosen bed, having stripped off a blanket. 'The pitchforks'll be got out ready. And the haymaking scythes. Charlie Bishop can't wait to slice the head off a German. And the Home Guard'll have their day after all. Nobody'll laugh at 'em if there's only them and a few tractors stuck across the roads ...'

Georgie fumbled in a pocket for another cigarette she'd

248

managed to slip from the Kommandant's box. 'Those whale-size tanks'll soon mow down whatever our lot put in their way. Imagine 'em clattering up Duck Lane, though. Hope our Pa's don't try and take pot-shots . . .'

Painfully easing herself on to her bed, Misha shut her eyes and remembered the rumbling sound of tanks and how it had throbbed through her body, becoming part of her. She could feel it again, now.

'Look, you two,' she said, 'my papers do state my place of birth as Montpellier. If I just get the things out of my moneybelt and show them, they'll be satisfied. What difference does it make anyway what nationality we are?' She couldn't open her eyes, couldn't fight anymore. The pain would be gone then, her balloon-like floating head also, and the clutch of horror around heart when she dared picture Frou trapped tight in a basket under a bed in a cell. 'What difference can it make?' she said again.

'The difference is,' Georgie said, striding to the doorway, 'the difference is that the French nation is conquered, vanquished. They can do what they like with 'em. Justice will be the least of it. But it's not going to be a simple matter to keep forty million people in order so they've got to make an example of anyone who dares raise a finger of protest. Look at the Poles. They've become dumb slaves or they've died.' She banged on the door. 'For the moment, though, they haven't got to England so they must observe international decencies. They know they ought to send British nationals home or let them go to a neutral country. That means Switzerland and we wouldn't mind a bit of Swiss hospitality, would we?' The door opened and a soldier appeared. 'Give me a light, my man, if you don't mind,' she said, 'and after that, I want *wasser*, d'you get it? And *essen* too. My friends are starving and so are my wounded.'

'Swiss chocolate,' murmured Patch. 'Oh, God, chocolate layer cake with chocolate praline filling, chocolate powder dusted on the top, chocolate icecream, chocolate sandwiches served with hot chocolate and whipped cream melting in it, pancakes stuffed with chocolate custard.' She groaned. 'The Swiss've got cheese too, ain't they? I'll have a fat slice of toast with cheese on it, pickle, one or two baby onions . . .'

249

Her eyelids flickering, Misha had a glimpse of George's sturdy figure, her chin up, facing the enemy guards. Somehow, she must make things easier for her. 'Let's not bother to insist on my leg wound being looked at,' she said. 'I mean, is it worth it?'

They pretended not to realise what she meant. And of course, how could they talk about her being condemned to death?

Chapter 34

Off the French coast, July 1940

'No good! The engine's dead.' Philippe turned the key once more. The little burst of sound the motor gave out echoed across the water, far too loud.

His fellow officer, Gautier, cursed. 'Let down by one of our own fishermen,' he said. 'As if there hadn't been enough letting down. France has earned its shame, my friend.'

'Maybe not.' Philippe eased himself from his position behind the steering wheel. 'The fisherman, I mean. The poor devil was desperate for his vessel to be used in the fight back. And since the rest of the village's boats were smashed by German troops, and all coastal fishing is now forbidden, he hardly had time to service his engine before we left. Heavens, what forethought, what planning, Gautier – in the first days of their occupation, the enemy has ensured every French vessel is out of action and every man-jack remains a prisoner. Except us, I hope. All is not lost yet. It'll depend on the tide and wind. Let's remain positive.'

Around them the black sea swayed. Philippe could hear it slap against the hull. He stepped a few feet to starboard to avoid Gautier. He hadn't taken to him but it would've been foolish not to recognise that a common purpose had driven each of them to the Channel coastline in search of escape – and that two would serve better than one on such a stretch of water. But they certainly couldn't swim it. He leaned forward to catch the feel of the cool, uncontaminated air. He could smell salt.

251

Gautier gestured towards the empty sea. 'To think we waited till it wasn't full moon,' he said. 'Now the sun'll show us clear enough come morning.'

'We haven't heard a single enemy patrol, boat or plane,' Philippe reminded him.

'Which doesn't help,' Gautier said, pacing to and fro on the tiny deck. 'So. What to do, man?'

Keep quiet, first, Philippe thought. 'Let's give the engine a rest,' he said. 'Maybe it was overheated.' He went on breathing in the clean air. He was enjoying the feel of the it on his skin, he realised, and the sense that he was unwatched, that he did not have to hide. Yet here he, was entirely exposed to enemy eyes, enemy planes, machine-guns. Well, he'd made his bid and got this far. The rest must be left to Fate.

'Hey, Constantin!' Gautier called. 'A coastline. Come and look, damn you.'

Philippe stirred himself and scanned the dark water.

'Over there,' shouted Gautier. 'D'you see? Cliffs, I tell you, cliffs. It's got to be England.'

He stared in the direction of Gautier's pointing finger. Yes. 'Cliffs,' he said.

'And we weren't making for Dover. Our luck's changed, Constantin.'

'Oh, I don't think it can be Dover,' Philippe murmured. 'I think it must be one of those seaside towns on the south coast, with a promenade, children paddling, teashops.' Sunny Bournemouth, he thought. Where no bombs will ever fall. So will it be that Fate leads me to arrive in the place where Misha was so unhappy? Well, one day then, I'll be able to tell her about this dark, still night when I felt that all was lost. A little chugging steamer came out and picked us up, I shall tell her, and that was the moment I started to make my way back to you.

Chapter 35

Misha gazed up at the black mass of flies over her head. Jerome, the old kitchen porter in the basement, had found flypapers down there and Georgie had fixed them to the light fittings. This meant a further reduction in their discomforts. Now she had nothing to complain about. Her operation was done – and Georgie and Patch had insisted on watching the German doctor conduct himself with care. He'd removed a piece of nail from her leg apparently and, Georgie said, half a pound of pus. She'd somehow recovered from this after a number of very feverish days. She didn't know how many. But it didn't matter.

Today she was resting in wonderful ease in a different, dry bed, one further up from the other patient, Madame Criblier, a fact for which she was also glad. Their second expectant mother had been taken home by a horrified family who hadn't realised their local hospital no longer contained a midwife, much less water or disinfectant. The ward was therefore to be spared another childbirth.

And she had to go on resting in this clean bed. It was part of the plan, because Georgie was convinced they'd be taken to the prison in Paris as soon as any of the guards saw her walk. She hadn't even been allowed to help make up the fresh beds. Sheets had been discovered in the abandoned nurses' quarters and a morning of unusual turmoil had finished with the ward almost resembling a proper one from the old days. None of them spoke of that time. This was the world now. If you had survived, Misha thought, looking down at clean socks and a nurse's pair of ugly black court shoes, every tiny step forward could give the most intense pleasure.

Her skin could feel the soft cotton of the mauve dress Patch had found in the same nurse's wardrobe. Even the old lady colour, mauve, didn't displease her. In fact, the only part of her not comfortable was her waist where the money-belt had to remain. Patch had scrubbed it but it still felt scratchy and too hot. The money it contained, though, must be kept safe.

Other trips would bring knickers for them all, including Madame Criblier, because it was Georgie's contention that these were the next most essential item, after food and water. Their own had already been rolled in the dirty sheets and thrown from the window to land on the heap of soiled linen and dressings which had lain there since before their arrival.

'I expect George'll be bringing you a nice, clean dress soon,' she offered conversationally to Madame Criblier. 'Aren't they wonderful, these clean sheets?' She stretched out her legs to keep the muscles from weakening, lifting the left one and turning the knee in a circle. The scar matched the mauve dress.

Madame Criblier groaned. She was exhausted, thinner, the baby lodged near one naked breast. She evidently thought it no more than her due that Georgie and Patch could organise extraordinary happenings under the eye of the guards and let her benefit from them. Her new baby didn't seem to want to feed and gave out a thin wail.

The sense of repose was astonishing, Misha reflected. She could almost fall asleep again and sleep properly, without waking from nightmares, shouting and sweating. There might be cardigans or jackets from George and Patch's next foray into other people's rooms. They'd need them, for the cool nights. They'd have to travel then, and rest in woods or empty barns during the day. This would only be until they reached the area where there were no more Germans – and how they'd run screaming and hooting with laughter and relief down the middle of the nearest road, because they'd be free! There might even be trains to catch.

Misha smiled to herself. It would almost certainly be

254

further south than the convent, so they had a long way to go. She wouldn't mind. She'd have Frou then. The nuns would have remembered where she was. They'd have fed her. They had good, generous hearts and anyway needed a mouse-catcher. Frou was probably at that very moment having a midday nap in the cowstall, eyes half-closed, gazing at Marguerite's lovely, heavy head, waiting, listening. One day, they'd both be waiting. They'd be home before the war started up again, when the Allies had been able to regroup. France *kaputt*, the ward guard, Hans, had said. And England *kaputt*. He'd drawn a finger across his throat to illustrate this and grinned, without malice. Both things seemed in order to him and what's more, possible. This was because he was quite stupid, Patch'd decided. He was also as smitten with Patch as a fifteen-year-old boy and therefore most useful to them. He'd said it wouldn't be long before they'd be taken to prison and indicated his own feelings by rubbing mock tears from his eyes.

They might not have much time left. This was her only anxious thought, if she let it in. She stretched her left leg again. I hope, she thought, that my new cardigan or jacket is not mauve like the scar and the dress, otherwise I have no requests. I shan't mind what type the knickers are, they can be made of artificial silk, Celanese or whatever it's called, as long as they aren't too big and need a safety pin.

'Is the plump friend of yours getting the milk for my baby?' Madame Criblier called weakly.

'She's made Hans go and demand some from the German side. They've got plenty, he said.' She thought, however, that Madame Criblier had neither the strength nor the love to offer her infant and it might be for the best if he died. 'What're you going to call him?' She ought to take an interest, having been a reluctant observor of his longed-for birth.

Madame Cribler shrugged. 'What does it matter? What sort of life awaits him? Shall we ever get back home? Who is there to help us? I don't know where my family is. Have they survived? Has our village?' She had the habit of reciting these questions regularly throughout the day.

As always, Misha had no answers. There were none. She

255

was about to suggest that George might be an appropriate name when a terrifying new noise seemed to burst up from the courtyard below. They stared at each other. Shots. There were shots and frantic, wailing screams, like an animal's.

'It's pigs,' Madame Criblier announced finally, shifting the baby to the other breast where it failed to search for the nipple. 'They have collected pigs, rounded them up from the countryside and are killing them for meat.'

Misha eased herself into a sitting position. She leaned across to the paneless window and peered down into the courtyard. Near the kitchen entrance stood two sinister loaded carts. A third was being hauled in to join them. 'There are bodies in carts,' she said. 'I think they must be animals. The corporal I've seen out there before, he's shooting into them. I think they are not quite dead.' She didn't hear the screaming. She wouldn't hear it. 'Some are trying to get out.' She wouldn't look. She'd seen some ginger fur.

'What?' Madame Criblier asked, with indifference, trying the baby at the other breast.

Misha lay down. She didn't feel as well as she had. 'I expect they'll make stews,' she said.

'Boeuf bourguignon,' Madame Cribler said suddenly, her fretful voice almost dreamy. 'Navarin of lamb. Blanquette of veal. Rabbit civet. You know, I shouldn't mind just a little taste of anything at all.' It was the first time she'd seemed to soften. 'What's your favourite dish, Mademoiselle?'

'I don't really like meat,' Misha said. The animals had been dogs and cats. 'You can have my share, Madame, if there is any brought up here.' She mustn't let herself think of it and above all, mustn't breathe in any of the warm, decaying smell that would soon be drifting their way. Were the ovens big enough for so many? Who would skin them? A clutch of fear had taken the place of her contentment. How could she have been so foolish as to let herself be almost happy? They'd round up the rats next. It *had* come to this then, as she'd told Philippe it might that last precious day. And he had joked about it. He wouldn't have believed it would happen. I shall take Frou to the country, he'd said.

She'll have less chance of being eaten. He wouldn't have joked about it if he'd thought it could happen.

She was struggling with unbidden, unwanted memories and the familiar flutter of nausea when their guard, Hans, burst through the doorway. 'Cats and dogs *kaputt*,' he said, drawing a finger across his throat. 'Starving all over town. Bad,' he added. 'We bury in earth.' He put the jug he'd been carrying on Madame Criblier's bed and mimicked the action of digging. 'Or maybe roast dog for supper,' he said, grinning.

Madame Criblier pointed at the jug and at her baby. 'Baby starving,' she said, 'Give me milk.'

Misha lay back. Let them manage between them. Me too, sick, she thought, but everything was going to be all right. Frou was not an abandoned, scavenging cat. Frou was safe. Philippe was safe. He was a prisoner-of-war and they never shot officers. She was safe. She'd soon be running down a road with no Germans in it and shouting for joy with George and Patch.

A soft touch on her arm startled her. Hans wanted to speak. 'What?' she said. She was tired of being translator and interpreter. Peering through her lids, she saw Hans standing by her bed, his blond eyelashes fluttering in a mock display of something. 'What?' she said again. 'George and Patchie,' Hans said, one finger representing a tear slipping down his cheek. 'All gone, Hans sad. Prison,' he said. 'Truck drive away. No more George and Patchie.'

Chapter 36

'I should like you to have tea with me, Mademoiselle,' the Kommandant said. He was smiling but his flat blue eyes were blank.

Standing in the room next to his office, Misha kept herself upright. There was no one to prop her up now, no one to speak for her. 'How kind of you,' she said. She'd show him no weakness.

He sat down in one of the hard chairs grouped about a low table and indicated she should sit opposite him. This she did, bending stiff knees and biting back a gasp of pain. Then she saw an extraordinary sight – an entire tea laid out on a silver tray with plates and cups and saucers. One of the plates held a delicate arrangement of sandwiches made of white bread. Where had this come from? There'd only been hard, green stuff for so long! The sandwiches weren't quite English, being round. Then she saw they were made of baguette bread, from the old days. The crusts had been cut off. The scent of white bread was far too strong and if she dared look down again, she'd have to look at the plate of biscuits. These were the shiny slivers called cats' tongues. She could smell the sugar from them. There was even of a bowl of it – a matching silver bowl on a silver plate with silver tongs. A rush of saliva filled her mouth. She mustn't look at any of this. She was beyond hunger and must remain so.

'Will you pour, my dear?' the Kommandant asked. He was watching her. He seemed to fill the room with his lead colour and the metal and leather pieces on his jacket.

She couldn't look at him so looked back at the vision on the tray and leaned forward to grasp the handle of the teapot. It was too hot. She should have known this. She was supposed to be English.

'Use a napkin, my dear,' he suggested, taking a cigarette from the silver box beside the tray.

There were white damask napkins. Misha stared at the beautiful cloth and picked one up. Her mother... her mother's napkins, starched. These were one of her perfections, the napkins folded in the cupboard, used only by Misha at supper-time. She could see the supper laid out by the cocoa tin: half a baguette, a morsel of Brie, a tomato. She jammed her teeth together hard. She'd cry later for everything that was lost. 'D'you take milk?' she said. The teapot shook a little as she poured, but then she had been ill. She'd allow herself this.

'Just a drop,' the Kommandant said, blowing smoke upwards. 'But no sugar, thank you.'

Misha added the milk and placed his cup carefully on the table, not too near his lead-coloured breeches. Was she now supposed to pour herself tea? She didn't care for it, but seeing the pretty liquid in its fine china cup made her long to swallow some, piping hot. She'd had nothing hot since the convent. She swallowed a mouthful of saliva instead. He was leaning across and offering her the sandwich plate. 'Bread and butter first,' he said, laughing. 'I'm sorry I have no cake, but if the biscuits can count as cake, Nanny wouldn't let us have them first, would she?'

Misha stared at the circular sandwiches. The bread had a wonderfully even texture. She'd learned about bread from the Doucets. She had to take a piece of it, and did so. She also had to find an answer to this remark. She knew there must be one. She held the soft thing between two fingers. She could smell the butter in it. George, she thought, can I let myself eat this or not? And then she realised. Thinking of Georgie had helped her. Georgie never took their words at face value, even Hans's, and he wasn't all there. She let out a long breath. 'My nanny certainly wouldn't let me eat cake until I'd eaten the crusts as well,' she said, and stuffed the white, moist wonder into her mouth. She'd done it. She could go on doing it. It was easy. She just had to think first. 'If my Nanny Birchell could see me,' she added, plucking an English name from nowhere, 'she'd have something to say to you for keeping me here.' She wanted very badly to cry now. Her eyes prickled. But she'd done it. She'd realised he was trying to prove she wasn't English.

The Kommandant threw back his head and laughed. Some of his teeth were gold and the flesh bulged over his collar. It was not a pleasant sight. He took several of the rounds for himself, and crammed them into his mouth. 'Help yourself, do,' he said.

Misha shook her head. She'd only allow herself a second reward if she managed not to be fooled by him again. Anyway, the bread was stuck somewhere in her throat, which was strange. She'd always been able to force down the hard, green rations they'd been given. But she'd pretend, in order to have something to look at that was not this man. She poured herself a pure, clear, steaming cupful of the tea where it sat very prettily in its bone china, and considered the brownish lumps sitting in the sugar bowl. Would one cube count as a reward? I'll have one, she thought, and one mouthful of tea, for reasons of health. She was about to lift the cup from its saucer, when Kommandant spoke again.

'Which of your friends knew how to send the messages back to England?' he said.

'I beg your pardon?' This was a genuine surprise. Misha felt her mouth drop open. 'What messages?' she said.

He gazed into space, a toe tapping on the floor beneath the table. 'The English are very arrogant,' he said, and sighed. 'Yes. It is this arrogance which has been your friends' downfall. They have imagined we could not guess they have been in the pay of the British government. Still, no matter. There is nothing of any strategic importance they could have sent back. France belongs to the German nation now and shortly we shall be in England. The advance of our forces has been so much beyond what the Allies could have imagined, hasn't it?' He picked up biscuits and began to crunch them one by one.

Misha didn't look at him but knew he was smiling. A

trickle of sweat ran down her back. George and Patch spies? They'd be hanged.

'Miss Fitzgerald and Miss Montgomery have been most helpful to us but they cannot remember where they left their radio equipment. They say you will be able to remember this.'

'I know nothing,' Misha said. 'Because there was no radio equipment.'

'Very well,' he said. A spray of crumbs landed on the table beside his empty cup, and he rose to his feet.

Misha watched them fall. She could smell biscuit. She waited.

'Guard!' he shouted. A soldier appeared and saluted. 'Heil Hitler!' The Kommandant answered this lazily and strolled to the door, muttering something in German. The soldier took his place against the wall behind the chair the Kommandant had just left.

'I shall return in an hour or two,' the Kommandant called to Misha. 'Do make yourself at home whilst you are waiting, Mademoiselle, won't you? And use this quiet time to remember one or two matters which have perhaps slipped your mind. Miss Fitzgerald and Miss Montgomery are very stubborn. The English are very stubborn, aren't they? Don't they call it pig-headed? You can see this, can't you, Mademoiselle, because you are not one of them? If you can be sensible and remember your real identity, I think I shall find it it my heart to forgive the very pig-headed nature of Miss Fitzgerald and Miss Montgomery.'

He was gone. Misha looked at the guard with his still, blank face. He too seemed to fill the room with woollen cloth and all that leather and metal, the heavy boots, the helmet. He must be hotter than her and she was very hot. Sweat had begun to trickle down the backs of her legs. These were shaking. She put a careful hand on each knee to steady them.

She could hear a clock ticking. There was the clock, fixed to the wall to her left. Five past two, it said. That was early for tea. No wonder she hadn't wanted any.

Twenty minutes to eight, the clock said. Misha turned her

head from this to her hands, stiff on her painful knees, and then on to the silver tray with its cold silver pot. The white rounds of imitation English sandwiches looked quite hard now, and greyish. The cats' tongue biscuits had lost their glaze. The sugar still looked tempting. It was the rough kind, like tiny rocks or those bullseye sweets she and Janet had bought on a Sunday coming back from church.

She didn't feel well enough to think about Janet.

Her mouth was full of saliva every time she thought about the sugar.

She looked from the sugar across to the soldier. He hadn't moved either. He was still looking at her. Perhaps he would rather do this than look at the tray. Perhaps he was hungry and thirsty too.

Saliva was dribbling from her mouth and on to her chin. She ought to wipe it off, but her knees had begun to shake again and she had to keep her hands there.

Had the soldier looked down at her knees to see this? She thought she had almost heard, or perhaps felt, the merest movement coming from his direction. He seemed to be made of stone though. They all did. And yet they slept at night. Georgie had wondered how they did. They slaughtered babies from the skies and then they went home and kissed their own children goodnight.

I have seen all kinds of death, she thought, and I have seen a hanging also. Or rather, I have seen someone after he'd hanged himself.

She stared at the soldier's blank face. She would like to ask him something, anything. It wouldn't matter what but she couldn't ask because she had begun to cry. The tears joined the dribble on her chin. She tried to manoeuvre a shoulder round to wipe them off.

This occupied her for a minute or two. It must have for when she looked up again, the soldier was leaning across the table. He held out a handkerchief and his face also was wet.

Chapter 37

How long before she realised the guard had approached
the table again? She didn't know. She could no longer
see the clock. It was night in the room and almost night
outside. But she could make out his shape, bending over
the tray. He was picking up sugar lumps and then the biscuits. The sugar made a particular little sound in the bowl.
She knew he must have wrapped them up when he reached
towards her and placed a handkerchief bundle on her lap.
She could smell his sweat. She heard him place his heels
very carefully together without the usual click. He didn't
want to make a noise. And then he resumed his position
against the wall.

She could barely make out his outline by then and could
assume therefore that he couldn't make out hers. So it was
time. She put the bundle into one of the mauve patch
pockets the nurse had sewn onto her dress. The woman
must have been a good seamstress because she'd chosen
a pattern which had buttons from neckline to hem. The
buttonholes were well done. She could tell this for her
fingers found it easy to unfasten the two or three she needed
to unfasten around the waist.

The money belt was damp from her hot skin, as it had
been since she left Paris. 1940 had been the best summer
for years, people said. Hitler's weather, the better to bomb
by. It may have rained once or twice but otherwise the sun
had been relentless from dawn to dusk.

The wallet was damp also and felt heavy with the card
and notes and there were a lot of these. Thousands of francs,

she had. Patch had been delighted to find them when she was scrubbing the belt whilst George had washed her hair. It'd buy train tickets right down to the south coast, hers for Montpellier, theirs for Marseille and even the boat home to England.

It would have been wonderful to buy them train and boat tickets. Though she owed them much more than money. Think, Mish, Patch had said, maybe somewhere trains are running. The whole world may not have stopped.

The effort had made her breathless. She paused, fingering her fortune. This was no use to any of them now, but the card they concealed would be, because she was described on it. Height: 1 metre 73. Colour of hair: light brown. Colour of eyes: grey. Special marks: None. Father: Michael Henry Martin. Mother: Yvette Marie Martin. Place of birth: Montpellier, L'Hérault.

When the Kommandant returned and allowed lamps to be brought in – or perhaps they'd had the electricity put back down here and the switch would work – then he'd see very clearly that she had been lying. She was French. She'd remembered. And he'd be able to find it in his heart to forgive the pig-headed behaviour of George and Patch.

Keeping the notes in one hand, she felt about on the tray for the teapot and the milk jug. She had surely earned a second reward. Pouring some in both cups, she placed one on the other side of the tray, in case the guard would dare to drink also. She herself drank three. She could hear herself gulping the cold, bitter stuff. She thought she could hear him make a movement too but he certainly didn't drink. Finally, removing a sugar lump from the bundle, she put it in her mouth and sat back.

She felt better.

'What's all this, sitting in the dark?' The Kommandant's voice was so sudden, she almost dropped the wallet. 'Sorry to have kept you waiting, Mademoiselle.'

Some orders followed. Her guard left and two more arrived, one carrying a brass lamp. This he placed on the table, sliding the tray off it with one deft movement as the Kommandant sat down.

Misha did not wait. She swallowed the last grains of sugar

and said, 'Here is everything I have. When will my friends be freed from the prison?'

'Tut, tut, what girlish impatience,' he said, accepting the wallet. The lamplight made his face seem skeletal, his eyes and mouth black. He hummed to himself, flicking through the notes. 'How did you come by so much money, my dear? I hope you didn't take all this from your savings bank. You could well lose it, you know, and you have nothing to fear from the German nation. Interest will be paid as it always has.' He was smiling. 'But where is your identity card?' He flicked through the notes again. 'Now, I am positive you would have gone nowhere without this, so where is it? I want your real name and place of birth, not this false thing.' He'd taken out a piece of paper from between the francs. It was a damp and flattened envelope.

Leaning towards the lamp, Misha peered at it. 'Oh, that's nothing. It's the pass we were supposed to need to get out of Paris when the panic started.' Monsieur Pierre had given it to her. She'd never even opened it.

'But this pass tells me you still have much explaining to do. You have gone so far as to have your false English identity put on it. What is the reason for this?' He flapped the paper in front of her and Misha saw English written in ink amongst print she didn't have time to read: *Miss Michelle Mary Martin, presently lodging in the rue Bonaparte whilst studying French, is to be allowed access to any transport which will enable her to return to her home in London*, it said. Monsieur Pierre must have written this himself.

But she didn't blame him. He'd have thought it for the best at the time. And it might have helped her. There were a lot of official stamps all over the sheet. He meant well. So did Patch and George when they decided to remove her identity card from her moneybelt so nothing could say she was French. Hadn't they seen the envelope? Perhaps it had been stuck to one of the thousand-franc notes. The damp would have caused that. Probably they'd asked their contact in the basement to burn the card. And she couldn't save them now.

'We shall have further questions to ask you, Mademoiselle.' The Kommandant put money and paper back

265

together and stood up. 'You will assemble at o-five hundred hours in the courtyard, from which place you will be transported to Paris.' He bowed and slapped his heels together. 'I remind you also that as a French citizen you will stand trial on a charge of committing a hostile act against the German Army, which is punishable by death. Your money will be passed to your next-of-kin once we have established who this is. Goodnight to you.'

Chapter 38

Returning from the washroom to her cell, Misha placed the tin mug containing her water allowance on the shelf over her bed and took off one of her shoes. With the heel of this, she scratched a clumsy square on the wall. This was the nineteenth, marking the nineteen days of her stay in the Cherche-Midi prison. Before nightfall, she'd put a figure nineteen inside of it. There was always the chance she'd be called for her trial and therefore not finish the day. Marie, her washroom friend, had had hers. She'd been given two years for muttering 'filthy swine' at a group of German soldiers who'd strolled to the front of the queue in a grocery shop and demanded butter. She much admired Misha's own hostile act. In fact, their whispered conversations during the five-minute washing period had given them both support. Conversation was forbidden, but sometimes the guards were lax at wash-time.

Today, they had whispered goodbye. Marie was to be transported to the prison of Fresnes to serve the sentence. Being a Parisian, she'd heard the enemy was using the Cherche-Midi for arrests only. It was her contention Georgie and Patch would already be at Fresnes. She'd promised to get a message through somehow if she could. Visitors would surely be permitted there, and perhaps letters.

Misha stood longer than usual, adding an F for Fresnes and an M for Marie under the day's square. Unless Marie was replaced by another congenial woman to share her five-minute wash allowance, she would forget the sound of her own voice. But if news could get through that Patch and

Georgie were in a pleasanter place, their trial done with, it'd be worth it. And sometimes the guards spoke a word or two if they dared. Being themselves prisoners for misdemeanours like drunkenness in the street, they had to be careful. Yesterday, one had pushed a bar of chocolate into her pocket whilst escorting her along the corridor to the central landing for the 2 p.m. *Essen*. This was the first meal of the day, a greasy, colourless soup ladled from a white enamel bucket with the words CHERCHE-MIDI round the rim, as if it were the name of a famous restaurant like Maxim's or the Café de la Paix.

The meal was a long way from 6 a.m. *Waschen*. She now had seven and a half hours to pass before this diversion. Replacing the shoe, she moved to her next task: smoothing down her sheet to cover every inch of the mattress which was made of something she couldn't identify. Without the sheet, she might not have been able to lie down. The kitchen porter at the old hospital camp had crept up the basement steps while the driver of the car that was to take her to Paris was revving the engine and the guard polishing his rifle. Neither had seen Jerome slip the linen bundle through the car door. Fortunately, they also hadn't noticed that she'd entered the car in the hospital courtyard with nothing to carry and had stepped from it in the courtyard of the Cherche-Midi with a rolled-up clean bedsheet containing assorted pairs of knickers and three woollen cardigans. And without these items of clothing to wrap herself in, she'd probably have died of cold before the trial confirmed the sentence of death.

Maybe today they would fetch her for it. Marie had said trials took place on the ground floor, with a Kommandant and other officers present, and also the witnesses to one's crime. Perhaps her motorcyclists needed to be brought to Paris and her trial would take place as soon as they were. Everything was in German, Marie said, so there were interpreters, and then there were typists because every word was typed out at once. You had to sign a number of papers, but she herself intended to sign nothing until she had made it quite clear that Patch and Georgie's freedom had been bargained in return for her honesty. She wanted the chance to be honest. If only the trial would begin, she'd stand up and shout that yes, she was of French nationality, she had committed a crime, but Patch and Georgie hadn't and should be sent to Switzerland.

Thinking of Patch made her tuck in the sheet and remove her handkerchief bundle from the pocket of her mauve dress. It had the chocolate in it, rather too soft, and the piece of cheese saved from yesterday's 7 p.m. *Essen*, when they received this and a portion of bread. She bit off a corner of the chocolate and sat down, wrapping a navy blue cardigan round her legs and a pair of peach-coloured outsized knickers round her neck and head. These had probably been destined for Patch and were a surprising comfort. Now she could lie down on the sheet she considered still to be clean, having only her own blood on it, from the bug bites. The bugs scurried from the plaster between the bricks as soon as it was dark and were the worst night-time torture. The worst day-time one was the extraordinary length of each hour.

From this position, she could see the tiny section of sky the high barred window permitted her to see. In a moment, she'd begin her journey, the one in her mind which took her across every inch of the Paris she knew, step by step. On a good day, she could see people about their daily routine: her mother yawning on her satin pillows, the Blanchards at the counter in the Bonaparte, the baker sitting over his breakfast wine. Perhaps they'd already been questioned about the real identity of one Miss Michelle Mary Martin?

In this imaginary travelling, she never allowed herself to step through the doorway of her own flat. For her, all was lost. Sometimes, though, she'd be surprised to hear bolts being shot back along the corridor because it was almost time for 2 p.m. *Essen*.

Wasn't this her own bolt now? But she could still taste the chocolate. It couldn't be later than nine o'clock. She sat up as the nail-studded door flew open and a plump, different guard appeared. '*Promenade?*' she enquired, getting to her feet and hurriedly removing knickers and cardigan. He didn't answer her until she'd reached the door and he'd slammed and bolted it behind her. 'Orders,' he said, and indicated she should precede him.

All right. Not one of the wonderful exercise periods in the courtyard There'd been three of these. Her trial then.

She had to pause by the steel door that led to the central landing at the top of the stairs. This always took longer than the passage down the corridor because there was a guard on each side of it. They had to study the prisoner before finding the right key to unlock the door though this appeared to be their only responsibility. Her guard wasn't in a hurry. He and the two door guards had a conversation. Perhaps they were exchanging accounts of their own misdemeanours. They were laughing.

Finally, the steel door men stood aside and for the first time she saw the other section of the second-floor cells and some of its prisoners being led out for their turn at *Waschen*. Vaguely, she noticed the same, silent shuffling disorder of the women in the assortment of clothing that she was used to from her own area. Then she saw a khaki sleeve. Were there other ambulance drivers then? She dared make a small, leaning movement the guards didn't notice. She'd like to indicate something if she could, that she too . . .

It was Patch's sleeve. Patch's face was over it, or almost Patch's face. It was pale instead of heartily pink. But then, she'd be hungry.

Misha lifted her head, desperate to make some sound that would make Patch look towards her, to utter some innocuous word that would bring a reprimand but incriminate neither of them. She found it. 'Frou,' she said in a loud whisper and made it straight away into a cough.

Patch's chin shot up. She clapped a hand over her lips to stop herself yelling a reply and removed it to mouth something instead.

Misha coughed again. What? She tried to indicate this question with her eyebrows.

Patch decided to stand slightly out of her queue and show Misha what she wanted to say.

Misha didn't see at once that this movement actually revealed Georgie because something unnameable had happened to her. Georgie had shrunk.

270

Raus!' her guard shouted and she felt something push her in the back. But she didn't care. 'Hold on,' she shouted, 'I'm getting you freed!' She tried to turn round. The push came again and she was forced to take several steps down the stairs. She turned her head, holding on to the wall. She must look, once more. She hadn't made a mistake. It was Georgie, Georgie with her hair gone brown, and blank, dead eyes staring down at her.

For herself, it didn't matter. She was lost but they mustn't be. She shouted again, fingers scraping along the bricks as her guard lost patience and forced her downwards. Her last words, 'Hold on,' echoed through the stairwell until the familiar, chill silence resumed with only the sound of boots and the metal clang of bolt and key to break it.

By the time she and the plump guard had reached the ground floor, they were both running. Here there were many other soldiers striding about, in and out of doors, carrying papers.

Her door was the largest, black, with studded nails. Misha took a deep breath. She must be ready. She must be stout and British, the way Philippe knew she could be.

Then the door opened and a burst of sunlight hit her. This she couldn't understand. She stood blinking. The guard took her elbow and guided her down some steps. She was in a courtyard, in the sunshine. Ahead was another wall, another studded door. This also opened and she could see a street.

The guard released her arm and pointed. She was to go towards the second door. Giddy from light and warmth, Misha went towards it and saw her mother standing on the pavement.

Chapter 39

'Don't utter a single word in French, the officer understands it.' Yvette Martin put shaking arms around her daughter and kissed her. 'Pierre's only been able to get you freed because you're on your father's passport.' She was whispering. 'You're British.'

Misha felt her knees shake too. Her mother's face was a stiff mask under her blue veil, and her eyes had the same blank look as Georgie's. Things had happened, then, outside the hospital, beyond the prison. And she had ceased to wonder about them. 'I am free?' she said, and looked along an ordinary street with shops in it and one or two German trucks. She looked at the black vehicle behind her mother and at the German officer and his driver sitting in the front seats. 'They've let me out?'

'Thank God. Get in the back, quickly. They might change their minds.'

The leather seats burned her skin. Misha felt heat and sunlight and an overwhelming thirst. 'Are we allowed something to drink?' She thought, The Bonaparte. I shall sit at my table in the corner and there'll be pomegranate juice, then coffee and maybe a piece of bread, perhaps a wedge of omelette, and half the street will come in to have a look at me. But I'll never be able to describe what has taken place since I last sat there. She turned her head and saw her mother climb in beside her. There was a cream silk flower in the brim of her hat. This was blue, darker than her dress, a cornflower-coloured crêpe with a bias cut. People had been putting on pretty clothes and walking in

272

the sunshine. But her mother was shaking so much, the veil trembled.

'Not in Paris, darling. Another place perhaps. The officer has promised we shall stop somewhere so you can have breakfast and change.'

'We're to leave Paris? I can't go to the Bonaparte?' Glued to hot leather by heat and weakness, Misha knew that neither mattered for the moment. Anyway, there might be German soldiers at her table in the corner. Monsieur Jules might be forced to serve them. She wouldn't be able to bear it. Better then to wait until the war was over and everything returned to near-normal. It would just seem more precious, because so nearly lost forever. If Philippe were not a prisoner-of-war, he was probably even then taking part in some Allied regroupment and Paris would be freed. They only needed more tanks and more cunning, as Georgie always said.

'We have to get away at once, Mish. You must realise.' Yvette put out a cool, slender hand and held her daughter's skeletal one. 'Listen, darling.' She bent her stiff face closer so that Misha had to look at her. 'Absolutely everything is dangerous now. It's changed here since we last saw each other. You must barely open your mouth until we've reached where we're going. You won't see your friends at the Bonaparte for quite some time. I have everything you'll need packed into suitcases. I've also been to see those café people and the old Widow Libaud to tell them you're going to be all right. I knew you'd want me to. Soon you'll be able to make friends of your own age, I hope.'

'I've got Georgie and Patch.' Misha could feel the tremor in her mother's hand but perhaps it was her own tremor. Vaguely watching unfamiliar streets pass by as the car set off, she said, 'You remember Georgie. She and her friend Patch were arrested too, just before I was, and the Germans put us together. Their only women prisoners, we were. They kept taking photographs of us to send home. It isn't fair Georgie and Patch are still locked in that place. They can't have had their trial yet but they didn't commit any hostile act like me and I've got to try and get them out.' Breathless from the unaccustomed effort of saying so much, she

273

managed the vital question. 'D'you think your Pierre can do the same for them?'

Yvette started to fidget with the handbag on her lap. 'I cannot begin to tell you, Mish, how foolish this idea is, so if I just pretend I didn't hear it, that'll do. If you knew what Pierre has had to do to get you freed!' She dropped her voice to a whisper. 'Everything is in turmoil, not only what you've seen, the bombing, the refugees. I mean everything.' She opened the bag, took out her powder compact, dropped it, replaced it. 'Can you imagine what it was like for me in the midst of it all to hear an officer knock on my door and tell me my daughter's been arrested for committing a hostile act? It's on all the posters, people are being warned, anyone trying to hinder them in their task of getting the country back to normal, is liable to be executed. Then an officer comes to my door! Oh, Misha!'

'I'm sorry, Mum.' There should be much more to be said but she couldn't manage it for the moment. Leaning her head against the comfort of leather, Misha noticed that only German troops in their green or lead-coloured uniforms were walking along the pavements. She'd seen no Parisians except a single waiter setting out tables and chairs on a pavement. Soldiers were wanting to sit down. 'Has everyone gone?' she said. 'Is that why we're in such a hurry?' The larger buildings had red swastika flags flying over them. There was probably one over the Eiffel Tower. She mustn't look back at this. She mustn't look back at Paris but leave it with hope, as she'd done the first time. It wouldn't be for long. What emotion could she also name for being released from a sentence of death? There could be no name.

Reaching an intersection she recognised, she saw the street directions were new, in black German lettering on white boards. But she wouldn't look. 'I think,' she said, 'that we're taking the same road I did with Frou in her basket. D'you remember? How long ago was it? What's the date?'

'It's the 22nd or 23rd,' her mother said, 'I've been too busy to notice.

'Of August?'

'July, silly!' Yvette didn't even manage a smile. Misha glanced across at her rigid profile and the set frown between her eyes. Her mother would never be able to realise her daughter had been trapped in places where there was no time, only night or day, heat or cold. And she was still thinking of clothes. Misha knew she should be grateful for this, the mauve dress now being so thickened with grime, it would probably stand up by itself. 'I've packed a winter wardrobe for you,' her mother was saying. 'The summer'll soon be over. I bought a nice pair of slacks in the Galeries. Women were wearing them last winter. Did you see? They'll suit you, with your long legs. They're navy. I couldn't find a navy jumper, there was so little time. Oh, Mish, if you knew what I'd been through since that knock on the door. Still, it's all over now.' She took out a handkerchief and blew her nose. She wasn't crying. Misha realised her mother was beyond crying, as she was herself. Tomorrow, or the next day, she'd be able to comfort her. She'd tell her how very sorry she was, and how grateful. For the moment, she was able to do no more than reach out to hold her mother's hand again.

'So I got hold of some navy wool, a proper dark navy, quality it is, and a pattern. Mémé'll knit you a jumper.'

'Mémé?' Misha tried to sit up. 'You mean we're going to Montpellier?'

Yvette gripped Misha's hand and turned to look at her with her rigid, older face. Misha thought she'd need time to get used to this changed face but they'd have time at Mémé's. Her mother would have nothing to do in the country. 'Don't mention place names, darling, or say anything else on that subject, please. Soon we'll be stopping at a café. I asked the driver particularly. I want to see you being all messy with that horrible milky coffee of yours and that soggy bread.' Now she smiled and her eyes had something of their old sparkle.

Misha too felt herself smile. She was free. She wasn't going to die. 'Isn't everything looking pitiful?' The car was out of the Paris area now because the verges bore witness to the bombing and Paris hadn't been bombed. The same trucks lay on their roofs, there were buckled farmcarts, wheelbarrows, countless family cars, military paraphernalia of all kinds. And on each side, the same villages had their

275

flattened air, roofs and people gone. 'Why haven't they cleaned up?' she whispered. 'I thought the Germans were supposed to be fanatically clean.'

Yvette dug her knuckles hard into Misha's thigh. 'Haven't you understood, Mish?' With a frantic movement of her head, she indicated the backs of driver and officer guard.

'Sorry.' Misha felt she'd wasted the last ounce of her strength. She surely knew more about mistrust than her mother did. And this was not a social occasion. But a feeling of happiness was hovering somewhere. Once she knew how she was going to get Patch and Georgie freed, she'd let it in. Because, oh heavens, she was going to hold Frou in her arms again and also perhaps learn that Philippe was safe in a prisoner-of-war camp until the Allies regrouped and freed *him*.

Her mother raised her voice. 'I've packed you a pair of sensible shoes. I could only get brown. I expect you'll be helping Mémé with the chickens. I found a pair for Félix too, though I'm not sure of his size now. The last letter from Mémé was nearly three months ago so I've estimated the next size up from his last ones. If they're still too big, he'll have to wear two pairs of socks or he'll get blisters.'

Misha thought, I am going to see Félix, I am going to see Mémé and Pépé and I'll be sleeping in a proper bed with a feather eiderdown. There'll be big bowls of *café au lait* for me and rabbit for Frou. She sat up and released her mother's hand. 'Is it true, then, that the whole world is not lost? That we are in a car travelling down the same roads I took and soon we'll be near the place where I lost Frou?' She'd been feeling too weak to register these momentous truths but was gaining in strength with each new recognition of approaching possibilities.

'Don't mention any place names,' her mother said. 'I was wondering about that cat of yours and hoping I'd heard the last of her, actually.'

'Frou's sheltering in a convent, looked after by nuns, but I shall be wanting to stop soon and look at a map. Surely the officer can't refuse a simple request like that? What rank has he got? The lower the position they have, the nicer they are. At least, that's what I've found and I've had plenty

276

of experience. We've had food slipped to us, all sorts of things, cigarettes for Georgie, even wine. Only yesterday a guard put chocolate in my pocket. Do ask, please.' She leaned forward to look at the officer in the passenger seat. From the array of metal on his tunic, she supposed he had a high rank.

'I'll try later.' Her mother caught hold of her elbow. 'Just relax, darling, please. There's time for everything later. Lean back and rest your head on my shoulder. The first thing you need is some sleep. I never thought I'd live to see a child of mine looking like a living skeleton, dressed in filthy rags and smelling like a tramp.'

Misha took a deep breath and did as she was told. She closed her eyes. Everything was floating. She'd sleep if she could, and when she awoke she'd be nearer to Frou and their haven with Mémé. They'd both earned it. Frou. She could dare think her name now and imagine her freed from under the bed, pretending to be a rat-catcher in the cowstall. 'The convent's in a nice little village which wasn't bombed. Only the wood was. Georgie and Patch'd been camping in it with their French troops. I couldn't believe it when the nuns said they'd been feeding two English ambulance women. I have so much to tell you, I don't know where to begin.'

Chapter 40

'Wake up, Misha.'

Her mother's voice. Misha opened her eyes and remembered at once. No more cell doors being slammed back. No more shouts: *Waschen!* And she was baked in heat. She'd never have enough of heat, after the Cherche-Midi. 'Is it breakfast or lunch? I'd like a pint of clean water first, please, then a bowl or two of coffee and a whole baguette.' She watched the driver hold open her mother's door and her mother trotting round to open hers. 'Are we anywhere near the convent, d'you think?' She put her legs out into warm air and sunlight. She was going to enjoy the sound of her mother's scream when she saw the scar.

'We're at a railway station, darling. And it's nearer suppertime actually. I didn't waken you for our first stop.' She helped her daughter from the seat but was too occupied to notice the scar. 'Now, she said, 'whilst I organise one or two things, you find the lavatory in the station buffet. You're going to wash and change in there first or they won't want to serve you.' She trotted round to the car boot and disappeared.

Misha decided she could almost produce one of her silly grins. She'd forgotten that her mother didn't always spend the day lying against satin pillows. She stood up and looked about her. It was true. The old world did still exist. This was an ordinary, whole railway station with the words BUFFET DE LA GARE and ENTRÉE written over it. People were going in and out. None wore a uniform. Their officer and driver seemed to be the only representatives of

278

the enemy. A small boy was staring and pointing at them. His mother was dragging him away and she was staring at Misha.

I look like a skeleton, she reminded herself, walking towards the buffet. She could smell tobacco, garlic, Pernod. France as it has always been, she thought, my world, and Patch and Georgie's too. They'd dreamed of finding it intact. Somehow, she must find a way to get them out of prison so they could go running down the street together, shouting for joy.

Three old men sitting over a bottle of red wine and a game of dominoes stared at her, and so did the waitress as she made her way round the interior tables. From the bar counter, a genial drunk called out something rude. She didn't reply. She wasn't ashamed of the dirty mauve dress or her dirty hair. Prison, she thought, did rather tend to wear away the usual vanities. But she'd had very little vanity in London. Survival had been the issue then, and in the Cherche-Midi, waiting for death. I have come through both, she thought. Perhaps she should thank her father for lessons in endurance and fortitude.

But she was startled at the sight of her own face in the lavatory glass. She did look like a skeleton. Her eyes and mouth were sunken. Her hair was flat with oil and grime. The bug bites covered every inch of the skin on her face and neck with bloody lumps. She splashed water on as much of it as she could as her mother's voice called out, 'Hurry, Misha. Open the door, take this bag in and push out everything you've been wearing. I'll throw it away. Be quick.'

The bag her mother had prepared contained silk camisole and knickers, a pink cotton dress, a straw hat with pink ribbon, brown sandals. Fingering these things with the beginnings of delight, she realised nothing could make her well again so quickly as a stay at her grandmother's. She must first persuade her mother to ask her Monsieur Pierre to use his power to have Georgie and Patch released. Whilst waiting for them to be brought from Paris, she'd fetch Frou from the convent, take her to Mémé's, make them both well with good food and being together.

Then Georgie and Patch would arrive, and fresh air, sunlight, duck cassoulet, goat's cheese, cherries, peaches, apricots'd soon help them forget the Cherche-Midi. Georgie's eyes'd be clear and blue again, her hair the blondest blonde. Patch and Frou'd lounge together on the terrace spreading out bit by bit into their intended shapes with the aid of shared titbits.

Soon after that, the Allies'd regroup and begin the fight back but if they had to wait until they could go home, there'd be no better place than Mémé's.

Chapter 41

Misha finished the bottle of water and burped happily. She'd had tomato vinaigrette followed by sauté potatoes and a wedge of cheese. Her mother had ordered it for her but had barely sat at the table to eat more than a mouthful herself, claiming to have much to do. A chemist's shop had to be found, for calamine to soothe the bug bites and much more in the way of washing materials than she'd packed.

Misha thought of Yardley's lavender soap and clean teeth, gazing round at the other diners who still took these things for granted. There must have been shortages here too but they appeared clean enough. She'd seen no soap since the hospital when Georgie had used the last on washing Madame Criblier and her new baby after the birth. Georgie herself was in need of soap now, and someone to help wash her hair.

She looked down at her plate where a crumb of cheese remained and licked a finger to pick it up. There hadn't been much bread and the coffee was imitation, made of ground acorns. Suddenly, she didn't feel quite so well. She'd been greedy and sat too long.

Getting to her feet, she went to the window to look for her mother's return. She wanted to get on. She also had much to do. Fetch Frou, first. Settle them both at Mémé's, second. And then somehow reach Monsieur Pierre in order to plan the release of Georgie and Patch. Offering him a brief apology in her mind for her misjudgement of him for he certainly must be someone high up in the government, she decided she would be able to offer him a very cordial hand-shake when they met next time.

Her mother was back. She was standing on the pavement by the car, talking to the officer. The shopping must be completed. The driver was in his seat. Good. They were setting off again. Hurrying to the doorway with new strength, she met her mother, who'd also been hurrying. There was sweat on her upper lip and at her temples. She looked frantic. 'Quickly, Mish, take this jacket and shoulder bag. They're yours. Pick up one of the suitcases from the pavement and follow me.'

Infected by her mother's agitation, Misha accepted jacket and bag, ran to the suitcases, took one and began to run towards their car. The officer smiled, saluted her genially and picked up the other himself. He pointed behind her. Her mother was disappearing through the station entrance.

Misha followed her mother and the officer followed her. She hadn't understood the rest of the journey was to be by train but was delighted. Now she'd be able to recount her story to her mother in absolute detail, beginning with the heat and the soot and the shelling on the roads. There'd be no listening ears. She'd let her mother be horrified, and proud of her daughter's endurance. She'd let her put on the calamine with cotton wool and they'd both feel better.

On the platform, her mother was looking at her watch. 'Hurry, darling, do.' The blue veil was askew and she'd lost her gloves. The officer saluted again and left.

'I suppose we ought to thank him,' Misha said. She felt a wide grin stretch across her face. This made the bites hurt more. 'Have you got the tickets? Where're we going?' She had to shout because a train was steaming into the station. 'Direct to Montpellier? What about Frou?'

'Your ticket, Mish, darling.' Yvette used an urgent whisper. 'Come closer. This is your train and the ticket for it is in the shoulder bag. It arrives in Montpellier around dawn. Have breakfast in the station there, then get a taxi for Mémé's. There is plenty of money. Spend what you need. If I can, I shall get down to see you soon and bring some more. You'd better open a savings account with it to keep it safe. Tell Pépé I don't believe in keeping money under the mattress. And while you're in town, go to the Commissariat, tell them you've lost your identity card and they must get you another. There shouldn't be any problem, you were born there.'

Her back aching with the effort of holding on to the suitcase, bag and jacket and keeping her face near her mother's in order to hear the urgent whisper, Misha tried to interrupt. The train was slowing down and spitting out smut and steam. Yvette coughed but hardly stopped for breath. 'You may be with Mémé some time. You must try and make friends there. Forget those odd people at the Bonaparte, forget the crush you had on that professor. You're nearly a woman now and you've learned a lot, I can see that, darling.' Steam and smoke were making her eyes water, and still she didn't stop.

Misha saw with distress that her mother's perfections were lost. Her dress crumpled, sweat making powder and rouge mix with the smut from the train, how would she be able to bear it when she looked in a glass? Her own mouth as if stuck open for her questions, she couldn't make her mother listen. 'What d'you mean, my ticket? Where's yours?' she yelled finally.

'Misha, I have to go somewhere else, to be with Pierre. It's top secret, everything is now. I can't bear the country, you know that, and anyway I might be trapped there.' Eyes watering, more agitated with each passing second, she spoke faster. 'You must go to Mémé's this minute, or you'll be trapped here and I shan't be able to help you get out.'

Desperate to hear, Misha leaned closer. 'What d'you mean, trapped?'

'There's to be a border. The Germans'll have the north, a new French government the south. Pierre's helping form the new government to try and make France a great country again. The German authorities are going to help with that. They're quite satisfied with the territory they've gained. Everything's going to get better for everyone.'

They were so close to the train's cab, Misha could feel the heat of the boiler. A stoker jumped onto the platform near them and hurried off. 'A frontier in the middle of France?' she said.

'Misha,' her mother said, 'you might not reach your cat. You'll never get back to Paris. Accept that. Try and make a life at Mémé's.'

'Never go home?' She could understand nothing.

Her mother shook her head, fumbling for a handkerchief to wipe her face. Misha regarded this new mother with smudged soot down her left cheek and tried to understand. 'But where will you be, and whoever heard of such a thing?'

'Look out, the stoker wants to get back in.' Yvette bent down and picked up a suitcase. This she flung through an open carriage door. Misha automatically threw hers in too, following it with her jacket and shoulder bag. 'I can't understand!' she shouted. There were sparks in the air now. Her heart thumped as steam shot out of the engine and the train began to throb. 'Get in with me, *Maman*, please. I need you to help me. How shall I know where you are?'

'Trust me, I know what's best for you, though you're nearly a woman. Think what you've been through already. I'm proud of you, darling. You've been so brave and British. I couldn't have done it.' She grasped her daughter's arm and manoeuvred her after the suitcases. 'Give everyone my love. Trust me.' She didn't have to whisper now. These were ordinary farewell words, or almost.

Stumbling through the door of the carriage, Misha looked down at the extraordinary spectacle of her mother's dress damp with sweat. A hot hand reached up to take her arm again and draw her close a last time. 'I shall be with Pierre in a place called Vichy. Remember the name but don't mention it to anyone, not even Mémé. You won't be able to come to me but I may be able to come to you. Be happy, Misha. You deserve it.' She paused and looked about her. The platform was still empty but for one porter at the other end who was starting to slam the doors shut. 'Find a nice man to look after you. Forget the professor. Listen, darling, old Widow Libaud, she learned he'd been taken prisoner-of-war and escaped. He went through Paris on some wild idea to try and find the battle lines or something. He convinced her the Allies'd regroup but of course he'll be caught.'

284

Dropping to her knees on the carriage floor, Misha held on to the seat. 'No,' she said. 'No.'

'And darling, think, if he did fight on French soil now the new French government has declared an Armistice, that'd be treason, so he'd never go home either. Do try and understand.' She attempted a smile and stepped back onto the platform. 'Life is utterly changed, you see, Misha. I've been trying to tell you but Pierre says it may be for the best. Good-bye, darling, keep being brave, help Mémé and Félix, they need you . . .'

A porter ran up. Misha released the door. He slammed it. She got to her feet and from the window watched her mother disappear.

Part Three

Chapter Forty-Two

South of France, November 1942

Misha settled herself at the terrace table, lining up the writing box her brother had made, the pen and bottle of ink, the letter from Dorset and those from her mother and the nuns. Beside them she laid the postcards. The low afternoon sun was warm enough for her to sit without cardigan. On the steps near her feet, Frou tapped at a dead vine leaf. Soon she'd curl up for her nap in the tub of lavender and a faint snore would join Mémé's louder one coming from the bedroom where bronchitis had kept her for the last week.

Her grandfather and brother were at work with the donkey in the field up by the Palavas road, grubbing out old vines. She'd have an hour or two of quiet, enough for a proper letter to the Sisters. Another glorious Languedoc summer had passed since she'd had theirs, and another exuberant grape harvest.

Arranging the cards and letters in date order, she prepared to re-read them. This she allowed herself before replying to the nuns, as a kind of pre-reward, a moment when she let herself draw back an inch of curtain on the past.

The first card was from Patch, dated 26 August 1940. A smudged postmark revealed it to have been sent from Marseille, so she and Georgie must have been freed from the prison not long after her.

Darling Mish,

Here we are at last like we dreamed about, catching trains and things. Haven't run about for joy, George still not well. Soon will be, though, where we're going. Hope you're safe with granny. Stay there until the world's back as it should be.

Much love,

Patch and George

Next was one of the official postcards which had been the only mail allowed across the border after the German military authorities took control of the northern section of the country. Designed to allow families and friends to communicate after the great exodus of refugees fleeing from the German bombardments, you had to fill in the blanks in printed sentences and cross out where appropriate. Its date was 4 September 1940 and it came from the Blanchards. Their pencil marks had faded with time but the print remained as stark as ever. On the line FAMILY WELL NEEDS FOOD MONEY NEWS LUGGAGE, they had indicated FAMILY WELL. And around the list of suggestions IN GOOD HEALTH TIRED SLIGHTLY/ GRAVELY WOUNDED KILLED PRISONER DIED, Misha could still decipher the 'professor' and the two pencil circles around the SLIGHTLY and the WOUNDED.

After receiving this, she'd sent several official postcards of her own to the Blanchards, trying to make questions from the bald statements. She'd never had another from them but that didn't mean they hadn't sent one.

Neither did it mean that Patch and Georgie's letter from their home in Dorset, dated December 1940 and arriving in April 1941, had not been followed by many others. Or indeed that her frequent ones to them had ever reached the giant censor's office which must exist somewhere. In this place, decisions were being made on what to pass, what to open. On what basis, no one knew, but she recognised the guarded tone Patch and Georgie used. It was the same as her own – and her mother's in the regular notes she sent from the town of Vichy, Monsieur Pierre being a member of the French government set up there with enemy permission.

Patch's letter had begun:

Home at last, old love. Don't ask how we got here, just imagine our first view of white cliffs with bright green grass on top! We didn't half wish our friend from sunny Bournemouth was with us to shriek with joy the loudest. Anyway, we're doing our bit at home, getting up at dawn to chop mangel worzels. I put in for war work in a *food* factory but was told to do land work instead. Now mangel worzels ain't tasty, Mish. Then Georgie insists on these French lessons in the evenings from the schoolmarm when I'd much rather be cosy down in the village pub scoffing cider. Make sure you eat plenty, for me. Are there still *oeufs* dripping mayonnaise? *Salade Nicoise* in a sea of olive oil? Cherry pancakes? Peaches, apricots, God I can't go on, Mish, wish you were here or we were there, don't know which.

To this, Georgie had added:

'It was a shock to realise I was weak, Mish, and I didn't know I could hate. It's taught me something, I can tell you – frightening to know I couldn't trust myself. Am working on this. Stay where you are (if you're there, which we hope) and EAT, please. Send proof of both with photo if possible.
Lots of love,
Georgie.

It was Georgie's words that still had the power to make her weep and it was at this point she usually picked up the pen and began her own letter.

My dear Sisters,
So Marguerite has calved again? Who'd have thought she'd ever recover! Did Prudence make the special pudding from the first milking? I think Frou misses the dairy. She'll accept a bit of the goat's cheese my grandmother makes but it's as if she's doing us a favour. She's grown thinner since I brought her down here last

year and has an air of desperation about her, as if she'd not sure where her next meal's coming from. She's forever rustling about in the vines and fruit trees in search of something tasty from the insect world. My brother Félix works hard for her, doing secret fishing at night, trapping frogs as well. These he has to roast on the outside spit, Mémé refusing to deal with such lowly meat. She can never understand why it's supposed to be a delicacy. What jaded, decadent palates the rich must have! she says. On both these points, of course, we're in agreement, but she adores snails. Frou won't touch them and neither will she go anywhere near the bits of goat stomach my grandad pretends should be her lot in life.

Can you imagine, I had to cook for Pépé's hunting party the other day because Mémé was in bed with a bad chest? I'd better draw a veil over the event actually. I overcooked the unmentionable item which was the main course, the worst of sins as you know.

In fact, I've had a very hard summer. My back! I can't tell you how it protests during the grape harvest. I'm too tall for grape-picking, I've decided. I claim that work on the vines has produced generations of short-backed, short-legged people like my Pépé who's as bent and twisted as the vines themselves. It's pruning time at present and he'll be all winter on it with Félix. They use a donkey and cart to bring down the prunings for our fuel. Today they're grubbing out a small field, roots and all. He'll be planting fresh ones in there to last another thirty years. Thank goodness we don't depend on coal because there isn't any, just like there isn't anything else.

I still find the lack of coffee and the paltry bread ration the hardest to bear but Pépé misses his Pernod more than anything. Soon he'll be bringing the donkey down for the night and since he can't go to the café for his Pernod like he used to, he'll probably start shouting about the Vichy requisition officers taking the food and drink from our mouths to transport up to the Germans, Mémé'll shout from her sick bed that

292

he'll have a heart attack if he's not careful and he'll march off through the little orchard to the outhouses where he's been cosseting secret tobacco plants. Félix doesn't like shouting so he'll take his dog Choco round to the scrub land beyond to fetch the goats home and I'll be left to gather in ducks and hens before it gets too dark to see.

Anyway, I write on this special date . . .

Here Misha paused to wonder how frank she dare be. Was there really some vast censoring office where local postal employees and spies sent doubtful envelopes? How many people knew she was half-British and had once committed a hostile act against the German military machine?

'What are you doing out there, child?' Her grandmother's voice coming from the open bedroom window behind her chair startled her.

'Sending a letter to my nuns, Mémé,' she said. 'There's time before I get the soup on.'

'Don't put in anything dangerous. You never know if the authorities'll decide to open it, you might be on their lists.'

Yes, Misha thought bitterly. 'Authorities' was a word used only by Mémé. She herself and Pépé referred to a 'they', which covered all the Vichy government, known to be German lackeys, the man who'd tried to sell Pépé a photograph of the hated Vichy Prime Minister, Pétain, the requisitions officials, some of whom were really black marketeers inflating prices and demand, and the Vichy police. These were no better than the Gestapo who held the Occupied Zone in fear. The increasing number of obviously German police of various kinds in their region could not be referred to at all.

But now they must be. Listening for Mémé's cough, Misha stared at the date at the top of the page: 11 November 1942, the day the rulers of the Occupied Zone were to sweep aside all pretence of a French government under Pétain and take over themselves. Shortly their uniforms would be everywhere. She'd have to keep her eyes on the ground as soon as she left the vineyard boundaries. At this recognition, Misha felt a rage like Pépé's begin to rise in the area of her chest. I shall say what I want to say, she thought, just this once, because soon I shan't be able to look at our own sky. She gripped the pen harder, making it scratch across the paper.

I'm not sure I'll be able to bear it with such visible reminders that we are not at home in our own land. They'll be like a blight on us with their uniforms the colour of lead and that truly distasteful green. Such ugly heavy wool, so many buttons, and the belt with *Gott mit Uns* on it. When I learned this actually means 'God with Us' I wanted to laugh. To think of God being on the side of so much slaughter and suffering!

And she hadn't remembered the uniforms until recently. But that very morning she'd woken with the clear image of the Kommandant, all dark cloth and breeches and flat blank eyes, sitting on the other side of a teatable with English sandwiches on it. She'd thought she could taste sugar in her mouth. She added quickly:

How to bear it? We did at least have the south free of taint if you didn't look too carefully, though to Pépé and his café cronies, and to *me*, the Vichy lot are already enemies. What else could they be? They've collaborated with the enemy. The awful Pétain shook hands with Hitler! To us, Vichy officials and Vichy police have *chosen* to follow the enemy with all the meanness of requisitions, their spying activities, and the way they allow a semi-official black market to operate. The police never catch the black marketeers coming out here demanding forbidden food, making prices impossible for the rest of us, flaunting their thousand-franc notes. I can hardly contain myself when I think of profiteers living like the enemy on the best of everything whilst innocent people starve and freeze to death all over Europe. Pépé says the shame of it all is that the war has brought out the worst in those who didn't know they had bad in them.

I think it's brought out a kind of simmering *anger* in

294

me and a terrible restless impatience because I am trapped here in this beautiful place, protected, fed, safe. I lie at night, comfortable in my feather bed, Frou snuggled up close, listening to the ducks muttering in their outhouse and the frogs calling, and I long to be suffering again, cold and hungry the way I was in London and in prison because then, you see, I'd be on the side of good. I'd be earning my right to freedom the way Britain is doing. It is daft, isn't it? You'd think my knowing what it's like to cross off the days to my own death would be enough, but it isn't. That little episode was such a long time ago and was such an extraordinary shock, I mostly forget it except in my dreams. Now the uniforms are going to be here to remind me.

Imagine it, if the Allies don't come soon, they'll be striding about these hillsides, under our sky, inspecting the vines and the peaches and our animals, wanting everything for themselves. My proud Pépé and Mémé and the people who've owned this land for generations will have to stand by and – even worse for Pépé! – accept the paltry payment they offer because they use our money. Did you know France has to pay them for occupying us? Billions of francs a week, Pépé says, and all our gold reserves and so on gone forever.

If only the Allies were ready to come and drive them out! This is why I'm writing to you, really. I've heard rumours some resistance organisation is starting, made up of groups of people prepared to help the Allies by sabotaging German war factories in France, so there'll be fewer tanks and 'planes when the invasion comes. The Germans call them terrorists and shoot them so it must be true. Don't write and tell Mémé, please, but I feel I'd like to be involved. There must be a way I could help. It's not a silly dream of nursing the wounded. I did have those at the beginning of the war, I admit. I've seen the real thing now and I've certainly learned I've got stamina, I can go hungry and thirsty. Best of all, most useful in that kind of work, is that I've already faced my own death and I can do so again. But down here under our Languedoc sky, in the great heat where

295

only the mosquitoes move fast and all human and animal life just *basks* – well, who'll be getting a terrorist group together?

Paris must be the centre for them and I'd like to travel up there as soon as I can. I suppose they have removed or will remove all the military and police controls from the border? I'm a bit worried it's not done yet and I'm therefore wondering if you'd be good enough to put me up for the night? I could get the lie of the land from there. I'd love to see you all again. You've been so much part of my life since the war began and you took in me and Frou. I'll look forward to meeting my Paris friends as well – the Blanchards at the café who were like my family, the old lady, Madame Libaud. She must be 91. I've been wondering if she's survived the last winter. Then there's Monsieur Steiner and the Schwarzes from the fashion house I worked in. They're Jewish and I feel an awful chill of dread whenever I think of them. Even here, the Vichy police have collected non-French Jewish people and put them in buses going to camps. What's to be their fate there? They say mothers were torn from their children and you could hear the screams all along the route . . .'

'Who did you say you were writing to?' Mémé's voice came again, startling her.

'I told you, the nuns, Mémé.' Misha dipped her pen into the inkwell and surveyed the filled pages with astonishment. She'd dared put thoughts into black and white. She felt better.

'Pépé won't let you go off to that convent a third time, don't think he will. If his heart wasn't broken already with the thought of the enemy on his land, it'd surely break if we lost you again.' Mémé put on her sick old lady tone.

'You didn't know you nearly had till I got back in one piece,' Misha called, a sudden shiver at her back.

'You were story-telling to your own flesh and blood,' Mémé reminded her. 'You travelled up to fetch that Frou, then you said you'd like another trip for a holiday and all the time you had a wild plan to get up to Paris. You lost ten thousand of your mother's francs with it!'

'Well, I think the man who was going to help me across the border lost his life, Mémé, and the priest was arrested on the same day. I don't care about the money but I did admit it afterwards, I went to the convent a second time because it's so near the border, and I had vaguely understood they were helping people get across it when I went for Frou.' With a jolt, Misha saw again Sister Honorine's ashen face in the kitchen doorway of the convent, saying, 'They have taken Father Berriat away.'

And then, shortly after arriving home, she'd learned she no longer had the same reason to try and get to Paris. Pulling out one of her mother's letters from the pile on the table, she at once returned it. Later. She'd finish writing the letter she'd never send first, then allow herself one glimpse behind the curtain before locking out the past.

Anyway, I feel that if I make some attempt at finding something useful to do, I'll be able to look my friends in England in the face after the war's over. Georgie and Patch *chose* to drive the ambulance right up to the front line, d'you remember? They saw horrors, they were imprisoned, and now I suppose they're living on subsistence rations still, two years later. If I have to say to them I suffered *paradise*!

'I think I can hear that dog barking already, it must be time to put the soup on.' Mémé had raised herself in the bed and was fiddling with the catch on the window.

Misha stood up and leaned through it to adjust the bolster on her grandmother's bed. 'Have another doze and when you wake up, you'll smell the soup.'

Grumbling, Mémé eased herself back and closed her eyes which must once have had the foxy prettiness of her daughter's. 'If you write too much, you'll have nothing left to write your next ones on. Even your mother can't get you paper.'

Gently closing the window and pushing the shutters against it, Misha sat back at her place, needing to have done with her task. 'Waiting to hear from you with my usual impatience,' she scribbled, 'I send you my most affectionate best wishes.'

Now, she thought, now I shall allow myself the moment of pain. Picking out the letter of her mother's dated June 1941, she read:

Pierre took me with him to Paris last week, darling – such a business, I can't tell you! A special train there and back just for the government people and still we had to have a pass. It was glorious at the Ritz, everyone was staying there, and all the smart set came in for cocktails before going on to Maxim's. I wore my little black, d'you remember it? A sort of halter neckline with back interest? I managed to order another from Berthe's and I got some shoes, high sandals, lots of strapping. This was lucky because I had to go to the races the second day, and the women there! Chic, darling, really chic, and me in my old stuff – and the hats! But I've done some sketches and hope to get things made up here. There are, though, going to be changes in town. I can't say anything yet but if I can, I'll get down to see you before the autumn.

By the way, I called in at the street, I knew you'd want me to. Those café Blanchards are just the same. I told them you were safe in the country but didn't say how foolish you'd been trying to ... well, I won't say what, you know what I mean. And it's not the money I care about, darling, it's your *life*. People caught trying to do what you tried have suffered very nasty fates. We nearly lost you once before and I want to see you safely married and settled with all your dashing about done with.

Pierre says we'll be going up again soon and I shall look for warm clothes for you and Félix. Your navy jumper and trousers have had too much contact with hens and ducks, darling, and do try and find a decent hairdresser in Montpellier. Stop scratching at those old mosquito bites on your arms and legs as well. You'll

298

have permanent scars and how will that look in evening dress or bathing suit?

By the way, dear, Madame Libaud told me they'd heard your professor was lost in the Channel trying to get to England last year. I said to her, Madame Libaud, if the poor man chose to be so foolish! After all, we have signed an armistice with Germany and it's England we're at war with now.

Yes, Misha thought, refolding the letter and adding it to the others in its place. Finally, she put the postcard from Marseille on top and thus the curtain was returned with the pain behind it.

She'd taken the writing box to the bedroom she shared with Félix, she in her mother's childhood bed, he in their Aunt Yvonne's, when she heard Choco's joyous bark announcing the return of the menfolk. She was in the kitchen just as the dog and Félix burst in. Félix was shouting, his braying incoherent boy's shout: 'Come quick, Misha, come quick! Dead man in field.'

Chapter 43

At first sight, the scene was the same as on any other evening. All was still in the smokey dusk, the sky turquoise and pink. Beyond the little orchard and across the lane, Misha could see the big field rising gently with its long rows of vine bushes in their winter hibernation. Up by the blank ribbon of the Palavas road were the silhouettes of the donkey and cart.

Setting off to run behind her brother and his eager mongrel dog, she arrived breathless at the spot where Pépé knelt in the rustcoloured earth next to the body of a man. Still disbelieving, she gazed at a dead man on their land. He was outstretched, face down, one arm twisted under him. His suit was of a respectable brown tweed covered in their earth and beside him lay a brown trilby and a suitcase.

'Not long dead,' Pépé announced. 'Must have had some sort of accident, but what sort, that's what we need to know.' Sitting back on his heels, skin, corduroys, beret all the same colour as the familiar soil, he passed Misha a wallet and a thick envelope. 'The case has a change of clothes, shaving kit, so he's not a tramp and he's not old. Blokes his age don't just drop dead, and he's not been hit by anything motorized. When did folks around here last have petrol? So you read out his papers for me, girl, and then we'll decide what to do.'

Hair prickling at the back of her neck, Misha held the items Pépé had taken from the jacket of a dead man and extracted an identity card from the wallet. ' "Name, Bertrand Baudry,"' she read. ' "Date of birth, 17 March

1910. Colour of eyes, brown, colour of hair, chestnut."' She
didn't look at the photograph but gave a cry of relief when
she picked out a business card in the name of some
company. 'It's all right, Pépé,' she said, 'he's a salesman, a
traveller in agricultural products. He was coming to sell you
something, Pépé, and here . . .' Fumbling, she held out a
folded piece of paper and a snapshot. 'A little drawing of
a girl, probably his daughter, and a picture of his wife or
someone. I shan't look at anything else, it's obvious he's a
family man.'

There was silence as Pépé digested this information. The
donkey yawned and a few seabirds wheeled overhead.
The sky had turned deep pink behind the slopes of the
Sérieys's place. 'Where's his bicycle if he's a traveller?' Pépé
said, clamping his pipe between his teeth. 'Boy, you
searched a good way along the road?'

Félix put an arm round the donkey's neck and nodded.
He wore his blankest face, Misha saw, his pale blue eyes so
like their father's darting about in fear, tufts of red hair
sticking up out from under his beret.

'I don't like it,' Pépé said, getting to his feet with a groan
of pain. 'How'd he die? Where's he come from with no
bicycle? Maybe he's running from something, or someone.
Maybe he's a spy. This is a war-zone now, girl. Me and the
boy could bury him deep and no damn' police will come
here asking questions then . . .'

'Wait, Pépé,' Misha said, 'look, this package, it's money,
I recognise the soft feel of it, bank-notes, don't do anything
hasty.' With a finger edged into the envelope, she made out
some high figures. She didn't want to recognise this. It
seemed too much for a salesman. 'Yes,' she said, 'So it's all
right, you see. He is a salesman. These are his takings.'

Thousand-franc notes they were, she thought, and she
mustn't let Pépé realise it. Today of all days there was
enough anger in Pépé to make him do something very
foolish. 'Felix had better fetch his bicycle and go for the
village police, they'll see to everything. Let's cover him up,
shall we? It's hardly decent to leave him exposed. Just think
of his poor wife . . .' Dazed, she stared down at the man's
body which Choco was still inspecting with excited dog-

301

interest. 'Call off Choco, Félix,' she said absently. 'He's licking something, maybe there's blood . . . it's not very nice. You must go for the police.'

They all heard the man groan. Delighted, Choco barked and snuffled around his face. And the man spoke. 'No police, please, Monsieur Tellier,' he said. He knew who they were.

Chapter 44

'You're all very kind, including your dog. It was he who woke me from my concussion and kept me warm whilst your menfolk were bringing me down in the cart.'

The man's words seemed to hang in the warm air of the kitchen. Mémé, up from her sick bed long since, dropped her ladle and turned round, hand to mouth in a signal of dismay. Misha knew her own face must echo this. Because the man had a slight accent. Which one? she thought, frantic.

Mémé must have had the same thought. 'You are not a local man, Monsieur?' she asked.

Misha placed a dish very carefully before the man at the head of their table as he replied, 'Oh, I go all over the country.' His grubby hand seemed to tremble as he picked up a spoon, replaced it and took up the wallet Misha had put there. 'Here's my card,' he said, passing it to Mémé. 'I was making for your vineyard when something went on my bicycle. You are the Domaine Tellier?'

It's in the U sound, Misha thought, forgetting to listen, and the R. They weren't quite French. Heat spread up from her toes and filled her chest, a red stain of heat that would mark her skin and betray her. Making for your vineyard. And the accent. German. German police. They were here already. She was going to be rearrested as one of their examples. They liked to set examples to instill fear and submission in the rest of the population.

There was sweat on her upper lip. She could feel it and he would see it. And in her bedroom was her writing box

303

with a letter ready for a stamp. Every page, every line of this, would be enough to incriminate her. 'Mémé,' she said, 'will you slip out and call in the men? They must have seen to the animals by now. I'll go and pack up my writing box on the terrace, I don't want the paper getting damp. Will you excuse us, Monsieur?'

Eager to comply, certain no doubt that outside there could be a whispered conversation about *accents*, Mémé made her way around the stranger's chair and through the kitchen door.

'Mademoiselle! May we have a few words alone?'

Horrified, Misha looked down at the man. He was smiling up at her. He had a fine set of teeth, she saw. He'd been able to afford dentists then. So he was no humble traveller. Here was her confirmation. Stifled with the desire to move towards the door and flight, she felt incapable of taking her eyes from his smiling, ordinary face, a nice face with a moustache and brown eyes. She realised he was offering her a piece of paper from his wallet. The drawing. He couldn't know she'd already seen it. Unable to abandon the usual courtesies due to a stranger, she took it and looked once more at the sketch of a girl sitting at a café.

He said, 'My friend claimed you knew that café very well.'

Staring, she saw the words BRASSERIE LIPP behind the girl. Not only that, she was wearing a puffy jacket and looked like the Michelin Man. She had bobbed hair under a beret and her eyes were far too big. Underneath, by the leg of a rather crooked table, were the initials of the amateur artist: P.D.C. And a date, October 1942. She hadn't known Philippe David Constantin could draw. And she thought he'd died. 'Where is he?' she said, suddenly blind.

The stranger didn't answer this but from his mouth issued the sweetest English words Misha had ever heard. 'Are your grandparents and brother to be trusted absolutely?'

'They are rock-solid,' she replied, and laughed. Her own English slipped out easily though it was so long since she'd spoken it. 'I thought he was lost in the Channel,' she said, giddy with shock. Her heart swelled. 'Where is he, please?'

304

'In London,' said the Englishman, taking up his spoon and trying to gather soup into it. 'Sometimes in Paris.'

'Paris,' repeated Misha in disbelief. 'Oh, I should have known you were English straight away! You looked nice, like an English air-raid warden or something.' Falling into a chair beside him, she stared at his ordinary face with its dusting of red soil from their field and said, 'Has he sent you here? Does he need me?'

'He needs to know you're in good health. I promised him I'd see if I could manage it when in the area on other business. Thing is, didn't expect it to be so soon. I've had no chance yet to begin what I came for. Had a bad landing, you see . . .' His voice faded and he dropped the spoon, letting his head fall forward.

'It's all right,' Misha cried, leaping to her feet, 'we'll get a doctor, we'll look after you. I can't tell you how honoured Pépé will be to offer you shelter. And trust? You can trust us all with your life, that's how much!'

She was trying to ease his shoulders back when the kitchen door burst open and Félix stood there, gesturing, agitated. 'Félix,' she cried, 'help me get this poor man to our bedroom. He can have my bed and one of us must run for a doctor. Get Pépé too, he's going to have such a wonderful surprise!'

From the darkness of the terrace, Pépé appeared behind Félix. 'Pépé!' she called. She knew she was shrieking, shrieking with joy at her news.'

Behind Pépé stood some other men. Pépé took the safety catch off his hunting gun and said, 'Here's your prisoner, Messieurs.'

Afterwards, she couldn't remember how many policemen had come for him. Two or three, she thought. She'd had to make way for them. They didn't take long. The Englishman's face had become the colour of Mémé's napkins as one took him by each arm. So there'd been three, because one stood in the doorway to keep Félix out of the way. He was dancing up and down with excitement. She shouted, 'The man needs a doctor!'

305

He groaned as they dragged him across the floor, one leg trailing out as if broken.

Misha watched this trailing leg disappear into the night as Pépé said, 'That soup hot, woman?' He lodged his gun with a clatter by the sink, a triumphant grin on his face for a job well done.

Unable to reply, her face as white as the stranger's had been, Mémé managed to stir herself from the doorway also and move to her place at the stove.

The door slammed. Félix lumbered to his chair, grinning too. Remembering to remove his beret, he went back to the door to hang it up.

Speechless, Misha watched this tableau of normal suppertime events. Then perhaps Pépé noticed the silence because he glanced at her. 'Pépé,' she said carefully, 'Pépé, our stranger's an Englishman looking for shelter. He's been flown to the area, I think. In an aeroplane. So he must be from one of those underground resistance groups we've heard about.'

Pépé stood up. His face had turned to stone, its ruddy colour ash. 'I thought he was a profiteer,' he said, 'a black market criminal with his packet of money, corrupting innocent people and I thought – there he was out on the Palavas road, looking for us to sell him something . . .'

He began to weep with noisy men's sobs, his whole body shaking.

Chapter 45

Lying in the hospital bed, the Englishman looked better. The police had allowed the doctors to put his ankle in a splint, he said, smiling up at Misha. They wanted him well enough for their questions.

'Pépé's planning to get you out of here,' she whispered, though they were alone in the small room. 'Once you can hobble with a stick, he's going to offer the policeman Grapas, some olive oil and a goose for New Year to arrange it. He's the one who let me bring you the suitcase.'

'Don't let your grandad even think of it.' The Englishman stopped smiling and coughed, trying to sit up. 'Much too difficult. Please. To them and to your family, I must remain a French travelling salesman possibly involved in the black market. If I can manage to make everyone believe it, I'll get away with a fine, maybe a few months in prison.' Urgently taking hold of her arm, he said, 'Did you find the package in that field?'

'The money? Pépé's hidden it in the wine press. It's so much, we realised you needed it for the underground work. They'll never find it, not if they come and torture him for it. I can't tell you how grief-stricken he was, knowing he'd betrayed an Englishman...' Remembering Pépé's desolation, Misha felt her eyes fill with tears. 'He says the money'll be needed for explosives and things. He never told me he'd heard rumours in his café about a parachute landing out past the swamps a couple of days ago...' She wiped her eyes with the sleeve of her jumper.

'Please don't cry, Misha, or how shall I ever able to report

307

to my friend when I get back that I made you cry? I hope he'll forgive me when he learns I've put you at risk by dragging my damned leg as far as the vineyard. God knows why I fell so badly. Everything was going well, parachute opened up nicely, no wind – but somehow I veered off course straight into a ditch. And no sign of the chaps supposed to meet me . . .'

'I'm almost glad you had an accident if it means I have news of . . . I mustn't say his name, must I, nor ever know yours, but you see, thinking someone to be drowned . . . He is alive and he's in London? Please tell me again. And he's doing the same work as you?'

'My dear.' He sat back against the pillow and released her arm. 'The less you know from me, the better. But he is indeed based in London and part of the same organisation. This year a number of the people it's recruited and trained've been got into France. Some have been caught by the enemy already. They know, you see, that we're everywhere, and they fear us. They watch and they wait and they pay for betrayal, but there'll always be more of us with the same objective – sabotage now and training in arms for the day the Allies invade.'

'To free France,' Misha said. 'I wasn't mad, was I, to think I might find something to do in Paris. I've been fretting here in this lovely place, belonging to a family for the first time in my life and restless, restless! I thought, I knew, I wouldn't be able to bear it when they took over here . . .'

The man closed his eyes and coughed. 'Misha,' he said. 'I have something to say to you and there isn't much time. Have you a good memory?'

'Too good, really,' Misha said, leaning towards him. 'There are things you push away, painful things, you want to forget and think you have until you waken one morning with a sense of something awful having happened, you can't quite remember what it is . . .'

'I think my friend will be glad to hear you do not forget.' The brown eyes opened suddenly and he smiled. 'I have also to tell you that he remains your friend, if ever you should need him although so much time has passed since you met.'

'Tell him me and Frou'll be waiting,' she said. She wiped her eyes again, clumsily, and saw the policeman Grapas standing in the doorway with his fingers raised. Five minutes left.

'Listen now, Misha,' the Englishman said. 'Afterwards, remember that if at any stage you feel uneasy or think you are being watched, go home without hurrying, without looking back. Remember also you know nothing of me but that a Monsieur Baudry, a travelling salesman, had some kind of accident near your top field and you found him there concussed. If you follow my instructions absolutely, there is nothing to fear. Then you must go back home to your grandparents and resolve to go on keeping safe. This I must tell my friend, you see, or I shall never dare admit to him that I did call at a certain vineyard, finding there stout hearts and a fighting spirit which I made use of for our cause.'

Misha went on listening until the five minutes had ticked by and Grapas signalled that she must leave Philippe's friend to his fate in police hands.

The Englishman's instructions had been very clear. Misha found the café he'd described at the left-hand turning off the main street of Palavas, facing the beach. She was in good time. Nine minutes to noon. The woman he'd called his contact would wait until half-past before leaving and when she heard Misha say the passwords instead of the expected Englishman speaking almost perfect French, she'd show no surprise. Resistance workers were trained to show no surprise. They were trained in England, at special centres, to keep a cool head and do many other things besides, use explosives, guns, parachutes. Philippe was one of them. That he was alive was already too much to take in but she felt that if she had not thought him dead, she'd have known he was working to help free France.

As she was. This realisation gave her an inward tremble she mustn't reveal. And all was in order. There was the woman, tall, wearing a bottle green suit with matching hat and sitting at a table near the door. She was reading a book and at her feet was a housewife's shopping bag. Fortunately the place was full of people taking imitation aperitifs and ordering meagre lunches. No one would notice either of them.

Misha strolled to the same table and sat down rather noisily, scraping back another chair and instructing Félix to sit in it. It'd been her own idea to bring him and act the part of a bossy sister with a brother not quite right in the head. 'We'll see if they have anything nice for you to drink,' she said, and smiled across to the woman in the green suit. 'This is my favourite place in the summer but I've never been to Palavas in the winter before.'

The woman looked up, as if startled. She wasn't supposed to be startled. Her mouth opened and closed, as if preparing the answer.

Misha thought hers had done the same. Because Georgie's face was looking back at her.

Chapter 46

'It's my first visit here,' the vision in the green suit said at last, an ordinary reply, the right reply. What was extraordinary was that Georgie made it – and in perfect French. Also that her eyes, meeting her dear friend's in such unlikely circumstances, were so perfectly blank. Then she opened the handbag on her knees, put her book inside, took out some sous and dropped them on the table. Getting to her feet, she caught up the shopping bag. This was where Misha was to have idly slipped the package. It was not the right action. Nor did she expect to see Georgie move past her.

'Felix,' she said, getting up also, 'I think I've left my purse behind. We'll have to go and fetch it.' It was fortunate she'd brought Félix. She could go on being bossy so no one would see she didn't know what to do next. She wanted very badly to shout, Georgie, it's me, *me*! Instead, the package of money like lead under her jumper, she touched Félix's arm. 'Come on, darling, it won't take a minute, I know you're thirsty.'

No customer in the café was watching them play out this tableau but she made herself finish it, taking Félix's arm and *not hurrying* to the door. Here, with the door still swinging behind Georgie, she understood – Georgie meant them to meet outside. Mouth open in a silent cry of distress at her own slowness, she flew into the street. But Georgie wasn't in it.

They searched every street in the small fishing port, Misha

311

trying to look casual, Félix looking worried because he knew his sister was worried.

She told herself she hadn't dreamed the last twenty-four hours. The Englishman existed. He was a member of an underground organisation. Georgie was too. The clues to this dizzying fact had been in the letter from Dorset. Georgie had been learning French. She was working on something. Yes, Georgie, Misha thought, turning from street to beach and back again, yes, I accepted it instantly, that you were my Englishman's contact. But why couldn't you accept that I was yours?

And how had Georgie been able to disappear so quickly? Also, what was she to do with the package containing millions of francs needed for the support of a new underground group in the area? Without the money, nothing could be bought on the black market, no bribes paid, no rent for hiding places, no food for the members to live on.

Turning a last time to look towards the café where she'd actually seen a Georgie restored to her old beauty, her excitement of the previous evening seemed far off. A chill desolation was lodged in its place. She'd made a mistake. She'd let down the Englishman. And Georgie. Where was Georgie now? How could she have left like that without a blink of recognition?

Somehow, she herself would have to get into the hospital again and admit she'd failed. Perhaps the money ought to be taken to some other contact? She'd do that. She'd do anything the Englishman thought necessary. She'd also go back to the café every day at the same time until there was no more hope Georgie would ever return.

Chapter 47

Mémé was standing in the chill air of the terrace, holding up the lamp up for them to see, Choco having announced their return from Palavas. In the kitchen the soup was hot. Frou was curled around the wine carafe on the table, her usual habit to ensure a proper greeting.

Misha was holding the cat in her arms as Mémé launched instantly into her own story without so much as a word of reprimand for their lateness. 'They came for Pépé just after you two left,' she said. 'They wanted to know where the money was. Pépé denied he'd seen any and they said in that case why did he suspect the man of being a black marketeer? They said he'd told them there was a wad of money in the suitcase and Pépé kept denying it so they took him up to the top field to look and then they came down and said the man was no travelling salesman, he was a British spy with false papers and we needn't think they didn't know you were British and that's why Pépé was helping a British spy.' Stopping for breath and coughing, she mechanically laid out soup plates and stirred the pot.

Turning to stone with a warm Frou cradled against the package of lead under her jumper, Misha said, 'I've never denied having a British father, they know it at the Commissariat anyway, what'd be the point?' Mechanically, like her grandmother, she went to the larder to fetch the plate of Frou's fish and rice Mémé had mixed. This she duly placed on the draining board. The three of them watched Frou gobble it, as Choco did, his chin resting on the edge. 'He's had his,' Mémé said.

'Are the goats and hens in, the ducks, the donkey ...?'

'It gave me something to do, how could I sit in that chair more than a second?'

Félix gave his dog Frou's plate to clean and suppertime proceeded with its usual momentum. Misha and Félix hung their berets on the pegs, they rinsed their hands in the bowl in the sink, they sat down and Mémé ladled their soup.

'You shouldn't have been waiting in the cold,' Misha murmured. 'I'm sorry we're late, things didn't go as expected.'

And then Mémé began to wail: 'Oh, whatever are they doing to Pépé?'

At this, Félix gave one of his braying shouts of distress. The hair stood up on the back of Misha's neck. She said, sensibly, 'We'll have our soup and save some for Pépé because he'll be back soon. Or maybe I'd better go to the police station and point out that of course I'm half-British but they've never bothered about it before, and as for Pépé. He can't even read, I'll tell them, he wouldn't be any good at helping spies. And he's an old man, they must let him come home, I'll say, I'll start to cry and that'll settle it. I tell you what, Félix must come with me on Pépé's bicycle, I'll ride his and Pépé'll be able to ride back with me on the cross-bar. We'll start off first thing, eh? But we won't have to, he'll be here shortly. Félix, tell Choco to go and wait in the lane, so we'll hear him come.'

They hadn't been able to eat the soup though it was full of precious rice. They stoked up the stove and put the pot over it. They'd enjoy it properly with Pépé. Meanwhile, Misha fetched some of their bedding and they installed themselves to wait a little longer in their chairs at the table, eiderdowns as shawl and comfort.

They were all dozing when Choco's bark came echoing through the little orchard. Misha sprang to her feet, grabbing the lamp and shouting with pleasure and relief. 'He's back, it's all right.'

It wasn't Pépé. It was the policeman, Grapas. He didn't speak to her. He went past her to where Mémé was trembling in the doorway. He said, 'You'd better tell the girl to get out of here and never return.'

Mémé showed no sign of having taken this in. She said, 'My husband, Monsieur?'

Grapas shrugged. 'I cannot help your husband, Madame. He's been taken to a different department. It's off our hands, the whole matter. And I say again, the girl must get out fast. A letter has already been received at the Commissariat denouncing her as a British spy, and now with that bloke last night . . . They're looking for his parachute so if you're hiding it, get it burned quick. Goodnight to you.'

He shook Mémé's hand but didn't look at Misha. In a few seconds, the sound of his footsteps through the little orchard had faded away.

Chapter 48

They half-packed the haversack Félix used for fishing, but what and how much should she take with her? 'It's lucky I'm wearing the jumper and trousers,' Misha said. 'And these walking shoes my mother insisted on buying me right in the middle of the Germans taking over Paris.' She was trying to be calm because Mémé was shaking and coughing so much she couldn't roll up the second sweater tight enough to force it in. Two changes of underclothes took so much space.

On the bed, they'd lain out toothbrush, flannel and a tiny towel, and these still had to go in. In the doorway, Félix suddenly said, 'My old rubber cape,' and went to his chest of drawers to take it out. Offering this, he sat on his bed, eyes losing their moment of eagerness and returning to bewilderment as he looked from his weeping grandmother to his sister in her whirlwind of activity.

'Félix,' Misha said, 'may I borrow your bike instead of Pépé's? It's much lighter and it's got a better carrier, the cape'll fit there . . .'

Dropping her assortment of toilet articles, Mémé suddenly cried, 'And where d'you think you're going on this bicycle if it's not up to the Sérieys' place, I ask you?'

'I don't know, Mémé, I can't seem to think. I'll have a bottle of water with a drop of wine in it, please, and any food that keeps.' She had done all this before, she thought. Maybe the first time was training for this worse one. Because it was going to be worse. She wouldn't be blindly following thousands of other refugees with the simple aim

316

to get south. There wasn't anything much further south than this little vineyard.

'Why not the Sérieys? Old Sérieys is a decent man. Surely we can trust him, from such an old family, all that land for generations? If you weren't so fussy, you'd be engaged to the son by now.'

Misha tried to laugh. They'd laughed about Julien Sérieys often in the past, in a nice way, for he and she were friends. 'You know he's shorter than me, Mémé, I can't help feeling awkward beside him. And he's overweight. In a man, it's not right somehow. He's too fond of his own jokes as well.' He was also too fond of her. She had to be careful not to encourage him. She liked him as a brother, they'd had good times together. He'd help her if he dared, she supposed, staring blindly at the swollen haversack. How had it come to this? How could she leave Mémé with her bad chest and all the daily tasks to do with only Félix to help? And what about Pépé, in a different department? Department of what?

'Puppy fat,' her grandmother was saying. 'And you make the boy nervous. Think of the size of their property, with another great vineyard up in the hills.'

'Think of his mother, Mémé,' Misha replied. 'She'd never allow him to marry a Protestant, and a half-British one at that. Think of the life I'd have to live if she did, that awful, stifling bourgeois life, going to church, confessing sins I don't have, being correct, always correct. Terrible! No dreams, no hopes, no freedom. Having to have those showy, perfect manners that hide a stone-cold heart. Perhaps Julien's mother is the one who's denounced me.' How extraordinary it was, this new war word applied to herself. 'She hardly needs the reward they pay for denunciation, but she hates Anglo-Saxon Protestants and probably thinks my father's a Freemason, whatever they are.'

'Catholic, Protestant, when did you last go to church? Your father's a heathen, your mother not much better, let alone Pépé. A woman can pretend what she wants if she has to and oh, whatever shall we do?'

'I don't know, Mémé.' Overwhelmed by sudden weakness, Misha sank on to her bed and drew Mémé's plump body

317

down beside her. 'Let's try and keep calm and plan things sensibly. I think you should go up to Monsieur Sérieys, or send Félix for him, he'll come here, in fact you'll have to promise me, I shan't be able to leave unless you do . . .' Her voice tailing off, she thought of her letter to the nuns where she'd put in black and white her restless desire to abandon her paradise. Beware of getting what you want, that was the old saying. Well, now she was getting what she wanted no longer. This forced reality had brought terror with it. And she'd already failed in her chance to be useful. Georgie was out there somewhere, needing the millions of francs that were still a lead weight under her own jumper. These she must hide also. She must think of everything. 'Monsieur Sérieys will let you have one of his men to help with the animals,' she said. 'Perhaps even to do some of Pépé's pruning. He's very much respected round here. He must go to the police station and demand Pépé be sent home. He must tell them Pépé's incapable of being a spy, he works hard day and night and anyway, he's too old to be put in prison . . .'

'If you don't hide at the Sérieys place, you'll be the one in prison, child. You've been denounced by some wicked heart . . .' Hands to her face, Mémé was a heap of trembling flesh, her red hair escaping from its bun.

Yes, Misha thought. If I don't run away, I shall be in prison again. 'I think I shouldn't stay locally, though, Mémé. I'd better get up to live with my mother in Paris. Our police won't tell the Paris ones about me, will they? I can't be that important. There won't be notices up about me all over the country!' She tried to laugh again, putting a comforting arm around the woman who was the shape of an English cottage loaf and as pleasing to look at. 'Whatever happens,' she said, 'you and Pépé must be here to welcome me when I get home. And you must somehow get on with your usual routine. I mean, what'll Pépé say if there's no soup on for his homecoming?'

'What'll he say if I've let you go off on some train journey across the country to a city where there's more enemy than people? You're not even sure your mother's gone back to her old flat or if she's still with that man of hers.'

318

'I'll be all right, my café friends'll help me . . .' Suddenly getting to her feet, Misha knew she'd already decided. There'd be resistance groups in Paris. 'Look,' she said, 'it's already light, Mémé. Félix must be seeing to the animals. I'll take his bicycle as far as Nîmes station. He can collect it later. Nîmes police won't have been alerted about this particular British spy yet, will they? I'll be on the early train if I hurry . . .'

They couldn't have heard Choco's bark because Félix startled them, lumbering into the bedroom with the bucket of goat's milk rattling in his hand. 'Man coming!' he yelled.

Mémé cried, 'Run, child, run!'

Chapter 49

And so Misha arrived at the Sérieys place without bicycle or haversack. At first, this seemed preferable. On foot, in her old jumper and trousers, she'd look as if she'd come to spend some time with her friend Julien as she'd done often before. She was a little earlier than usual, that was all.

Julien was about to leave on his morning ride. She could hear his horse clattering on the cobbles so skirted straight round to the back of the house and the stable yard.

He was saddling up the big grey horse and called out with delight when he saw her. 'What a bit of luck, Misha,' he said, dropping the reins and running across to shake her hand. 'D'you know, I was coming to call at your place and ask if you'd like to take a ride out with me. I've got all day, if you have. Long as I'm back by six for *Maman*'s cocktail party. You can come to that too if you want.' He placed a friend's kiss on each of her cold cheeks. She returned them on his full warm ones and waited for this astonishing remark to sink in. 'A cocktail party, Julien?' she asked. 'I thought no one had parties any more.'

'It's mother, you know what she is, she's invited the new Nazi Kommandant for drinks this evening no matter how much dad and me protest these chaps aren't quite the new aristocracy and anyway she has no more daughters at home to be married off.'

Staring blankly into his familiar face, with its distinctive black eyebrows that almost met over the strong nose, she said, 'It's a party for the enemy, Julien?' She could find no other answer. She'd been expecting to start at once on the story of Pépé's arrest and the denunciation, the urgency of her need to hide, but she couldn't hide here. And she'd even been going to trust Julien about the Englishman!

'Well, my father isn't keen, but I think it's probably better to keep on the right side of 'em. We take a drink together and they leave us alone afterwards, that's how I see it. Anyway, you know what my mother's like. Born practically fascist, she was. I can say that though I love her! She actually sees 'em as saviours of our dear old France. She wants some distant time back before there were socialists and communists wanting to slit the throats of people like us.' He took her hand again and said, 'Come on, help me saddle up Stella, you're best on her, then I tell you what, Mish, Geneviève's got some real coffee German orderlies brought up yesterday with other bits and pieces to help with the party. Shall we get her to put some in a flask? I must get out to the Lodève area. I think it's where I lost that leather jacket I'm rather fond of.'

Unable to protest, Misha felt herself being led towards the kitchen, gazing with horror at his thick-set figure, at the back of his handsome head. There was confidence and ease in every line of him, as it was in the beautiful pale stone house he'd one day inherit. This sat solidly in its place amongst the slopes of reddish earth under the vast empty sky, where it belonged. And enemy officers were going to be received in it as guests! The fact amused Julien. But he'd never been faced with hunger and death in the hands of the enemy or been pursued by machine-gun fire from aeroplanes. That she had, seemed to add to her charm for him. He wanted to look after her as if she were some rescued kitten, when she neither needed nor wanted to be looked after anymore. She'd grown beyond it. And she wanted to act. This was the measure of the gulf between them.

'Yes,' he was saying, 'you can almost see my mother's reasoning. The Nazis are the new powerful ones who also happen to be fighting Russian communists, thus confirming her view of them as conquering heroes. See, Mish?' He paused by the basement steps and put a brotherly hand on her arm, a gesture permitted since they'd agreed to remain friends after his marriage proposal in the summer. 'Still,

321

we'll get some real coffee out of this little do, so it's worth it.' He was smiling at her but Misha couldn't look at him.

'No, Julien,' she said carefully, 'it isn't. And I can't actually stay, not even for coffee.' At twenty-five, he was still a boy! She released herself and got as far as the corner of the house when she caught sight of a car approaching the main drive, a military car with a swastika flag flying from it. Turning on her heel, she began to run for the steps.

'Mish, whatever is the matter?' Julien was too surprised to move.

'I've been denounced, Julien, and Pépé's been arrested. Please don't tell your mother I'm here and come and open the cellar door, open it, Julien!'

Chapter 50

'Misha, you will have to trust us, my son and I. You have no choice. As for my poor wife, well, try and understand her if you can.' Seated opposite on a wine cask, Julien's father stuffed his pipe with tobacco and kept talking.

Misha, from her stool in a corner of the cellar by a row of some important vintage red, made herself concentrate on his words and the rather nice smell of pipe smoke. Over their heads was the murmur of voices from Madame Sérieys's yellow salon where the enemy was taking cocktails. At the unmistakable echo of laughter, Monsieur Sérieys raised his voice. 'My wife, you see, like many others of our class, welcomed the Nazi invasion. I know an English girl like you will find this hard to understand. But we French had socialist governments in the thirties giving power to the workers – or the mob, Misha! Imagine, the very kind of people who organised revolutions and slit the throats of the aristocracy. Royalty, for that matter. Think of France in 1789, think of the Bolsheviks and the Russian ruling classes!'

In the cellar darkness, Misha could see him smiling gently. He had the same untidy black eyebrows as Julien, the same short plump body. The same protective charm also, she thought. He was a proper husband and father who'd never query the need for a frivolous hat or a new pair of shoes.

'And so today she welcomes the Nazi Kommandant to our house with genuine pleasure. She doesn't choose to recognise what's behind the terrible illusion of good manners and correctness these high-ranking officers bring with them. Can I condemn my wife for her choice? I cannot, Misha. For I too have shaken hands with the enemy. D'you know my greatest shame up there just now?' He paused and leaned across to her. 'It was the little tremble of excitement I felt to know my cellar harbours a British spy. Yes, that is my shame, dear girl, because I've lived the last two and a half years with my head firmly in the sand.'

Eyes pricking with fatigue, Misha gazed at the blur of whiteness from his shirt. Refusing to accept the truth that France was an abjectly conquered nation had been sensible of him. Most people had done the same because they didn't have Pépé's nobility of heart. Monsieur Sérieys at least had the excuse of age. His son did not. Julien should be feeling a raging humiliation which forced him to try and throw out the Nazis who defiled his land.

'You realise one of your own neighbours has denounced you as a British spy?' Monsieur Sérieys was saying. 'I learned that in the town today making enquiries about your grandad. I learned much else besides that I'd rather not know. I've been hiding up here in the vineyard quite a time. I understood that also today.'

'I wonder who it was?' Misha said. But she didn't wonder. It didn't matter. What mattered was the sound of laughter from the room upstairs. There'd be smoke drifting from fat cigars into Madame Sérieys's yellow silk drapes, dark wool and breeches settled into the yellow silk chairs. If she were not so weary, she wouldn't be able to sit still because maybe Madame Sérieys might decide to show the guests her husband's rare vintages and therefore reveal what was rarer, a spy.

'This afternoon, I felt I had aged ten years,' Monsieur Sérieys said, pouring himself a second glass of something. 'Because I had to admit to myself that we have our very own French Gestapo now – we have adopted brutality instead of German music, order and discipline . . .'

'And clean streets,' Misha said, remembering another conversation from another world – with Philippe, in a Paris as yet untainted.

'Perhaps we do have the clean streets,' he said, smiling. 'Still, it seems I might be able to negotiate the release of your grandfather in due course. Nothing's certain. People are questioned and requestioned for no good reason, thrown into some prison and more or less forgotten. Many are passed to a different department where the sadists and thugs get their pleasure. Whatever happens, child, I shall not let your Pépé be forgotten. I spent a couple of hours with our old family lawyer and asked him to start talking a bit too freely about the disappearance of the Tellier grand-daughter – you, Misha. To spread the rumour, in fact, that you've left your innocent grandad to his fate and've run off to your resistance cronies in the hills, the ones probably involved with the Englishman. They'll be paying more for rumours now because they're terrified of an Allied invasion on our south coast after the successes in North Africa mean there's only the Mediterranean to cross. That's why they've taken over down here, and they'll be absolutely ruthless with any local resistance groups preparing to help the Allies. But they don't yet realise how much our hills and plateau areas can hide . . .'

'So British agents being sent over by 'plane are doing work that really counts?' Misha asked. She wanted to be sure the Englishman hadn't risked his life for nothing; that Georgie, somewhere needing hundreds of thousands of francs for the cause, wasn't also risking hers in vain. Oh, Georgie, she thought, where did you run to?

'Certainly,' he said. 'It would be pointless for Frenchmen to face the Nazi tanks and modern armaments with a few hunting shotguns in their hands. Proper weapons are needed, explosives, and these must come from Britain. Of course, I haven't asked you, Misha, if you actually have been helping bring in arms. If I'm discovered buying you a new identity, you see, I'll be due for the same treatment as your Pépé.' He laughed.

Misha didn't answer. A sickening weariness threatened to overtake her from somewhere in the pit of her stomach. Monsieur Serieys was a kind, protective sort of man but an immense gap of different experiences separated them, as it did her and Julien.

She might be going to vomit. She wouldn't mind. Then he'd leave her in peace to listen for the sound of voices

325

coming from the yellow salon over her head. They must be like the ones questioning Pépé. She'd thus be nearer to him, better able to imagine the cell, the chill air, Pépé being stubborn. Pépé would never give in. Please, Pépé, she thought, tell them anything, everything. It won't matter. Get home to Mémé and Félix and I'll be all right with my new false identity. She hoped Pépé realised, as she did, that the Englishman was already lost.

Geneviève, the housekeeper and former nurse to Julien and his elder sisters, had made her up a bed in the far corner of the cellar, behind the dustiest, most ancient wines. Geneviève was also to be trusted apparently. Misha knew she had to accept her help anyway. She couldn't stay in the cellar without it and she couldn't move outside until she had a different identity, a different appearance. The fact that the tiny, bony Geneviève kept clutching her arm with such fervour during the bed-making process, hissing, 'The Allies are coming to free us?' and 'They've said so on the BBC?' was, she thought, as much as she could ask for. And she was inexpressibly tired. She found the energy though to sit up in the mound of feather bedding to eat four slices of enemy bread and butter. This wasn't of course really enemy property, as Geneviève pointed out, it was French, purchased by force with French money and they were therefore only taking their due.

The bread she followed by one of Geneviève's hot toddies, which had honey in it. She got to the end of the glass just as she finished recounting what she'd learned from the BBC broadcast announcing the Allies invasion of North Africa.

Geneviève then insisted on tucking her into the bed, wrapping a blanket smelling of lavender around her shoulders because it was a cold night. 'Tomorrow you'll have the coffee,' she was muttering. 'My boy made me promise. "Coffee for Mademoiselle Misha," he said, "and anything tempting you can find make her swallow it, she's too thin, but no meat, mind . . ."'

'Where is Julien?' Misha said. She'd temporarily forgotten

him after he left on his horse at lunchtime, still wanting to search for something he'd lost over Lodève way.

'Not back from fishing,' Geneviève said, placing a precious torch on the nearest cask. 'You can use this if you get frightened, but remember batteries is like gold dust . . .'

Fishing! Misha thought. She was still thinking this, that Julien away fishing on such a day only proved his frivolous character, when she must have fallen into a deep sleep.

The sound of a voice woke her, a voice saying over and over, 'Oh, my dear boy, my darling boy, whatever shall we do . . .'

Struggling with too much blanket, Misha grabbed the torch and was halfway into her trousers before she made out Geneviève moving towards her dragging a bundle.

'Quick,' she hissed. 'Help me get this hidden.'

The bundle was half as big as Geneviève herself and covered in thick canvas. Taking hold of it by the rope which tied it, Misha hissed, 'Where?' She hadn't heard the door open, and wouldn't again find it so easy to fall asleep. This she had time to think before Geneviève snatched the torch and pushed her to her knees. 'Take this key,' she said, 'and open the lock you'll find near the floor behind that crate.'

Feeling her way, Misha's fingers caught on rough wood and an iron grating which did indeed cover a lock. The space revealed seemed just wide enough for her to push in the canvas package. Still prostrate and breathless from the task, some impulse made her reach under the camisole she'd kept on beneath one of the housekeeper's nightshirts. The money felt warm and slightly damp from her body. Shortly it was stuffed through the opening and she'd closed and locked the hatch.

'He wants you to go and say goodbye,' she heard Geneviève whisper.

'Who does?' Heart thumping, Misha got herself on to her bare feet. Who but Pépé? Pépé had escaped and the bundle was to be hidden for his sake. 'Pépé?' she said.

'My boy,' Geneviève replied, shining the torch into Misha's face. 'You let him kiss you, d'you hear?' she said again. 'You give him a proper kiss.'

327

'Julien, you mean?' Straightening, Misha returned the key. 'We're just friends, Geneviève, you know that.'

'You do as I say,' said Geneviève, making for the corridor outside the cellar.

'But where's he going?' Almost laughing with the shock of her awakening and the strangeness of the bundle, she heard Julien say, 'Not far, Mish, and not for long, I hope, but I think you may be gone before I get back.' He was standing in front of the kitchen door wearing his leather coat and a cap.

'You found your jacket then?' She whispered.

Geneviève prodded her in the waist. 'He wasn't looking for no jacket, Mademoiselle Misha.'

Julien laughed. 'I'll see you in a minute, Geneviève,' he said. 'Give my two friends a second tot of that *eau-de-vie* and pack us up anything we haven't eaten, will you?'

'Another fishing trip?' Misha yawned. 'Heavens, surely this household doesn't need fish to survive like some people!' She put an arm over her eyes and rubbed them. 'Can't I see you when you get home? I'll still be here unfortunately, your father won't be able to get my papers that easily.' An unreasoning irritability threatened to overwhelm her. 'You can't imagine how tired I am, Julien.'

'I'm glad my father's so keen to look after you,' he said. 'I've told him who to contact about false papers, it's a mate of mine.'

'He's being very kind, Julien. I am grateful, truly. I'm tired though and it isn't surprising. The last few days have been a terrible upheaval and it'll take me time to adjust. I mean, if your father can't get Pépé freed, whatever shall I do? He says Mémé didn't even recognise the sort of police it was questioning her this morning. And I can't help her, I can't go and comfort her, I mustn't show my face anywhere. I'm trapped as badly as if I were in prison.' She could hear an unpleasant whine in her voice and couldn't change it.

'Darling.' Julien took both her hands in his. 'You're cold,' he said. 'Get Geneviève to give you a drop of the *eau-de-vie*, it'll warm you and help you get back to sleep. Dad'll see to everything, I promise, because he's promised me.'

'And you're going off on some fishing trip?' She asked, removing her hands and hearing her tone rise.

'Sshh, you'll wake my mother and that won't help.'

Behind him, the kitchen door opened and Geneviève's head appeared round it. 'Your friends say to hurry,' she whispered, before vanishing.

'Geneviève's instructed me to give you a kiss and I will, Julien,' Misha said, placing a sisterly one on each cheek. 'There,' she said. 'Why are you so hot?'

'I've been riding home fast. Didn't you hear us bring the horses in?'

'I was asleep.'

'Good, then you'll sleep well the rest of the night and the next and the next, dear Misha, until my father's organised everything. You'll be all right till then, won't you?'

'I shouldn't think so,' she said. 'In fact it's hardly likely, but I am grateful for the shelter, Julien.'

'You'd have done the same for me.'

''Course I would.'

'Goodbye then, dear Misha.'

'Goodbye.' She offered Julien each of her own cold cheeks and watched the door close behind him.

She'd reached the makeshift bed a second time and taken off her trousers to get back into it when Geneviève appeared beside her.

'You've given him a proper kiss?' she demanded, gripping her arm.

'Yes, I did. I always do,' Misha said, climbing into feather down. 'And you ordered me to. I'll be glad actually when Mémé's been able to send up my nightclothes . . .'

'Only you might not see him again.' Geneviève stood like a pale crow, pulling at the tassels of her dressing-gown cord.

'Why ever not?' Misha said, leaning back against the bolster.

'Because they're coming for him.'

'Who is?' Misha sat up.

'Police, Gestapo,' Geneviève answered.

'You're saying Julien's wanted by the police? Well, it can't be Gestapo. It must be for buying something on the black market.'

Geneviève shook her head and crossed herself. 'You think he'd be be able to stand them wicked ones on his land?'

'He was certainly prepared to shake Nazi hands at his mother's party, so it isn't the Gestapo sort of police.'

'You think he didn't work out how he was going to fool 'em? He'd got it all planned, my boy. And if I ever find out who's betrayed him, I'll kill them with one of my boning knives! I've promised him that and he's laughed at me. I'll do it, though, Mademoiselle Misha, because if he's gone, I'll have nothing to live for.'

Misha stared at her, a chill of horror creeping from the pit of her stomach to her throat. Julien. Of course. Of course he wasn't a boy. Only someone with her own blind arrogance could ever have thought he was.

Chapter 51

The hat well over his forehead, Philippe forced himself to keep his eyes on the pavement. It had become a habit exclusive to Paris and was especially useful when having to pass one of the cafés Nazi officers liked to frequent. The stick helped him stoop slightly, the pebble inside his right shoe also. A worn overcoat, the badly trimmed moustache and cheap spectacle frames declared him to be a school-teacher sent to the city on supply work. His papers matched this identity of course, though he would rather not be stopped. A teacher was too easily checked on.

But he was almost at his rendezvous. Once past this place with the sound of laughter coming from the open door, he had only five or six metres to go before turning into the courtyard and finding the flat where his new contact should be waiting.

His mind occupied with a flicker of anxiety about this man, he slowed his pace to make way for a tramp searching the ground for cigarette ends. He almost put a hand in his pocket for a few sous but that would be a gesture from the old Paris, his and the tramp's.

There was more laughter as a cigarette end landed on the pavement and the tramp pounced. He thought, In a moment I shall ask the tramp his name and the corner where he normally sleeps, and one day when this is over I shall take him a kilo of best tobacco. This I promise myself. A longing for the sweet taste of a Gitane rose most unexpectedly in his own mouth.

Someone laughed again and a pair of black boots came

into his view. Looking up to waist level, he recognised the dagger attached to the front of a black leather belt. Gestapo. He must show no sign. Nor must he move away. He must allow the Gestapo man to kick out at the tramp for daring to defile the view of Nazi officers and their ladies and he must go on his way.

The tramp's face was looking upwards, waiting for the kick. He too knew he mustn't move until this was received. Philippe waited also, his heart surging with shame and disgust. Get on with it, my enemy friend, he thought, or I shall betray myself. A light, playful touch knocked the cigarette from the tramp's hand. The boot withdrew and rose again, finding the neck through his mat of hair and pressing very carefully down on it. There was a sound, a splutter, a cough. A little foaming patch of blood appeared. Some fingers clicked. A voice said in excellent French, 'Take this body away. We must be free of useless parasites. It is our work.'

Did he hear more laughter? Philippe didn't know. He'd become blind and deaf. He'd seen nothing, heard nothing. Holding hard to his stick, he stepped casually into the street as if to make way for the removal party.

A black arm barred his way, and the voice said, 'Your papers, please, Monsieur.'

Without haste, Philippe reached into his jacket, a mechanical movement. 'Certainly, Monsieur,' he replied, smiling and adding the merest suggestion of a bow. As always, he refused the sullen response so many others chose, though it was vital not to go far enough to be accused of impertinence. He almost liked to see the controls, the constant checks because it meant they were not at ease. Yes, he thought, the pebble suddenly painful under his right foot, I am glad to be reminded you are never at ease, can never be at ease in someone else's city.

'You do not approve of our work, Monsieur?'

This question was unexpected. It could have no answer. He nodded vaguely, smiling, smiling. A space had appeared along the pavement. People had been careful to turn away. An elderly woman wearing a yellow star with the word

JEW on it had stopped, as if remembering something she'd forgotten. Face rigidly blank, her eyes met his. Terror he saw there, and pity. Be proud, Madame, he thought, to be of a race they envy and fear so much they want to be rid of you. They were sharing a moment, he and she, a moment he was grateful for when the man spoke again. 'Well, Monsieur Schoolmaster,' he said, 'I trust you are instilling in your pupils the Führer's teaching on the value of hard work and healthy minds? Heil Hitler!'

Philippe nodded vigorously, holding out his hand – but it wasn't finished. The papers were not being offered. Looking up to smile again, he saw the sharp little teeth of Eveline's lover smiling back at him.

Then a voice came from the café entrance, a high-pitched, female voice. 'Eric, darling, don't be long. Me and Friedrich want you to come to the Commodore. You did promise and it's been so long since you came anywhere with us. There'll be nice girls . . .'

As if in a dream, he heard these words and saw a fur-covered arm reach towards the impeccable black shoulders of Gestapo Eric, a delicate gloved hand brushing at the cloth in a familiar, female gesture. He had made a mistake. What a waste of his training, the work he longed to do – and would have done! He so had hoped to see them depart! An immense sorrow rose in him, to know that he would not. He was lost, and much else with him.

'Eveline, please.' Eric drew himself up.

Of course. The voice. The perfume. The fur. The woman turned towards him. He saw that Eveline's face had the same perfection of beauty as before, as if made of something inanimate, the beautiful eyes expressionless below her dark fringe of hair. Stifling an intake of breath, he tried to make those eyes read his. Please, Eveline, I am no longer Philippe Constantin. Think, think of the only possible reason for my being dressed like this today . . .

There was no glimmer of recognition. Instead, and better, far better, she spoke the right words. 'I feel I know you, Monsieur.'

Stifling a release of breath, he made himself bow. 'I am a schoolteacher, Madame. Louis Moquet. I have perhaps

333

taught a member of your family.' He stared at her slender legs in their silk stockings, a symbol of her choice. We are on different sides, Eveline, he thought, but thank you.

'Of course,' she was saying, 'You were my little sister's history teacher. She was a bit in love with you, I remember.' She offered him her hand and he shook it, bowing once more.

Gestapo Eric must have felt he'd lost a little of his position. He clicked his fingers towards the black car waiting on the pavement and it slid towards them as Eveline cried, 'Till later, Eric, you can bring a girl if you want to.'

So I have not been betrayed, Philippe thought; by the woman who once shared my bed. Perhaps this was a good omen. He must take courage from it.

Chapter 52

She was Catherine Elisabeth Fournier, an orphan brought up in a convent and kept on as an assistant teacher until being sent to care for a sick grandmother in the Languedoc. And now she was going to Paris to stay with her Aunt Yvonne. This meant she would very much miss her grandmother's cat, Frou, her hardly-known brother, Félix and a neighbour's son she'd become friendly with.

Sitting by herself on the dark station platform, Misha embroidered on her new identity, mixing half-truth with lie until she and this Catherine arrived back at the same point – the goodbye to Mémé, Félix and Frou whilst Monsieur Sérieys waited tactfully outside on the terrace.

He hadn't been able to get Pépé freed, but it was early days. Pépé had only been arrested a few weeks before. Bribery took time to work its way through several palms, he kept saying on their journey to the station by horse and cart. He was trying to reassure her, being a kind man.

It had seemed a long trip and a cold one and there'd been little to say, everything having been endlessly discussed already. But she'd thanked him again for the trouble he'd taken on her behalf. He'd found her a new name from a graveyard and had paid for a complete set of identity cards and ration coupons with the appropriate number of tickets torn off. And even if he were wealthy, this was a generous action. He'd risked his own life by it. She also repeated how much she wished for Julien's safe arrival in Spain and his return home after the war was over. And how she'd like him to thank his youngest daughter, Madeleine, for releasing a

335

set of her old convent clothes without being given the reason why. Madeleine was thus enabling her to be warm in Paris as well as unusually well-dressed, this fact alone being enough, she said, for none of her Paris acquaintances to recognise her.

They were good clothes, Madeleine's, a fine grey flannel suit only an inch too short in the skirt, a woollen blouse, lisle stockings, sturdy pre-war shoes. Underneath, there was a flannel vest and knickers down to the knee of the sort she'd longed for in London and a cape she was already glad of. Pulling it around her shoulders on the station bench, Misha also pulled down the sensible felt hat and returned to the same moment – the goodbye to Mémé, Félix and Frou. She'd been down to the house for the last time and Mémé'd helped her dress for the new identity. The quality of the cloth had pleased Mémé apparently, but they just hadn't been able to speak. Now it was too late and they wouldn't meet again until the war was finished with. She could think of many things she should have said. They couldn't be said in a letter either. The enemy had done this too, ruled that family members should have no intimate communication by correspondence when apart, a ruling which seemed more and more extraordinary the more she thought about it.

In fact, she decided, feeling eerily alone after the frequent company of Geneviève, the entire war was bit by bit revealing itself to have an extraordinary and unique nature. Whole countries and their populations were directly involved in it though they held no gun or bayonet and there was no battle field. And here on this station platform, released from her cellar cocoon, she was in the war zone. To the temporary conquerors, she was the enemy. Of course they must hunt her down.

'Papers!'

Waking with a sickening start, Misha fumbled with the handbag on her lap. The uniformed figure in the train carriage doorway would see at once it wasn't her own.

But he worked along the three people to her right first and she made herself keep calm. In the gloom, he wouldn't notice, nor would he see the subsiding flush of her skin. And he did no more than glance at her cards. They'd passed.

Sitting upright, fiddling again with the clasp for the show of it, she took out the convent prayer book. She'd relaxed enough actually to begin turning the pages and was therefore all the more startled when a second shout came. 'Shoes!'

The elderly lady in the corner, having just put away her papers, gave a cry of distress. There was a surge of movement from the others. Misha felt this whilst carefully replacing the book and staring down at Madeleine Sérieys's lace-up shoes. The Gestapo wanted to inspect them.

'Not you, Madame,' the Gestapo officer shouted, pointing a black-gloved finger at the elderly lady. She seemed not to have understood and continued struggling to lift one leg.

'You!' The black glove appeared in Misha's sight. She offered up Madeleine's right shoe. 'Both!' the officer commanded, producing a small file and with it scraping at the soles of the lace-ups. A little dry dust fell off them on to the old lady's skirt. Misha's heart thumped as she accepted the return of the shoes and told herself she'd learned something important: expect the unexpected. And of course, show neither surprise nor hesitation.

The old lady wasn't managing either. She was allowed to go on trying to bend to feet she could scarcely reach before the officer said again, 'Not yours, Madame.' Misha saw a few weak tears fill her eyes which she dared not or hadn't the strength to wipe away.

Of the middle-aged couple opposite her, only the man's shoes were inspected. But he too had passed, it seemed, because shortly the officer had slammed the door behind him. The train picked up speed and swayed on.

Suddenly, the middle-aged man spoke. He said, 'There must have been a parachute landing from England last night near our last stop. And it must have been raining. That bloke was looking for mud on our shoes.' He nudged his wife. 'Obviously considered you a bit overweight for undercover work, dear.' She prodded him to be quiet. The old lady smiled, holding up the underside of her bag, as if casually. Stuck to this was a strip of blue, white and red. The

337

French flag in miniature. Misha smiled. Resistance could be no more than a little piece of cloth.

She settled back into her seat with an odd sense of peace. She was really on her way now. There could be no turning back. She wanted none. This episode had encouraged her quite unexpectedly. She'd learned about the warmth of fellow-feeling between strangers, for one thing. That Catherine Fournier's papers would pass, for another. She also had innocent shoes. In fact, Catherine's wholly innocent identity would enable her to have the privilege of joining the endeavour to drive out the enemy. It wouldn't only be a privilege. She'd also be sharing somehow in the experiences of the Englishman, Georgie, Julien, Philippe, and thus feel a little nearer to them.

Chapter 53

The colours of her beloved city had changed to black and grey with patches of the green she'd always found so displeasing. But the uniforms Misha stared at weren't all of this military green. Many other uniforms were contaminating her Paris streets, black ones, police and Gestapo black. Black also seemed to clothe all the ordinary businessmen and clerks scuttling to what must still exist, ordinary work. Mostly though, she couldn't avoid noticing the green and black uniforms getting to their work.

There were splashes of red, just on the edge of her vision. The flags. There'd be black on these. The swastika was always black. But she didn't look up to the top of the buildings so didn't see it. It did cross her mind, however, that she'd never realised before how pretty the blue, white and red flags had been.

In fact, it was inconvenient she had to pause quite so long in front of the station, and in a northern wind she wasn't used to. But her legs had been weakened by her long incarceration in a train and before that, a cellar. Yet all she had to do was start walking. Even if she hadn't known the way to her mother's flat, the signs banked up on giant posts would have told her. They did indicate the direction for the offices of the military commander of the city, for instance, and for many other places, the Ortslazarett, whatever that was. But German had never been her strong point, even in the Swiss school she'd attended.

She could take a taxi, as there were some. A smart woman was making for a notice saying VÉLO-TAXI and getting into a cart behind a man on a bicycle. The only thing the woman lacked was a smart little whip to encourage on the human beast of burden.

This sight seemed to make her move. Grabbing her suitcase and not hurrying, not looking up at anything, she set off for her mother's. It would be as well to arrive there before mid-day. Her mother would have taken her bath by then. She'd be in good humour, planning some pleasure for herself, luncheon, window-shopping for wooden-soled shoes, a hat. There'd still be hats, for officers' wives, the chic set of the Ritz and her mother.

If she timed her arrival well, her mother would be pleased to see her. It'd have to be quick, the exchange of information in the doorway of the flat, so her mother didn't shriek the wrong thing, like Oh, my beloved daughter, since she was supposed to be her orphaned niece. The first moments would be difficult, she reasoned, quite unable to hurry with her cold and shaking legs, but after that it'd be wonderful. She'd let her mother run her a hot bath and sit on the bidet whilst she herself recounted her adventures and the story of Pépé. Monsieur Pierre would have his old influence, since'd he certainly be in with the smart set, and instructions would be sent down that Pépé was not to be touched and his half-British grandaughter had escaped to England so no one need bother with her either.

Did the enemy realise what extraordinary difficulties were caused by fear of their censorship? Probably they did. If she'd been able to write frankly to her mother, the bath'd be ready, and coffee, and maybe black market bread to dip in.

She had kept her eyes more or less on the pavement after leaving the station, so she came upon the entrance of her mother's apartment block rather by surprise. Vaguely wondering at the time whether Monsieur Pierre himself might be with her since the day had crept into its afternoon, she hesitated. Afternoons he sometimes visited. She didn't want to embarrass them, but on the other hand, she'd need to meet him as soon as possible to begin the process of helping to get Pépé freed. Monsieur Sérieys was an amateur in such matters, whereas Monsieur Pierre had proved his real power with the enemy by having her released from the prison.

Her thoughts having reached this point, she made up her mind. She'd be embarrassing if necessary.

She had one frozen foot on the first step when she thought she recognised a drift of her mother's scent and looked up, delighted. Her mother was coming, there'd been no need to hesitate. A late luncheon was evidently to be the order of the day and if she were careful, she'd be able to stop her mother crying out her name. Her own mouth was just about to form the words, 'Aunt Yvette, it's me, Catherine!' when she heard a German voice saying the same word, Yvette. And then, 'Yvette, my darling, all morning I wait for this very moment.'

She stayed long enough for her mother and the Nazi officer to run down the steps together. Neither had eyes for anyone but each other. He had quite a handsome face. Under the cap, his hair was probably blond. He was younger than her and much taller. Their arms were entwined and her mother was dressed in her dark sable coat and her pre-war leather boots.

Noting all this, she watched them stroll off down towards the rue de Rivoli. By then, she'd realised she had to make for her only other possible sanctuary. Someone in the street would take her in, Madame Libaud, the Blanchards. The difficulty would be in first avoiding anyone who might shout, Mademoiselle Misha! and thus betray the presence of a British spy.

There'd be no hot bath of course, no complaints about the lack of pretty silks or doeskin gloves either. She was almost glad, except for Pépé's sake. In the humble street across the river where people were no doubt suffering properly from the enemy in their city, she'd feel she belonged.

Chapter 54

Every crack in the windows of Madame Libaud's flat was stuffed with newspaper and only one shutter was open in the kitchen to give her light enough to see. But for the gloom however, she and Misha, side by side near the empty stove, might have been in the street. Removing only her gloves, Misha laid out on a stool the food Mémé had packed for her, baked potatoes, goat's cheese, a jar of peach compôte, goose pâté.

Her face skin and bone, Madame Libaud watched this happening in silence, the first pause in her recounting of more than two years' worth of gossip. 'And you people down south have been having such feasts every day?' she said, easing off a corner of the eiderdown she was wrapped in.

'Only in the country,' Misha said, passing across a plate containing half a potato and a spoonful of the pâté. It was almost like old times, except that the elderly widow's chin was blue with cold.

A trembling hand took the plate and Madame Libaud drew a deep sniffing breath. 'I don't know as I can eat all of this today, my dear child,' she said, 'What with the shock of you come whispering outside my door . . .' She put the plate on her eiderdown-covered knees and considered it.

'Go on with the story of the Nazi officer strolling in here demanding your sheets.' Misha wasn't hungry. The food smelled of Mémé's kitchen. Leaving her own plate until later, because she'd certainly have to hide here until she could make new plans, she got hold of the coffee grinder and the bits of ancient cabbage root and tried to turn the handle. She'd started her old managing ways, she realised. It would be as well to have something to do. How foolish she'd been not to think beyond her mother and Monsieur Pierre's help! 'So these officers went all up the street, into every flat?'

'They did!' Madame Libaud hugged the cover around her and snorted. 'Then they rang my bell. I saw two of 'em standing there, nasty pale skin, nasty little eyes and proud of themselves, you know, boys showing off, strutting about with toy guns, I nearly called the head one "lad", would have probably till he said he had an order allowing him to inspect my linen!'

'But whatever for?' Misha said, struggling with the tiny handle. 'D'you actually drink this cabbage powder?' She felt a strange unaccustomed languor in spite of the cold. She needed sleep first of all and some chink of reassurance, which she knew she'd have to find for herself, and very quickly.

'That's what I said to 'em after I got my wind back. What for? I said. He said Frenchwomen had been greedy for too long, they had far too much and German women nothing. With that, the head one pushes past me and indicates his minion should go ferreting in my bedrooms, spare room and all, in the wardrobes, the trunks. Choking over my lavender dust he was, and I stood there watching, and he shouts out how many I've got, my lovely thick yellow linen sheets, the set my grandmother made for her dowry, the ones her mother embroidered as a girl with *fleur de lys* all along the edges.' Rocking with remembered anger, she was still angry and couldn't go on. Instead, she put a finger on the spoon of pâté. 'Herbs,' she said. 'Garlic,' and began to cry without sound.

'How many sets did he leave you?' Misha pretended not to notice the tears.

'One set for each bed, two blankets, one eiderdown, and no soap anywhere to have it washed anymore. Those clean people, they want us to live dirty, I tell you that!' Little puffs of vapour appeared as she spoke faster, wiping her face with eiderdown. 'Anyway, they counted it all out again on the landing and some more underlings came and carried it down to the street where removal vans were lined up ready. And it wasn't just us, we heard later, they were doing it all over Paris and ransacking all the empty flats, the Jewish ones of course, all the fine stuff, our fine French stuff, gone to German housewives so two sets of my beautiful linen is all you'll get for your trousseau, child.'

Hiccoughing, she suddenly picked up her plate and took a mouthful of potato, one of pâté, and went on eating until the tiny portions were gone. 'Oh, my dear girl,' she muttered, as Misha hesitated over the question she wanted to ask the most. 'Oh, my dear girl, I think I could die happy now with my shrunken belly full up, too full, and you sitting there like you used to, making things better for me. You always did, you've a good heart though I don't know where you got it from. I saw that father of yours the other day, shouting in the courtyard he was, always a noisy man, wasn't he? I think he wanted that Bassas woman to open up your old flat for him, he'd lost his key. Offering her a few francs to do it, he was. Whether she would have done it or not, I don't know, but she does rush off to her cubby-hole as if she's going to. Next thing I know he's making for the archway and the street so I get into my parlour quick as I can and there he is, running off towards the boulevard. I suppose he hadn't offered her enough. She'll get 50 francs for denouncing an Englishman to the police, he should have been in that camp where they all are long since. Englishmen're in one near Paris I've heard, the women and girls in some cold place in the east, Besançon I think. You'd have been sent there if you'd stayed.'

Rendered speechless by this particular item in Madame Libaud's list of news, Misha tried to conjure up the image of her father's heavy body dressed in his fine clothes, his cashmere coat, his hat from Jermyn Street – and running.

'He must have some of them false papers people keep talking about, you can buy them as well and call yourself something else,' Madame Libaud muttered. 'How much did you have to pay for yours?'

'Our neighbour paid,' she said, faltering in her grinding of the cabbage root. 'But how can my father be managing?

344

Especially with false papers. I mean he'd have to be careful, follow the rules and regulations, collect his ration coupons, keep the curfew. He was always too grand for rules.' Tomorrow, she thought, tomorrow, when I am settled in Madame Libaud's spare room and have had a night's sleep, I shall think about my father's extraordinary reappearance in a place where he shouldn't be, and shall try not to imagine my mother in her peach-coloured silk négligée, a Nazi officer's cap on the bedside table. Whatever could have happened to Monsieur Pierre?

'Anybody see you coming up the street?' Madame Libaud said, her voice slowing with tiredness. 'Only the ironmonger and his mother have set themselves up as a little nest of spies of the meanest sort. They even told on that nice baker of ours for selling his bread hot to a poor soul who was going on a train journey. Baker got fifteen days in prison for that. Hot bread's not allowed. Then the butcher, of course, when he's not buying in black market calves and killing 'em round the back of his shop so as to sell more meat than he's permitted to do . . .'

'I think my new clothes fooled Denis,' Misha said. 'I didn't dare look up but I saw him standing in the shop doorway and he called out, "Mademoiselle, don't cross there, you have to use the special crossing." ' Remembering the thud in her heart at Denis's call, Misha put down the grinder. She was exhausted. There was already far too much to mull over. 'I can't tell you how strange it was creeping along the street like a criminal. I know I am, yet somehow, I hadn't realised what it could feel like in my usual places. Of course, I assumed my mother would be at her old flat since her last letter came from there. Silly of me, really . . .' She had not revealed all her news, that her mother had a different protector. This was going to be kept to herself.

'The Blanchards'd have recognised you,' Madame Libaud said, her head nodding. 'Jules Blanchard mentioned your father as a matter of fact, said had I seen him. Naturally he and that hot-headed son of his are involved in some sort of spying work of the right kind, spying on the enemy they are and blowing up things, about time too. That café's a meeting place, there's people and parcels going in and out of the cellar soon as it's dark. I sit up here watching it all and I think if I see that Bassas woman or anyone else of the wrong sort creeping about, I can get down to warn 'em. Blanchard knows I know but he trusts me...'

Recognising she was about to fall asleep as she used to do in the old days, Misha asked her question. 'And the professor?'

The widow stirred, hugging the eiderdown tighter. 'Thought you'd have found someone your own age in the country, with the church and them village dances...'

'Have you seen him?'

'Oh, I saw him that June. June 1940. Then he came last year in April and I told him you were down there in the Languedoc. Pleased about that he was. I told him all about them coming for my best linen. He was hoping to use my spare room for a night or two, he's mixed up in something... Anyway, I said to him, those beasts have taken my best linen I meant for Misha's trousseau. That made him smile. He said he hoped you weren't planning a trousseau yet because he'd like to be at your wedding. Misha must wait to be married until after the war, he said. I did put his note somewhere with the other one...' Her head had fallen so far into the eiderdown, she looked like a bird. 'Of course, he couldn't stay here...'

'Notes from the professor to me?' Misha said, disentangling herself from coffee grinder and flannel cape. 'Shall I fetch them?' She was startled when the doorbell rang, but being already on her feet, almost went towards it.

'That'll be my lodger,' the old lady said. 'Open it dear, he must've forgotten his key. Put here without so much as a by-your-leave, he was. Can't you smell his boots in the spare room? I can, and his nasty green uniform. I just want to live long enough to see him and the rest of 'em driven out. I often wonder what he thinks he's doing, living in someone else's flat in someone else's city.'

'Don't forget I'm your great-niece, Catherine Fournier, he'll see the food,' Misha hissed, grabbing her suitcase and making for the front parlour to crawl under the tablecloth.

Chapter 55

'And as soon as the soldier'd changed his uniform or whatever he wanted to do, I ran up here to you, Reine,' Misha finished, the little puffs of vapour coming fast from her mouth.

'You did right, darling Mish. We'll sort something out, don't you fret. You'll kip down with me and Isa for tonight, the bed's big enough for three.' Like the Widow Libaud, Reine was wrapped about in clothing, a rabbit fur coat, fur hat, and on her feet, men's socks and felt slippers.

'If your daughter doesn't mind,' Misha said, looking across the kitchen table to where Isabelle sat also encased in fur. At fifteen, she seemed already a woman, with the same full red-headed beauty as her mother.

Isabelle shrugged, leaning her elbows on the table and pulling tendrils of red curls around her hat.

'She don't mind,' Reine said, 'She can't. She should still be in the convent. If I hadn't weakened and let her come home, Misha, there's where she'd be today but if she thinks she's going to sit around in the cafés much longer, she's mistaken.' Turning anxious loving eyes on her pride and joy, she added, 'Yes, Miss, I ain't spent all that money on your education to have it wasted. When this war's over, you're going to university, that's where you're going.'

'Well, now I'm going out, *Maman*,' Isabelle said, her lovely face set in the adolescent sulkiness Misha recognised only too well. 'Eric's coming for me at two o'clock, I told you.'

'That Eric,' Reine snorted, 'He's the enemy and consorting with the enemy is just what they want . . . And you ain't finished these noodles I cooked for you, you can't go out with nothing in your belly, it's good honest food, noodles. I don't want you eating what he gives you. Chocolate it was the other day, Mish, and I try not to blame her but when I see that crowd of pretty young French girls like my Isa hanging round with all those strutting uniforms in our best cafés, it makes me mad.'

Isabelle sprang to her feet, scraping back the chair and pushing her plate across the table. 'These aren't cooked anyway, you only poured boiling water on them. In the cafés, there's proper food if someone pays for it.' She took a compact from her pocket and glanced at herself, pouting her full mouth and teasing out more hair. 'Anyway, *Maman*, you've been consorting with the enemy!'

'That's business,' Reine snapped. 'And I had no choice when you came home. That German sergeant's the only regular I could get.'

Trying to find something to say in case Reine should be embarrassed by this exchange, Misha was about to open her mouth when the doorbell rang.

'Eric!' Isabelle cried, making for the door. 'Bye!'

'Hope he's not like that awful cousin of Eveline's, d'you remember him?' Misha asked, watching Isabelle throw up each leg in turn and peer backwards at it. She willed herself to stay in her seat. She was perfectly safe as Catherine Fournier. And she must get used to the enemy.

'I drew them stocking lines straight,' Reine said, 'If you catch your death, don't blame me. And don't forget Mish is called Catherine Fournier and she's out of a convent just like you. Don't be telling that Eric any different . . .'

'I couldn't be bothered to!' The door slammed.

Reine absent-mindedly began to spoon Isabelle's noodles into her mouth and sighed. 'It is that Eric, Mish,' she said. 'Gestapo he is. Spying already back in the old days. What fools we were, eh, making jokes about the Fifth Column dressed as nuns and all the time a real one in our very own block of flats. 'Course, he dresses smart, she likes uniforms, kids do, don't they? I tell her, I say, them Gestapo, they're the worst ones, the killers . . .'

'Yes.' Misha felt a strange panting feeling in her chest, and tried to ease her stiff limbs. 'Quick, Reine,' she said, 'Can you watch to see which way he goes? He's like the ones after me. I'm a wanted British spy and you'll be shot for harbouring me, remember.' Struggling with a muddle of grey flannel, she put cold hands to her cold face. 'I'd have been better off in my grandad's fishing hut or up in the hills at my Aunt Yvonne's. But you know me, I thought I could come up to stay at my mother's, blithely assuming she'd be there, then I'd do something useful against the enemy like some of my friends are. D'you remember Georgie? Well, she . . .'

'Oh God, Mish, what did you say?' Reine tugged open the windows and turned round. 'Do something useful against 'em? You mad or what? This ain't no American film with the gangsters in the nick at the end. This is real life and if you got a death wish, I shan't let you keep it . . .' Leaning perilously from her tiny balcony, she hissed, 'I can see his nasty black cap and my little baby holding his filthy black arm. She's going to the bad, Mish, and I must face it, yet I can't. She's like me, you see, making up to the boys. If it wasn't for this damn' war, I'd have kept her safe longer.'

'Don't lean too far, Reine,' Misha said, going to sit on the rabbit hutch by the window in order to hold on to her fur coat. 'Which way are they going? If I leave in a few minutes, I can hurry in the opposite direction.' Except that she had nowhere to make for. This was the stark truth. And there'd be no point in knocking at the Steiner's flat on the third floor. The entire block must remain out of bounds; the street itself for that matter. 'You don't think Eric might fail to recognise me from two and a half years ago? And perhaps I was silly about the soldier billeted on Madame Libaud. He only sleeps there, they eat in canteens apparently.' These were just words. She was talking to herself, wanting a glimpse of hope. Yet she knew not a soul beyond the street except her mother.

'You think no one'd recognise you in that old maid's outfit?' Reine said. 'Darling, that's why they would. You don't match it, see, you don't look humble enough, as if you're always on your knees praying. You keeps your head up too much, and your eyes, well, them eyes is too like, *interested . . .*' Withdrawing from the edge of the balcony, she shut the windows and sighed. 'Gone striding off towards the boulevard, that peacock has,' she said. 'And he won't be eating in soldiers' canteens, Eric won't, only the best cafés and restaurants for them, black market food and silly girls like my Isa hanging round 'em. Still, when you see some of their Nazi women, ugly as sin, they are, you can understand the blokes. Oh, I can't bear it, I feel like a cuddle . . .' Kneeling on the floor, she opened the rabbit hutch and took out a big white animal. 'Chap who sold me this said it was a pregnant doe, so I got done, Mish. Now I have to find someone to lend me a doe and we'll go halves on the little ones. As long as the electricity keeps going this winter, I'll have rabbit stews on the hot plate.' Kissing the animal's nose, she let it snuffle into her fur collar. 'Maybe if I feeds my Isa better, she'll stay at home more. I have to think of meself as well, I can't get too thin, my regular won't like it. Twice a week I go to his hotel, Mish, now Isa's here.' She laid her face against the rabbit and added, 'He's not one of the killers, he's only in the quartermaster stores. I can't stomach what some of the girls are doing. I mean, we sell our bodies, Mish, that's the job, but not our souls.'

Unable to move from her place on the hutch, though the rough wood had snagged her skirt, Misha recognised the forlorn expression on the face of her friend and changed the subject. 'Is Eveline living there with Eric, in the professor's old flat?' she said, with an odd thump in her chest at this further echo from the past. She'd forgotten Eveline and would quickly forget her again. Philippe's two letters, though, were hidden unread in her jacket, a promise of consolation in worse times. Even if they held no more than words of friendship, they'd be a consolation. He had continued to think of her. And worse times did lie ahead – she'd shortly have to leave Reine to go to some other place where there'd be no safety either.

Sitting back on her haunches, Reine held the rabbit tight. 'Eveline moved on,' she said. 'She got herself someone higher than that Eric at the beginning, after the owners of the fashion wholesalers where you used to work decided to get out and sold her the place. They say she had all the addresses of their Jewish customers and they were looted soon as the Nazis came in.'

Misha thought of the hours ticking by in the hot workroom, Eveline shut away from the rest. 'The girls always claimed she was writing instead of drawing.'

'There you are then.' Reine was triumphant for a second. 'I wasn't surprised. That blank face. No heart. I used to wonder what he saw in her and why she ever thought he'd do as a husband.' She put out a cold hand to touch Misha's. 'There was a man, eh, Mish? And what a pash you had on him in the old days.' She laughed. 'I wish my Isa had a pash on some special sort of bloke like that professor. Now you can't imagine him consorting with the enemy, can you?' Suddenly, there were tears in place of the laughter.

'No,' said Misha, breathless, watching this change, understanding it.

'He must have been doing grand and noble things in this old mess. Such a pity they got him.' Reine sniffed and lay her face against the rabbit's.

'Got him, Reine?'

'Yes, arrested he was, in some disguise, so he must be in one of them resistance groups, spying on the Nazis, trying to get their war factories bombed and that. There's some people hiding guns, ready to settle a few scores when the invasion begins and the Krauts start running. I'm going to get myself a weapon, as a matter of fact, and make sure I get a chance to kill that Eric personally. If he touches my Isa, he'd better watch out for me.' Reine sniffed again. 'I'll ask Jules Blanchard how to use it, too. I swear him and that Robert Blanchard are mixed up in something. Old Blanchard's so damn' full of jovial friendliness with his new uniformed clientèle, he's got loathing of 'em written all over him, if you see what I mean. I hope no one else recognises it, or he'll be the next . . .'

Heart beat suspended, Misha watched Reine frantically kissing her rabbit from its nose to the top of its head. The Blanchards, of course, she thought, and Eveline and Eric. She might have set out their future paths back in the old days if she'd been perceptive enough. But Reine, Reine,

351

leave the rabbit and tell me again, I must have misunderstood, I want to have misunderstood . . .

'The baker was passing it on,' Reine said, as if she'd recognised this silent plea. 'He heard it through some police friend. Our nice professor was stopped and taken in. For insolence, apparently. He'd been staring at a Nazi officer killing a tramp with his boot.'

'He tried to stop it, of course. He would, he wouldn't be able to bear it.'

'God, no. He wouldn't be so daft,' Reine said. 'That sort of guts is useless anyway. No, darling, we keep our eyes down here, and that's my advice to you. Keep your eyes on the pavement and don't look at anyone, not even your old friends. No, I expect the professor just stood there *not* looking at the bloke killing the tramp, and like, didn't laugh and cheer him on. That'd be enough to be taken to the rue de Saussaies.'

'The rue de Saussaies, Reine?'

'Worst place that,' she said. 'Here, give my substitute baby a cuddle for a minute. I got to go to the lavatory.'

'What's it the worst place for, Reine?' Misha accepted the animal bundle and crushed it against her shoulder where Frou used to lie. She knew, of course, and must sit there and hear it.

'For getting information out of people, darling,' Reine said.

Misha felt the cold seep further into her body as if she had entered a darker, icier place.

352

Chapter 56

Philippe allowed himself a deep breath of sleet-filled air. They'd released him. He was *outside*. This fact was as extraordinary to him as the feeling of rain on his skin when he'd been expecting to die. Why had he been released? Why only four days of the same questions that never went any further? You do not like our work? How is that? You expect us to believe you are a humble schoolteacher with such an arrogant demeanour?

And all this from a bored man sitting in an office with a typist to record these questions and his answers, always the same. Then two weeks and three days of being left entirely alone.

His head thumped. He would most like a strong drink. Glancing sideways at the nearest café on the corner of the street where they'd kindly dropped him, he saw it was a Without Alcohol day. No matter. That he could walk in there and say, 'Coffee, please, Monsieur,' or perhaps 'Cinzano, please, Monsieur,' was enough to make him feel drunk.

The imitation aperitif actually made him cough but he felt a little better, his mind ticking on as he watched the street. First, he thought, I shall prove to myself that the chap in raincoat and homburg on the pavement opposite pretending to stare into the shop with a solitary lady's shoe in it, is more interested in me than in shoes.

Forcing himself to take his time, he ordered vegetable soup and savoured the warmth it gave his body. He'd forgotten the pleasure of hot food. Careful to lean back in his chair and yawn from time to time, he paid the barman with the money they'd returned to him. How meticulous they were on one's arrest, sealing up money and other effects whilst one signed a paper to state these were accurately listed. Yet they took a life without so much as a flicker of an eyelid.

Next he bought a *jeton* at the counter and picked up the directory from which he quickly discovered the number of Maison Schwarz, fashion wholesalers. Situating himself by the telephone so that neither customer nor barman would be able to make out this number, he asked the operator to put him through.

Eveline herself picked up the receiver. He recognised her voice. He said, 'Have I you to thank?'

'Yes. It wasn't easy. Be careful. You'd better leave here.'

'Yes. I am grateful. Goodbye.'

It was enough. So then, if the chap opposite made his move, he'd know. Cat and mouse. They knew what he was. They'd bide their time. He was freed only on higher orders and it'd be temporary. They'd be pleased to play this game. He'd lead them to others.

Slipping back into the street, he made for the hotel lodgings where he'd booked in as one Louis Gaston Moquet, schoolteacher on supply work. Yes. The man opposite took his eyes away from the lady's shoe and strolled casually in the same direction.

Now his own way was clear. Walking smartly past the hotel entrance, he dropped into the Métro station. He'd shortly be moving so fast in and out of various carriages journeying to various destinations, the poor plain-clothes devil on his trail would lose it. He'd done this before. It'd be good thinking time. Because he'd been betrayed. He suspected this already and the trail put on him made it certain. Gestapo Eric had had the car ready, he was waiting there, watching for him to turn into the courtyard. The tramp had been a mere diversion.

The sole person to know the exact time and place of this rendezvous was the new contact himself, code-name Savoy.

Savoy would have to be caught and destroyed. If not, the whole group could be lost.

*

354

It was dark when he reached the street and the barber's shop where another identity and set of clothing were hidden. Fearful in spite of leaving the policeman well behind, he nonetheless walked twice up and down the pavement past the shop, looking casually at his watch. On cue, the barber opened the door and shook out a blue towel. This was the all-clear signal. He had no client but one of the lowliest.

Philippe strolled in to take a seat at the second mirror. 'Cold day, Messieurs,' he said, glancing at his own image and refraining from any expression of surprise at the untidiness of his beard. He'd only been allowed to shave twice during his incarceration and that by feel. Smiling, he added, 'I'll ask you to take this lot off, barber. My wife doesn't like it.'

'And didn't I tell you she wouldn't, Monsieur?' the barber said, whipping the cape from his client's shoulders and picking up a glass to show him the back of his head. '*Danke schön*,' the client said, admiring the new pink smoothness of neck and head.

Philippe watched the meticulous brushing-off of hair from the green cloth uniform, its badges and epaulettes, barber dealing with the top half, the soldier with his own breeches. It took some time and the barber did not hurry, had never hurried a client. What safer house could they have than this, a meeting place under their very noses? And yet, he thought, his chest tightening with anguish, with the weight of his present and necessary distrust, what if this courageous little Normandy barber had also been taken in? Had also been released but then touched, corrupted, turned around, offered his own life for his comrades'? This was how their cleverness increased the spiral of shame and degradation. I do not think my barber friend is capable of betrayal, he said to himself as the soldier departed, but if I am wrong, they will be waiting for me upstairs.

He got to his feet, immeasurably weary, and moved to the beaded curtain at the rear of the shop. Without a word, the barber took out a key and opened the door leading to his staircase. 'Chartier'll see to you,' he whispered, pushing him through it. 'I'll come as soon as I close.

And am I glad to see you!' As if overcome, he grabbed Philippe's hand and shook it. 'We assumed you'd been lost with the others.'

So it was done. He had been right, Philippe thought with profound sadness. How many lost? Very nearly the worst had happened. The barber and Chartier remained for the present but like him they were in greater danger than ever. Any other remaining group members must be dispersed at once.

Knocking four times and saying his own code-name, David, at the door on the landing, he was soon securely inside the kitchen and being embraced by Chartier, the policeman he used to see from time to time at his old flat and who was now the agent code-named Guêpe. Moving with infinite delicacy so that no sound could be heard in the shop below, he sat down at the table. Chartier put before him a plate with a portion of *saucisson* and cold potato on it, which he did not attempt to begin eating, though he supposed he was hungry. He had much to find out first.

'So which of our group did they take in?'

'Diderot and Toulouse,' Chartier replied. 'Diderot's family have had his clothes sent back to them. We can assume the poor chap refused to give anything away so they went too far.'

'Went too far,' repeated Philippe slowly. Where could so much bitterness come from, that a man could torture another to death? And that with the extraordinary purpose of trying to retain possession of the man's own country. 'What about Toulouse?'

'No clothes sent as yet. Maybe he's broken and they've got the information they need, maybe he's been deported – who knows? There's never any sense to it.'

'There was no sense in leaving me alone,' Philippe said. 'And it worries me. Now the waiter, Voltaire. Wasn't he the contact between Diderot and this Savoy man I was on my to meet when I was taken?'

'He was,' Chartier said, 'but he knows nothing of either of us but our appearance and our code-names. He's not at work at the hotel at the moment, but the barber hasn't been

356

able to find out why. I've been lying low here, I knew I had to after your arrest, and of course London HQ's due to send the 'plane to pick me up next full moon, Thursday it'll be, provided the weather's right. The farmer's still prepared for us to use his field. We got a message through about that.' Here Chartier paused and put his head in his hands. 'I'm not sure I'm cut out for this game, Constantin. With you gone, it's not been easy.'

'Bear up, Chartier, remember how much you've done already. Arms and men like you are vital to the work and you're particularly needed to get thorough training in the new Sten guns. They'll be useless to us if men in the field don't know the mechanics of the things.' Philippe wiped his hands on his shirt and picked up a round of *saucisson*. 'You haven't long to wait, and you'll be sent to another group. This one will no longer exist very shortly, everyone must be dispersed right down the line from contact to contact. I'll see to that myself since I'm the one who got them together.'

'You must get out, man, you must come to England with me!' Chartier was almost shouting. 'If you're right about this Savoy, you're marked, marked bait! Or else why did they let you out?'

'I'll leave once I am convinced Savoy did not engineer that rendezvous with me on orders from his masters. And yes, if they killed Diderot and possibly Toulouse, why not me also?'

'Maybe he has no masters, Constantin, maybe the man's a genuine possible group member who could do us a lot of good. Diderot and Toulouse could've been trapped by another informant and you could simply have been taken in for insolence, as a warning.'

'It's what I must find out, Chartier,' Philippe said calmly. 'Tell me what you know about Savoy from the beginning. I know I've heard it before we fixed the rendezvous but I've had plenty of time to wonder why this man was prepared to take the risk of approaching Voltaire, who might himself have been an enemy stooge and why Voltaire was so sure he could become one of us.'

'He's some kind of dealer,' Chartier said for the tenth time. He was getting tired. 'A dealer in this and that, gold, diamonds, guns, heaven knows. He's been mixing with all sorts since before the war. He carries false Swiss papers and hotel rumour had it he'd got several people across the border into Switzerland. Voltaire knew him vaguely from before the war and the days when he himself worked at the Lipp. The man always wanted credit, just for the show of it, you know the sort. Anyway, they get talking about old times, without either of 'em mentioning the fact the hotel's mostly full of high-up Nazis apart from Savoy. One day he asks Voltaire if he knows anyone in trouble who'd like to get out of Paris, because he could help. All in a roundabout way, of course. It worries Voltaire a bit but meanwhile he learns from hotel staff gossip that Savoy actually did get a pass for a bloke who strangled a Nazi major and pushed him in the Seine, the one they took those hostages for. This impressed Voltaire naturally because the assistant manager got a postcard from the bloke, posted in the south of France.'

'Savoy's motive would be money, would it?'

'No, Constantin, it seems it's patriotism.'

'Swiss patriotism?' Philippe laughed. 'To make up for his countrymen salting away the gold the Nazis have stolen?'

'But he's English by birth,' Chartier said. 'Didn't I remind you? A true blue Englishman, no less, with false Swiss papers and a comic accent that'd fool no one but the Germans. He said he was ashamed to be living amongst the Krauts, that's what he calls them, and wishes he'd gone back to England to do his duty before it was too late. He wants to help in some way and this is the way he can. Of course, he let it be understood by Voltaire that he was dealing with the Nazi profiteering fraternity. What better way to stay protected after all? That's probably why he's holed up in that hotel and hardly steps outside. Someone'd soon denounce him as British for 50 francs and the local police'd put him in that camp.

'It might take him some time to get back amongst his Nazi friends. Maybe none of them'd bother to get him out!' Chartier sighed and poured them both another drop of the barber's Calvados. 'In their madness, they despise collaborators.'

'I don't like it,' Philippe said. 'And I blame myself. I
didn't check up on him enough. Easy to say that now,
I know but I tell you that Gestapo creature was waiting for
a schoolteacher type to be coming along and there I was,
about to turn into the courtyard to meet Savoy. The car
also was waiting, I repeat. The tramp was a mere diversion.'
He drank his warming reminder of home in one gulp. 'I
want him brought in.'

'Not so easy,' Constantin said. 'Who can we send into
that place that isn't one of us? And we can't take the risk
of being seen talking to him. Neither dare we send in a
note to suggest a meeting. If only Mademoiselle Misha were
in Paris, it'd be easy . . .'

'Mademoiselle Misha?' Philippe slammed down his glass.
'Whatever made you think of Misha?'

'Because Savoy's her father, Constantin, he's Misha's
father. Yes, Voltaire knew his real name was Michael
Martin. I think that's why he was prepared to trust him,
really. He used to see him at the Lipp, always nagging at
his wife and daughter, he was, a definite family man. I didn't
think anything of it until you disappeared on the way to
meet him.'

Chapter 57

Damp from Madame Blanchard's tears, Misha sat on the bed in the café's dry goods storeroom, laughing weakly from relief. Fear was briefly postponed and the whirl of impossible ways and means gone over and over with Reine postponed also. Monsieur Jules, older and thinner, stood nonetheless like a pillar of remembered strength, offering her a tray. A drift of something scented reached her. 'Not real coffee, Monsieur Jules?' she said, breathing in.

'Just for you, my dear Mademoiselle Misha,' he said, leaning towards her so she could see her own bowl with the green rim and the family napkin ring she'd always had, a wooden one with most of the green paint rubbed off.

She took the tray and lowered it on to her knees and saw something extraordinary from the old days also. '*Café au lait?*' she said. 'With cow's milk?'

'Sshh,' Madame Blanchard said, blowing her nose. 'My boy brings us milk, and don't ask me how my heart stands it, him living like he does! Drink it quick, they'll smell it downstairs. The day you left Paris with that haversack and that cat, I put some coffee beans in a sealed packet and I said to Jules, if ever she comes home, that's what we must have ready for her . . .'

'You are so kind and I'm so sorry to be putting you at such risk.' Misha lowered her face and picked up the bowl with red, stiff fingers, taking a sip of something so bitter-sweet, she couldn't swallow it.

Monsieur Jules smiled. 'It's our Robert's bolt-hole,' he said. 'He sometimes has need of one. You might say it's been as useful to us lately as when it held flour and rice. Just remember the hatch into the attic is behind the stack of broken chairs. You must get into it fast and draw the chairs across it if you hear either of us bring anyone up the stairs. If we also shout, "Ah, Messieurs, I'll have to fetch the key from the kitchen for this door," you'll realise it's police and you stay there until one of us confirms it's all right again.' He put a hand on her shoulder and patted it. 'You understand we have to lock you in? It's a safe system we've devised for Robert – the wireless is in there too so we never get caught listening with the dial turned to the BBC.'

'I understand,' Misha said. 'And I'll leave it all back to Robert once Reine's found me lodgings where I can be Catherine Fournier and no one'll recognise me. I'd never have dreamed there'd be a soldier and a Gestapo man in our block of flats but I did intend to stay with my mother.' She took another mouthful of the coffee and her eyes watered. 'I was so foolish about Paris in this war-time winter, I assumed she'd be able to offer me a long, hot bath.' Still she'd failed to reveal the truth about her mother and it was almost as if her mind refused the truth: her mother was offering her body to the enemy and this apparently without Reine's fine distinction. Her man was one of the killers. He plotted torture and death from his office in between thinking of her mother. 'It's a shame she's away,' she said. I would like somehow, she thought, for my mother to be hiding here with me, on the run, on the right side. We'd be proud of each other then.

Monsieur Jules moved to the door and put his ear to it. 'I'll close the bar now. My wife will fetch you what you need, Misha, water and so on to wash, a bucket. You will not have to be shy with us. If no one saw you slip in the kitchen way dressed in Reine's fur coat, we'll have nothing to worry about, and you'll stay here until we find some solution. Trust me, I shall find one.'

Looking up into his concerned face, she said, 'I know I can trust you absolutely, but I don't want to be the cause of your being arrested, and not just arrested. If that Eric or even Denis recognise me as Michèle Martin, British spy, you'll both be shot. If you can help me find work and a place where I can be Catherine Fournier, I think I'd do best to lie low until the Allies come and forget helping. What good would I be? They shouldn't be long now they're in North Africa. Have you heard?' She held the tray with both hands to stop it rattling on her trembling knees. She needed very badly to sleep, to forget.

'He's heard!' Madame Florence said. 'D'you think I can prevent him crawling into that attic space where he's hidden the wireless? When you left Monsieur Steiner took over the translating, but of course after he was taken in July, my husband managed to find someone else I'm not supposed to know about to crawl in there with him and it's six months in prison for listening to the BBC.'

'The less you know, my dear wife!' Monsieur Jules straightened his jacket and apron and slipped out.

'Oh, Mademoiselle Misha,' Madame Blanchard said, letting a few more tears fall. 'He's mixed up in something awful and I can't stop him anymore than I can stop my boy roaming the countryside with papers that say he's thirty-three when anyone can see he's twenty-five. If he's caught, he'll be sent to work in German factories, they're rounding up boys under thirty-two, but they'll do worse than that if they find out what else he's up to.'

Taking very nearly the last sip from the bowl, dizzy with unaccustomed caffeine, Misha said, 'What did your husband mean, Monsieur Steiner was taken? Reine said the same thing but I didn't have time to ask what she meant.' Of course, she did know and didn't want to. He'd been arrested.

'Oh, that lovely Monsieur Steiner and his shy little wife were rounded up with all the other foreign Jews in Paris last July. Thousands of them there were, all taken to that big sports stadium and left in a terrible heat without food or water or lavatories. There was nowhere for them to sit much less sleep. Days it went on and many started screaming and howling like animals to get water, to move, anything and then some began throwing themselves off the top to die to get out of it.' She put both hands over her face and moaned. 'To think of such things happening to a man you'd been serving with his aperitif for the past ten

362

years, whose wife you saw pass by every morning to fetch her bread.'

'Did Monsieur Steiner throw himself off?' She felt very sick. She'd known it was going to be awful.

'We never could find out, my dear. Jules went down there to try and pass in food but he couldn't get close enough. When he came home, he vomited down the cellar steps and wouldn't speak of it for days. I'm only glad they got that big son of theirs down south in time.'

'Yes,' Misha said. 'Monsieur Steiner must have been glad too. He did love him so. He wanted him to do some good in the world, be a doctor, save lives . . .' Her old friend's face came to her very clearly, cap pulled down to his eyebrows, pipe clamped in his mouth. No, not the pipe, of course. His mouth open, and howling into hot July air with the smell of urine and faeces in it. He'd be frantic, trying to protect his wife and fearing that if this were to be their end, it wouldn't come soon enough.

'Then they began to send them off in buses, the ones who hadn't been stifled or crushed to death, child, and if you want a glimpse of hell, try and picture it, though it's better not to.' Madame Florence paused and rubbed her face with her sleeve. 'There's worse, you know, and we only learned about it because of the policeman, Chartier – you'll remember him, he lived on the first floor. He sent his wife and kids south before you left and being lonely, poor chap, he spent many an evening in the café. Well, after he was sent to round up the orphans, he couldn't wait to unburden himself to Jules and me . . .'

'Which orphans?' Misha asked, staring into her bowl at the last drop of milk fat. What had Monsieur Steiner and his wife to die *for*? she wondered.

'The ones left behind. The order to collect the foreign Jews didn't include their children so these mites were left about and another order was given that they be taken to the sports stadium too. Oh, I wish I'd never listened to Chartier, but I had to, he was so upset. He was one of the policemen sent to round them up and take them to this stadium, and a sight more terrible you'd never be able to dream up, he said. The bodies and mess'd been cleared away, there was just a bit of grass and a few flowers left in this sort of wasteland with a pall of terrible heat and a stench over it. The kids were dumped there in vanloads, all ages, lots hardly more than babies, toddlers of two or three. He and his colleagues stood about watching them wander around and start to pick the flowers, like kids do. There were no more orders come through to tell anyone what to do next but some Red Cross sort of women were trying to organise a supply of nappies and milk. Yet it seemed somehow, Chartier said, as if it were a *normal* kind of event. Anyway, he takes a mite by each hand and starts to wander about with them and soon there's dozens wants to hold his hand and when Chartier sees he's the only adult there weeping, he makes up his mind. He rushes in here that evening and says he's never going back to work if that's what his work's supposed to be.'

Gazing into space, she said, 'If you imagine all that with a mother's eye, Mademoiselle Misha, you can't ever clear it out of your mind. My Jules, that's when he admitted what he'd seen. Of course, we put Chartier up here in our Robert's hiding place.'

'Where is he now?' Misha asked. It was the only possible question at this point. She knew where the orphans went next. To the same place as any surviving parents.

'Gone underground,' Madame Blanchard replied, getting to her feet. 'And now I've told you enough to keep you well awake all night. I'll fetch up some hot water from downstairs, there's still electricity, thank heaven.' She was about to unlock the door when Misha asked her own question yet again, hoping against hope to hear of rumour and counter-rumour and possibilities. 'Have you news of the professor?' she said. 'Reine did say something but . . .'

Slowly, Madame Blanchard straightened her stiff back. Misha heard the squeak of her stays and in the gloom saw her shake her head. 'I'm glad I wasn't the one to tell you, child. I know how much he meant to you though you'll have mixed with some nice boys by now, won't you? A first love . . .' She turned and put her cold hand on Misha's icy one. 'Keep it as a lovely memory to look back on,' she said. 'The poor brave man! It's always the best who go young, you know. The day my husband told me, I saw him weep at last.'

Trying to articulate another question, Misha could not.

'Three or four weeks ago, it was. He was arrested by the Gestapo. And I keep thinking of his mother alone in the country getting a parcel of her son's clothes.'

'A parcel, Madame Blanchard?'

'That's how they inform the relatives their dear one will never go home again.'

Chapter 58

In the kitchen over the barber's shop, Philippe watched Blanchard, his friend and first group member, lean his elbows on the table. 'Nobody in when I passed through but the barber's got two square necks booked in for later. Then he'll close for lunch and come up to join us,' he whispered. 'God, Constantin, I can't tell you how delighted I am to know you got out and in one piece!'

Philippe felt both his hands taken up and shaken warmly a second time. 'I am delighted to see you, Blanchard,' he said. He felt himself relax a little. There was something about this man which gave comfort. Maybe it was his air of certainty – that their clandestine, risky work was simply necessary, a job to be done. He was without doubt a natural for it, as he himself had reported to London HQ. Blanchard, he'd said, had taken to it like a duck to water. He wished he'd found more like him.

'Is everything ready for the pick-up?' he heard him say to Chartier without asking for date, time, or place that Chartier was to be collected by the 'plane being sent from London. None had understood the principle of cut-off better than Blanchard. What an agent didn't know, he couldn't reveal, even under the most brutal torture. And may you be spared that, my dear Blanchard, he thought in distress.

'Magenta's checked the landing-field and the farmer's quite happy with the amount of arms being dropped though it's more than expected. I'm trying to persuade Constantin to come with me,' Chartier replied, 'but he won't budge.'

'Chartier's right, Constantin, you're a marked man. Get

366

out now. London'll send you to a different area to set up new groups. There's work to be done all over France, you know that.'

Philippe felt Blanchard's steady gaze on him and smiled. 'I do indeed, old chap,' he said, 'but I shan't have finished my work in this one yet until I have convinced myself Savoy is not a set-up. The only way to find out is to ask him a few questions ourselves.'

'All right, Constantin,' Jules Blanchard said gently. 'Given we must take in this man, why d'you have to be involved yourself? You've always said personal revenge must never be in our vocabulary. Hot heads equal loss of security, you told us. You even said outright that London HQ was fearful of we French indulging in too much of both, and some at HQ would rather send out British agents . . .'

Philippe watched his friend's pale tired face flush with the warmth of his feeling. 'I am glad I've taught you so well, Blanchard,' he said. 'And honestly, it has nothing to with the fact that I spent three very unpleasant weeks contemplating my own death as a probable result of this man's probable double game. No, it's because he must be stopped. He's been successful in our group, with two, three lost already and me perhaps bait for the rest of you. If we don't get to him before he's moved on, there'll be more clothes parcels being received by families and a crack in the enemy defences sealed up also.' He leaned back and yawned as Chartier began his reasoning again. But they'd all said enough. And he was decided. He would not leave until Savoy was brought in. It was not personal. No. He was also decided on that. It was not because the image of Misha's father was so displeasing to him.

Head thumping from fatigue and bad air, bad food, he gazed at the top of Blanchard's white head with his big peasant's hands cupped around it. He had had a sleepless night, and in his half-waking state had dreamed that Misha was a faint ghostly presence tapping on a window and calling, calling. He wanted to get up and run to her but something invisible was between them, and anyway he was bound fast by a weight on his chest.

He found he was about to get up from his chair with

remembered, helpless anguish when Blanchard's voice penetrated. 'But Chartier,' he was saying, 'Why on earth did you just remark it was a pity Mademoiselle Misha wasn't still living in Paris? Whatever made you think of her?'

'Because Savoy's not just any Englishman, Blanchard, he's Misha's father,' Chartier replied. 'If anyone could get through to him safely, it'd surely be his own daughter.'

Jules Blanchard groaned. 'Constantin,' he said, 'Chartier. Perhaps I should have told you a simple fact earlier. Mademoiselle Misha is at present sheltering in Robert's hiding place, our dry goods storeroom, having been chased from pillar to post by the enemy as a suspected British spy.'

And so he did get up, his head bursting.

Chartier raised his voice and said, 'Constantin, we can do it!'

He himself said, 'Chased by the enemy, Blanchard, hiding, frightened? And here in Paris?'

'All those things, Constantin,' Blanchard said. 'Sit down, man. It's got to be talked through.'

'No,' Philippe said. 'She'd be at tremendous risk. I can't sanction it.' The dream came vividly back to him, her ghostly presence, her voice calling him. He eased himself back into the seat and put his head in his hands. Misha, half a kilometre away, less. 'How long has she been in trouble?'

'Weeks. Down at her grandparents, an injured British parachutist made his way to their land. It's a long story, but they took in the grandad for it and she was warned to get out fast. A neighbour bought her false papers and she came up here hoping not to be recognised. Of course, with Gestapo Eric on the premises and that nasty little nest of spies on the other side of our street . . .'

Philippe thought, John Keating, his friend Keating, having fallen badly, went there for help carrying the wordless message he himself had foolishly entrusted to him. So it was his fault, caused by his longing that she should remember him as he remembered her. This was the result – her grandfather probably brutalised to death and she pursued from pillar to post. Misha was on the run, terrified, alone. Half-listening to the debate between Blanchard and

Chartier, he made up his mind: he'd get her away from the city. He must go to her now and organise it. In his second disguise, there'd be little risk. But he'd take it anyway. He'd promised her he'd always be her friend. And he'd let her down.

'I tell you, Constantin,' Chartier was saying, 'If we act fast, Misha can travel to London with me next Thursday, London'd be delighted with her. Think of the good work she could do, bilingual like she is, they could use her at the transmitter station getting messages here, just think . . .'

Staring at Chartier's excited face, he thought, London, England, Misha being so happy to be useful, Misha being as safe as houses, in England. He drew up his chair.

'I think she can do it, what's more,' Jules Blanchard said. 'She's got guts and there's absolutely no doubt about her moral fibre. Where she has it from, with those two parents of hers, we'll never know. She was arrested way back in 1940, June 1940, for making a hostile gesture against the enemy – throwing a beer barrel out in front of their motor-cade, no less – and they took her in for it. She was in the Cherche-Midi for weeks until her mother's protector had her released. We had no idea of course but she's been telling my wife all about it since we offered her shelter . . .'

Philippe gazed at Blanchard's mouth uttering these extra-ordinary words and felt the band of pain tighten around his chest.

Chapter 59

'So my father might be a double agent working for the Germans and may have betrayed your agents who've died under torture?' Misha said.

'That is what we think, my colleagues and I,' Jules Blanchard replied. He was sitting on the floor of the storeroom, his back against the door. 'Those of the group who are left.'

Misha stared down at him from her place on the bed. 'And I must go and speak to him and bring him to you so you can question him?'

'Nothing quite so risky as that, my dear. But if you agree, we'd like you to approach him at this hotel he hardly ever leaves, and where mostly Nazi officers are staying. You approach him as discreetly yet as casually as possible and tell him you'd like him to meet you. We'll give you an address where you must pretend you have a room. None of us in the group dare go near that hotel, but you must think carefully before you agree to act for us. There's a real element of danger in it for you. And he is your father.'

'He wasn't much of a father,' she said. 'If he's staying amongst Nazis, isn't it obvious he's with them? Why did your agent Voltaire think he was all right?'

'Ah, well, under their very noses is often the best place to be. They don't look there! And he'd need to work with them if he wants to remain a dealer. He was buying and selling gold, guns and so on all over Europe before the war, wasn't he? We think perhaps he's been mixed up here with the Dutch and Belgian profiteers who've infested Paris since the Occupation. If he's reneged on a deal and those gangsters are out to get him, he'll also feel safer where he is. That could be why he approached our agent Voltaire and was angling to exchange passes and information on the enemy for underground help to get out. Whatever!'

He smiled across at her. 'Me and my friends need to ask him a few questions anyway. We'll do it in Paris once we get hold of him. And we shall be absolutely ruthless, Mademoiselle Misha. If he is proved to be a traitor, we shall kill him unless London HQ think they'd like to use him from there to send the enemy false information. In that case, we'll persuade him into a 'plane with assurance of our protection. Certainly they'll have more time to extract what they can from him, but he'll be put in prison probably and have to stand trial at the end of the war . . .'

My father, thought Misha, trapped, nowhere to run to anymore, making his deals to the end. This war'll give me the break I deserve, he used to say. But he hadn't been clever enough. She'd understood that at once. Her father was a very small fish lost in a big murky pond.

Jules Blanchard eased himself to his feet and sat down beside her on the bed. 'Your part in this involves you in a moral dilemma not many have to face, you know. He is your own flesh and blood and I have made it quite clear what will become of him if you are successful. Moreover, only you are likely to be so. I shall do nothing to help persuade you. But I can say one of us will escort you out of Paris shortly afterwards. I'll say nothing about our plans for this arrangement in case you're stopped. The less you understand, the better.' Pausing, he added, 'I hope I haven't upset you too much. I should hate my own daughter to be faced with such a choice!'

'Your daughter's chosen,' Misha said, 'She's helping Robert with food supplies for starving people from her farm in the country although she's a mother with two children and risks their being hurt. Sometimes they beat little children to make mothers confess things, don't they?'

Jules Blanchard put a hand on her shoulder. 'I hope she'd betray me if she had evidence I was betraying my own kind,' he said.

'Except that you wouldn't, Monsieur Jules.' Staring at the

371

door behind which she was in effect trapped, she wondered vaguely where her next hiding place would be after she'd been taken out of Paris.

'We do not judge your father yet, my child. Anyway, shall I ask you to sleep on it? Sometimes the mind at rest solves one's problems.' He stood up, as if to return downstairs.

'Yes,' Misha heard herself say. 'But I've already made up my mind.'

'Florence will bring you up the hot water and a little drop of something warming.' He was hesitating, fiddling with his keys.

Misha saw he was concerned about leaving her alone. 'You're both so kind to me, Monsieur Jules, goodnight.'

He was obliged then to unlock the door and go. Hearing the key turn again, Misha thought, yes, and my father is trapped also, as good as behind locked doors, and by his own making, his bluster, the big schemes he was never big enough for. He'd been a petty dealer all his life and in a war had chosen to deal with what he'd see as the big shots, the smart set mixing with enemy big shots, betraying his own kind. Only they weren't his own kind.

Her father was on the other side, or rather on his own side. If she had wondered far enough about his past behaviour and his disappearances, she'd have realised this. Now she did.

It hadn't taken long for Monsieur Jules's words to open up a great pit of anguish. Her father had helped send men to their death in the rue de Saussaies. People like him had caused the suffering of the Englishman, Pépé, the Steiners, the orphans in the sports stadium wept for by a solitary policeman.

And thousands more like them, she thought, thousands more, millions, until she reached the bottom of her particular blackness and thought his name, Philippe.

Chapter 60

'Ain't Madame Florence got something better in the way of a looking-glass?' Reine cried. 'How can Mish see this face I done her?'

'Oh, *là là*,' said Monsieur Jules from the doorway. 'A feminine boudoir in my dry goods store. Well, the war brings me nice things from time to time. My wife has had the very same thought, my dear Reine, and has made the sacrifice of her powder compact with a dust of pre-war powder in it.'

'I don't want her seeming wrong,' Reine said, snatching it. 'Put up your head, Mish. Oh, this light!'

Helpless under Reine's ministrations, Misha did so. 'It won't attract notice, Reine, just me and you going into the hotel without an escort?'

'This place ain't for provincial couples on a night out, Mish,' Reine said, dabbing powder on her friend's cheeks. 'This is the smart world. There's girls going in there and blatantly offering themselves to Nazi officers, titties all over the tables, skirts hitched up, disgraceful it is. And I don't mean girls like me, I mean ones like my Isa and the friends she's made in the cafés. Instead of staying little innocents, they're out there younger than ever, like as if this war's made 'em desperate for some enjoyment before their bloom's gone and it's too late. You got to have principles, really, to stay home in the cold with nothing in your belly when your only chance of fun in life is in them lovely lit-up places, even if they is full of the enemy.' She sighed, dabbing her own face after an expert glance in the mirror. 'And they're handsome in their uniforms, them officers,

373

they're strong, they're male, they're *conquerors*, Mish.' She sighed again and snapped shut the compact, sitting down on the bed beside her. 'Give us a recap, Monsieur Jules,' she said. 'Tell us again exactly what we have to do because we can't make any mistakes, I know that.'

Monsieur Jules leaned against the door. 'You have to go into the hotel bar, buy yourselves a drink with the money I've given you, chat to the barman perhaps, but don't get involved with any other guests, that's essential. Wander about as if looking for the Ladies sign, glance into the restaurant and so on. Misha will be the one to spot her father, of course, and when she does, she'll have to make a signal that she wants to speak to him alone. Let's hope he's aware of her risk as well as his own and isn't daft enough to say something in English.'

He could well be daft enough, Misha thought, because in public places he was all bluster. He was a show-off. He wanted people to notice him. He'd be quite likely to address an enemy officer in the French or German equivalent of 'My man'. Which language could he be using? His accent in both was comic enough to be used in one of those films about the English abroad.

'And if he's not there, we must go through it again tomorrow evening and the next?' Reine asked, linking her arm through Misha's.

'We have three evenings to try it before it'll be too late for the special arrangements we've been making for Misha's escape from Paris and if he's not there by then, maybe we ought to assume he's done a bunk of his own or been moved on by his enemy masters, if that has been his game.'

It will have been, Misha thought. She had only briefly doubted it. And he had got in too deep. He'd been wanting to get back into their old flat to hide the day Madame Libaud had seen him with the caretaker. He was frightened and had nowhere to run to. Perhaps he'd be pleased to see her. 'Don't forget to call me Catherine, Reine,' she said, trying to straighten the hat perched on her head. It had been concocted from bits and pieces by Madame Florence that afternoon and felt like a dried pancake.

'Leave that alone do, Mish, I mean Catherine, heavens,

374

that's going to be the hardest part. These new shapes is being worn forward, I told you.'

Misha stood up. The hat was too far forward, the canvas base unbalanced over her left eyebrow. 'I'll never be able to get into the Métro carriage with it on, and your fur coat's really too big, Reine. Can't I go in my cape?' She felt so alien to herself in her disguise that maybe it was going to be easy to commit the alien act of sending her own flesh and blood to prison or death.

'Into that place, certainly not,' Reine said. 'We'd be laughed out of it. Here, I'll put a bit more into this safety pin, hold on. I match you, anyway, the jacket Madame Florence lent is flapping round me, proper country cousins we're going to look.'

The moment has come, Misha thought, giving herself up to Reine, breathing in the mingled scents, lavender and mothballs fur. I must bear all this, she thought, bear looking ridiculous, over-painted, the lipstick like candle-grease on my mouth, and I must bear the journey underground which I have never borne before. I shall concentrate on these discomforts and my fear that hundreds of tons of earth and the entire River Seine will cave on to my particular Métro carriage, so that when I come to the moment I have to seal my father's death, I shall not hesitate. I shan't have worked myself up to it and it will be easy.

'My word,' Monsieur Jules said, as Reine finished meddling with the coat, 'you'll be so busy fighting off male attention tonight, you'll forget what you're there for.' He smiled at Reine and added, 'Remember the places Nazi officers frequent are often raided by their own military controls who'll order any females not German wives to attend for a medical inspection the next morning. They can't have their men catching anything.'

'Pouff!' Reine said, 'They can medically inspect me if they like, I'm used to it but let 'em trying touching my cousin Catherine just out of a convent. Ready, cousin Cath?' she cried. 'Ready to go out into that street and fool that Alibert and Lagrue? If they ever finds out they've had a proper eyeful of British spy without realising it . . .'

'I'm ready for anything, Reine,' Misha said, accepting her arm.

She was ready. And when she'd finally carried out a task in the cause of resistance, a vital one only she could do, she'd make herself open and read the notes Philippe had written her so long before. These messages from the past would thus add pain to pain and all of it could be sealed up to bury deep and be forgotten.

Chapter 61

The most astonishing thing about the hotel was its warmth. Misha felt it as soon as she and Reine had passed the controls at the door and had stepped through the layers of thick blue curtaining which was Paris's version of blackout. After that, it was the amount of wasteful light. She couldn't remember when she'd last been aware of more than a dim blue bulb.

There was music also. A piano was being played somewhere at the far end of the foyer. Around the pianist there was pre-war laughter. Also evening dresses, fur stoles, white military uniforms, gold epaulettes, jewellery. No plain suits, from her first glance, but she wouldn't stare. She must be casual and come upon her father as if by accident.

'What did that woman say to you, Catherine my love?' Reine said, holding tight to her arm as they strolled along the carpet. This was their agreed conversation, Reine's idea, to prevent her adding the word Mish to every sentence.

'That I was far too uppity for an apprentice schoolteacher,' Misha replied, glad to feel the steadiness of her friend's support through the layers of bulky fur. She was almost used to the fur, almost used to the hat. It was the glare of light and the acres of white tablecloth spread with pre-war table silver in the restaurant to their left that had startled her for a moment. And the fact waiters were proferring menus. There were menus here, choice, food. There had been all the time, whilst people screamed under torture in dungeons and toddlers wandered over a wasteland with

377

only a policeman to grasp their hand. She just hadn't imagined it.

I am in the wrong place, she thought, with a chill sense of desolation and helplessness. I am in the wrong place for me but I am in the right place for my task which I would like to have done with.

'Look at 'em,' Reine hissed. 'Get your friends at home to send over a few thousand bombs as soon as they can to clear out these Kraut gangsters – and their women. I swear I can smell beefsteak . . .' Pulling Misha into the bar on their right, she cried loudly, 'A Cinzano for my little cousin, Monsieur, and a little something nice for me if you can spare it.'

They were shortly leaning on the counter whilst an attentive barman found something special for Reine and Reine pulled out a cigarette. This was also for show.

Misha took a deep breath. It was gloomy there. She was used to gloom. It was also practically empty though a dark shape or two sat in a corner. She felt better. Reaching up to push the hat firmly to the back of her head, she also felt more comfortable. She needed to, for her task. Reine had successfully got them both to this point. Now she must take control of herself. Accepting the glass, she held it to her lips, letting Reine carry on her flirtation with the barman. Another figure was being drawn into Reine's impressive act, she noticed. A man had risen from his seat in the corner and was saying, 'A light for your cigarette, Madame? And may I also pay for those drinks?'

He had some kind of heavy accent. Plain-clothes police probably, she thought. This was to be expected. He was off duty obviously. There was nothing to worry about. In fact, she felt enough, at ease to swallow some imitation Cinzano. Then she looked up and saw her father's face looking at her, horror written on it.

Chapter 62

Reine had led the way down to the basement cloakroom where anyone could stand talking for a moment without looking obvious. The three of them arrived there somehow without a word of either language having been spoken. Reine then strolled towards the cloakroom lady of the usual Paris kind, elderly, with a face of indifference because she had seen it all.

Misha stood beside her father watching Reine begin a conversation and said clearly, in best French, 'It is so nice to see you again, Uncle Michel, Reine was only saying to me just now, "Cousin Catherine," she said, "I wonder if Uncle Michel's there tonight, he'll be able to give you a hand." '

There was no change in his expression and he gave no reply. She could smell his familiar cologne mixed with the lavatory smell. Had he understood? She couldn't see. In the dim light, his face was paler, thinner, but it bore a trace of the sulky schoolboy, the way it used to do when he was displeased and determined to get his own way. His blue eyes seemed to have no colour, gazing at Reine and the cloakroom lady. The gingery moustache hadn't its old sharpness and there was a slight suggestion of wear about his tweed suit. This she had time to take in because he seemed unable to respond in any way. Must she begin again, try another direction? She and Reine had worked out several.

He shifted his cashmere coat from one arm to the other as a chain was pulled and a man in a suit emerged, throwing a coin into the saucer and muttering, '*Bonsoir, M'Sieur, 'Dames.*'

'*M'sieur,*' her father replied sourly. His first word.

Misha felt encouraged to continue. She'd like it to be over quickly. '*Maman*'s still living in the flat near here,' she said. 'She went to Vichy in 1940 but came back recently.'

'Good.' He managed this also. It was a strangulated sort of sound and he went on staring at Reine who'd reached the stage of asking the cloakroom woman to look in her left eye. There was a lash in it.

'I'm so glad we met tonight, Uncle Michel,' she said. 'Because I'm in a bit of trouble, actually. Could you call and see me at my new place later? It's quite urgent but I don't want to go into it here. About ten would suit me, or the same time tomorrow. It's been hard on my own, I must admit and if it weren't for Cousin Reine . . .'

'Where?'

Twice she told him the address Monsieur Jules had given her. 'It's not far,' she added. 'You could be back before curfew.'

'I don't need to keep the curfew,' he said, gazing down the corridor where signs announced AIR RAID SHELTER and also CLUB DE JAZZ. There was a gleam of sweat on his forehead.

She had to swallow the urge to make the peremptory remark she'd have made to him in the old days: 'Could you repeat that, Dad, to be sure you've got it?' And almost as if she had dared to do so, he turned a little further round and glanced at her. 'That hat is particularly ridiculous on you,' he said.

Slowly, his heavy body moved towards the stairs. Without his London smartness, he had the air of a man in reduced circumstances, of a man quite alone. Watching him, she had to blink away tears. But no one could ever be lonelier than a traitor. The Nazis despised traitors. She wouldn't pity him. There was never any pity from the side he'd chosen to join. In view of their different characters, though, it was quite remarkable both her parents should have made the same choice.

*

380

'That eye's real sore, Cath,' Reine said, leaving the cloak-room. 'Uncle Michel's gone, has he? Shame he didn't stop to buy us a drink.'

'He's agreed to come to my place later,' Misha said.

Reine prodded her and winked. 'Here, let's try that night-club, it's just opening. I couldn't half do with a sit-down.'

Blindly, Misha followed her friend. She too wanted to sit down. They were probably exhausted. Much effort and planning had gone into the scene just played out and they wouldn't know its result until Monsieur Jules had made his telephone call after ten o'clock. Her own part was done. Shortly, she'd begin to feel relieved.

The room served as air-raid shelter and nightclub, being low and dark and packed all round with sandbagging. The pianist from the foyer also served two purposes. He'd installed himself at a second instrument and was drinking beer. A singer in a long sequined dress was trying out a few bars of a song between puffs at a cigarette.

Reine fell into a chair near the door beside a notice asking clients to remain seated until they heard the all-clear sound. This sight pleased Misha. Good, she thought, wrapping the awkward fur around her so she could sit down, they maintain the shelter's set up because of their bombing, now they have to expect Allied bombing, which they will shortly receive. Paris will not remain theirs.

'Christ!' Reine said. 'I'm damp all down my spine. I was afraid you'd never have done with it. I could almost smoke a fag now. We are sure, are we, he isn't telling on us upstairs?'

'I hope he isn't, Reine,' Misha said. 'He didn't seem to want to open his mouth but I'm certain he took me at my word. I mean, a father wouldn't suspect a daughter nor-mally, and he certainly wouldn't consider me capable of undercover work. He didn't think I'd be up to trapping a husband, let alone a traitor . . .' And that is why it has worked, she thought, and I must remember that my own betrayal of him is a tiny step towards the freedom of this city.

'We'll stay here a bit to get our nerve back,' Reine said, 'then we'll make our way out. We'll get one of them *vélo-*

381

taxis if there is one. He'll go as far as the river. We need a treat. Won't be far by Métro after, will it?'

'No,' Misha said, forcing herself to relax and watch the club preparations. This was a world she'd never see again. The singer yawned and leaned on the piano. A waiter appeared from a door behind it and put down a tray of glasses on a table near the dance floor. At most two people could dance on that, she thought vaguely, transferring her gaze to the only other occupants, a couple at a corner table. The man looked like Gestapo but it didn't worry her. They'd passed all the controls and no one but her father had glanced at them. Anyway, the officer was occupied by his girl, running his fingers down her neck and into the bodice of her dress, easing off her fur coat and furthering the procedure with his mouth.

'Disgusting, in public like that,' Reine said, and got to her feet with such suddenness Misha's heart thumped from shock. It was very fast, what happened next, yet afterwards it seemed to her that Reine had been frozen to the spot with the chair overturned for a minute or more. But it couldn't have been that long. She was silent, opening her bag and finally moving, skirting round the table and on to the dance floor. Misha heard her heels tap, one, two, three, four, on the wood.

The Gestapo man hadn't heard them. His entire upper body was occupied in his ministrations to the girl. So Reine had a clear angle.

It was only because she hadn't understood that Misha remained glued to her seat. Otherwise she might have followed, thinking their act wasn't finished.

Isa screamed first, though quietly. 'Eric!' A restrained sort of scream. She too, though, could not have understood what her mother was about. Only Reine herself did and she was very deliberate in the thrusting movement she made.

Misha herself had a flash image she was never to forget: Gestapo Eric's head rolling sideways, blood gushing from it all over everything, and the singer trying to push Reine through the door behind the piano. She didn't see what happened next because she'd slipped into the corridor and was carefully walking past the cloakroom towards the stairs.

*

Philippe forced himself to take his eyes away from the hotel entrance and stroll casually in the direction of the queue of bicycle-drawn contraptions everyone else took for granted but he could not. Nonetheless, he'd have preferred to have the place Chartier had now, waiting for them to emerge. Only he'd been voted down, and Chartier had simply refused to allow it. His was the contact as a former policeman and anyway, the *vélo-taxi* owner would countenance no one but an ex-colleague on that saddle. There'd been some debate on the issue, Blanchard being violently opposed and refusing to tell the girls Chartier'd be there in order to allow him the chance to reconsider. Still, the bicycle and its mock-carriage would enable Chartier to travel safely to the rendezvous with Misha's father.

'Get out of it, man,' he heard Chartier hiss.

He got out of it, reaching the café and ordering coffee he didn't want. The stuff appeared before him as he sat at a table by the window staring at curtains which prevented him from seeing into the street. Without them, he might have been able to catch sight of Misha as she emerged with her friend. Not an unsuitable friend, either, he reminded himself. A stout-hearted and useful one. She was helping Misha carry out the task he'd so foolishly, carelessly allowed her to be given.

The result of this foolishness was that he and Chartier were taking further risk to themselves by being near the scene of the action.

Except there was no action. A girl was going into a hotel to speak to the father she'd lost sight of before the war. It was simple, a family matter, and against no regulation, new or old.

Swallowing something scalding, he threw down a few sous and returned to the pavement. He also was perfectly safe in the new disguise declaring him to be one Marcel Frédéric Latour, dealer in fine art, specialist in seventeenth-century Dutch painters. He should have chosen this one before. They were less inclined to stop those with a prosperous air since prosperity in this war meant you were a collaborator.

Fearing to hear the sound of running, of whistles and cars around the hotel entrance, he was surprised at the silence.

Chartier was feigning the inspection of a tyre. It was early still, of course. The cyclists would have few clients until the diners re-appeared. Misha's father dined sharp at eight, they knew that and had hoped she'd be able to speak to him whilst he was in the bar having his aperitif. Whisky, that was his drink. They knew much about Misha's father. Well, he wouldn't be having whisky. That was the only thing he could be sure of, he realised and he should never have let the things reach the planning stage.

He'd gone so far as to imagine himself strolling into the hotel and ordering dinner when in his agitation he crossed the road a third time. This was such a foolishness, he made himself stop. He must appear lost. He must cross back and ask one of the other *vélo-taxi* drivers the direction he'd need to take for some other hotel. Hesitating, cursing himself, he was about to do so when he saw Chartier was opening the door of his ludicrous contraption for a woman stepping towards it.

He wouldn't have known it was Misha. She had on a woman's hat and a bulky fur coat. Her disguise. It was a good one. But it was so long since he'd seen her!

Chartier was taking her arm. There was a pause. She was saying something to him, removing her hat, putting a hand to her mouth. There was no mistaking her slender grace as she stood there. He could almost see the shape of her face, the shadow of her eyes as she leaned down to get herself inside. Chartier was protecting her head as she did so. This should have been him. He'd go forward now, quickly, and come upon her as an old acquaintance, gather her up, embrace her, kiss her at last. 'How wonderful to see you again, Catherine,' he'd say. Chartier would move up to the café to wait there whilst he and she took a drink together . . .

The door of the contraption slammed shut. Chartier threw a leg over the saddle and pedalled off.

He waited until the thing had disappeared before he collected himself and his heart resumed its normal beat.

She was out of it. She was safe. And then he realised there was no Reine. Something had gone wrong.

'The word I have received from my telephone call is Yes,'

Jules Blanchard said, locking the door of the storeroom behind him.

'This means my father went to the address I gave him?' Misha said, hugging Reine's fur coat around her knees. It smelt of Reine.

'It does,' Jules Blanchard said, sitting on the bed beside her. 'It also means, very probably, that your father has been permitted to leave that hotel and after the murder of a Gestapo officer in its basement . . .' He shook his head.

'That my father is working for them.' She wrapped the old Blanchard family dressing-gown further round her shoulders. She could find no touch of warmth in any part of her body and shook so much, they had had to offer her precious cognac from the stock kept in case Robert should be injured. 'Will they have killed Reine at once?'

'I doubt it. That'd be too easy for her. They could decide to hush it up completely from shame, I suppose. I mean, with their officers in every corner of that place! Or they might take fifty hostages and shoot them, as an example, followed by a mock trial for poor Reine . . .'

'She'll be tortured first?'

Jules Blanchard paused. 'It won't be easy for her.'

'It's our fault.'

'Tonight, yes, but perhaps something like it would have happened anyway. My wife was sure the girl was pregnant, she had the look of it, she said . . .'

'And Reine loved her so.' Her hand holding the brandy glass shook and her teeth seemed to be rattling. She'd never be able to sleep or find a moment's rest.

'She put fifteen years of love into the only pure thing she ever had, or thought she had. That girl had sexuality in every pore, just like her mother. Reine didn't want to see it.' He held out the plate of onion and potato slices made for her by Madame Florence. 'Try one, food will warm you.'

Misha took a slice for the show of it. 'You say there's a chance Reine got away?'

'Every chance. If that singer pushed her through the door, it means her heart's in the right place, though she'll need every ounce of her courage to keep on claiming she didn't see the killer or didn't see where she went. There could be all kinds of secret corners in that hotel where Reine might be hidden.'

'What if Isa betrays her mother?' A new image flashed into her mind as she said this: Eric's blood spattering on to Isa's bare shoulders. It seemed dark, black against that white skin.

'Oh, if Reine has escaped, she will never appear in Paris again. We shall do our best to find out what's happened to her, she'll be able to go underground or we'll get her out of Paris anyway. As for Isa, she'll be sent to a nursing home in Germany. It will be a Nazi baby so they will care for mother too, though they prefer mothers also to be blond and blue-eyed, the Nazi ideal.'

He kept talking and Misha went on hugging Reine's fur coat round her knees. She could smell Reine through the onion. Reine was her fault because it was her father involved in the task. She should have gone alone. The same sense of desolation and helplessness she'd felt in the hotel seemed to spread like an icy band around her chest. It would always be like this. She'd always be helpless, they all would, and they would always lose more of their own kind in the unequal fight against the enemy.

'Anyway, my dear,' Jules Blanchard was saying. 'Preparations are in hand for your departure from Paris. I shall tell you no details as yet, just in case, but on Thursday evening you must be ready in your convent outfit with a small suitcase. You will not leave alone, an old friend will be there to see you off ...'

Chartier, Misha thought, without feeling, though he'd been a tiny comfort outside the hotel. There'd be no other comfort for a long time. And how could there be? After Pépé, there was a whole list of friends lost already or facing capture and death. And now there was Reine.

Chapter 63

With infinite stealth, Chartier edged open the farmhouse door. In the moonlight, they could see the ghostly shape of the barn and beyond it, the low, flat land essential for an aeroplane landing. 'No sign of David yet,' he whispered, closing it with the same caution.

'He's your leader sent by this SOE organisation in London?' Misha asked.

'Yes, and one of the first agents Special Operations ever trained and dropped out here – that's a word you'll soon learn. There's drops and pick-ups, postboxes for left messages, safe houses which might be no more than a store-room where we can hide.' Chartier yawned and returned to his packing task at the kitchen table. 'Special's a pretty apt word as well, since any poor devil prepared to risk life and limb must be, including you and me.' He grinned, laying out the city trousers he'd just changed out of. 'But for David there isn't any other. I'd say he has a kind of nobility you don't meet often. Blanchard has it too. Nothing escapes them, no detail of our undercover work is too small for them to weigh in the balance and every action has to have a value. Slitting the throats of a couple of soldiers on patrol is just self-indulgence if it leads to the shooting of fifty innocent people.' He looked across at her, managing to keep the smile on his thin, drawn face. 'Now, blowing up an electrical sub-station will retard one of their factories making essential ball-bearings or tank parts and even if it means a town council having to pay a huge fine in recompense, well, money isn't lives.'

'And this SOE has been sending out the explosives and the guns and the agents . . .' Misha let her voice tail off. Her Englishman. Philippe. And she herself. She watched vaguely as Chartier shook out the flannel suit she'd also changed from, folding it with a policeman's precision. He'd been kind to her throughout the train journey from Paris to some country stop and then their walk to the farmhouse where food had been left. She'd remained Catherine Fournier, convent girl, and he'd pretended to be her Uncle Alain.

'It's been such a shock, I can't tell you,' she said, 'arriving here to be flown to England by this SOE when I was assuming I'd be helped back south to lie low there. If SOE turns me down, I shan't be able to bear it. As soon as you told me, it seemed as if all my war experiences had been fated to bring me to this point.'

Gazing up at the strips of moonlight through the window shutters, she thought of her first anti-enemy gesture. 'I've even been interrogated,' she said. 'The Nazi officer had a tea-tray laid in front of me with English sandwiches on it.' A sudden wish to cry made her long to sit down again. But there was no time for this or any other weakness. The 'plane was due at any moment. In a few hours, she'd be in England. There'd be English sandwiches again, real ones with square bread and crusts. She'd be able to cut off the crusts and dip them in hot milky tea.

'Heavens,' Chartier said, rolling up the grey flannel cape, 'when David heard from Blanchard what the latest occupant of his hiding place had been through, he said, "We must get that girl to London at once."' He edged the cape carefully between her nightdress and underclothes. 'HQ might want you to come back with this outfit. It's French, you see, stiching, labels. Even the thread counts. They're using French tailors to make agents' things in London. The Nazis miss nothing. If you're arrested, everything you have on you will be gone over. Even tobacco dust in pockets could give you away as coming from England.'

'They'd better train me in folding jackets,' Misha said, as he dealt with hers. 'I've always been hopeless at it and my mother wouldn't let me bother trying . . .'

She'd almost asked to telephone her mother from the

railway café, to say goodbye, she supposed. Goodbye, *Maman*, I am leaving to join the right side. How is your new protector and did you know the hats you fuss over, your chic little dresses, are paid for with torture and death? That you and Dad did after all have something in common? Maybe they had actually met, moving as they did amongst the same smart set. Perhaps her mother had been one of the diners in that restaurant. 'It must be nearly time,' she said, again, stifling the stubborn wish to cry. She was very tired.

'We'll give David another minute,' Chartier said. 'If he's behind schedule, he'll go straight to the site. It's one he set up himself, dealing with the farmer and so on. It's the farmer who'll have organised his helpers to get the containers away and hidden as fast as possible. Enemy ears are listening for 'plane landings, local people too. Betrayal is one of our worst problems. It's astonishing what people will do for a few francs.'

'Shall I help with these containers?' Misha tugged her beret into shape and pulled it over her hair.

'Not if they're the steel ones – six foot long they are and too heavy for you. There'll be all sorts in them, guns, ammunition, plus the sweeteners, coffee and chocolate, and cigarettes, for the helpers. London's always generous. Every single helper is risking his or her life, even that farmer's wife who put out our food and let us use her house to change our clothes. If caught, they'll be sent to a German concentration camp or shot – the better option.' He clicked shut the cases and put them on the floor. 'Not afraid?'

'Not for myself,' she said. 'Though that's strange, isn't it? I waited nineteen days for my own death once and after that . . .' She shrugged. 'I'll go on worrying about my grand-parents, and my brother Félix, I expect. I keep imagining he's gone quite mad with worry about Pépé. Then there are the friends I told you about, Julien and the English one, Georgie. At least now, if I'm to get proper training, I'll be doing something for them.'

'Like me,' Chartier said. 'SOE will try and train the emotion out of us, which is all very well, but I shan't forget I'm fighting for my wife and kids, and for those orphans. When this is over, Misha, I shall go in search of them and if I find any, well, I'll apologise first, on behalf of all the French people who were part of that particular disgrace. Not a word was raised against those harmless, ordinary families being dragged apart . . .' He shook his head. 'D'you know what? You and me and the other resistants, we represent France's only hope for the future. If there's no one prepared to raise their eyes and look at what's happened to their own country, it must be a Nazi state they actually want. Imagine being a Frenchman and signing a form to order me and my colleagues to round up little kids and dump them in a wasteland. Imagine being me, Misha, realising I'm the only one to say to himself, "No, not the children, that's a step too far and now I must act . . ."'

Misha saw that he was trembling. 'Yes,' she said, shivering herself from cold and so many glimpses of other people's torment. 'And then, if you think about Monsieur Steiner himself, without even knowing what a kindly and wise man he was, even if you decide he was a rogue who was unfaithful to his wife, say, whatever kind of man he was, what have they killed him *for*? What benefit have they gained from murdering him?'

'Ah, never ask yourself that, Misha.' Chartier wrapped a scarf round his neck. 'Because that'll mean you have to look into the Nazi soul and no matter how deep you look, you'll never be able to understand or accept it. You know the worst of it all? It's the way what they do has become normal, everyday, like it's normal to collect thousands of innocent people and their children and send them off to rot in some awful camp somewhere, *discarding* them as it were. Discarding people, robbing of them of their dignity, their pride and their children first of course, that's become normal.'

'Not to me, not to us,' Misha said, taking a deep breath. 'I'd like to stand up and scream that it isn't. Years ago, back in the beginning in 1940, I used to wonder what sort of minds could have asked themselves how to kill people quickly and hit upon the idea of laying down lime in railway carriages so the fumes would stifle them to death.'

'You're an unusual girl, you know, if you don't mind me saying so.' Chartier moved towards her and put a friendly

390

arm on her shoulders. 'I'm not the only who thinks that either. We are going to stand up and tell the world one day. We can't scream it yet, though. Quietly does it for now, biding our time, fighting by every single possible undercover means till they're forced back to where they belong and the world is free to hear us. You ready to start?'

'Yes.'

He dropped his arm and picked up their cases. 'We'd better be off,' he said. 'David may have decided to go straight to the site. Edge that door open, will you? Have a look round. We can be caught even at this late stage in our escape . . .'

Misha turned the door knob with caution and put an eye to the gap. 'No one . . .' she began, and with horror freezing her body, saw the shape of a man standing outside. He spoke before she could slam the door in his face. 'Our Father which art in Heaven, Hallowed by Thy name,' he said.

This was such unlikely statement to make in such a place, she knew at once it must be the password. 'It's David,' she whispered.

'You're almost late,' Chartier said. He reached the door and stepped in front of her. Misha saw him smile as he added, 'Not my fault, Misha. David forbade me to tell you who he is.'

Staring at his departing figure, Misha felt her mouth open to form a question as the man spoke again. 'Yes, Misha,' he said, 'I wanted you not to have to consider our past friendship when you had a difficult decision to make about your father.'

It was his voice, Philippe's, low, measured, never forgotten. Philippe stood there in the doorway and shock took away her breath.

Misha said, 'It wasn't difficult to decide about my father.' And then, 'They told me you'd been driven to the rue de Saussaies. I thought you were dead.' She put out a hand to shake his. It had been such a long time. She'd be like a stranger to him.

'And I thought you were safe, dear Misha.' He accepted her cold hand in his warm one and held it.

She stifled a gasp. She'd thought him dead and as if in a dream he stood near her in the moonlight, in extraordinary circumstances, so like a dream. Yet she felt his skin on hers.

He removed his hand and used it to take off his hat which he threw down somewhere.

'It was hard,' she said, drinking in every movement, every gesture, his face, its shadows against the navy blue sky behind him. He seemed much taller. 'It was hard,' she said again, 'twice to think you dead.'

'Yes,' he said. 'It was foolish of me, Misha, to think you safe, and to send my friend to you.'

'I was so happy when our Englishman told me you hadn't been drowned in the Channel.' The words were slipping out quite easily though she very badly wanted to cry, to lean against him and weep for the years of her own suffering, and his.

'I was happy to hear from Madame Libaud you were in the Languedoc with your grandparents. That's where I wanted you to go, d'you remember?'

'Yes,' she said. 'Frou's there now. I managed to get Frou out.' Of course she remembered. She remembered everything about him, all that he'd said in their special evening times.

'Yes! I've often imagined you carrying our little cat in her basket all that way, so many miles, and under machine-gun fire . . .' He was smiling. Misha saw this clearly though it was so dark and his face was in shadow. His smile lifted all the lines of it, the way it used to do.

'Half way,' she said, wanting to move, to offer him a chair. They ought to sit down. She couldn't move. An over-whelming weakness had affected her legs. Her knees seemed to be shaking. 'I left Frou with some nuns and fetched her later.'

'And since then you've had to come back north. Did you read the notes I left for you with Madame Libaud?'

'No. I was keeping them. They're in my case. It was painful, you see, to know, to think someone dead and have

392

their . . .' She heard herself tail off. This was more than silly. She couldn't think sense much less speak it.

'But you remember what I promised you, that I'd always be your friend?'

'Yes.' And the day you said it, she thought. I've forgotten nothing, especially not my ridiculous longing for you to say more. He hadn't changed in any way. He stood as still and firm as he used to do, listening to her, patient, her friend.

'Well,' he said, 'if I have agreed you be sent to England, it's because I'm sure it's best for you. I've asked HQ to try initial training in wireless transmitting. You'll be good at that, I'm sure.'

She'd always known that if he were alive, he'd be in the resistance. And of course, he was their leader, a special man, a noble man. He was David. 'Yes,' she said, 'but Chartier thinks I'd be invaluable if I were to be trained to do real underground work, as a courier, a messenger for groups back in France . . .' Why didn't he move? She wanted to sit down with him.

'Ah, not that, no. Listen to me, Misha.' He leaned close enough for her to feel his breath. 'You've been lucky to have come through what you have, but luck never lasts. It's a kind of superstition amongst agents. They survive something tricky once, twice, then . . . D'you understand, Misha?'

She took a deep giddy breath, hearing words that didn't matter. 'Women are the most useful, Chartier says.'

'It's a man's job just the same.'

From behind him, sudden, startling, came Chartier's urgent whisper. 'Time's up. I can hear an engine, I think . . .'

'Ready, Misha?' Philippe moved at last, taking off his coat and stepping towards her to ease it round her shoulders.

This too was actually taking place, she thought, hugging it to her with his warmth, his tobacco-and-cologne smell.

'We'll walk across the pastures,' he said, 'keeping very quiet. You can tell me all about our little cat and your life together in the sunshine so that I can remind myself there were those happy years for you after the Cherche-Midi.'

She was to have a few more minutes alone with him. Misha drew another deep breath and steadied herself. She

393

must show him how calm and sensible she'd become in those years, how much she'd learned about the world, about herself, yes, her own courage, her endurance. These she'd offer him, if they'd be of any use. She'd become his messenger, his helper, the one who was his friend. She wanted to lay something of hers around his shoulders, to give him ease and warmth and comfort. She wanted to shout, 'Remember you've had two lucky escapes,' but he was taking her arm and indicating the path they must take past the barn and onwards under the moonlight.

He seemed able to move across the fields in his city shoes without a sound. She, clumsy, stumbling, breathless, muttered a jumble of details she could barely recall, the Sérieys' wine cellar, the buying of her papers in the name of Catherine Fournier, her innocent shoes in the train, her mother and the Gestapo man. He knew about her father so he was easily left out.

He, rock-solid, with a steadying arm and his coat wrapped round her, listened and finally said, 'You know that I was the one who decided your father had to be brought in to answer our questions? That we must be absolutely ruthless about the fate of anyone guilty of betraying our men to the enemy?' He paused and looked into her face.

'Yes,' she said, looking back into his, every part of it remembered. 'And it's all right.'

'Good.'

'I would have liked to say goodbye to my mother.'

'I'll see if a message can be got to her somehow.'

'Thank you.'

Then came the unmistakable whine of an aeroplane.

At the landing field there were dark shapes moving about, the murmur of voices, torches flashing. And a whine that became a rumble like thunder, shaking the earth beneath their feet.

'You are coming to London with us?' Misha said, straining her voice to be heard above it.

There was a shout from someone. 'Get into position!' and

394

more lights flashing; with the noise bearing down on them like a leaden weight.

'You are coming with Chartier and me?' Misha said again.

He didn't answer. His arm went round her shoulders once more as the juddering metal monster circled over their heads and finally came down.

Everything began to move fast, the men, the lights. A hatch opened up in the machine and long gleaming containers rolled out. She wanted to shout it, You are returning with us? Because it must surely be a dream that they stood together in such a place.

Chartier's voice came through to her next. 'Misha! Quick! We have to get in now.'

She saw him half crawling across the grass towards her and responded, 'All right!' remaining glued to the earth.

Chartier stood up and grabbed her hand. Philippe took the other, throwing down his coat. 'Goodbye, Misha, until we meet again,' he shouted.

'You aren't coming too?' Relentlessly, between them, they were pulling her towards an opening in the machine's belly.

'Not this time,' Philippe said, supporting her by the waist as Chartier released her and climbed into it. Then he lifted her up, both hands around her disgraceful jumper, and she fell inside. Turning round instantly on her knees, she saw his face again, smiling at her, turbulent air catching at his jacket. 'Chartier will tell you what happened to your father, Misha.'

'I don't care about my father,' she tried to shout. 'Please don't stay behind. Third time unlucky!'

'Goodbye, Misha.'

Chartier urged her away and closed the hatch. The machine was giving out a roar which meant it was taking off. Despairing, she caught at Chartier's wrist. 'Please! Make him come with us!' she shrieked.

Chartier shook his head and mouthed, 'Watch from the window.'

Crawling into the dark centre of the thing, Misha put her face against a circle of rattling plastic. Philippe was still there, waving. She too tried to wave, uselessly. He couldn't

395

see her. And now she couldn't see him. Leaning her head on her arms, she finally began to sob.

Mechanically beginning to retrace their steps, her steps, Philippe held his overcoat to his mouth, hoping to find there a trace of her, a scent. The sound of the engine faded. An owl hooted. The helpers had vanished. Good. As a drop and as a pick-up, it was well done. But he wouldn't call in and thank the farmer, not tonight. He wanted his solitude, this cold air, the silence.

She had been so cool when she saw it was he in the doorway, offering her hand as if to a stranger. Well, he was a stranger. She'd been embarrassed to be confronted with the real figure of her first love. She was probably wishing even now that he'd remained a youthful dream. As for his gaffe about the letters, of course she'd been embarrassed. Yet she didn't want him to feel left out. Her sweet nature had made her keep asking if he were to travel with them. It was fortunate he'd held to his former role of concerned neighbour and friend.

He paused, staring vaguely at the blank round of the moon. She'd soon be seeing it hanging in an English sky. All in all, he was glad not to have her father's blood on his hands. Chartier had insisted he be the one. And he mustn't mind about the letters. If ever they were to meet in London, she'd give them no mention. That would be best. But, oh, how touching she'd been with the same vulnerable slender figure she'd always had, and her grave, grown-up face under the boy's beret!

Chapter 64

A Dorset hillside, Summer 1943

'Bet they've put you on wireless operating,' Patch said, picking another daisy and slitting its stem with her thumbnail.

'You know I'm forbidden to say anything about what I do,' Misha replied, holding up her completed daisy chain and draping it round her khaki shirt and tie. Her FANY officer's uniform was only a cover for the SOE training but she was proud of it. It marked her, she felt, both as part of the world's huge collective effort in the fight against the Nazis and as one of the chosen few.

'Well,' Patch said, yawning, 'it's daft us pretending I'm ignorant of the existence of SOE and resistance work when I applied to join it same time as George did. It was only my French that let me down. That and the fact I couldn't stand the thought of always being on my tod out in the field, or whatever the word is. I mean, there you are, a gun in your knickers, a lethal tablet to kill yourself with hidden in your top button for when they get you, running about the countryside carrying explosives, and not a damn' soul you're able to talk to night and day. If George and me'd been promised we'd be able to stick together . . .' She peered into the grass and chose a daisy. 'So I chickened out and here I am, driving for top brass. I've got an American general at the moment. If I wanted, I'd probably be able to tell you all about the invasion plans and D-Day itself.'

'I'll expect you to,' Misha said, smiling at her friend.

397

Patch's cheeks were reddened by the sun like an overheated baby's. They'd sat on the grass too long and couldn't be bothered to move. 'Then'll I'll spread it all over France when I get there.'

'Hah!' Patch said, grinning. 'You just told me something.' She dropped the flowers and leaned back on her hands, squinting down to the valley where her family home lay bathed in sun. 'Hoping to see anything of that White Knight of yours whilst you're there?' she asked in a casual tone.

'I may not have passed for operational missions at all,' Misha said quickly. 'I'm to do the parachuting course again. I'm no good at it. It's the awful dark emptiness you have to throw yourself into I can't bear, and sitting waiting for the right second to do it with your legs dangling through a hatch in the 'plane.' She shuddered. 'Twice I've been sick thinking about it, which pleased the men on the course, as you can imagine. I'm to have another go, anyway. But I wish SOE wouldn't keep on about my parents. Chief'll say, sort of off-hand, "It is clear to you, Suzanne, that your father was acting as bait to trap some of our SOE agents?" Or, "How d'you feel, Suzanne, about your mother's connection with the enemy?" And this I can't answer, Patch. I don't know how I feel about her. Shame on her behalf, I suppose. Yet not shame *of* her, as I did at first. She just needs someone to look after her, like a lot of women, and the Nazis are the ones with the power and money now, even if it is other people's.' She's not the sort to feel she must support herself whatever the circumstances. Sewing in a garret for a pittance is about all she'd have managed anyway, apart from being a shop girl. I'm positive that if she really thought about the Nazis' terrible, deliberate brutality, she'd have found herself another Pierre type of man. I miss her fussing over me, actually. I'd like to tell her what I'm up to. She'd have been proud of me in her way. As for what I did to my father, I think she'd have been proud of that too. Given the chance, she might have done the same, I think. She'd have loved the drama of it all.'

'All right, Mish,' Patch said gently. 'SOE know about your mother and father. You dared ask 'em about White Knight?'

'I've dared,' Misha said. Too many times she'd dared,

until the weekly reports on her had begun to read: 'We fear Suzanne is allowing the personal to intrude.' And she'd accepted it: the agent David was missing, believed arrested, his wireless operator Magenta also. 'He's missing, Patch,' she said suddenly. 'Believed arrested. Probably tortured to death. Third time unlucky, you see.' She gazed blindly at clumps of daisies. How long had he endured the degradation, the daily beatings, the solitary pain-filled wait until the next? A fresh stab of anguish pierced her heart. She was never free of this, carrying it with her from hour to hour with the other things, memories and regrets. They were almost as tangible as the two letters he'd written her long before and which had their permanent place in her shirt pocket.

'Oh, God, I'm sorry, Mish,' Patch said. 'And you never told him how you felt about him!'

'No.' And worse, she thought, worse, she hadn't even spared him the embarrassment of hearing about letters she hadn't dared open. He had taken her bald statement of fact at surface value, without realising she'd been trying to save herself the recognition they'd contain too little for her to hold on to. And now it was all too late. There could be no more burdensome words than these, except perhaps 'never more'.

'Because you weren't sure of his! Cripes, how much clearer could he make it, coming over to see you in London in the middle of a war?'

'I convinced myself he felt sorry for me and must've been coming over anyway on some war matter. London was full of French officers at the time. There was also that Eveline woman in his life, remember. Heavens, she was chic, Patch. She was everything I wasn't and he'd chosen her. And most adults did regard me as a sort of waif and stray to be looked after. Apart from my parents, that is. I mean, the Blanchards fed me. Monsieur Steiner tried to educate me. Philippe seemed to think he should as well. He even once sent me money for train fares.'

Patch groaned. 'Sorry, old thing. But the missing ones do turn up. If you ever so much as catch a glimpse of Philippe again, you shout it out, d'you hear? With a war on, how much time will anyone have left?' She grabbed a blade of grass and chewed on it. 'Me and John, we had three days' honeymoon before he caught it in Libya and I wouldn't take them back. I gave him that. Gave myself a few memories to hold on to as well.'

'And now you're a rather young widow, Patch,' Misha said, watching her friend twist the wedding ring round and round. 'But I'm glad you and your John had the honeymoon.' Three days, she thought. Oh, to have had three days with Philippe, lying at last in his arms, hearing his voice say the words he'd written to her:

I am so fearful that we shall never now be together. Yet how joyfully you'd have come to me that August day last year when I thought you too young and wished you to be certain of your feelings, as I was. Most of all, I wanted you to be safe in England and so I turned you away. Forgive me. I felt your pain in my own heart, watching you run across that courtyard and out of my life. But safe in England I know you were for a while, my darling, though not happy.

That brief hour we had in Paris this spring, well, all I could do was gaze at you and show you I had kept to my promise. I shall keep to this always, you see, and look toward the day we have our world back and I have no longer to dread that hurt may come to you, only that you have given your heart to someone else.

How could she ever forget a single word?

'The thing is though, Mish,' Patch was saying, 'your chap's only missing, believed arrested. They told George's family the same but I'm sure she's still alive. She wouldn't want to die before seeing off the Germans. I never saw anyone so angry about 'em as George, and like we've been hoping, she must be in Lisbon. Her group lost their wireless operator so they couldn't get news through. Maybe they lost other members too. She'll have managed to make her way across the Pyrenees somehow. Then she's had half Spain to travel over. We know the Spanish've got their own camps, Franco being more or less a mate of Hitler's, but with them it'll be

400

a simple matter of how big a bribe you can offer not to be put in one. Now there's been no shortage of money being sent over, you said . . .'

'Yes, and I also said George might not have any left and that I failed to give her the Englishman's package. It's still hidden in the Sérieys' cellar wall, I imagine.' She and Patch had been through the Palavas episode many times but neither could find a sensible reason for Georgie's instant disappearance.

'I still think she saw she was being spied on,' Patch said, 'and got out quick to avoid your being involved. And maybe she did go back the next day, same time and place, like agents do.'

'Not if they're being followed or notice anything suspicious. Then they leave the entire area very fast indeed and never go back.'

Patch brushed an insect from her skirt and sighed. 'It's not knowing that's the worst, but I say she's holed up in some Lisbon hotel, waiting to be brought home. The British Embassy have given her plenty of cash and there she is, boozing every night, orange juice for breakfast, laughing her head off because she's free again. Maybe that gorgeous bloke of yours took the same route out of France. Got into a bit of trouble with the Gestapo, say, so decides to hop it down south to trek over the mountains and there *he* is, waiting in the same hotel with our darling George for the next flight home.'

'They're sometimes ships out of Lisbon,' Misha said vaguely. This was the most impossible of all possible scenes imagined by her and Patch countless times. But she accepted in fact that Georgie was dead, as Philippe was. 'Your maid's waving up at us, Patch.'

'Time for tea,' Patch said, not stirring. 'You will let me know the final departure date, Mish?'

'Of course. Thanks for coming to Bournemouth with me yesterday.'

'I wouldn't have let you go on your own. Glad to have those ghosts from your past sorted out before you leave?'

'I did want to. I suppose if the grandparents haven't died, they're in some nursing home. I shan't bother to find out.

With the neighbours not knowing and the house sold, it wouldn't be easy anyway.'

'I'd have most liked to hear you inform that foul half-sister of yours that her dad had his throat cut by the resistance and was thrown into the River Seine. I wouldn't put it past her to be a traitor, same as him.'

'Nor would I but I can't really feel bothered about her. She did keep knocking me down but I learned I could get up again. And what could be worse than being someone like her? I mean, waking up in the morning and plotting all the nasty things you're going to say to people, being pleased with the ones you managed the day before. I've accepted my past, I suppose, father and all. Growing up means you do, if you're sensible about it. Against her and my father I can line up the ones who've been good to me. Joanie, for instance. I'd have liked to have seen her again. And your parents, Patch. I am grateful to them for offering me an English home to return to. It would have been strange to have had no next-of-kin sort of address to leave with SOE in case I don't come back.'

She gazed down the hillside to the house with its rich covering of ivy. She had no ties of her own. This also she'd accepted. Only Mémé, Félix and Frou remained to her. And they must manage without her until the war was over, as they had before. An agent without ties was the best sort.

'My pa and ma and brothers have adopted you,' Patch said, getting to her feet. 'Just don't forget it. Soon as you return from where you're going, you make SOE have you driven down here. Your room'll be ready, biscuits in the barrel beside the books and flowers all over. Just don't forget it. Promise?'

'Promise,' Misha said, standing up and inspecting her skirt for grass stains. 'I've been lucky in my friends, very lucky in fact.'

'Your friends've been lucky in you,' Patch said. 'Come on or I'll start howling.'

'Patch,' Misha said, 'I shall be going out soon, wait. They have told me, asked me rather. They had to ask, it's a bit special.'

'What way special?' Patch stood stock-still.

'I'm going out to where I used to live, to the Languedoc.'
Slowly Patch turned round. 'But they can't expect that of you, Mish. You were betrayed in that area, you're known by sight and for being English.'

'Yes.' Misha tried to avoid her friend's stare. 'But SOE'd like me there because I can do the local accent. The group was started last year. Our Englishman was supposed to have been met by them. George was a courier for a circuit just to the north and had gone to the café in Palavas to collect some money he was taking in for that circuit plus the new one. The chap who was setting up the new group not only failed to meet the Englishman for some reason, he also caught it just after Georgie disappeared and he thinks . . .'

'You mean it's the actual same circuit as George was connected with?' Patch was shouting. 'Are SOE mad?'

'No, Patch,' Misha said carefully. 'They think it was because George's accent was too precise, too perfect really, that she was noticed.'

'She worked at that, my God, didn't she work at it and now they say . . .' Patch put a hand on each of her plump hips. 'My God! Isn't being perfect enough for 'em then?'

'Seems not.' Misha felt her eyes fill with tears, for the perfection of Georgie and the once-broken will Georgie'd had to rebuild. Wiping her damp face with an arm, she added more, because there were no listening ears on this hillside, nothing but sweet summer air and daisies. 'Patch,' she said, 'The group leader who caught it got out in the end. They couldn't break him in prison so they released him. I expect he's lost a few fingernails, that's a favourite torture. Well, he wants a girl to help him, a courier like George was, but a blending in sort of one. He's going to build up a whole circuit like he was going to do with the Englishman. Couldn't be better work, could there? And with a chap who's been through it as he has. He's got to lie low himself, of course, having been taken in once . . .'

'Blend in? You?' Patch shrieked. 'You'll stand out like a sore thumb living with those short-arsed grape pickers and goatherds in their stony old mountains. That's obviously how George copped it.' She shook her head. 'No fear!' she said. 'I'll make Pa go to SOE and have you stopped.'

403

Half laughing, Misha said, 'Don't be daft. And think, Patch, I'll be able to find our exactly what happened to George. That's why I've given in and told you what I shouldn't. I want you to realise we shall know the truth about her. I'll find out the truth about my Pépé as well.'

Patch shouted again: 'You mad or what? Find out about your Pépé and George? That's personal, that is, that's emotional and emotion out in the field is forbidden. I'll blab everything you've said to Pa and he'll get a pal of his in the House of Lords to make a fuss with SOE. Extra risk, that's what they want you to take. All very well for them, nice and cosy in their offices.'

Misha couldn't help laughing outright at Patch's face becoming redder and redder. 'SOE are meticulous about risk, you know that. Being a wireless operator's far more dangerous than a courier anyway. Once I've got my safe houses established, I'll be free to work things out for myself, where I must avoid going and so on. Liaising'll be my job, between the circuit leader and our wireless man, between him and all the groups in their villages and camps. There's lots of camps growing up since the Nazis started the forced labour transports to Germany. Any chap under thirty's likely to prefer undercover life in the hills to slave labour in a German factory. As soon as I can report back to HQ they're worth it, a saboteur will be sent out after me to train them in armaments and explosive.

'Wonderful,' Patch said. 'So there's these blokes having their nails torn out and keeping their spirits unbroken whilst they get all excited playing with their new guns and start letting 'em off in the wrong places. This alerts the enemy to the fact they've had the proper stuff sent in from London and aren't just polishing up their grandads' boar-hunting shotguns. Five hundred Gestapo and military then go ferreting around and come across you, little Miss England if ever there was one, and it occurs to 'em quite quickly you're not there for your holidays and must be the one responsible for getting in the weapons that're aimed at their nasty fat selves . . .'

'No one's getting excited anymore, Patch. No one's playing games, not even the *maquis* chaps in the hills. SOE says they were a bit hot-headed to start with but they realise they have to accept training in modern armaments. Training and leadership as well as arms, that's what SOE is offering. I mean, they even send out money to sustain the groups and their families, and boots as well, an army can't march without boots and it's an army we have to form, a guerilla army to help the Allies drive the Germans back to where they belong at the same time as the Allies invade from the coasts. They can't invade the entire country all at once.'

'No need to give me a lecture.' Patch sighed and put a hand through her hair. 'I'd just prefer SOE to use local women if they want local accents. Why can't they, come to that?'

'You know why. It's a question of security. We're trained as well as any soldier. We are kind of soldiers, in the resistance. Advance ones. We're part of the Allied High Command invasion plan and essential to it. Anyway, when did you last see a French girl doing so much as going on a hike? There aren't many who'd take to explosives or parachuting, much less roughing it without lipstick or a hairdresser. Imagine my mother contemplating the mechanics of a Sten gun!'

Patch looked upwards at Misha, her sturdy figure outlined by the sunshine, the blue of her eyes more intense than ever. 'If you go the same way as George . . .' she said.

'I shan't.' Misha shaded her own eyes against the glare. 'I'll be George's revenge. I'll be her anger, Patch. Remember Georgie, how she was in the Cherche-Midi?'

'I remember every second of the Cherche-Midi, Mish.'

'So do I. And that wasn't even the beginning of the misery for us, was it? I'm not afraid anymore, you know. I'm just glad I've got my chance. I won't waste it, I promise.'

Chapter 65

The Pyrenees, Late Summer 1943

Ahead of him, the SOE agent Laurent was inching his way along some ancient unused path towards a resting place near the top of the ridge. Philippe could hear the tug of blackberry thorn against his shirt and the in-out of his laboured breath. It was a steep path, with many more to come. If he hadn't known it, the near-vertical wall of rock of the next ridge to their left was reminder enough.

Laurent let out a gasp as his boots dislodged a small boulder. Catching at it just in time, Philippe stood stock-still, listening. In these mountains, the tiniest noise could echo down as far as the villages below.

But it was all right. No answering sound came up. He rolled the boulder aside, released his tightened chest and read Laurent's silent gesture made with fingers held out. Fifteen minutes more and they could pause.

Wasting energy flapping at a cloud of mosquitoes, Philippe pulled the beret into a peak over his eyes and blindly edged himself on. The climb had already cost him more strength than he could spare.

Life could still hold small pleasures, thought Philippe. The slender birch trunk supporting his back, for one. And the natural summer sounds he'd forgotten. He could hear the rush of the stream as it broke from the rocks somewhere and the high shrill music of the grasshoppers.

He'd survived then, to the very borders of France, after

so many near-captures he must have nine lives, like fat little Frou who'd travelled to a vineyard not so very far from his present position. She'd be fretful in this heat, and dozing in some cool place under the vines. Misha was almost certainly enclosed far from them both, in a wireless transmitting station in England, feeling the same hot sun as they but from behind window-panes as she worked the keys, so grave, quick and clever. Maybe she'd be the one to take the first coded message Laurent's borrowed wireless operator would send back in a day or two: David passed to guide, arriving Spain next forty-eight hours if all goes well. She'd give a start and be pleased for him. It would make her think of him again.

Laurent laid out a picnic on the ground between them. 'I've brought a few of the last peaches,' he said. 'And there's plenty of sausage but not much bread.'

'It's good of you to have managed so much,' Philippe said, accepting the greasy rounds of meat without distaste. 'And at such short notice. I wasn't expecting to find myself in the Pyrenees and having to climb mountains in order to get back to HQ, not once I'd managed to pass through a number of our safe houses and most of France. I thought fate'd be good to me and allow the Provence circuit to arrange my pick-up without incident. I only hope the whole lot of them haven't been arrested. Hope my Spanish holds up as well. I have a few contacts over there from my university days but I know it'll take me weeks more to get across to Lisbon. I'm anxious to go on with my work . . .' Preferably with direct involvement in the invasion, he thought. He'd wasted enough time. After the war, of course, life would be different and he could imagine no future for himself but the one he'd imagined too often before. And that wasn't going to come about.

'Feeling all right?' Laurent asked, his mouth full of bread. He too was seated on a fur-lined jacket which had been a torment to carry in the heat but which they'd need for the cold nights at higher altitudes.

Philippe nodded. 'Not too bad, thanks,' he said, though in fact exhaustion had threatened to overwhelm him more than once. Determination must carry him forward, and pacing himself. If the bomber for his pick-up had arrived, he'd be in England by now, probably in a hospital with a cup of warm milky tea beside him, and a step much nearer his goal. 'Know the mountains well?' he asked his companion, flicking a grasshopper from his sausage.

Laurent shook his head. 'Only what I've needed to learn to help SOE escapees like you. You're the ninth or tenth I've led part of the way. Someone who's used to the treachery of 'em will take over tomorrow. That's if my message has got through all right and if the Gestapo or local militia haven't got hold of my chap or the Spanish police for that matter. I was once thinking of getting to Spain myself and spending the war there but I didn't fancy a Spanish jail if I were caught!' He finished his bread and from his jacket took out a small thin-bladed knife which he laid on the grass. 'That's for the dogs,' he said, 'if a patrol spots us. Trouble is, Alsatians squeal a lot and your only hope then is to know the pathways better than their masters. If they're Gestapo that's easy, but if they're local French militia working for the Gestapo . . .' He shook his head. 'Much worse, they are, as you'll have heard. Even the Nazis despise traitors. An odd point of honour, isn't it? They admire any one of us who stands up to their worst but loathe our French turncoats. It'd make you weep if you thought about it enough.' He sighed and leaned against his birch, squinting down to the green plains below.

Philippe saw for the first time that this was a man who'd had his fingernails removed. He looked with fresh appreciation at his thickset figure, the broad solid head and shoulders. At first glance he'd seemed a very ordinary member of the French middle class, a hunting and shooting property-owner with a sharp little wife chosen by his mother and five or six children to follow. A man, in short, accepting without question the traditions of church and family. As for the Nazi Occupation, well, one day it'd be over with and meanwhile the Nazis were usefully re-establishing clean streets and a discipline which kept the workers down, with strikes and demonstrations forbidden on penalty of death.

Yet Laurent sat there with the rare sign he'd also noticed

408

when the beret was removed – a patch of hair grown white. 'How long did they keep you in?' he said.

'Only a few months,' Laurent replied, plucking another blade of grass. 'Back in the early days it was. I'd messed up a drop and was on my way into the hills to lie low for a while when they took me in on suspicion. But I'd covered my tracks. They couldn't prove a thing. My mother's friendships got me out.' He sat up and rolled a peach between his hands. 'She's a fascist sympathiser,' he said.

'Ah,' Philippe said. 'What, then, made you decide on resistance?'

'A girl,' said Laurent, tossing the fruit in the air and catching it. 'She was just so indignant about the Germans, you see. Couldn't stop talking about their particular iniquities, the non-battle things, like putting lime into railway carriages to stifle the wretched Polish soldiers to death. She'd been through a lot herself one way and another but to her mind, if men want to indulge in war, they should fight it out on battlefields. As for them taking over down here ... well, by that time she'd made me feel so ashamed at my own lack of anger, I'd started talking to a few chaps and before I had time to think, one of the early SOE agents approaches me and I've fixed up a landing–field. I was planning to lay all of my exploits at this girl's feet ...'

'And have you?' Philippe picked up a peach and bit into it.

'Nope. I realised she'd be only too eager to join in and I didn't want her mixed up in it. Anyway, she's left the area and it wouldn't have been any good. If a girl doesn't care for you, she doesn't, and nothing changes that ...'

'No,' Philippe said.

'And now resistance is a way of life. I don't see my parents anymore but I've got three hundred men to call on after D-Day, some *maquis* lads in two small camps in wooded areas near my second property, some in the higher village there, with only one road up suitable for motor transport. The military don't venture there much.' He grinned. 'Then I have seven group leaders with a number of men each in the main town and the smaller ones on the coast. I've a wonderful old man with me, sixty-eight he is. We call him

Grandad with the greatest respect. He was a neighbour of ours at the house near Montpellier. They had him in on some pretty strong suspicion, pulled out his remaining teeth without dental charges when he wouldn't talk, slit the soles of his feet and made him stand on salt. My father bought him out in the end and since he was a bad way, took him to our hills place to recuperate. First thing he demands is proper training in the latest arms so he can pass it on to the youngsters, and SOE tell me to send him up to the Auvergne circuit for it. Very anxious he is for my new courier to get dropped in with a load of Stens . . .'

'A useful man,' Philippe said, easing his legs out straight and rubbing the left one.

'The leg troubling you?' Laurent drank his fill of stream water from a flask.

'A bit,' Philippe admitted. 'I was lucky it happened near the place I was brought up. It was my own fault too, not that it helps to realise it. I was dawdling in the countryside after a very successful pick-up, as I thought. Next thing I know, lights everywhere, cars screeching along the lanes and I have to start running. Tripped in a ditch and sprained something. That slowed me down otherwise I'd have got to the railway bridge quicker and wouldn't have fallen awkwardly trying to get under it.' He gazed into the prettiness of birch trees in sunlight and remembered the darkness, the cold wet bricks and his dangling leg. 'My mother's farm wasn't far off and I'd been vaguely deciding to go there shortly to see if she'd be prepared to take in and hide a woman who'd done some good work for our circuit. I made my way there once the noise had died down.'

I crawled there, he thought, from ditch to ditch, like a wounded animal at bay. It'd taken him five nights. 'Our old family doctor came up to do the splint and so on. Christ, how I cursed the lost time and my stupidity!'

'Mother was pleased to have you under her wing again, I expect.' Laurent ate a peach with one mouthful and ground the stone into the grass with his heel.

'Yes. Also furious at me for failing to stay in England. But she did want to help the woman who'd helped us, though she was a lady of the streets.' Philippe let himself smile, thinking of Reine. 'Who now, believe it or not, has turned her hand to the making of butter and cheese. And that, after once stabbing a Gestapo officer in the throat!'

'War's brought out the best and the worst . . .' Laurent's hand paused over a peach. 'Listen,' he said.

Philippe began cautiously to re-pack his haversack. Flask first. His ration of the bread. He was listening. He could hear nothing but the stream and the insects. Perhaps a rustle of breeze in the birch trees. He got to his feet with care, every muscle of his limbs stiff and painful.

'Yes,' Laurent hissed. 'Dogs.' He too rose to his feet. 'Get as ready as you can.' He moved forward as far as the next birch.

Philippe shrugged on the fur-lined leather jacket. Easier to wear than to carry. It'd soon strike chill. The afternoon sun was fading.

Laurent was on his knees, peering down to the valley. He turned. Yes. He nodded. It's them.

Philippe was ready. And now he could hear them. Dogs. Dogs barking and faintly, the shouts of one man to another. He must wait no longer. And there was no time. 'As we arranged then?' he whispered. 'You stay and hold them off. Sure your papers will match your story?' They had sat too long.

Laurent nodded, crawling back to his place, checking every inch of the ground for evidence that two had sat there. The knife he crammed hard into the grass so it glinted no more. 'Shan't use that unless my story doesn't hold,' he said.

'*Merde*, old chap,' Philippe said. 'And thanks.'

'*Merde!*' replied Laurent as Philippe set off at a run, tearing his way through the brambles and on up to the top of the ridge and down again for the next peak. At some point he should come upon a climbers' refuge hut where a proper mountain guide would be hovering, if the message had got through. If not, he'd have to find his own way with the map. But if Laurent could convince the dogs' masters he was a rock-climber on a few days' solitary holiday, with the boots, rope, haversack to prove it, then he himself might

411

not be pursued. And above all, he'd be grateful for that. More than he dared accept, he was infinitely tired of the chase.

Chapter 66

The Languedoc Hills, Late February 1944

Her padded knees locked over the open hatch, Misha gazed down at the beautiful, ominous panorama of hill, gorge and valley coloured purple and black in the moonlight. She could even make out the pale winding strips of goat and sheep paths and the dark shadows of the woods.

'Remember what your granny told you,' shouted the bomber's crew man from his safe post in the belly of the thing. 'Keep your legs together.'

'Shut up,' Misha yelled. 'Just shut up.' She was tired of English jokiness, in fact, and would be glad to get down to join the silent hill people in their tight little villages lodged on the edge of nowhere. Only she couldn't jump yet because if she did, her frozen hand wouldn't reach the slip-cord in time. There were the flares laid out in the right L-shaped pattern. The long flat ridge between the two valleys seemed a perfect place for a drop. And the weather was in order. She wasn't though. The will that had carried her this far was gone like the breath from her lungs and she couldn't release the grip-handle.

'Ooh, duckie, this is it,' bellowed the wireless operator, Bertrand, headed for the same circuit. His Michelin-man parachute suit covered all but his face.

Misha could make out his mouth drawn back as the wind thudded at it. Bertrand, she thought, leaning dizzily forward, listen . . .

'Toodaloo, ducks.' Bertrand's hand moved from the grip

to the cord of his 'chute and he disappeared. The white nylon billowed up, his boots swaying to and fro under it.

She leaned further out, the familiar surge of nausea snatched away by currents of air. 'I can't,' she shrieked and let herself fall into the howling eeriness of space.

Keeping her legs together, she rolled on to the rough scrubland and instantly scrambled to her feet. I have done it, she thought, taking deep, gasping breaths, and lifting her head to the navy blue sky. I am here and my fear is done with and finally I shall be of use.

Relief and exultation made every movement suddenly easy, one following the other in the right sequence. The harness was off in a second, the cap, the suit itself, and she threw it all into the long stream of nylon which was her 'chute, falling to her knees to begin hauling it in. Oh, a good jump, she thought, what a good one, and when I had to, I could do it. Bertrand was safely down also. She was aware of him dealing with his 'chute fifty or so yards ahead. Behind them both along the ridge were the darting figures of the circuit helpers collecting the packages the bomber's crew was still releasing. Each on its own miniature 'chute, they made a pretty picture, like giant balloons set afloat to celebrate some festive occasion. She'd be glad when they were all down. They could be spotted for miles, just as the bomber could be heard for miles. Seeing it bank and turn overhead, she waved. A wing dipped in goodbye as it set off for home.

The rumbling sound of it faded, leaving scrambling noises and the subdued mutter of voices. The flares were being doused, one by one. An efficient group then, so far. Getting to her feet, a hand on the pistol at the waist of her trousers, she stood stock-still, listening. This would be the moment the enemy burst out of hiding with their dogs and their shouts. Nothing yet. But she'd rather get off the scrub.

She was looking about for a sheltering tree to make for as she heard her name called, 'Suzanne!' and then 'Bertrand!' 'Bertrand,' she hissed, 'reception committee approaching. I hope.'

'Coming, ducks,' he replied. He was more encumbered

than she, having jumped with his transmitter set strapped to his body. This he held like a piece of luggage as he ran towards her. He'd even put on his beret and would pass for a salesman anywhere if this hadn't been the middle of the night. What she had under her blouse, however, was even more incriminating than Bertrand's wireless.

'Pecker up, eh!' He gave her a hug, put his case under his arm and slipped away behind Didier, the man who was to conduct him to his safe house. 'We rendezvous two days' time via these chaps.'

'Cheerio, Bertrand,' whispered Misha as he disappeared along the ridge. She set off beside her own guide, Raphael, who was making his way in the other direction to the point where the flat earth sloped downwards. 'Shall I be meeting your leader Laurent tonight?' she asked. He had a glorious wine, sweat and garlic smell, exactly like Pépé's, though he was young, not more than twenty-five. He wore baggy corduroys, earth-covered boots, a very old jacket, and a wide grin of pride because he'd been entrusted with the task of conducting the SOE agent Suzanne to her safe house.

Raphael paused and shook his head, eyes like black pebbles by the light of the moon. 'Boss'll come and see you tomorrow,' he said. 'I'm taking you to your lodgings at the shepherd's house in the valley. They're very proud to have you in their son's room. Gestapo took him two months ago. Only fifteen he was and he'd done no more than help us remove a bit of railway line to hold up a few of the labour transports to Germany. We wanted to storm the police station to get him free but the boss said we'd lose too many more by it. Those devils worked on him a whole day and a night while we argued with the boss and in the morning the boy's cries had stopped so we knew he was gone.'

Misha took her eyes away from the desolation she saw come and go on Raphael's face, a look she recognised. 'Then I can't lodge with them, they'll want to keep their son's room exactly as it is . . .'

Raphael gently touched her arm. 'Suzanne,' he said, 'please allow Gaston and Violette the privilege of harbouring you. You're the only person they could bear to have sleeping in it. And the boy, Gilles, would want if he could know. You're from England, you see. We can go on murdering a few Nazis or blowing up something they need here and there but we must be organised for real guerrilla warfare if we're to help the Allies drive the lot off our land. We all realise that and for our circuit to have our very own courier from London, well, it means this London HQ place believes in us, that we will be used when the invasion comes. It will come, won't it, Suzanne? We resistance blokes aren't just living on hope?'

'I can promise you it'll come,' said Misha. She'd have liked to tell Raphael the exhilarating news detailed in the envelope around her waist so that he could spend the next days shouting it out from the hilltops.

Chapter 67

Dawn, the first dawn of her return, and the sky was pale lavender, just as she remembered it. Standing by the open shutters of her bedroom in the shepherd's house, Misha contemplated this sky and the vast stretch of hill and valley rolling out to meet it. Below the cottage, the land dropped in terraced layers of earth cultivated for vegetables and the vine. Leaning out, she recognised its stunted rows. A road had been built down there, she could see a bridge as it passed over the river. It was the only one capable of supporting motor vehicles apparently so she'd be very quickly aware of enemy arrival from this side.

Now for the rest. Her back escape route was going to be a problem. There was a tiny second window opposite, no more than a square set into the criss-cross of ancient trunk-thick beams and stone the house was made of, but it had no opening frame. Running a finger round its edge, she thought age and grime held it in place as much as anything. She'd have to ask Gaston or one of the men to put a wire mesh in there instead of glass so she could easily pull it out.

Continuing her exploration, she inspected a trunk containing schoolbooks and the walls themselves. On one was pinned a school Certificate of Merit in Composition, Summer 1936. Next to this a drawing of a sheep was claimed in faint crooked letters to be the work of Gilles Bonvin, aged six. Over the bed was something bigger, a map of the Languedoc hills so old it was cloth-backed. It must have been Gilles's pleasure to learn the paths around his home because he'd marked them with little symbols of his own, goats and eagles, rabbits, wild pigs. He'd been an animal lover.

She liked knowing this of him, she decided, and felt oddly at ease in his room. And better me than anyone else, she thought, finally splashing her face in the washbowl Violette had put ready for her. For I add you to my list, little Gilles, my personal one. Pépé is on it, Georgie, Monsieur Steiner and his wife, the orphan children in the sports stadium, Reine, and now Gilles Bonvin, schoolboy, aged fifteen, tortured to death in the cellar of a police station. Also Professor Philippe David Constantin, manner of death unknown.

Checking the security of the packet around her waist, she pulled on jumper, trousers and the lace-up shoes she'd arrived in. She'd feel happier when her suitcase containing two woollen skirts and the dresses for the summer was brought up to her from the dropped parcels, In these hills, where modern life had yet to penetrate, she'd stand out like a sore thumb in trousers, an English sore thumb, as Patch had kept reminding her. I am here, Patch, she thought, everything's in order so far. Fingers crossed though. And today I meet the man who might know what happened to Georgie.

First, breakfast with her hosts at the table in the low, beamed place which was kitchen, scullery, living-room and nursery for young animals. The night before she'd sat with them by the hearth after a supper of soup and she'd had there a flash of memory so painful that to ease it she'd told them about her suppers in Mémé's kitchen. As they sat carefully listening, side by side, she realised Gaston and Violette might be taken for brother and sister. They were both short, spare and bony-limbed, with the same surprising clear blue eyes in dark-skinned, weathered faces. Their grief, she thought, showed in their wakefulness. They rarely went to bed, they informed her, and she couldn't therefore disturb their daily life. Animals were their routine, they said, and in their eager shyness, their old-fashioned courtesy showed her without words, which they used little, that they wanted nothing better than to offer her the house as shelter, harbour, comfort. And even then, that night, she'd felt a sense of rightness in her presence there.

Gaston had taken the billy goat, Bleu, and his dog, Rif, and gone off to his sheep on the other side of the ridge. Misha was helping Violette with the milking of Amélie, Sabine and the youngest goat, skittish little Fleur, when she was startled to hear the sound of an engine. 'Quick, Violette,' she said, instantly alert, 'I'll run up the back way. Perhaps I can catch up with Gaston and mingle in with the sheep . . .'

'It's only Laurent coming to see you, Mademoiselle Suzanne,' said Violette in her slow, gentle southern voice. She hadn't raised her head from its position against a goat's belly. 'That's his *vélo-moteur*.'

Misha stood in the doorway of the milking shed and took in every corner of the yard, the outhouses, the cottage. She'd have had time to get across to the back slopes. 'Won't the entire area hear him, though?'

'Oh, Laurent goes where he wishes to go, he has genuine papers in his own name,' Violette replied, squeezing out some last drops, removing the bucket from under Amélie and getting to her feet. 'He was in prison for a long time during the winter of '42, but I believe his mother was able to buy him out. She is a Nazi sympathiser, Mademoiselle Suzanne, but please . . .' She put down the bucket and put a rough hand on Misha's arm. 'Laurent, or the Boss as some of the men call him, is to be trusted. And he no longer sees his poor mother . . .'

Misha looked down at her clear blue eyes and smiled. 'If you trust him, Violette,' she said, and moved into the yard, leaving the shepherd's wife to her tasks. She felt uneasy. Why on earth did a circuit leader choose to announce his arrival by *vélo-moteur*? For one thing, he was also announcing his ability to obtain petrol. How did he get it? An agent in the field must always be anonymous, silent and anonymous. He was neither, being both noisy and a member of a wealthy family with a known Nazi sympathiser in it. Squinting down the hillside, she caught sight of a fur-lined cap with earmuffs and a fur-lined jacket approaching in winding fashion up the terraced paths. The pop-pop sound grew louder. She wasn't going to like this man. That hat! He was the showing-off, I-am-in-the-resistance kind, who gave themselves away. She'd been warned about them in training. She'd hoped for a solid, responsible circuit leader, one she could trust.

She was recognising her disappointment just as the irritating noise stopped at the corner of the outhouses where a goat had appeared and was snatching at dry twigs. The man got jauntily off his scooter as if it were some splendid motor-cycle. He hadn't seen her. He was having a word with the goat and with Violette in the milking shed and then he paused in the yard, rubbing a hand over his face with an air of such weariness that Misha rebuked herself. Training hadn't reduced her arrogance. Here was a brave man, who'd worked in the field since the early days, who'd been tortured and withstood it. Yet SOE would expect her to find a tactful way of suggesting he be less blatant in his travelling, however many friendly eyes and ears the hills contained. And did they know about his mother?

'Good morning, Laurent,' she called.

He was taking off the hat. 'Good morning! Suzanne? They told me you'd arrived safely. Where are you?'

He couldn't see her in the doorway. But she could see him. And she'd have known him anywhere. He had the same thick-set figure, the same sturdiness of shoulder and neck. A patch of white had appeared at his left temple, that was all, and perhaps his face was thinner. He certainly wasn't a boy now though. But he was still Julien.

She stepped into the yard and waited for Julien to see it was she.

Chapter 68

'It'll be all right,' Misha said. They were sitting at the kitchen table over cold coffee. 'You must just remember never to call me by my real name. For code purposes only I'll remain Suzanne. I've decided to use my country-cousin identity first, so I'm to be Brigitte Marchand, born near Nîmes illegitimately of a mother in service, and employed as a chambermaid in a hotel in the Alps but dismissed after a long bout of pneumonia this winter. I'm staying with my mother's second cousin Violette, to help her while I benefit from warm air and good food. I'll be working out a few family details with Violette later and she's already been saying down in Castelnau that she may be having her cousin's daughter to visit. You must remember to tell your men that I'm to be Brigitte and not Mademoiselle Brigitte either. I'll save the Mademoiselle for my other identity where I'm a student . . .'

Julien shook his head again, cupping the bowl in his hands. 'I shan't be able to use you in my circuit at all, Misha, you haven't understood, it's too dangerous an area for you, you might be spotted, and the job itself . . .'

Misha stared at his fingers. Their tips were reddened stubs. Of course, she'd been told her circuit leader had been an early sufferer of this particular treatment and had forgotten. She almost wanted to get up and do something, bathe and dress them in bandages, when it was far too late for this and much else. Julien would have had to endure weeks of bleeding wounds, alone in a cell. She said, suddenly losing patience and very nearly shouting: 'Well,

421

you certainly need a courier, getting about yourself on that noisy *vélo-moteur*. Whatever are you thinking? That they won't take you in again? Why wouldn't they? Soon as I heard you arriving, my heart sank. I thought, I've come to a circuit that won't last, I'd better ask SOE to send me somewhere else.' It was a relief to say it and she felt a ridiculous desire to cry.

'I'll get you sent to another circuit, don't worry, Misha.' Julien slammed down the bowl. 'Because I won't work with you. As a former friend, I wonder why you aren't prepared to accept the value of the judgements I make. I've been in this business a long time. Naturally I avoid road blocks and controls as far as I can. We hear about most of them through one or two friends we have in the *gendarmerie*. I've also bought a little garage in Lodève which means I can deal in black market petrol, charcoal, and the charcoal-driven vans we need for transport. It's also a useful meeting ground, my customers are often my contacts.'

Misha opened her mouth. She wanted to say that she was sorry, they were both tired, they'd talk later, but Julien didn't stop. 'May I ask you why you've been so long getting here? SOE promised me a courier who knew the local ways and local accent last summer. And as for my mother, I gave a report to London through the Auvergne circuit about her Nazi friends and my relationship with her. Since they've continued to send me armaments, and now you, I imagine they have made their decision about me. Of course, when I started this work, the first thing I had to weigh in the balance was the fact of my mother's Nazi sympathies but since I'm well aware how much I mean to her, I believed it unlikely she'd denounce anyone I work with. At the moment, I no longer see her and she accepts that. She daren't contemplate the possibility of the Germans losing the war and thinks I'll one day have to come to my senses and recognise the glory of being part of the German New Order.'

As a former friend, Misha thought, I can see how very upset you have been about your mother, Julien, and how very upset you are now, about me, though a stranger would think you merely angry. 'I am late getting here,' she said, her voice as sharp as his. 'And partly through my own fault. I couldn't manage the parachuting. They offered to send me by submarine but you know my claustrophobia . . .' She waited for Julien to reassure her, to tell her such weaknesses did not matter, especially beside her strengths, as he'd once have done. Then she realised she didn't need reassurance from Julien. She knew her frailities – and how to balance them against her courage and her will. 'So it had to be by 'plane to Gib,' she went on in order to fill the silence though such past trials really had no importance. 'And from Gib I was supposed to take a fishing boat to the south coast. But after two failed take-offs, one a crash on the runway which gave me concussion and a cracked rib, I was so late getting to Gib, the fishing-boat captain'd been arrested. You can't just land on the coast anymore.'

'I know you can't, Misha,' Julien said. He was blinking, eyes over-bright. Taking in a breath as if to speak again, he released it.

'We must talk sensibly,' Misha said. She felt the air between them held something tangible in it, his old love for her perhaps, changed to hatred.

'Yes,' said Julien. 'We really must.' He reached into the fur-lined jacket and took out a pipe which he proceeded to clamp in his mouth.

'You didn't used to smoke,' she said, surprised.

'Your Pépé taught me,' Julien said, getting slowly to his feet and going to the hearth.

'Pépé? When? He certainly didn't, Julien! You surely haven't forgotten Pépé was arrested before I had to leave home, and you weren't smoking in 1942.'

Julien stirred the embers of the fire for a suitable piece of hot wood, and didn't reply.

'You surely can't have forgotten when Pépé was arrested?' Misha said, irritated by the slowness of his search and by the shrillness of her own voice. She and Julien would need time to adjust to their extraordinary predicament. What would SOE say to it?

Julien found Violette's fire tongs and picked up the piece of wood he'd chosen, delicately balancing it over the pipe. He puffed like an expert pipe smoker, carefully and with satisfaction. 'I haven't forgotten when your Pépé was arrested, Misha,' he said, suddenly turning and looking at her. He withdrew the pipe and added, 'Nor the day Dad brought him to our vineyard over Lodève way. That's not far from here, if you remember. A Monday in July it was, July 1943.'

Misha saw a reluctant smile on his face as she leaped to her feet. 'You mean Pépé? Pépé didn't die? He's alive?' Her heart thudded. 'But he can't be. I thought for sure he was dead, all this time, I thought . . .'

Julien laughed. 'You always did think you were right about most things, Misha, but about Pépé you were not. He's living at the vineyard and he's my saboteur trainer, going from group to group. Dad's sent that old Herbert of ours, you remember him I expect, to run Pépé's place . . .' He went to the doorway and kept his back to her.

Misha sat down and put her head in her hands. Pépé, not tortured to death. Only a few fingernails lost perhaps, but he'd have borne that all right. It would have made him more angry, but he was in the right place to put anger to good use, thanks to Julien and Monsieur Sérieys. 'We do need to talk, Julien,' she said, because she could find nothing else to say. Niceties about gratitude wouldn't be enough.

'Yes,' Julien said. 'And first I want to see your papers.'

'What?'

'Your papers,' repeated Julien, turning to face her. 'D'you think I'm going to allow you to run about my circuit putting us all at risk without being absolutely certain your identity will stand up round here? D'you honestly think you'll pass as one of Violette's relations? There's a good twelve centimetres' difference in height between you for a start.' He held out his hand.

Misha stared at his hand and got to her feet. 'For a start,' she said, 'I was a Father Unknown baby so he could have been any height, but Violette's going to mention down in Castelnau that her gangly relation keeps hitting her head going through doors. But you can have my papers, the ones I'm using for the moment, that is.' Fingers trembling, she fumbled in the pocket of her blouse. She supposed she was angry herself but wasn't used to the feel of it. 'Here.' She threw her identity card, clothing and ration coupons on the table. 'There's a bicycle permit in with them. I presume you have been able to buy me a bicycle, a decent one? I'll need good tyres for these hills and when you've checked all that, you can sit down again and give me a list of your circuit's requirements. I'll need precise foot sizes as well as numbers of pairs of boots, also ages and family circumstances of all your men. We'll pay 20 francs per day subsistence plus essential extras like support for children, wives and elderly parents. I also have authority to buy food in bulk if it can be got. You'll have contacts with various farmers, I imagine?'

'Of course.' Julien moved to the table and picked up the cards.

'I'll want to begin drawing up lists of viable landing-fields as well,' she said. 'There must be at least thirty and that'll only be the start. Each one must have more than twenty helpers available. Drops'll be coming in day and night once the invasion date is set and more saboteurs'll be sent with the full panoply of arms, but unless you're up to the task, we shan't waste our resources on this circuit.' She sat down with a thump. SOE had been right. An agent mustn't carry emotional baggage. She hadn't realised she felt emotion about Julien but obviously did. And for her, he still felt something, almost certainly hatred, she decided, watching him throw her papers back on the table.

'These are well copied,' he said calmly, 'but I'm not sure whether the regional stamp on the bicycle permit will hold up. I'll have to ascertain that through one of my men. Now, I've a number of other matters to attend to this morning, so I'll leave you to acclimatise yourself to house and area. You can go down to Castelnau in a day or two, not before. Any stranger in such a small village will be connected with the 'plane of last night. When you're there, you'll be able to see if anyone stares at you. Which they will. I'll return by the end of the week with lists of our requirements.'

He leaned across and held out his hand to shake hers without so much as a glance at her face. 'By the way, Mémé and that fat little cat of yours are also staying at the vineyard. Of course, you won't be able to risk the rest of us by

425

going to see them.' He turned and made for the door. 'Goodbye, Misha,' he said.

'That cat?' cried Misha. 'She does have a name.' But Julien was gone.

Blindly, she went to the doorway and heard the sound of his cheerful goodbye to Violette. The nasty scooter noise started up. She didn't watch the ridiculous hat winding back down the hill. Frou, she thought. Mémé. All right. They were safe. She wouldn't go and see them. She'd send a message via Raphael to say she wasn't far away. No. She couldn't do that and reveal who she really was. No message then. And no visit. It was going to be difficult. But they were all right. And Pépé was.

Stumbling into the yard, she knew she must somehow get herself back into the professional manner with which she'd arrived. She was a professional. Julien was also. So they should be able to work together. She must ensure they did. Really, their past friendship could be an advantage. She must make it into one.

Then she realised she'd failed to ask him about Georgie, and he wouldn't return until the end of the week.

By that time, she'd have adapted to many things and all those months of training would come into play. She'd only been set a little off course. Julien would soon understand she was no longer the girl he remembered, the one who thought she was always right, who was over hasty, impatient, cocky. She was going to be very patient, very steady, utterly meticulous, and above all, absolutely in charge of herself.

And the first matter she must attend to was the stowing away of the items in the package around her waist.

Violette had found her some of Gaston's used tin tacks without asking why she needed them. Laying them out on the floor beside the sealing tape and scissors from the suitcase Raphael had just brought up, Misha removed Gilles Bonvin's map of the Laguedoc from the wall. Laying that also on the floor face down, she took the fine sheets of paper from her waist package and began with infinite care to tape them to the back of the map. This done, she levered the whole, heavier thing against the beams and held it in place with her shoulder whilst she knocked in the tacks with her shoe.

Next she stood back and regarded the map from all angles, first with the daylight and, with the shutters closed, by the light of her torch. No obvious thickening, no lumps at all, she decided, but she'd check it daily for signs the cloth wouldn't hold. As a final touch, she covered her fingers with a little of the cobwebbed grime on the unopening window and smudged it over map and beam.

There'd be no map at all for her to make temporary use of, she thought, if Gilles hadn't gone to work on the railway lines without his identity card and hadn't then, once caught, refused to admit who he was. After they'd killed him, the Gestapo had taken a photograph of his swollen face. This photograph had appeared at all the local police station, offering a reward for the whisper of his name. But the villagers had kept silent as a tribute to Gilles who'd kept silent to spare his parents the ransacking of their house and their own journey to Gestapo cellars.

Contemplating her work a last time, she felt as sure as she could the map would remain in place. Otherwise, the detailed planning by thousands of people in secret offices all over England might spill out, be caught up by one of the rare winds of the Languedoc and be swept away, straight into the wrong hands. Her PERSONAL TO SUZANNE message coming over the air from the BBC French Service or via Bertrand's wireless transmitter might then contain some very sharp comments from Churchill himself, because all the schedules for D-Day would have to be changed.

Before the morning had become afternoon, she made a minute inspection of the main room, finally settling on a crevice high up in the walls between stone and beam for a second hiding place. Here she placed the five million francs destined for the expenses of the new circuit. The pistol she wrapped in a piece of rubber sheeting from her case and buried it by the root of the climbing peach tree near her bedroom.

For the lethal pill which would bring her quick death if

she were captured, she chose the fire in the hearth. She was too much of a coward ever to choose that way out.

During these activities Violette had kept herself busy in the yard. Whether she disturbed the hiding places Misha never knew because they never spoke of the matter and that was for the best.

Chapter 69

Squatting in the ruined tower of an old monks' retreat beside Bertrand and his wireless transmitter, Misha said, 'Nothing to report to SOE as far as I'm concerned except that I'm established in my safe house with D-Day plans stashed away and escape route worked out. What about you?'

'Same.' Bertrand sucked in his breath as he fiddled with the trail of wire he wanted to fit high on the crumbling stones above the window-slit. 'Nice old dear I'm with. Grandson's a PoW. She keeps hens, a goat, the usual, so I'll be well fed, thank God. Keeps hinting the entire village is fiercely pro-resistance but since I'm supposed to be a mad botanist professor in search of rare species, I'd better stick to that for the moment. I think I'll only use this place when things hot up, or if they do, I suppose. Give me some electricity and an anonymous town anyday. Blasted batteries don't last long and the generator's such a weight. That Didier bloke says there's one or two safe places they've got me in Montpellier so I'll flit about down there 'long as I can.'

Misha gazed down the hillside to Bertrand's village, Pic-L'Eglise, a pretty collection of fifteenth-century cottages bunched above the wide flow of the river. Layers of stone walling seemed to be holding it up and the bare trunks of trees. 'It's true we can feel sort of unwatched in a town,' she said. 'I'll have to get a second safe house sorted out down there because our Laurent claims that's where he needs me, to move between his group leaders in the small

429

towns and villages along the coast. He says he's all right up in the hills.' Her voice tailed off.

Bertrand was not fooled. 'Nothing wrong with this bloke, is there? Because if he's a loose cannon, we're getting out, ducks.'

Misha drew in a breath. 'No,' she said. 'No, honestly.' After all, a discussion with Bertrand would change nothing. She and Julien must adapt to their peculiar position and that was that. 'He has a garage of his own, also genuine papers. The Nazis appear to tolerate him more or less and he uses a *vélo-moteur* around the paths. He seems to be some sort of local hero . . .'

'Which can have its disadvantages,' Bertrand said.

'Yes.' Misha got to her feet and passed him a second wire. 'Anyway, you don't need me for the generator. I'll be off for a bit of reconnaissance. Rendezvous same place, day after tomorrow?'

'Yep. Transmission time for Thursday's 9.23 so don't be late.'

'What's our signal?'

Bertrand pulled out a white handkerchief. 'If you spot this tied to the first tree above the village, get out quick,' he said. He looked up at her and winked. 'Smashing goatgirl you look. Mind you don't get any goatherds after you.'

Misha grinned. 'The jacket's Violette's and the scarf Gaston's. They smell of garlic and smoke.'

'S'pose the goats you got tethered out there have names and you're fond of 'em already?'

'Of course, and I'm grateful they're prepared to take me round their paths and little secret places, though they won't realise that's what they're doing.' Watching his practised fingers testing the keys, she thought how much she liked his airy theatrical mannerisms, his teasing, knowing they hid the profound loneliness and courage of a man prepared to be always on the run, always hunted. Each time he started his transmission to London, he risked detection by the Nazis' powerful listening devices. 'That beret makes you look more French,' she said. 'And your letting the moustache grow bushier, especially as it's come out so black.'

'And there's me thinking my short fat little figure and

bandy legs were enough. Get off on your jobs, duckie, I got mine . . .'

Misha grinned. 'Cheerio, then,' she said, leaving the tower, untying Amélie and Sabine and persuading them up to the top of the ridge. Here she paused and considered her position. Half a kilometre below, the village of Pic-L'Eglise. Along the valley beyond it to the west, the larger one of Castelnau. On each side of the valley, the mix of rocky ridge and wide sweep of undulating land covered in rough scrub. Ridge, peak and valley dipped and rose in its volcanic contortions with oddly perched hamlets and dense woods of the peculiar dwarf quality caused by harsh, long heats. Nothing could grow tall and free in the Languedoc. But its air was like crystal. She drew in a deep breath of it. This was where she'd spent the longest period of her life after all, two years. This was more her home than Paris.

Gazing on up to an area of woods to the north, she thought she saw a drift of smoke rising from it. Almost certainly that must come from one of the circuit's hill camps and if so there'd be a pair of binoculars trained on her by a sentry that very minute. What would he be deciding about the stranger on the ridge? Not that she was the boss's new liaison officer from London, that was for sure.

Smiling to herself at the thought, she rejected the impulse to wave and set off for her investigative ramble and its final destination, the gentle irregular tinkle of the goats' bells echoing down the hillside and up into the vast clear sky.

It was dusk, a cold misty dusk. By her reckoning, she and the goats had covered a good twelve miles of very uneven territory. But she'd found what she wanted: some escape paths she might need, one or two barely accessible hiding places between boulders. And now she'd reached the house. Tying the animals a few hundred yards away, she returned to station herself behind a water-butt at the corner of the long stone barn which served as dormitory for the vineyard's September grape-pickers. The house itself was below her, a one-storey building with a roofed veranda forming an L-shape to the wine-pressing sheds. Its occupants were getting ready for an early supper. An elderly man was chopping

431

wood, a younger one drawing water from the well, his dog beside him panting for a drink. Smoke rose from the chimney in homely fashion. It was a homely scene. She could hear the thud as the man's axe reached the block and the slight splintering sound as he threw the wood on to the pile.

She remembered these sounds from another time. And the next one, Mémé's shout, 'To the table, you two!'

Misha stared down, hoping for a glimpse of Mémé. Did she and Pépé and Félix sometimes still think of her, worry for her, wonder where she was, where she was having supper? Of course they did, all three of them. And perhaps in Frou's dreams, she too heard a familiar voice, calling her.

Pépé and Félix were going in, their boots quite loud on the cobbled yard. She thought she saw Choco lift his head towards her as if he'd caught her scent.

Then she realised she could smell smoke, not chimney, vine-wood smoke, pipe smoke. She turned casually round to meet the owner of the pipe, slowly and casually round because she was Brigitte Marchand, walking the goats for her second-cousin Violette, and she'd lost her way.

'If you put any of my people at risk, Misha, I shall shoot you.' Julien hadn't gone so far as to have a gun his hand – he held a pipe – but Misha had no doubt he meant it. And he was right.

She said calmly, 'I'm merely getting to know my area, Julien. I'll have another walk with the goats tomorrow and again on Thursday after I've rendezvoused with Bertrand. If you have any messages for him, I'll read and memorise them now if you wish.' Her heart was thudding from shock. She hadn't heard him creeping up on her and she was supposed to be trained in absolute alertness at all times. She'd been wrong, of course, to allow herself a weakness and it must be the last. She eased herself away from the water-butt and waited for Julien to answer. As he was too busy staring at her she spoke again. 'Shall I come up to the garage on Friday? There's a bus from Clermont and Raphael says you have a bicycle ready for me to get about the roads here. Then I'll need the address and contact for

432

my second safe house in Montpellier. I'd better get down there soon to meet the other contacts so I can save you the need to move around the coastal areas . . .'

Julien fiddled with his pipe. 'Come to the garage on Friday by all means,' he said. 'I'll have my messages for Bertrand ready, also your bicycle. I've been giving it a coat of paint to cover the rust. There's another rather ancient one at your other safe house.'

'I'll see you about half-past nine, then,' she said. Nothing more is to be said between us, Misha thought. We are to adapt to each other gradually and that'll be the best way. She made as if to walk past him. 'Goodnight,' she said.

Julien failed to move aside. 'You may as well stay to supper now you're here,' he said, the thick band of his eyebrows very dark in his pale face.

Misha paused. 'Certainly not,' she said. 'If Mémé knows I'm a resistance agent, she'll worry herself sick, Félix'll go on one of his walks to try and find me, and as for Pépé . . . well, if he's arrested again, I'll be one more thing for him to have to keep quiet about. If Pépé's your saboteur, I'll have to meet him, I expect, when things hot up, but I don't intend Mémé or Félix to know I'm here until the war's over.' She turned away and set off by another path towards the one she'd arrived by.

'Misha! Come back!'

She didn't stop, beginning to cross an area of rough scrub which she hoped was the right direction for the goats. 'It's getting dark,' she said.

'Misha, please try and understand.' Julien caught her up and she was obliged to stop for fear his voice would carry too far. 'Try and understand,' he said again. 'I'm worried about you because we lost one English agent here. In Palavas it was. The café owner who saw her arrested is one of my chaps. He told me she couldn't be anything but English, really tall and fair, with a distinct English sound to her French. Anyway, the Gestapo got her outside the café when she was waiting for a contact. She walked straight out into the arms of the Gestapo, Misha. And she could have used his back exit. He saw them on the pavement so she must have.'

Misha stopped, one foot half in a rabbit hole she was trying to avoid. 'What was her code name?' she asked. Here it was. At last.

'Dominique.' Julien also stopped.

'And what happened to Dominique after she was taken in?'

'I'd rather not tell you, Misha. You don't want to hear things like that.'

'Julien, I'm a trained agent. What happened to Dominique?'

'She was taken to the same police station as your Pépé. And never came out.'

'Never?'

'Well, she came out in a pretty bad way and we think she was sent to a camp in Germany after a few days in the hospital.'

'It's for sure? Who told you, Julien?'

'A police contact.'

'All right. Thank you for telling me.' Misha removed her foot from the rabbit hole. 'I understand your concern. I just wanted to see my family and now I've seen them . . .' The foot hovered over another rabbit hole. She could barely make out the ground. Georgie had walked into the arms of the Gestapo to save her!

'Let me come a little of the way with you, Misha, please.'

'No, thank you, Julien. Goodnight.' With application, she put first one then the other foot in the right places and began to walk off. 'Dominique was my friend, Julien,' she said. 'I told you all about her, Georgie her real name was. She and our other friend, Patch, they were the ones who picked me up with their ambulance. June that was, June 1940, just before we met.'

She didn't hear him following her but thought she could smell his pipe smoke for some time afterwards, right up to the point where she found Amélie and Sabine. Their bells had guided her.

By the time she'd arrived back the shepherd's house, she'd put to rest the little bit of hope about Georgie that she'd kept close to her heart. And Georgie, she kept thinking to herself, over and over again, Georgie, it has

taken me a long time to get back and continue your work.
But here I am.

Chapter 70

'Honestly, Julien, I didn't feel I had ENGLISH stamped on my forehead the minute I stepped into the bus at Clermont. In fact, all those gossiping women coming up to market with their live hens and their dead rabbits barely gave me a glance. And don't forget I'm half-French.' She was sitting in the cubicle he called his office in the back of the garage and the atmosphere between them was cool. 'But if I can't actually read these lists of contacts you've given me, that's just a matter of your hand-writing and not my incompetence as a liaison officer.'

'I don't have a secretary or a typewriter, Misha.' Julien cleared a space on the table where tools were piled up along with stale ends of grey bread, half a sausage and what looked like his dirty washing. 'Real coffee,' he said, putting down a grimy bowl of something he'd made over his bunsen burner contraption. 'Black market and it cost me 400 francs the kilo.' He seemed different in his overalls covered in oil and charcoal dust, but the set blankness of his face and the frown of his heavy brows was the same.

Misha drew in a breath. She felt she wanted to cry, which was both foolish and unexpected. 'Isn't it strange our being together like this?' she said suddenly, the words also unexpected. 'Who could have dreamed it?'

Julien stared back at her for what seemed like several minutes, his eyes over-bright, a flush of emotion staining his skin.

'It's quite extraordinary, isn't it?' she said, and felt her eyes fill with tears.

'Yes,' he said finally. 'And I'm very sorry about Dominique. If I'd known she was your Georgie, I'd probably have
tried to storm the prison to get her out.'

'Julien, I'm glad you said that. It's something I decided
in the night to talk to you about. Promise me you'll never
try and save me from anything if you're likely to be putting
yourself at risk. You're more important to the cause than I
am. I'm a messenger, you're the organiser and the leader
of all those men. I'll try not to be too cocky and managing
and just help you wherever I can. Will you promise you
won't be, well, recklessly brave on my behalf, because that
might end in our both being lost . . .'

To this, Julien couldn't seem to find an answer. He picked
up a rag and wiped his hands like a proper mechanic.

'Anyway,' Misha said, 'I'll write out your lists in capitals
and have them memorised in an hour or two. I work by
visual memory, you see. There's nothing complicated here,
not like the D-Day schedules. I had to bring them with me
on the finest scraps of paper and my first job was to find a
temporary place to hide them.'

'D-Day's on? Good heavens!' It was a shout. 'When,
Misha?' He stopped wiping and gazed down at her, his
whole body transformed with his excitement. 'And you are
right, who'd have dreamed you'd be bringing us the news
we've waited for so long . . .' Misha smiled, avoiding a direct
answer as to date, knowing that both March and April were
likely to pass first. 'We'll get an A-message warning over
the BBC French Service,' she said. 'Then the B-message a
few days later that it's definite. Forty-eight hours after the
B message, the Allies will land and you must put your men
on to the programme of attacks laid out in the schedules.'

'Which I'll have to run through well beforehand in order
to allocate the jobs . . .' He began to turn to and fro in
the tiny space. 'We've already worked out where to cut the
communication cables the Nazis have been burying out of
sight for fear we'd strike. Our making them worthless will
be the first of many shocks.'

'After the cables, then the other communication points
are to be destroyed,' Misha continued, feeling a lift of
pleasure at Julien's response. 'Finally, there'll be a series

437

of general sabotage acts for you to carry out, based on the information you've been sending to SOE via the Auvergne and southern circuits. Any particularly big job they want you to do to reduce the load of RAF bombing in this region, SOE will let you know three weeks before.' She forced herself to take a sip from his grimy bowl. It was going to be all right. They were making it all right. 'Now these lists,' she said. 'I see my second safe house might be with the group leader Prosper over his chemist's shop by the bus station in Montpellier?'

'Yes, he's a good solid man and his wife is brave enough to offer us a spare room for anyone who needs it. There's a back exit and a shed where she's had her girlhood bicycle stored for years. Raphael's cleaned it but the brake pads are rotten. Don't ever go fast, even along those flat coast roads. The shop's also next to a hairdresser so a bit of coming and going by women is usual.'

'Hair!' cried Misha. 'That's a point. I want to develop some kind of *zazou* look for the towns. SOE have heard it's still around. Girl's hair is long at the back, rolled up at the front and worn with very long dangling ear-rings, is that right?'

Julien laughed, his old, frank laugh. 'Heavens, Misha, you know I never look at what girls are wearing. I never noticed what you were wearing, did I? Well, I suppose I didn't mind.' He stopped. 'But you look nice as a goatgirl. Just too tall.' He laughed again and she made as if to throw his lists at him. 'All right,' he said. 'Raphael's got a girlfriend, you'll have to ask him what the student fashion is.'

The lists and messages for Bertrand memorised, the scraps of paper burned, Misha stood in the street with her new bicycle. She was about to ease herself on to the saddle when she felt a vibration under her feet, barely noticeable, familiar. A convoy of trucks was approaching. It was something she'd felt many times before. In fact, if an aeroplane were to shriek across the sky now and rat-tat out its machine-gun fire, she'd make for cover with barely a flicker of surprise or fear. All her war experiences had made her right for this work.

438

She stood waiting. The rumbling sound grew louder and suddenly there it was, her first enemy truck since Paris, filling the street with gritty dust and the smell of petrol. Another followed it and another and another.

She occupied herself retying shoelaces and yawning, and finally allowed herself to glance into the last truck as it rattled off. Two young men in green uniforms were watching her, kneeling behind their guns. She gazed idly back, sending them a silent message: Go home soon, go quietly, or it will be too late and thousands more of you will die and thousands more of us.

Part Four

Chapter 71

1 June 1944

Heat was baked into each stone and into every patch of dusty earth on the hillside, into the cobbled yard with its fringe of lavender and thyme, into the little table under the shelter of the porch where Misha sat stunned and silenced by heat. The vine, as if moulded around the trellis-work frame over her head, seemed deadened by heat though its umoving bright green leaves proclaimed life. A matching bright green chameleon flicked its tongue as it scampered past her shoulder, making for the peach tree fixed to the wall under her bedroom window where lizards basked on the dead-seeming boughs in the shade of leaf and fruit. And the cicadas shrieked on in their unceasing summer chorus.

'You are to sit down to this meal, my dear Brigitte?' Violette emerged from the open door carrying a plate of radishes and a heap of Gaston's early tomatoes sliced with onions.

'With the utmost pleasure, Violette,' Misha said. 'I wish I need never get up.'

A panting Rif appeared on the path leading from the vegetable garden on the slopes below. 'Have you left that village lad alone with the goats and the sheep, Rif?' she said. 'You'll never make a proper sheepdog.'

Rif gave her a grin from his yellow eyes and flopped in the shade by her feet as Gaston himself appeared and sat down.

'Good drop last night, Gaston,' Misha said. Neither of them had slept more than an hour or two.

Gaston nodded, pouring them each a glass of his own vinegary wine. 'Store number 3 won't take much more,' he said. 'Laurent or Raphael'll have to get some of those youngsters on to digging out another instead of standing about pretending to be sentries.'

Misha grinned. 'Pépé won't let any of them get their hands on the new bazookas,' she said. 'Bazookas send up rockets, Violette,' she explained. 'If we ever do have to fight it out on the plateau here, it'll give us a better chance against enemy weapons.'

Violette served the radishes and cut them each a generous portion of the real baguette Raphael had brought up that morning from a raid on a collaborator's bakery. 'The young men have been disappointed by another month slipping by,' she said. 'But we must all be patient.'

'Yes,' Misha said, feeling the heat reach into her very bones. She was exhausted. The last weeks had seen a definite increase in the number of drops to their circuit and she too had been expecting the month of May to be glorified by an announcement of D-Day. Eyes pricking against the blaze of sun, she leaned forward to turn on the radio she'd put ready by the wine carafe. 'Nice little set, isn't it,' she said. 'SOE've sent them out to all their agents apparently, so we can keep up with our BBC messages wherever we are, also the general war news, to give us hope, I presume. But it can't be long. I mean, think how many times the BBC has warned the French people to avoid travelling by train at night because the RAF will be bombing junctions. There can't be many of the big junctions left. Best not to think of all those old wooden train carriages being splintered to bits with French people in them whilst German troops are travelling much more safely in our modern metal ones.' She went on talking, having developed the habit in their early days together of telling them about Allied progress. They themselves had little custom of speech, yet seemed passionate listeners whenever she was inclined to spare the time, and would sit side by side close to her, their faces set in lines of grief and resolution. 'To me,' she said, 'the huge increase in RAF bombing is one more sign it won't be long. I suppose without American help we wouldn't have got this far. I mean, look what the enemy is going to able to throw back at the Allies. All these war years, they've been stealing iron and coal reserves from most of Europe and turning out their tanks and their armaments in other people's factories . . .'

'And they've been stealing our men,' added Violette unexpectedly.

Misha finished her radishes and began on the tomatoes. 'Yes,' she said, her mouth full. 'Another lot of poor chaps were collected off the station platform yesterday, Raphael heard. They didn't even discard the older ones. The poor devils'll find themselves slaving in some German hell-hole in a week or two.'

'So many men, so many wives and mothers left without knowing what becomes of them . . .' Violette shook her head. She'd eaten nothing.

Misha gazed anxiously at the woman who'd known the exact nature and extent of her own son's suffering. It seemed to her that Violette and Gaston would be unable to follow the natural course of grieving for their child until they knew his torturers were gone forever from the place where he had spent his short and happy life; that this would the nearest they could hope for to his murderers being brought to justice. 'Let's see if the lunchtime news has anything fresh to tell us,' she said, gazing out into the blaze of sunlight on the landscape of hill and valley she'd grown to love as the recitation of personal messages for people in the field began.

She'd almost forgotten to listen and was half-dozing when she jumped up with a start and stared at the set. She felt her mouth drop open, but there it was again. THE CIGARETTES ARE GREEN followed by THE PIANIST PLAYED ALL NIGHT. 'Our A messages,' she said. 'Oh! Violette! Gaston! In a few days' time the B messages will be sent and forty-eight hours later it'll be D-Day – the invasion. The Allies are coming!'

With the same spontaneous gesture, Gaston and Violette

stood up and reached for her hands to hold them tight. A
solitary tear ran down Violette's face.

Chapter 72

D-Day, 6 June 1944

At the back of a restaurant in a little Camargue village, Armand's wireless had been removed from its hiding place and was sitting next to the stove, its dial blatantly set for the BBC French Service. The *Marseillaise* had finished again and it was the turn of the *Star-Spangled Banner*. 'This morning, my dear Suzanne,' said Armand, 'Eisenhower himself spoke to us and then our very own De Gaulle. Now I wait only for Churchill's voice in his wonderful, terrible French and I shall know it's true, the Allies have landed in Normandy.' He kissed her soundly on both cheeks for the third or fourth time.

Already thoroughly kissed by the other two contacts she'd called on with Laurent's orders that morning, Misha felt a welling of tears in the face of Armand's happiness. His eyes were red, his bushy southern moustache quite damp. 'No more champagne though, thank you, Armand,' she said. 'I drank a glass with Romain and had a very wobbly trip here on my bicycle, I can tell you.' She picked up the roll of detonating wire. 'Prosper needs this. Delivering it will be my last job then I'm catching a bus back to the hills for more orders, and I'm not sorry. There's an awful lot of troop movement about and I haven't been stopped yet. Bet I am with this stuff on me! Sure you have everything for tonight's jobs?'

'Unless you have some nice whole tyres with rubber on them for my van . . .' Armand said wistfully.

'Tyres!' Misha said. 'You'll be lucky. Maybe there'll be some in the next series of drops. Things'll really start coming in soon.' She packed the wire in her handbag under the sheets of toilet paper on which Romain had scribbled a last-minute message for Laurent. She hadn't had time to memorise it. 'Not too disappointed it's not an airborne landing from the south-west?' For weeks she'd been dreading the men's reception of the fact of a Normandy landing, which she'd had to keep very quiet about.

'A little.' Armand shrugged. 'We'd have felt more important down here if we'd had some immediate real fighting to be getting on with instead of just cutting communication points and cables and blowing up a few things. But we understand. We can't chase out thirty thousand armed soldiers without some proper military support, so as soon as British and American troops get to us, whatever way they do, we'll be ready. And meanwhile we'll do our best to make life very uncomfortable for our unwanted, uninvited guests.'

'And how!' Misha said. 'Meanwhile, try and keep your chaps from doing anything silly from sheer excitement . . .'

'Today, my darling Suzanne,' he said, 'we shall just be happy to bring our wirelesses out of hiding, let them play too loud and rejoice in the music, the music, Suzanne, of our national anthems. Who'd have thought these simple tunes could fill a cynic with joy.'

As the sound of *God Save the King* rang out yet again, Misha said, '*Merde*, then?'

'*Merde!*' Armand replied, offering her another damp embrace.

Thank heaven! Misha closed her eyes against the glare of the sun through the window of the bus and pretended to doze. Had they gone? Yes. The bus was starting again. It'd been most unusual, a bus stopped and controlled half way between villages. They must be getting uneasier. Perhaps this lot had already been informed about D-Day. It certainly wouldn't have been described as a huge coastal onslaught, though. That would have been too much to swallow. Reopening half an eye, she watched the uniforms take up

448

their places by the roadside, the girl they'd taken out for a closer inspection of her papers having been allowed to resume her seat. The nasty green ill-fitting cloth was stained with sweat, the faces above them pinker than ever. Who were they looking for?

Still, she'd survived with the help of the hot baby in the lap of the young mother beside her. The little thing had vomitted all over the handbag Misha had been about to open at the request of a sergeant's thick finger pointed at it. The sergeant had hastily passed to the seat behind them as the poor mother had fussed with embarrassment and Misha had laughed with relief. It was worth a little vomit, even the awful smell, for the entire duration of the journey, for the pieces of toilet paper to sit crumpled but untouched by enemy hand in the depths of her handbag. The incriminating message would reach Laurent instead of the spiteful eye of some Gestapo officer – and she'd reach Clermont instead of enduring a slow and painful death in some cold dungeon. Or hot one, she reminded herself. They'd invented a new kind of torture in one of the prisons, having had an asbestos floor made in a special room and lighting coke fires under it. Anyone not answering their questions would be pushed in there to dance about for a while on bare feet. Not long enough for death by burning at once, of course. They'd be revived and pushed back in several times before that release was allowed.

She must be grateful for a lucky escape, not her first, she decided. A feeling of luck did not pervade many days. She smiled at the baby and the mother. It was only baby vomit, she assured the woman, and her skirt was due for wash. The bag didn't matter at all, being an old one, and things never mattered, only lives. In fact, she had already made up her mind to throw them both away as part of that afternoon's impulsive gesture to be rid of her *zazou* look. She'd thrown both the blue plastic sunglasses and the ugly dangling brass ear-rings that pinched into a drain outside the hairdresser's parlour, and in the hairdresser's she left behind most of her long hair. Trying to catch a glimpse of her reflection in the bus window, she realised she looked disconcertingly different with a short bob. She'd been

449

longing to be rid of the hair for weeks but had once thought she'd seen Julien's mother sitting under a drier in that shop and had never been near another. The men were going to laugh at her, she realised, but she wouldn't mind a bit. The hot sun felt wonderful on the liberated skin of her neck, and soon she'd have the great happiness of arriving home to supper with Gaston and Violette. As a celebration of D-Day, she would wish for no other.

At the bus stop in the square of Clermont, she saw one of the men from the hill camp at Pic-L'Eglise idly appearing to take his ease on a bench.

Casually, she joined him and took off a sandal as if to shake out a stone.

'Boss sent me,' Luc said.

Misha's heart sank. No chair in the porch for her just yet. 'What's up?'

'Gestapo,' Luc said, producing a mock yawn. 'And military, the works.'

'Where?'

'Up at Gaston and Violette's place.'

Misha blindly replaced the sandal and got to her feet.

'Boss says you're not to go there. The enemy has finished, Didier watched the whole thing from the peak so Boss has put the sentries round but he says no one's to go in yet because of booby traps. He says you're to get straight up to Pic-L'Eglise.'

'Thanks. Tell Laurent I'll see him at the camp,' Misha said. Calmly, she made for the grocer's shop behind which she'd hidden her bicycle. Of course, there was no hurry.

Turning left along the road, their road, the one she'd been so confident she'd see them coming on, Misha hid the bicycle again on the other side of the bridge where she found a sentry, Frédéric. Stiff with sympathy and reticence, he hadn't understood at first and therefore made no attempt to stop her. He was only a lad.

She crossed the road and began to climb, avoiding the usual paths, taking one of her own the goats had shown her, past the dry little fig trees and the giant tomato plants,

450

Gaston's pride, on through thistle and round bush until she had to drop to her knees and begin crawling with infinite stealth in the dry dusty soil. Soon she was covered in it, her sweat acting like glue. A tiny lizard had got caught in the rolled sleeve of her blouse. She paused to flick it off and crouched, listening. Only the cicadas' relentless chorus. What she was expecting to hear? It was all over, she thought, bar the booby-traps. Eyes pricking, feeling her way, she looked for the thin, fine wire they may or may not have left as a goodbye present. But somehow, she didn't expect to find any. She felt she knew they'd done their worst.

And they had. She could smell petrol, could see a faint trail of soot as she edged herself up to the tiny window at the rear of the cottage. Removing the wire mesh, she got herself inside. Cooler here, the smell of burning very dense. Waiting to get used to the change of light, she looked first for Gilles's map. They hadn't touched it. Even the flames had left it alone, having made the merest scorch marks on one corner. Why was this important? She didn't know. The D-Day lists had gone from it long since. Yet she was aware of a faint sense of relief. The bedding was scorched, Gilles's trunk overturned with the books spilled out. These too had escaped the flames. Her suitcase was also upturned; the clothes she'd kept there lay in a scorched trail towards the kitchen.

She made herself follow this trail and with the utmost caution enter the kitchen.

Here, Violette's dresser had been attacked with an axe. Pots and dishes had been thrown about in a mess of goat's milk. She pushed her feet through this towards the centre beam where the body of Rif was hanging, his belly split open, dead eyes gummed shut with his dried blood. Finding a whole patch of fur on his back, she stroked it gently. 'I am sorry, Rif,' she said.

Next she searched for a whole chair, stood on it and retrieved the package she'd hidden in a crevice between beam and stone. So far then, she'd seen nothing of hers that could condemn her as a British spy. Stick to your story, Gaston, she thought to herself, and Violette, tell them my

451

mother's name over and over again and all about my rather ungainly Swiss father and how poorly I became working in service in the Alps.

She almost didn't bother to put the package inside her blouse, but did so. It contained the much-needed ten million francs just sent in for the month's expenses. It'd be needed even more now because they'd have to live at the hill camp, she and Laurent and all the other members who'd so far been able to get about more or less normally.

Because the circuit had been betrayed.

Finding the same spot on Rif's back, she stroked him for a last time and made for the kitchen door. Strange they'd left it closed, but maybe they'd planned to as a nice surprise for Gaston and Violette returning from their ordeal in a month or two. They'd open their door and find the rotting body of the dog. The enemy liked surprising people.

The door was heavier than usual, she thought, but her climb in the heat and the shock of seeing Rif had left her rather weak. Dragging it open an inch or two, she was about to turn away and leave by the way she'd come when she caught sight of something put to dry outside – one of her dresses that Violette had washed that morning. Hesitating over the task of getting the door open and maybe risking a booby trap just for a dress, she saw it wasn't hers. It was a grey dress, a grey she'd mistaken for blue. And hanging there in her grey dress on wire fixed to the trellis over the porch was Violette. Beside her was Gaston, dead eyes staring out from the bright green leaves of the vine. The blood from their torn bellies had formed a thick brown river across the cobbles.

Reaching past Gaston's poor tilted head, she found the little wireless set she'd had the recent habit of jamming between the tight hold of the vine and the trellis frame. It had been such a good place, not even a hanging had dislodged it. She told herself that should the occasion arise, she'd use the vine again.

After that, she was somehow sure her pistol would be untouched. And it was. She pulled it out from its burial place by the root of the peach tree, blew off the dusty soil

452

and allowed herself the tiny comfort of knowing that the enemy had discovered nothing to betray the presence of an English spy in Gaston and Violette's cottage.

Chapter 73

That afternoon they had put to rest the bodies of Gaston and Violette in the circuit's burial ground by the river at Pic-L'Eglise, next to the other twenty-seven resistants lost during the past weeks. A pall of subdued expectancy now seemed to lie on the camp. Was Laurent going to order their evacuation to a more inaccessible area of the hills?

Misha sat on a bucket in the clearing by her new tent – no more than a sheet of parachute nylon stretched over the branches of a dwarf oak. Beside her Bertrand, called up from his safe house in Montpellier, knelt on the ground by his new home, an equally makeshift affair with a trail of mountain rose over it. Whistling quietly between his teeth, he set out his wireless and generator ready for transmission time to London. 'A little bird told me Raphael and Didier have gone off on the scent of something nasty,' he said suddenly.

'The place is full of rumours and all Laurent seems to do is collate the reports coming in on the sabotage stuff . . .'

'Well, London will be waiting for those, ducks, and I did hear him ordering out some reconnaissance parties . . .'

'Yes.' Misha brushed at the cloud of insects round her face and gazed across the clearing to where Pépé sat in front of the official training-in-arms tent. This had been his for a month or more, ever since Laurent had decided he should be on-the-spot and close to store number 3 in the monks' tower at Pic-L'Eglise, half a kilometre below them. 'At least I've seen my Pépé again,' she said, eyes filling with tears. Pépé hadn't been able to speak when he'd seen her arrive, a spectre of exhaustion and misery, covered all over in scratches and dirt. He'd thought she'd been in an accident, and anyway that she was in England, so there'd been explaining to do.

'If Laurent got me up here, he must be planning some kind of move,' Bertrand groaned. 'And for my part, I wouldn't mind, as long as we'll be allocated barns at least instead of having to burrow in dense old woods like a lot of badgers or something. I hope he'll persuade the villagers to evacuate up to Clermont, or further if possible. I don't want my nice landlady strung up for going to so much trouble to feed me.'

'You think the enemy will make their move on us, Bertrand?'

He shrugged. 'Here,' he said, and pointed to the camp entrance where Raphael and Didier were having a word with the sentries.

Misha stared. Between the two of them stood another figure, standing sharply to attention with an air of importance. Grapas. 'Heavens,' she said, 'the third one's a policeman I knew at home, before all this, well, just as all this began, I suppose.'

'Here.' Bertrand nudged her again. 'There's a woman with her hands behind her back in charge of Simon and Luc. Bet that's our betrayer.'

'Well,' Misha said, watching the entire group of six move slowly across the clearing towards Laurent's tent two down from hers, 'if she's only a collaborator, they'll be in trouble. SOE said definitely no collaborator revenge parties yet and Laurent's been really firm about it.'

'We'll keep out of it,' Bertrand said 'But I'm staying put. Don't want to miss anything.'

Julien appeared in front of the tent and the group lined up there – Raphael, Grapas, Didier, then Simon, the woman, Luc. The captive wore a blue silk dress, torn at the hem and damp with her sweat. Her feet were bare in the dry, dusty earth. Misha stared at these feet. It must be the first time, she thought, that the manicured toes of Madame Sérieys had ever been in contact with the soil.

*

Raphael threw Misha a glance of despair and cleared his throat. 'This is our betrayer, Boss,' he said.

Julien did not answer. He stared down at his boots, hands in his pockets. Misha stared at his bowed shoulders and finally looked into the face of Julien's mother. There were two angry red patches on her cheeks and her eyes blazed out of the black mess of her mascara.

From pity, from courtesy, because they were both women perhaps, Misha said, 'Would you like to sit down for a moment in my tent, Madame?' There'd be a delay, or a proper tribunal because even Didier wouldn't be prepared to torture the boss's mother for information on her contacts with the enemy, and the woman surely wouldn't be shot either.

She had time to think this because Madame Sérieys was taking so long to answer. She regarded her steadily and waited.

The first surprise was the splash of spittle on her own skin and then the words which burst forth: 'It's all your fault, English bitch!'

Misha wiped off the spit with an arm and heard Julien finally speak. 'No, Mother,' he said, and looked up at her, his eyes blank. 'Not her fault, or rather, her fault only in the sense that her spirit and anger forced me make the right choice.'

Madame Sérieys began to sob, her mouth an ugly gash.

Embarrassed, with much fumbling, Simon and Luc undid her manacles so she could wipe away the tears which she made no attempt to do.

Julien said again, 'Mother, listen to me. Yesterday our friends Gaston and Violette were hanged by the Gestapo on the trellis of their vine.' He paused. 'I wish you could have seen them there. Today we buried them.'

Her sobbing sounded across the clearing, louder than the cicadas, louder than the clatter of the ammunition Pépé was packing into a crate.

The policeman, Grapas, stepped forward and coughed. 'Monsieur Laurent,' he said, 'this is the woman who sent a letter to the Gestapo headquarters about the English girl,

Mademoiselle Michèle, way back, end of 1942 it was. I have seen the letter. She is also the woman who sent another letter on the same subject last week. I have seen this in the report book at the station and I also read there a resumé of the telephone conversation she had with the duty sergeant when he told her he'd already passed the information to the Gestapo.'

He paused and reached into a pocket. The assembled company seemed to hold its breath, as if the letter itself or the report book were going to appear for them all to see. 'I have here my credentials,' Grapas said. 'A set of blank vehicle permits and a list of the road blocks and troop movements expected in the area over the next few days. Also,' he said, 'information on a number of other denunciations. I wish to join you.' He handed Raphael the envelope as Julien did not seem inclined to take it.

All the men stood as if rooted to the ground after this statement.

Madame Sérieys's sobs had become hiccoughs. Still she did not wipe her face or move to brush at the mosquitoes round the sweat on her face. She went on staring at the figure of her son and finally said, 'Julien. Julien! You believe this riff-raff rather than your own mother? Your own mother, Julien!'

Julien raised his head and nodded once at Didier, his face without expression, the colour and texture of stone.

Misha watched him walk carefully round his tent and disappear into the tangle of bush and bramble behind it.

Didier had stepped back. He held out his hand to Simon for the manacle, tying it once around the left wrist of Julien's mother and indicating with a gesture she must accompany him.

Waiting until Madame Sérieys could bring herself to tear her eyes away from the place when her son had vanished, and following each bare-footed step in the dirt, Misha saw her out of sight at the camp entrance. Then she slipped away behind Julien and with caution followed the solitary path he must have taken.

She came upon him suddenly, standing on a grassy ledge. The rock dropped down just there into a crevice where gentians grew and little tufts of mountain buttercup and rose. Into this crevice, Julien was being very sick.

Julien, she thought, you don't realise yet that we do have something in common. One day I shall tell you what it is.

Silently making her way back, she sat down again on her bucket. It was time for her to turn the handle of Bertrand's generator otherwise London would be waiting for their message at the appointed time, 5.53, and it wouldn't come.

When the shot rang out, Pépé said loudly, his voice reaching across the clearing, 'You have to be careful how you place the rocket, otherwise it'll jam on you . . .'

A couple of older men, just back with reports, seemed to have been given another job to do, for they picked up spades from the collection by Pépé's tent and slipped off again past the sentries.

'Going to give Didier a hand,' Bertrand remarked, pushing the generator towards her.

'Yes. They won't put her anywhere near Gaston and Violette and the others, will they?'

'Christ, no,' Bertrand said. 'That's as good as sacred to these chaps. I'm surprised they're burying her at all, actually. It can only be for Laurent's sake.'

I shall always remember this night, Misha thought, sitting sleepless outside her tent. I shall remember the hot, still air, the nightingale singing, and waiting for Julien to come back to camp. I'll remember I had no pyjamas of my own and sat on the ground in Bertrand's that were about a yard too big in the waist and pleasantly scented with his cologne.

From the gloom she saw Raphael appear and make his way stealthily towards her. He didn't speak at first, settling on the grass and whistling between his teeth a tune she didn't know. Then he said, 'Laurent's burned his house to the ground.'

Misha let this statement sink in. 'Which house?' she said.

'The main one near the town.' He scraped his left heel into the earth until he'd made a little ditch to rest it in.

'Who told you?'

'He did.'

Misha thought of the splendour of the Sérieys house and

458

the way it had seemed to belong where it was. 'What about his father?'

'Didn't mention him, but Geneviève, the housekeeper, he took her up to the other place, the one where your Mémé is staying with the boy Félix who's apparently your brother.' He nudged her. 'You've kept all that pretty quiet but I'll go on calling you Brigitte, I expect. No wonder you found it easy to call Pépé Pépé!'

'Mémé won't like Geneviève in the same kitchen . . .'

Raphael began forming another ditch with his right heel. 'Seems that Geneviève was the one who went to find Grapas and it was she who told him about the telephone call Madame Sérieys had made to the police station.'

Misha didn't reply. Instantly, she'd remembered another night she'd spent awake and heard Geneviève promise to slaughter anyone who hurt her boy. Well, she'd kept the promise in a way, though without the use of a kitchen knife.

'You know it's my fault, the betrayal?' she said.

'Don't be daft.' Raphael gently touched her arm. 'It's all part of the game we're in,' he said. 'Might as well suggest it's the boss's for having a Nazi mother. This is war – and resistance groups are being betrayed in every district, in all kinds of different ways. I mean, look at what we've heard about the Dordogne and the Auvernge circuits, hundreds lost in them. So far we've done very well. There's been no one lost by our own carelessness, thanks to you and Laurent forcing us to be meticulous in everything we do. Think of it like that. And we're ready to get out, you know, soon as Laurent gives the word. It'll all be done like a proper military campaign, you'll see, and that'll be thanks to you and Laurent as well . . .'

'Yes,' Misha said.

Raphael went on talking and she felt her tears trickle into the neck of Bertrand's pyjamas.

Chapter 74

The short night was coming to an end. Over the hill camp the sky was just lavender. Misha sat on the bucket by her tent, waiting. The sentries had heard shots, very faint, coming from the direction of Castelnau half an hour before and reconnaissance parties had been sent out. But they all knew the attack had begun. Grapas had warned them. It was probably the most useful piece of information he'd offered to establish his good faith, not that anyone was prepared to accept it yet. He'd have to prove himself. Their world of enemy occupation was based on suspicion and deceit, containing no certainties but those of self-interest, brutality, the bullet.

Laurent had ordered the dispersal of the Castelnau camp, though, and thirty or forty of its men had arrived to join them. The rest had gone to positions around the Mas Noir area further up the plateau where a new command post would be set up if the ridge didn't hold. Mas Noir was perched on rocks with no accessible road to it. Attacking troops would never venture as far, but once there, the circuit wouldn't easily get down again.

Half dozing, the pistol at her waist, a Sten slung over her shoulders, Misha cursed the heaviness of her clothing: a pair of Bertrand's underpants, some black cotton trousers belonging to one of the lads and a shirt of Pépé's. It was already hot. The day would get hotter and it threatened to be a long one.

'I imagine Laurent's going to keep that Grapas chappie up in these woods for the duration,' Bertrand said. They'd been watching him drag a bazooka across to the edge of the clearing and begin manhandling it through the undergrowth.

'He could slip off to the enemy even now,' Misha said, yawning. 'Laurent'll want him practically tied to Pépé, I should think. Still, he is a good arms man and Pépé might need help blowing the bridge down by Gaston and Violette's. That's if we seem to be losing Pic-L'Eglise.'

Bertrand drained the last of the cold coffee from his tin mug. 'Call your brother over for another tot, ducks,' he said. 'You sure all the Pic villagers left in the night?'

Misha searched for a glimpse of Félix over the heads of the men hurrying in and out of tents getting themselves ready. 'Well, they did,' she said, 'but that old landlady of yours wanted to come up here and help. Laurent practically had to force her into the van in the end and she shook her fist at him as Simon drove her off.'

'Félix is over by Laurent's tent, fetching some more of the good stuff,' Bertrand pointed.

'So it's not coffee you want, then, Bertrand?'

'Not with the chance before I die of tasting what Laurent's had brought up from his family cellar. Battle orders include giving it out in morning tots anyway,' he hiccoughed.

Misha waved to her brother. She hadn't dared speak to Julien about the burning down of his house or about his mother. Would they ever become subjects to speak about? she wondered. For the moment, they had become an irrelevance. One day, she might bring herself to mention the matter of the two million francs she'd stuffed behind a hatch in the cellar of the house. Money would always count.

Félix arrived and knelt beside her, refilling her mug and passing Bertrand the newly opened bottle of something rare.

'Félix,' Misha said, 'you know the guns are going to start soon?'

Félix nodded, face set in its most determined and earnest mould. Only his darting, pale blue eyes showed his agitation.

'Stay with Pépé,' Misha said, 'unless he tells you to run, when you must. Meanwhile, give me a kiss.' She had to get to her feet to reach up to him. He was well over six feet tall now, with a heavy man's body which didn't match his mind and limbs too long for his clothes. 'When the war's over,' she said, 'we'll be together again at home with Mémé, Choco and Frou. And *Maman*'ll come visiting and absolutely scream at the sight of us. She'll have to go on a huge shopping spree, she'll have our old stuff off us in seconds and we'll be scrubbed all over . . .'

Félix grinned and shook his head, lumbering off to the next tent with his jug and his bottle.

A sudden commotion at the camp's entrance made its occupants pause. Silence fell as every pair of eyes watched the three reconnaissance lads run across to Laurent's tent.

'This is it, ducks,' Bertrand said, standing up and pulling on his beret. 'What about a kiss for me, eh?'

Misha put her arms around his neck. 'Thanks for the comfort, Bertie.'

Bertrand hugged her and planted several alcoholic kisses on her cheeks. 'Me too,' he said.

Laurent appeared from his tent. 'It's on,' he announced, not needing to shout. 'You all have your orders. It's a pity it's come before the biggest series of drops we've had yet, which will set us up in the full panoply of arms we desperately need. But we must do our best. They've started on the Castelnau camp and I imagine they'll destroy the village itself in their fury at finding us dispersed. I'm sorry some residents chose to stay behind in spite of our warnings last night. We don't expect them to reach Pic-L'Eglise before noon. We make no move until they do. If they start to drive through it, the bridge will blow and they'll have to scatter across the ridge on the other side as we open fire. Remember, we have the slight advantage of altitude. As you know, the command post remains here unless we have to retreat when it'll be in Mas Noir. Keep in small groups around there. Feeding will be a problem so you'll have to get into the villages to ask for help. No threats please and no looting. As soon as we assemble at Mas Noir, if we have to, Brigitte will organise some bulk purchases. Remember all of you that this ridge is the front line and anything behind us to the north is ours. Any walking wounded must make for the first-aid post . . .'

'He looks a fine figure of a leader, standing there,'

462

Bertrand said. 'I just don't like the colour of him somehow and the real stuff's not started yet.'

'No,' Misha whispered. Only, she thought, the real stuff of condemning his mother to be shot with a nod of his head. She felt a familiar sense of anguish grip her around the chest. She wanted Julien to glance her way, to smile at her as he used to: a perfectly ridiculous desire at the start of their first guerrilla battle.

As if he'd sensed something, he called, 'Bertrand!' and came towards them both. 'I want you to start off for Mas Noir at once, on foot. I don't want to risk you or the set being captured. When you get the transmitter fixed up, keep calling London. Tell them the attack's started as expected and that we are now the occupiers of this plateau unless we're driven out.'

'Heard and understood, Boss.' Bertrand shook his hand and winked at Misha before launching himself with transmitter and generator into the general mêlée. '*Merde*, Bertie,' called Misha.

'*Merde*, ducks.' He was gone.

'You have your orders clear, Misha?' Julien's eyes had leaden marks of weariness around them and seemed flat, indifferent. Impulsively, she reached forward and gave him four of her old natural kisses without answering.

He responded at once, kissing her in return. 'You will only do what I've asked, won't you?'

She thought he was trembling but couldn't be sure. 'Promise,' she said. 'But remember I'm the best trained of all of you.'

This made him smile, stiffly. 'Yes,' he said. 'But you're also Misha.' He shrugged. 'I can't help it.'

Misha rejected the desire to kiss him again. A shiver had crept down her back with the sudden piercing thought that she and Julien wouldn't meet again. Instead, she burst out with what was actually the truth. 'I couldn't have wished for a better leader, or one I felt I could trust as I do you, Julien.' And then she managed something else, also the truth. 'I'm sorry about my arrival and my rudeness.'

'And about your cockiness, Misha?'

'Yes,' she said. 'All of it. Shall we have a proper talk tonight when we regroup? If there's time? I'd like that.'

He didn't answer.

'Goodbye 'til then, Julien.'

'Goodbye, Misha.'

She looked round from the other side of the clearing. He wasn't watching her. He'd remained as if gazing into her tent. She made herself hurry across to Pépé and kiss him quickly on the back of the neck to the accompaniment of furtive grins from the men waiting for arms. What a silly thing to have said! 'Shall we have a proper talk?' She'd left proper talks far too late. She was always too late to recognise emotions, that was her problem.

She set off at a run down to Pic-L'Eglise where she had to get a van out of hiding and into action – a task not only useful but vital. For an hour or two, she'd probably find herself almost happy.

Chapter 75

Shuddering down the hill from Clermont, hands slipping on the steering wheel from mingled grease and sweat, Misha peered through the curtain of mortar-shell smoke floating gently towards her. Fat black drops of soot were spattering on the windscreen, on the rough scrubland, on the narrow band of road which she must soon get off. She could barely see her way. Slowing to a crawl, she veered right, rattling and juddering in the direction of the woods.

The van had two tyres gone. It wouldn't go much further but then nor would she. Every part of her body felt like lead. Her chest was enclosed in a band of steel. They were losing the fight. It wouldn't be long before their side of the ridge went quiet.

She had to walk the last few hundred yards. The van had rolled into a bush and she couldn't persuade it out. She'd become accustomed to the pall of soot now, as one always did to each new discomfort, each new horror. Well, there couldn't be many more because the enemy had won. Superior arms had helped them, as always. Dragging behind her the carton of melons a farmer had placed by the road-side with a child's French flag fixed on it, she heaved it under the tree where the red scarf was tied. Here was their first-aid post, or here it had been. She and Simon had carried countless seriously wounded up into Clermont and along to the village of St Jacques where the doctor was a resistance man. The walking wounded had had to make their own way as best they could. She'd seen Georges and

Olivier holding each other up and knocking on the door of the first house on the road to Clermont and having the shutters slammed in their face. Yet the next house up had hung out little scraps of rag in blue, white and red and so Georges and Olivier were presently lying in clean beds. They'd been lucky.

'Any more news?' she asked Luc. He was leaning against one of their trucks which had also made its last journey that afternoon. The nearside front wheel had spun off just as it was coming back to collect its next consignment of injured. These men had disappeared she saw, by what miracle she hadn't the strength to consider.

Luc squinted at her through sweat and soot. He shook his head. 'If there's any of us in there, they're dead. Or as good as.'

'I picked up some melons left out for us,' Misha said. She reached for one to cut into it with her penknife. 'Here.'

He was too weary to take it so she caught up his hand and balanced a slice on it.

Her stomach was heaving. How many times had she had to suck out the carburettor? She'd lunched on petrol in fact.

Lowering her head towards the warm green flesh, she sucked up pips, spat them out and started again. Her mouth couldn't take it, her throat retched, but soon fruit sugar was dribbling down her chin. 'It's good, Luc.'

He stared at her, melon balanced on his dirty hand, eyes drawn so far into his skull she could see the shape his skeleton would have.

She took hold of his arm and manoeuvred him into a sitting position, propped against the radiator. 'Try and have a sleep,' she said. 'Look, I'll leave another couple of melons cut ready. Eat them when you wake up. By then some of the runners may be along to help you up to Mas Noir. The aircraft's gone from overhead and I can't feel any vibration from the ground now, so I think I'll just creep into the woods and see what I can see. All right?'

He managed a nod. She felt his eyes following her as she made her way along one of the paths the men had made, ready for just such a day as this. They'd got themselves ready in every single way except in the matter beyond their

466

control: the supply of arms. And in two weeks' time, a series of fifteen drops was due, each of them involving twenty bombers and the mass of arms they needed. The attack had come too soon.

Wiping the dirt from her borrowed watch, she saw the hands showed 4 p.m., the worst, dead time when the world always seemed to come to a stop.

In the clearing, their makeshift tents had been blown into tatters by mortar shells. Strips of nylon hung from the trees, several boots were perched up there and a solitary tin mug. Making her way to her own patch, Misha counted seventeen dead bodies with faces beyond recognition. She found her torch, a bar of warm chocolate sent by SOE and her water flask. These she held in her hand until she'd picked out a suitable jacket from the debris. She put this on, stowed away her finds and went across to Pépé's tent, or where Pépé's tent had stood. Here she was lucky. A few hand-grenades lay about and a nice strip of ammunition for the Sten. Now she was even hotter, though the sweat on her back seemed cold. She stood listening. No sound, yet far off, or as if subdued, the chorus of the cicadas made the summer day, the hot still air of the woods, seem perfectly normal.

At the edge of the ridge over the valley Grapas lay dead, his body hung across a toppled bazooka. Lying carefully down beside him, she began to crawl on her belly through the undergrowth.

The monks' tower was no more than a scattering of scorched stone with a few slats from the packing cases she'd emptied that morning.

There was smoke coming from Pic-l'Eglise. Some of the pretty stone houses had stood firm and were still perched whole above the river. Their window slits were black gaping holes, stained all around with scorch marks. Inside there'd be nothing left but the charred remains of several generations of family life.

Misha put her face into the rough cloth of someone else's jacket, trying to stifle the urge to cough. There was too much smoke for her throat to take yet the merest splutter might echo down into the empty desolation of Pic-L'Eglise and up again to the opposite ridge where enemy ears, enemy eyes, might be listening and watching even now. She tried to look across against the glare of the sun at the darkness of bush and scrub where nothing moved, nothing glinted. But they'd be patient. And so would she. Reaching for her flask, she rested her head in a tangle of broom and thyme and swallowed a few drops of water.

Then with infinite caution, she moved far enough forward to be able to see the circuit's burial ground. They'd found it. They'd dug it out. They liked to disturb the dead as well as the living. A heap of bodies, twenty-nine she supposed, half-burned, were thus to lie rotting and exposed to scavenging wild boar and the rat.

By the time she'd edged her way back along the ridge to Gaston and Violette's, the sun had disappeared behind the enemy's ridge from where so far no sniper fire had burst across at her. Perhaps the snipers had been ordered back for the day. Certainly their dead seemed to have gone. Sitting in the cool of the billy goat's shed and peering out, she could see two of their trucks had been thrown back by Pépé's blowing of the bridge. Pieces of metal and wheels were scattered about down there, an entire undercarriage was lodged in the river. Didier had reported seeing at least sixty dead being carried away. So that would make sixty less for the Allies to face. Pépé would be pleased to know that. And they hadn't been able to get any further.

A little rested, some of the warm chocolate got down for the necessary surge of energy, she crawled from the shed and began to make her way on her knees along the paths the goats had shown her until she could hear the splash of the river water forcing its way past unfamiliar obstacles.

Pépé wouldn't have seen the shot coming. The wound was at the back of his head. He must have turned to get back up into Gaston's bushes just as he was spotted.

But Félix had received his shot full in the face. He was spreadeagled against a fig tree, his hands clutching at Pépé's

468

shirt sleeves. Pépé was lying face down between Felix's knees. They'd probably died at the very same second. A trail of ants was scurrying to and fro between their wounds under a cloud of flies.

Chapter 76

Well, she had far too much to tell Mémé now, but if she were lucky, Geneviève would have informed Mémé her grand-daughter was the subject of Madame Sérieys's denunciation, that she had in fact returned to the Languedoc as a British spy. This'd mean Mémé was already well into fretting about the matter and the shock of seeing her appear out of the gloom wouldn't be so very great, there being others to come. Her heart mightn't be as strong as it once was.

As for herself, she had nothing else to wish for but the sight of Mémé's cottage-loaf shape on the wooden seat of the verandah, her sewing box there, and Frou. And the best possible sound would be her scream of horror at the spectre her grand-daughter made, stumbling towards her in a man's clothes and carrying a gun. Of course, she and Geneviève would have heard the distant rat-tat of guns without dreaming anyone of theirs would be involved.

Deciding she'd allow herself five minutes of fussing before she released her other news, she was about to start up the paths when she heard a tiny movement of something – not river water. Rats? She squinted down into the mess of debris where the bridge had been. A German soldier was trying to edge down the opposite bank to drink.

She felt for her Sten and lifted it against her shoulder. His head snapped up. He was squinting across into Gaston's garden but certainly couldn't see her. She could see him well enough to make out the wound in the area of his left ear. In fact, she could see the flies buzzing at it and the pale blotch of his face.

He'd heard the click of the Sten. He knew she was there, sensed it, because he was staring in the right direction. He put up his hands, two more pale blotches. '*Bitte*,' he said.

The rat-tat of released fire burst out, sickeningly loud. Pausing long enough to see him topple forward, she thought she could decipher more green cloth, more human shapes in the bushes where he must have been, and there, oh, yes, beyond where he'd stood, was the merest hint of movement. So there were others like him waiting for her to show herself.

She stood up, flung the Sten across her shoulder, fiddled just long enough to get two grenades ready and lobbed them into the shapes.

She paused once more, a little further up her path, threw the remaining three into the cloud of smoke and with the last of her strength ran on.

There was no light of candle or lamp showing at the house. She had to use her torch to make her way past the barn and the water-butt and down on to the cobbles. At once she sensed that there was no living presence in yard or house. The shutters gaped open. Even the mosquito netting wasn't up. Mémé wouldn't sleep without those. Well, Julien had failed to inform her he thought the vineyard was at risk but he'd evidently sent Mémé and Geneviève up to Clermont with Choco and Frou, so he must have considered it was.

And they'd moved out in a hurry. Reaching the verandah, she sat down on the steps. She felt a decidedly tearful disappointment. There'd have been comfort here, rest, the relief of the day's events told and retold, and hours and hours gazing at Mémé's plumpness, her anxious face, her almost-red unsuccessful bun. For herself, she'd have been glad of a little fat for once. Only the skinny could know the discomfort of sitting on stone steps. Her entire body throbbed with pain. She probably had a bruise from the thud of the Sten against her shoulder. There'd be something in the house for bruises. Witch hazel. First, she'd better wash away some dirt.

Easing off boots, Sten and borrowed jacket, whose owner she'd never see again, she removed Bertrand's two pairs of socks, picked up the torch, replaced the Sten and walked across the warm cobbles as far as the well. If she were lucky, the bucket would be nicely filled and sitting near the top within reach, thus saving her the huge effort needed to wind it up.

On first sight by the beam of her torch, she thought the well had its lid in place, which was unexpected. Reaching out for the handle to lift it up, she touched cold flesh.

Perhaps they'd thrown in Mémé's body first because she was taking up most of the space, her right shoulder lodged over the well rim. Geneviève they'd tried to jam in upside down and had failed. She almost looked as if she were praying. Choco sat in the bucket, his mouth bared in a dead grin.

Maybe it had been Frou they'd thrown in first, before Mémé.

Anyway, there wouldn't be any well water to be had for a long time, years probably.

Chapter 77

A nightingale was singing. Back on the verandah, Misha listened to the nightingale. She was thinking about shrouds and flowers, and got up with dizzying suddenness.

Under her bare feet, all the tiles of the house were warm. This was rather a pleasant feeling, remembered from other summers. Moving from room to room, she eventually settled on the one Mémé had been occupying. Her old slippers were under the bed.

She'd been right in thinking clean sheets would be in the cupboard there, neatly piled up, smelling of lavender. Mémé was particular about sheets. These linen ones were of course Madame Sérieys's, or most likely had come from Monsieur Sérieys's mother's dowry. From feel, she thought they were oldish. Picking up three, she felt for lavender bags also and found two – better than nothing.

In the courtyard again, she decided the nightingale was more than irritating, being ceaseless. She didn't particularly want a mating song trilling out when she was occupied with shrouds.

She covered all three bodies and arranged the sheets in some kind of neatness. Next she broke open the muslin bags and scattered dried lavender over the sheets. Later perhaps she'd pick fresh lavender and some jasmine to make a wreath.

The effort of searching round the edge of the yard for stones to anchor the sheets exhausted her and she was soon back on the verandah steps, Sten lodged across her knees, listening to the nightingale.

She must have fallen asleep for a second but suddenly jerked awake. A strange noise had woken her – teeth chattering, something like that. Hand on the Sten, she drew in a breath. Yes. The faintest, faintest chatter of teeth. An animal, she thought, a rat, a hedgehog on its night's business.

She released the breath. Nothing to worry about. But there it was again, much nearer, and with it a soft thud sound near her bare feet. A rabbit, she thought. It was all right. A rat wouldn't come as close. It was a hungry rabbit creeping from the scrub to see what it could find. Perhaps Mémé had been leaving food out to make it friendly enough to catch for supper. She didn't want to think rat.

Well, she'd offer it something. She'd go into the kitchen and fetch food for them both. She herself was probably hungry. Reaching for her torch, she switched it on and looked down at Frou's dirty beautiful tabby body shuddering with fright.

Both full of dry bread and goat's cheese, burping from their sips of the Perrier water she'd found under the sink, Misha carried Frou from the kitchen and laid her on the bed in Geneviève's room where she fell instantly asleep.

Now for something else to occupy an hour or two. Inspecting the housekeeper's suitcase, which hadn't been fully unpacked, she chose a grey cotton dress with a piqué collar and also picked up a pile of handkerchieves and some lavender cologne, adequate washing equipment in view of the lack of water.

Soon she'd removed every item of clothing that had been stuck to her body for days and had wiped her skin all over. Rejecting the grey frock as too short though narrow enough, and padding off to pick out a pale pink one of Mémé's, this too-generous item was shortly tied like a sack around her waist, her pistol in its pocket, and she and Frou were re-established on the cushions of the verandah seat.

Before a minute had passed, another odd sound came up from the yard. Straining her ears, Misha lifted her hand from

474

Frou's body, though as the cat hadn't stirred there was really nothing to worry about. Still, she reached for the Sten and waited for the sound to move off, shining the torch beam cautiously to and fro on the cobbles. Then she traced the noise. A figure was dragging itself along, face down. The Gestapo didn't go in for charades, so this was one of their own. She got to her feet. 'Who's there?' she hissed.

A faint voice came back. 'Julien. Is that you, Geneviève? Mémé? Help me please.'

Chapter 78

She managed to help Julien into the house and along to
Mémé's bedroom, a patchy trail of blood marking the way.

It hurt him to lie down. He wanted to be propped against
the bolster. She fetched the entire set of bolsters from the
other rooms and made a nest of them round his head and
shoulders, placing another carefully under his right leg
where his wound showed as a dark mess of half-dried blood
on the upper thigh.

Around this area she packed a couple of sheets.

The nest effect made him smile. 'Cocooned, Misha,' he
said. 'Safe.'

After that, she worked fast with Mémé's dressmaking
scissors, cutting more linen sheets into strips, her mind fixed
on tourniquets.

It was wasted effort because the wound lay too far up
into his groin. She had to satisfy herself in the end by cutting
off the lower half of his trouser leg, removing the soaked
sock and shoe and washing away some of the blood with
several bowls of Perrier.

Julien's gaze followed every movement. 'When I've made
you comfortable,' she told him, 'I'm going to try and get up
to Dr Renaud in St Jacques. He must come and drive
you to the hospital in Montpellier.'

Julien gave a slight shake of his head. The skin of his
face was faintly blue, a colour not of human skin. 'Arrested,'
he said.

This was a blow she wasn't expecting. She eased a hand
gently under his neck and helped him take a few more sips

of sweet wine, watching the too brilliant shine of his eyes. 'I'm going to switch off the torch now,' she said, 'Or we'll waste the last of the battery.'

'Close the door first,' he said. 'Close all the doors, bolt the main doors, lock us in, will you, Misha?'

She'd almost shut out the song of the nightingale. Pulling the chair against the bedroom door, she lifted Frou from it and settled her in her own nest of rumpled sheet at the foot of the bed. 'All done,' she said, leaning over him and wiping his damp blue skin with cologne-soaked linen, gently rubbing at his eyebrows and temples where there was still dirt embedded.

'We smell nice,' he said.

'Yes. For a change.' She picked up the torch, walked round the bed, and lay down beside him.

'You and me, Misha,' he said.

'Yes.' She switched off the beam. 'We'll have a little sleep and tomorrow I'll get everything organised. If none of the runners are about, perhaps I'll get down to Montpellier on the bus . . .'

'Misha. Put on the torch, please.'

'What is it?' She shone the light across his shoulders.

'Let me see you.' He edged his head towards her. 'That's nice,' he said, closing his eyes at last.

Misha settled her feet around Frou and closed hers.

'Misha?'

'Yes.' She was instantly awake.

'What time is it?'

'I don't know. I left the watch somewhere.'

'Well, it doesn't matter.'

'No.' Her hand was still gripping the torch so she hadn't slept long. 'Shall I put this out now?'

'Not yet.' His head had fallen away from her and he was staring into space.

She reached out and touched his cheek. 'You're cold?' His skin was icy and his breathing seemed more rapid, shallower.

'So much killing,' he said.

477

'Yes. In the morning I must find someone to help organise the burial parties.'

'I killed my father, you know.'

'Did you, Julien?'

'I shot him before I burned the house.'

'It must have been because you had to, to save others.'

'It was because I wanted to.'

'Ah.' She hesitated. She didn't need to know but he might need to tell her. 'Why was that?'

'He said he would have hoped for his son to make the right choice.'

'But Julien, you did.' She sat up, stiff in every joint and muscle. 'Shall I put the torch out now?'

'Not yet. And lie beside me, Misha.'

She edged herself back again, easing a sheet across his body and her arm under his shoulders. 'You are cold,' she said.

'My father was one of those hesitators.' Julien coughed and gave a little cry of pain.

'Sitting on the fence, we say in England.' Misha laid her face beside his. Somewhere an immense sorrow was waiting to be felt, her sorrow for Julien and Julien's loneliness. One day, there'd be time for it and room for it amongst the others. 'But he did help me.'

Julien coughed again and shuddered. 'For my sake and for the thrill of it, I think. It made him feel brave and it got rid of you. He was afraid we would marry.'

'And I wasn't good enough.' Misha smiled, for herself, for Julien.

The light remark had distressed him. He made as if to raise himself and failed.

'Lie quiet,' she said. 'Soon I'll get up and make coffee with the rest of the Perrier, what's left after I put aside enough for the three of us for the day.'

'The three of us. You, me and that cat.' Carefully, he turned his head and brilliant gaze upon her once more.

'Ah.' She smiled into the too-bright eyes. 'Frou and me, we're together.'

'I could have the house rebuilt,' he said. 'Would you like that?'

Misha kept smiling. 'I think Frou and me would both choose this house,' she said. 'And think of our friends up here and all that we've been through together.'

'Here then,' he said. 'Mémé and Geneviève will be so happy. What a time they'll have with the furnishings . . .'

'Yes.' He'd forgotten. Or perhaps he hadn't been able to accept the last of the killings. And he'd thought the vineyard safe from the Gestapo, when nothing and nowhere was. 'I'd like an English sofa,' she said. 'A chintzy English sofa to rest on in the afternoons. I may have to go to London to find the right chintz. Pink, I want, different shades of pink and apricot, fat roses and swirls of sweet peas . . .'

'And when I come in from the vines, there you'll be . . .' He coughed again and his breathing quickened with a troubling, rasping note. 'It won't be long before the war's done with. But wait, Mish, wait. Find the paper in my pocket, my trouser pocket, quick!'

Fumbling, Misha withdrew a screwed-up ball.

'Read it,' he said.

With one hand, torch gripped between finger and thumb, she uncrumpled something she recognised – a public notice of the kind usually pinned to trees and displayed outside police stations.

'Read it out so I know you understand . . .'

'Reward.' Misha read this one word and her eyes slipped down to a smudged picture, a copy of one of her taken in July 1941 at the wedding of Julien's sister. She looked fifteen.

' "A reward of one hundred thousand francs is offered for information leading to the arrest of this criminal and British spy," ' she recited, 'Is that what I'm worth?'

Julien stirred. 'Don't joke, Misha. Hundreds of those were dropped from a 'plane last night. All over the villages, everywhere. Someone will betray you. You must leave.'

'Yes. Never mind.' She tried to hug him without hurting. 'In the morning everything'll seem different. To the world outside, it'll be a normal day after a small resistance skirmish in the hills which was nothing to do with them. The buses will run, the markets be set up. I'll try to look ordinary somehow and get down to Montpellier to my safe house

479

with Prosper and his wife. They'll help hide me for a bit. I've got clothes there, my other identity papers . . .'

He nodded. 'Prosper'll look after you as head of circuit.'

Misha wrapped her too-hot feet around Frou's hot snuffling body. 'Raphael and Bertrand'll help me too.' Also any circuit men not killed, she thought, if there were any. 'Go to sleep,' she said.

She'd decided Julien wouldn't speak anymore but some time later she felt his breathing get easier. He suddenly opened his eyes and muttered her name. 'Misha?'

'Yes. I'm here,' she said.

'I thought you were. I am very happy, you know.'

'And I'm happy, lying here with you, Julien.'

She watched the torchlight flickering across the bedclothes and went on waiting for him to die.

Chapter 79

'Is it supposed to be lucky or unlucky to feel you're reliving past experiences?' asked Misha.

'I dunno.' Casually leaning next to her against a wall in the railway station of Montpellier, Bertrand shook out his single-sheet newspaper and sighed. 'Bet only a woman'd think such a daft thing,' he said. 'And ain't you got enough to worry about?'

'Only I've waited for a train on this very station, new identity, praying to pass the controls, uncertain whether I'd get where I was going, the lot. Except it was cold then. November.'

'You told me,' Bertrand hissed. 'But you didn't have that blasted cat with you, did you? I mean, she'll pee in that cardboard box for a start. What did you say you had hidden underneath her?' He yawned and glanced around at the usual harassed, overheated crowd also waiting on the platform.

'The FANY uniform SOE sent in last month ready for the day of glory which I now shan't see. And my pistol. But Prosper's wife has wrapped them in rubber.'

'Yes,' Bertrand said. 'Rubber off parcels of explosives. They spot that, you know they do.'

'Yes.' Misha glanced down at Frou's box and its elaborate ties of linen sheeting. 'But they won't see in there. I'll put on the best act of my life if they decide to try . . .'

'You make sure you keep within your identity,' he said

481

sharply. 'You're supposed to be a student of philosophy not a poor-little-me, don't-hurt-me-sir type. What did you bring to be reading?'

'Something by the most fashionable philosopher of 1938, Jean-Paul Sartre, actually – and I won't have understood a word even by the time I get to the convent.'

'You do promise you're going to stay there?' Bertrand frowned into the glaring heat of the morning. 'Your PER-SONAL TO SUZANNE messages have each come through insisting on that. You're to wait for SOE contact and not move up home to Paris until after its liberation, which you're not to get involved in, d'you hear? With our RAF blokes increasing their bombing schedule by the day, everyone should stay put. And you've been through enough, in the process losing most of your family . . .'

'Yes.' Misha went on gazing down at the ties on Frou's box. They were quite grubby.

'Oh, Christ, ducks,' Bertrand said. 'Look here, all the best and pecker up, eh? Our pact stands. We meet at the Savoy for a slap-up dinner on me the very day the war's officially declared over. Another few months should do it. Oh, don't cry, I can't bear it . . .'

'I'm not crying, Bertie. And thanks for everything you've done to get me here. Thank all our circuit contacts for me, will you? Tell them it won't be long before they have Allied help to finally drive 'em out. There'll soon be lovely British Tommies striding along the coast road and on up into the hills. Tell them I'll be back to see them after the liberation.'

She'd said this before, certain she wouldn't return. But she'd never forget any one of the Languedoc people she'd known or any one of the events she'd lived through with them. And she'd remember with absolute clarity every changing shade of the Languedoc sky and the sweeping lines of its landscape. 'The train's coming, Bert. You'd better get off.'

Bertrand groaned and shuffled his newspaper. 'You bloody mind yourself,' he said. 'And that blasted cat, I suppose. But she certainly ain't the only thing you got left. There's half the SOE blokes dotty about you, all the circuit chaps have adored you from afar, then there's that friend

482

Patch who's been sending me loads of messages to decipher for you, and there's me.'

'Yes, Bertie, there's you and I love you. Cheerio.' Easing on the straps of her haversack with her own and Frou's supplies in it, she picked up the cat box, holding it in front of her to use as battering ram to get them both into a seat before every one was taken. They had a long way to go. But they were used to going a long way. It wouldn't be Paris just yet. First they were going to have a long sleep at the convent, a number of long sleeps lasting days probably.

Then there'd be Paris. Paris to see her mother was all right. And Paris to say goodbye to, the last of the goodbyes. The future would have to start somewhere untainted.

Chapter 80

'Enough!' Philippe cried, leaping from the truck and pushing his way through the mob in the street. 'Are we to show the same brutality as the enemy at the very time they finally leave us our city? Where is your pride, I ask you, Messieurs, Mesdames? And I warn you, you will remember this hour with shame . . .'

They made way for him, a little sheepish but with their excited righteousness unsubdued. His Free French uniform was enough to make them part but how many more of these taunting, chanting crowds were there in other streets? This was the first he and his lieutenant had come upon that afternoon and his heart had lurched with pity at the sight. He somehow thought he'd find Eveline amongst the half-naked women being prodded along like cattle. Instead, here was Misha's mother.

He took her arm, removed his cap and put it over her shaven head with the lipstick daub of the swastika on it. The others stood mute beside her, sun burning on the cruelly exposed skin of skull and breast where their bodices had been torn away. 'Come this way, Mesdames,' he said, turning towards the truck and shouting loud enough for the entire crowd filling the pavements to hear.

'Lieutenant! Help these ladies into the vehicle and let us hope we see no more of these disgraceful displays. And I remind everyone they have committed no crime,' he yelled

484

into the hot air. 'Are we French to replace the enemy's brutality with our own? Is that what you want?'

Shortly he and lieutenant were back in the truck and had resumed their patrol incongruously surrounded by six women who'd given themselves to Nazi lovers – one of them Misha's mother.

'Hold on to my arm, Madame,' Philippe said. 'You are safe with me and the truck has dropped us very close to your old home, we haven't far to go.' He smiled down at Misha's mother who gripped his arm like a vice. So far she hadn't raised her eyes from the ground. 'We'll seem very much part of the celebrations,' he added, 'especially if you keep my cap on your head and I remain without it. But be careful, here, look, the resistance have been blowing up enemy vehicles, half an engine lies in our way, there's also a barricade of barbed wire and paving stones and close to a barricade there is sometimes a sniper or two.' He paused, her fingers digging into his very hot flesh. 'You see, from that window up there over the bank? A rifle lodged on the sill and if I'm not mistaken a couple of young lads behind it wearing resistance armbands. This means there must still be an enemy presence in the buildings opposite. I'm afraid it is not quite all over but very nearly . . .'

He kept talking, leading her on, past the shuttered offices and shops, the rubble on the pavements, the drift of music and laughter coming from the cafés. She was so far fixed into her terror, she gave him no answer. Her face was a stiff yellow mask, her eyes brilliant with fear. And she was Misha's mother. Pity swelled in the tight, unfeeling area of his chest and with it a profound sense of loss he'd held at bay so long.

'Have you any news of your daughter, Madame? I first heard she was in England and then that she'd been sent to the south on a resistance mission, which I must say I was surprised at. She was not a sporty girl, if I remember, but rather a frail, slender one, and she'd have needed to learn to drop by parachute, to use a gun . . .' He paused in front of a group of small boys happily digging up paving to form a barricade of their own, and waited for Misha's mother to give him some sign of acknowledgement of this statement, some form of reply.

But Yvette Martin was incapable of speech, he saw, and her delicate body had begun to shake. 'Anyway, let us get on,' he said, offering a salute to the youngsters who'd smartly stood to attention to salute him. 'We're almost there, and if I'm not mistaken you'll be able to get into your old flat. The concierge, that Bassas woman, has disappeared, it seems, but the keys are hanging in the lobby. That surprised me, I don't know why. I imagine you'll find your rooms untouched, a little dusty perhaps. Shall you be able to settle there for a while? Madame Libaud is still on the first floor. She was determined to live long enough to see the Germans depart and she has. Yesterday I took her on a drive along the Champs Elysées and we were lucky enough to catch sight of American troops arriving. She wept . . .'

Good God, he thought, what tactlessness was making him pronounce such things? Well, he'd leave her now and get on for a drink with Blanchard. He could see the Bonaparte. They were at the corner of the street.

He'd have been happier, though, if he'd also been able to escort Eveline to a place of safety. She'd helped him once and he'd like to repay her if the need were there. Apart from Eveline, he had no personal debts or duties to see to. In fact, the liberation of Paris was going to leave a void he wouldn't know how to fill.

'Gee, it's sure been a pleasure, ma'am.' The American private helping her down from the truck she'd been travelling in for the past two days, went on chewing gum and shook his head in admiration. 'Gee,' he said again. 'We come here to chase out Germans and find ourselves picking up an English lady in a uniform and a cat in a cardboard box.' He grinned at her, his hot pink face sweating in the Paris sunshine.

'Pass me my cat, Chuck.' Misha grinned back. She hadn't thought it could be true, but her Americans had nearly all been called Chuck or Hank and were as friendly as they seemed in the films. 'See you in London sometime?'

'Sure thing, ma'am.' He saluted.

Saluting in return, Misha adjusted the pistol at her waist, picked up Frou and stared down at the Seine. People were swimming in it.

Well, so far on her journey through almost-liberated Paris, she'd seen enough blue, white and red to satisfy her, and no green uniforms. She'd seen the black and white street signs with their foreign lettering being broken into firewood. She'd seen a street mob prodding at some shaven-headed women, none of them her mother or Eveline. And she'd been cheered herself by pavement crowds cheering at the Americans coming at last. Everyone had been laughing and waving, holding out flowers for their saviours – having nothing else left to offer. The Americans had been charmed by the cheering and the flowers. The Americans had done such good work there were people swimming in the Seine on this burning hot afternoon. She was glad for them, and glad for the pavement crowds and their joy. They deserved these celebratory days. Paris was very nearly free.

She wouldn't have liked not to have reached this point, she decided. And she might as well press on as far as the street. She'd make for the Bonaparte first, to have news of her friends, then put Frou somewhere quiet, perhaps in the storeroom, before setting off to look for her mother.

These matters would serve as purpose for the moment. But she realised she was searching for a flicker of happiness impossible to feel ever again.

Standing in the doorway of the Bonaparte with Frou, she first caught sight of Monsieur Jules by the counter with a bottle of brandy and a muslin cloth in his hands. With these he was wiping blood from his son Robert's arm. Robert seemed to have had a cut from a sniper's bullet. It hadn't done much damage though, because everybody was smiling. Even Madame Florence was, in spite of the fact that Robert had been hurt at last and the brandy had finally served to clean his wounds.

Misha stared at this scene in a blur of tears. She put Frou's box on the floor and said, 'Is there anything to eat? I can't tell you what a day I've had.' This was what she'd often said in the past and it was foolish. She'd left them years before, not at breakfast. She amended the statement. 'I can't tell you what a time I've had.' It was a kind of joke she supposed, but everyone stopped smiling. Madame Florence screamed. 'Oh my dear professor,' she said. 'It's our Mademoiselle Misha, Mademoiselle Misha's come home! Oh, isn't she beautiful in her uniform, who'd have thought it, today of all days, Jules fetch the champagne . . .'

Misha turned her head towards the corner they'd all been smiling into until she disturbed them, towards the left-hand corner and her seat at the table by the window.

She saw a Free French officer get to his feet and heard Philippe's voice saying her name.

It seemed to her she'd been sitting at her old table for a very long time. Hours. And during these hours, her head had been leaning against Philippe's shoulder. In her half-doze, she'd been aware of his tobacco and cologne smell. Before that, they'd been staring at each other for a very long time. She'd taken in every inch of his face, the flecked brown eyes, the deep lines of exhaustion, the mouth that rarely smiled, that did not smile now, looking down at her.

Removing her glance from the extraordinary reality of him, she gazed at the counter where normal café activities were in progress and at the table with its two glasses of flat champagne. Next she gazed at Frou spread out between the glasses, grubby tie of her harness held tight round Philippe's wrist where one of his wounds had left a deep and livid scar. Half a baleful eye fixed on her master, Frou was pretending to be asleep, head lodged on his rifle, her tail draped across the SOE pistol.

She said, 'I used to dream Frou and me'd be watching the courtyard for you to come home from the war, and often that I'd be strolling along the boulevard and there you'd be, on some terrace. I never dared think further. Who could have dreamed we'd ever be here like this, a rifle and a pistol in front of us . . .'

He seemed unable to answer. He hadn't spoken much yet except to tell her Reine and her mother were safe. Then he said, 'I used to dream that one day I'd see you and

488

our little cat running again across to my window. As for our being together as we are now, who indeed could have dreamed it? I might perhaps wish there were no pistol on the table. I find it so hard to accept you have held and used it. But I know our long separation has been enough to last our lives and we mustn't part again.'

'We mustn't part again,' Misha repeated, finally allowing herself to study his face once more and read there the message he'd so often tried to pass her and she'd been too blind to see.